The Path of Flames

Phil Tucker

Phil Tucker

DEDICATION

This one goes out to my beta readers.
Jim, Will, and Paul, you guys are the best.

CHAPTER ONE

Asho

The wind plucked at Lord Kyferin's war banner, causing the black wolf emblazoned on the field of white to snap fitfully as if impatient with the delay. Asho shivered at the sight despite the quilted undercoat that he wore beneath his chainmail, and sat up straighter in Crook's saddle. For years he had only seen the war banner hanging above his Lord's high chair in the great hall, limp and still, but now it rippled and surged as if awakened and thirsting for blood. It was his first time riding into war with the Black Wolves. Even though he was at the back of the company with the other squires, he felt as vividly alive and terrified as if he were positioned in the vanguard.

Asho raised his chin. He'd die before he let the others see his fear.

"Asho!" Lord Kyferin's bellow carried over the cacophony of the great army arrayed around them. "Where are you hiding? Get up here, now!"

Out of the corner of his eye he saw Alardus and Cuncz smirk, could feel the cold stares from Cune and Tyzce. A squire he might be, but the others saw only his white hair and pale skin, the tell-tale signs of a Bythian. That he was free and rode by their side was an outrage they would never forgive.

Asho ignored them and dug his heels into Crook's flanks, urging him forward and through the ranks of the Black Wolves. There were thirty-three knights in his Lord's service. Lean, dangerous men with flat eyes and black mail under blackened iron plate. They loomed over him on their destriers, patient, waiting like coiled snakes for the word to strike. A few glanced down at him as he threaded his way between them. Their gazes were as disdainful as those of the squires.

Lord Kyferin sat astride his black mount at the very front, Ser Eckel his bannerman to his left, the cadaverous and terrifying Ser Haug to his right. Crook nosed his way forward, and Asho felt his stomach knot at the view that opened up before him. The Black Wolves were assembled on the lower slopes of a gentle hill, one of hundreds of similar companies that stretched out to the left and right to form the Ascendant's host. Never had Asho dreamed of such a gathering of might, and the air fairly trembled with hoarsely yelled commands, the neighing of thousands of horses, the fluttering of hundreds of brightly colored pennants and banners, the subdued gleam of armor and the plangent call of a fife over the thunderous roll of the great drums.

The Black Wolves were positioned on the very front line. The slope below them was clear, right down to the valley floor where the kragh were gathered. Across from them rose the opposite hill on whose summit the Agerastians were assembled. Even with the cloud cover the late afternoon stung Asho's eyes, and he resisted the urge to visor them with his hand. Doing so would only bring a rain of mockery down on his poor Bythian vision. Still, he could make out the long line of their enemy, their banners and archers.

"There they are," rasped Lord Kyferin, nodding up at the far summit. "Damned heretics. Finally forced to stand and fight." There was a quiet, vicious satisfaction in his Lord's voice. The past three weeks spent chasing the Agerastians across the fields and forests north of the great city of Ennoia had worn his temper dangerously thin. Day after day they'd trailed the fleeing enemy, tracking them through a swathe of burned farms, butchered livestock and pillaged villages. "Can you make them out, boy?"

Asho kept his expression neutral. After all these years, he'd grown practiced at revealing nothing. "Yes, my Lord."

"Must be less than a thousand men up there. Knights grown lean and brutal with hunger and fleeing. Archers with itchy fingers and yard-long arrows. Men-at-arms with their curved Agerastian butcher blades and black hearts." Lord Kyferin grinned down at him, all teeth, like a wolf baring its fangs. "You ready to ride up into their maw?"

Asho felt his heart quail. The thought of charging up that far hill made his pulse race. He resisted the urge to swallow, knowing how closely he was being watched, and instead simply nodded to the base of the valley. "Won't that be unnecessary, my Lord? The kragh will destroy them, won't they?"

The kragh. Two hundred of the monsters stood in a rough mass below, each nearly as tall as a man but easily three times the weight in muscle and piecemeal armor. With their pebbly green skin, lantern jaws with inch-long tusks, slit noses and ragged batwing ears, they were Ascendant Empire's shock troops, used to crush and subjugate the Agerastians at the founding of the Empire centuries ago, and a force against which nobody had been able to stand ever since.

"Yes, the kragh." Lord Kyferin stared sullenly down at them. "They'll knock a sizeable hole in the Agerastians, but there will be glory enough for us once they're done. I'll repeat my question. Are you ready to fight? To risk your life?"

Asho stared straight ahead. Any other squire or knight would be mortally insulted by such a question. He simply nodded. "Yes, my Lord."

"It's not too late." He could feel his Lord's heavy gaze. "Give the word, and I'll release you from your squiring. I'll have you escorted to Ennoia and sent back through the gate. Leave the fighting to us Ennoians.-. Go back to your own people, Asho. Return to Bythos. "

Asho sat stiffly in the saddle. The cold air whipped past, bringing with it the scent of torn loam, stale sweat, the tang of oiled metal and the stink of fear. The Ascendant's host seemed to pulse and throb all around him, eager for battle, eager for blood. There was not one other Bythian amongst those ranks, Asho knew. Some might be present as camp slaves back at the baggage train, but mounted and armed and squiring a lord? The very thought was laughable. Ridiculous.

"Are you ordering me to leave your service, my Lord?" He stared down at the kragh. As inhuman and feared as they were, at least they were respected for their ferocity and the role they had played in the founding of the Empire. He almost envied them.

"No, of course not." Lord Kyferin restrained a sigh and leaned back in his saddle, the leather creaking. "Just giving you a chance to save yourself before it's too late."

To save your honor, thought Asho. *To cease humiliating you with my presence.* "Thank you, my Lord." How did these insults still have the power to hurt him? "I wish nothing more than to repay your generosity by remaining in your service."

Lord Kyferin stirred uneasily, and Asho could tell he wanted him gone. His ploy to frighten Asho back to Bythos had failed, and now Asho's continued presence was galling him. Just then trumpets blew from higher up the slope. Turning, Asho looked up and saw the great white pavilion where the Ascendant's Grace was stationed. The second holiest man in the Empire had descended from Aletheia to lead the army himself. There was a bronze flash as the trumpets sounded again, and then he turned back as Ser Haug grimaced and spat.

"What the Black Gate is he doing?" Below, the kragh let out raucous cries and bellows, smashed their weapons against their shields, and began to surge up the enemy slope.

"Sounding the charge," said Ser Eckel on Lord Kyferin's far side. "It would seem."

Asho forgot his simmering emotions and watched as the kragh raced tirelessly up the slope. They seemed unstoppable, and ran with their legendary tireless, loping gait.

"At this hour?" Ser Haug sneered. "And with half his forces still bottle necked at the Solar Gates and spread out across the breadth of the Empire? We should wait for morning. Wait for the Gates to open at dawn and the rest of the army to join us."

"Enough. The command has been given. It is done," said Lord Kyferin, drawing himself up. "And besides. We do not need every Ennoian to be withdrawn from across the empire to deal with this rabble. We can crush them easily ourselves."

The other two subsided. Asho remained very still. He didn't want to be sent back to join the other squires. He wanted to watch from this vantage point, to see the kragh smash into the Agerastians up above, even if doing so meant straining his eyes.

A Black Wolf from behind them rose in his stirrups. "Why aren't the Agerastians firing their arrows?"

The other knights stirred uneasily. The enemy lines stood immobile, seemingly indifferent to the carnage that was working its way up toward them.

"You see that?" Ser Eckel sounded almost disinterested. "Their lines have opened up. They're letting some people through."

Asho couldn't make anything out. The far summit was wreathed in searing golden light, and held only intimations of forms, orderly lines, and kite shields. He could feel the beginnings of a headache coming on as he fought to make out more. He ached to raise his hand to block the sunlight. Then the Black Wolves tensed, gauntlets clenching, horses suddenly stamping their hooves, hoarse cries dying in a dozen throats. All of them were staring fixedly at the upper slopes where the kragh were disappearing into the clouds of light. Never had Asho so resented his poor vision. He knew from bitter taunts that the Ennoians around him could make out the details clearly enough. And what they saw had captured their full attention.

Terrible, deep screams echoed across the valley to reach Asho where he sat. The Agerastians? No. These bellows were inhuman, more akin to roars than yells. Yet they were rich with horror, pain, panic. Now Asho did gulp and raise his hand, frowning as he made out huge figures racing back down the slopes in disordered ranks, clawing and leaping as they fought to get away.

Asho glanced up at Ser Haug and froze. He'd never seen the old knight look so stunned. Lord Kyferin looked like somebody had stabbed him in the back, his brow deeply furrowed, lips pale, eyes slitted with fury and amazement. *What is it?* The question almost passed Asho's lips. *What's going on?*

Asho rose in his stirrups to get a better look just as a brazen yell sounded as clearly as any trumpet from the center of the army. A richly appointed knight in blazing steel armor rode forth, a gleaming sword raised high. "Ride down the cowardly kragh! Ride down the traitors!"

"Madness," said Ser Eckel. "What's he doing?" But others along the line began to eagerly ride forth, following the errant lord who led them down the slope. The orderly battle line began to break down. Trumpets sounded belatedly from the Grace's white pavilion ordering the charge. A roar of defiance flashed up and down the great wall of waiting knights, and then the errant lord urged his horse into a gallop, and the assembled might of the Ascendant Empire howled and followed after.

"For the Black Wolves," bellowed Lord Kyferin, urging his destrier on, and his thirty-three knights roared their response, "For Lord Kyferin!" They broke forth into a canter, passing by Asho on all sides. The thunder of their hooves filled the air and Crook stopped trying to turn and instead began to race forward alongside them. A hundred war cries echoed up and down the line, and everywhere knights were galloping, lances pointing skyward, pennants fluttering, the world shaking as the destriers pounded it to pieces.

Asho resisted the urge to yell and instead clung tightly to Crook, who was jostled by Ser Hankel on the left and Ser Merboth on the right. The host poured down the hill in glittering splendor, picking up speed until everyone was galloping, the line breaking apart as the swiftest and most powerful steeds pulled ahead. One Black Wolf after another galloped past him, and Asho was happy to let them pass; he could see the kragh gaining the valley floor just below, see their black eyes widening in horror as they saw the wall of glittering steel pounding down toward them.

Lances lowered and the forward edge of the knights sliced through the broken ranks of the kragh, shattering and colliding with them, horses going down with shrill screams and men cursing and shrieking as the enraged kragh swung their axes and curved blades up at them in self-defense. The momentum of the line was unstoppable, however, and like a wave crashing over a rock the host surged through and around the retreating kragh and gained the far slope.

Ser Haug's squire, Alardus, inched up beside Asho on one side, while Cunot rode up on the other. Glancing back, Asho saw the other squires grinning and yelling right behind them, spare swords and maces strapped to their saddles, eager for war, eager for blood, eager to prove themselves in the eyes of their masters. Asho tucked his chin and urged Crook on. He wouldn't be left behind. He'd be there when Lord Kyferin needed a replacement weapon; he'd be there to block the fatal stroke when it came toward his Lord's back. The euphoria and fear of the charge gave him wings, and Asho drew his sword, exhilarated by the terror and power of their attack.

From the late afternoon sky fell a rain of impossible bolts of black flame. Hissing like water cast into a red-hot pan, they scythed through the riders to Asho's left. Horses tumbled and fell as if their legs had been sliced out from under them. Asho looked back and saw an entire second wave of charging knights collide with the fallen, some leaping clear in a magnificent display of horsemanship, but most crashing to the ground.

Crook was flagging. The slope was too steep. The Agerastians had chosen their last stand well. Asho dug his heels in once more, but the Black Wolves were beginning to leave him behind.

Another hissing rain of bolts fell from the sky, slamming into a phalanx of knights riding under the azure and yellow banners of the Lord Zeydel. The bolts cut through their armor with the sound of bacon fat burning on a skillet, and with shrieks and cries they fell. Magic? Asho felt his stomach clench. Impossible. Looking past the other squires, he saw that entire swathes of the charge had crumbled under the ebon assault. The acrid stench of burned horseflesh and the cries of wounded men mixed with the battle cries and the sweet scent of torn earth.

"For the Black Wolf!" Lord Kyferin's cry was a bellow of defiance, a summons, but Crook could go no faster. The charge had been sounded too soon. Instead of approaching the enemy at a controlled trot, shoulder to shoulder, so as to break out into a devastating charge at the very last, they'd impetuously thrown themselves into a charge at the base of the hill, and now some knights streamed ahead of the pack, while others fell behind, with no order or unity to the attack. Asho felt fear grip him by the throat. This had had all the makings of a disaster—and then the black fire fell amongst his Lord's knights.

Horses collapsed, men were punched from their saddles, and right before him Ser Hankel's helm burst into molten metal and brains as a bolt caught him straight across the brow. The large man toppled off his saddle, dragging his reins with him such that his horse reared and fell right across Asho's path. Crook leaped, but he lacked the speed and the incline was too steep. With an outraged whinny Crook landed on the heaving flanks of Ser Hankel's mount and fell in turn. Asho threw himself clear, hit the raw earth with his shoulder and tucked himself into a roll. The world spun. Screams deafened him, and by reflex more than wit he rose to his knees.

His sword was gone. The fallen knights were acting like a breakwater, causing the attack to split around them. There—his blade. He scrambled forward on all fours and scooped it up. Where was Crook? Again that hated sizzling black fire fell from the skies. Magic! Used in battle! Impossible. Asho rose into a crouch, ignoring the pain in his wrenched shoulder. Where was his Lord? There! Only twenty yards farther up the hill, the remaining knights of the Black Wolf were embroiled in battle with Agerastian men-at-arms. Their horses reared and kicked as the Black Wolves laid about them with their swords, lances discarded or abandoned in the bodies of their enemies.

"For the Black Wolf!" Asho ran forward, exhilaration giving him wings. He leaped over a body, ran around a fallen horse, and then all his training abandoned him as he simply raised his sword overhead with both arms and brought it in a sweeping cut down upon the helm of a Agerastian foot soldier who was thrusting at Ser Sidel with a spear.

His sword screeched off the helm's curvature and chopped into the man's shoulder. The Agerastian screamed and dropped his spear, turning in time to receive an elbow to the face. He toppled to the earth, his fall pulling his body free of Asho's blade. Before Asho could finish him off, a horse sidestepped into him, sending him sprawling. His own steel cap fell from his head. Asho went to rise, and a blow nearly stove in his side. He cried out and fell again.

"For the Black Wolf! For the Ascendant!" The cry was muffled and seemed to come from a mile away. Asho took deep, ragged breaths. Around him plunged warhorses, massive Ennoians, accompanied by the hack and slash of blades. He'd never believed the tales told by the bards, but this was even worse than he'd imagined. The enemy should have melted like mist before the Black Wolves' charge. And magic! The Sin Casters were supposed to be centuries dead and gone.

Reeling, blinking away mud, Asho forced himself upright. There—the Black Wolf himself. His Lord stood, wounded, a space having opened about him, bodies at his feet. Only five knights yet stood by his side. Asho couldn't understand that number. Only five?

Asho stood and scooped up his sword. He turned to join his Lord and then froze as the enemy ranks parted to admit a man who stepped to the fore. He was dressed in purple and yellow silks, his hatchet face thinly bearded, a grimace of distaste twisting his lips. The air around him seemed to crackle with barely suppressed energy. He was slight, yet the Agerastian soldiers pressed back from him as if in fear.

Asho knew he should move. Should yell a war cry and charge. Yet he stood rooted to the spot as the enemy placed a black rock in his mouth, swallowed, and then raised a hand. His nails suddenly writhed and grew longer and twisted like ancient roots. Lord Kyferin raised his ancient family blade and bellowed his defiance, Ser Haug and his four other knights charging right after him. They didn't take more than three steps. The stranger whispered something beneath his breath, and black flame shot out from his fingertips. It scythed through the charging men, cutting through their armor and flesh like a heated knife through tallow.

Lord Kyferin and his remaining knights toppled to the ground. Asho stood there, stunned. The cacophony of battle faded away as he stared at Lord Kyferin's fallen body. Hatred, resentment, loathing, disgust, fury—all those emotions were smoothed away by shock. It was impossible that Lord Kyferin should be dead. He was a force of nature, the hub around which Asho's miserable life turned. To see him fall made no sense.

The strangely dressed Agerastian didn't even pause to gloat, but stumbled, nearly collapsed, and then gathered himself and turned to walk away.

"For the Black Wolf!" Asho raised his sword, not understanding his grief, his outrage, his furious denial. *Lord Kyferin was dead.*

The stranger paused and looked over his shoulder at Asho. The Sin Caster's eyes seemed to expand so as to swallow Asho whole, dark as the bottom of a well, and within them lay a single promise: *Charge me and die.*

"For the Black Wolf," whispered Asho, his arms shaking. The Sin Caster strode away, and as he did so he placed another black rock in his mouth, cried out a fell string of words, and bolts of magic flew from both palms to arc up into the sky and lance down somewhere else on the battlefield.

Asho lowered his blade. He was shaking so hard he could barely stand. He turned to regard the battle and saw the impossible. The forces of the Empire lay wrecked and ruined upon the slope that led up to the Agerastian position. A few knights had managed to reach the summit and engage the enemy in combat, but most had foundered long before, and either lay dead or were retreating down the slope, back to where the second wave of the Ascendant's great army was waiting to charge.

The wind stirred Asho's white hair. His sword was a dead weight in his hand. Streaks of ebon fire erupted from the Agerastian line here and there to fall upon knots of resistance. How many of those strange men were there? A dozen? Screams drifted with the wind. Horror caused his skin to crawl. Sin Casters, emerging from the most dreadful legends to walk the earth once more.

The Agerastian line was beginning to move down the hill. One of the soldiers ran at him, followed by three others. *I'm a coward*, thought Asho as he raised his sword, tip angled obliquely at the ground. At the last moment he stepped aside, and the man's downward chop slid down the length of his blade and buried itself in the dirt. His momentum carried the soldier on, and as he ran by Asho pivoted and brought his own sword up and around and down to cut through the man's neck. *I stood still as my liege Lord died.* He felt numb. The second soldier stabbed his blade straight at Asho's chest, but Asho parried and stepped forward, spinning up the length of the man's outstretched arm to crack his elbow into the back of the man's head and send him staggering to his knees. *But why should I have died for that monster?* The third man dropped his sword as Asho's blade sliced open his forearm and died when Asho ducked under the fourth man's swing, allowing it to catch the third full in the throat.

Shaya, I didn't avenge you. Kyferin died without knowing my hate.

The fourth man screamed a curse as he wrenched his blade free and spat at Asho. "Bythian scum! I'll send you back to the Black Gate!"

The numbness cracked and shattered. Asho blinked, seeing the man for the first time, and into the void of horror blossomed fury.

He stepped in, gripping his sword's hilt with both hands so that he could place all his strength behind his blows. The Agerastian was taller than he, of course, lean and whipcord strong, but Asho's fury was cold and total and he attacked the man's very blade, smashing it aside again and again, driving the bigger man before him, causing him to stumble back on his heels. Each time the soldier tried to raise his sword Asho smacked it aside, until finally the man dropped it and Asho speared his sword through the man's throat.

The man fell, gurgling and scrabbling at the wound. Asho stood over him, his rage sluicing away as quickly as it had come. Death was everywhere, given voice in hoarse screams and pleas for mercy. He thought of Shaya as he'd seen her last, her white hair plastered to her head, turning to smile brokenly at him before she rode through the castle gate and to Ennoia, to pass back once more into the depths of Bythos and a life of slavery. Asho shuddered and looked around him. He recognized one body after another. Ser Eckel. Ser Orban. Ser Merboth. Each as lethal and brutal a knight as could be found throughout Ennoia, and all cut down by a Sin Caster.

Asho looked up. They'd lost the battle. It was unheard of; the Ascendant Empire had lost. Around him as far as he could see, the flower of the Empire's chivalry lay wasted and ruined. The greatest knights of the age had been massacred.

"Asho!" The cry was thin, almost inaudible over the chaos, but he turned and saw Ulein, squire to Ser Orban, weaving his way drunkenly around the fallen toward Asho. His left arm hung awkwardly by his side, the chainmail torn at his shoulder. "Asho!"

"Here," he called back unnecessarily.

Back at Kyferin Castle, Ulein would rather have swum in the moat than talk to him. Now the other squire hurried to his side, expression a combination of relief and fear. Asho slipped his arm around Ulein's waist as the other youth sagged, and then they both turned as they heard the high, pure clarion call of the trumpets from the far hill. Asho felt his heart sink. "They've sounded the second charge."

Together they stood and watched as the second half of the Empire's army began to move forward, riding down the gradual slope of the far hill. The line was orderly, and this time the knights did not break out into a gallop but continued up the enemy slope at a trot instead.

"But why?" Ulein's voice was a hoarse whisper. "Didn't they see...?"

Asho watched as close to a thousand knights rode up toward them. They looked glorious, but their gallant bravery seemed nothing but cruel foolishness. The slope was strewn with the dead and dying. No orderly charge would be possible.

Ulein winced. "Maybe if they stay close together, maintain order..?"

Asho didn't have the heart to answer. He surveyed the enemy line just above them, which had come to a halt at the sound of the trumpets. "We have to do something."

Ulein hissed and shifted his weight. "But what?"

"Those bolts of fire. They'll destroy the second wave. We have to kill their Sin Casters."

"They can't be Sin Casters," said Ulein. "That's not possible."

As if they had been summoned, twelve robed men and women stepped forth from the massed ranks of the Agerastian army. They were spaced out equally across the line, clad in the same flowing purple and yellow robes, and the regular soldiers seemed to accord them all the same mixture of fear and respect.

"Whatever they are," said Asho, "we have to stop them." He paused. "Somehow."

Below, the knights had spurred their steeds from a trot to a steady canter. The great hooves caused the very ground to shiver. Their lances were still pointed at the sky, but Asho knew that soon they would lower their points, and that would be the signal to charge.

"Find me a sword," said Ulein with some of his former

arrogance. "Hurry!"

Asho stepped over to the fallen Ser Eckel and took the knight's beautiful sword from his dead hand, then hurried back and gave it to Ulein. The other squire barely had the strength to lift it.

"There," said Asho, pointing. "The one closest to us. He's the one who killed Lord Kyferin." *While I stood aside and watched.*

Ulein took a deep breath. "I'll charge him from the front. You come 'round the side. Wait till he's focused on me, then take him down."

Asho stared at Ulein's profile as the young man's jaw clenched and unclenched. For the first time, he felt admiration for the squire.. It was almost possible to forget the years of insults and disdain. There was no hope of success. Each Sin Caster stood in clear sight of their army. For Asho to reach the mage's side without being noticed was impossible. But what choice did they have?

"I'll see you in the next life," said Asho.

The dull rumble became furious thunder. The charge had been signaled.

"Don't kid yourself," said Ulein, voice thickening with contempt. "I'm bound for Nous. You'll be lucky to be reborn an Agerastian. Now go!" With that he started to limp straight toward the Sin Caster.

Asho's admiration curdled. He glanced at the charging army below. Already its ranks were breaking up as the soldiers rode around fallen knights.

"My soul to the White Gate," Asho whispered fiercely, and he took off at a run, crouching low as he circled around to come in on the Sin Caster's flank. He darted from fallen horse to fallen horse, pausing to check Ulein's progress. The other squire was dragging the sword, his face pale and drawn, but Asho saw ragged determination on his face.

Asho ran to the fallen horse that lay closest to the mage and crouched behind it. He didn't think he'd been noticed.

As one the twelve Sin Casters swallowed their black rocks and then raised their hands, palms toward the sun. As one they began to call out their incantations. They all looked sick, Asho thought, faces beaded with sweat, pale and fevered, spittle flecking their lips. They shuddered, and two of them stumbled and nearly fell.

Ulein screamed, somehow raised Ser Eckel's blade with one arm, and broke out into a run. "For the Ascendant!" Asho heard him cry.

It was now or never. *I'm a coward,* he thought, his stomach a greasy knot, but then he sucked in a deep breath, gritted his teeth and burst out from his hiding place.

CHAPTER TWO

Asho

Eleven of the Sin Casters finished their incantations and black fire streaked out to arch out into the sky and fall upon the charging knights below. The twelfth mage—their mage—saw Ulein's approach, and with annoyance lowered both arms so that his seamed palms were pointed directly at the charging squire. Ebon fire exploded from his hands and flew right at Ulein, who screamed and brought Eckel's blade down as if to cut the bolts in twain, but still his back burst out behind him, clotted pieces of flesh spraying into the air.

Asho bit back a cry of rage, trying for every chance at surprising the Sin Caster. He ran hunched over, as if that might hide him from the army, sprinting across the torn ground toward the mage. Numerous voices called out, and the Sin Caster turned to stare at Asho.

I'm not going to make it, I'm not going to make it, I'm not—

The Sin Caster fought back what looked like a spasm of nausea and raised his palm again. Deep lines of exhaustion were carved into his face; his eyes were sunken and hooded. He whispered a word and that sizzling, lethal sound filled the air as a single bolt of flame flew at Asho with unerring accuracy.

Asho screamed. He closed his eyes and brought his blade around as if to slice the bolt in two. He saw falling rain, Shaya turning away from him, felt terror and regret and loss engulf him, and then his sword shattered in his hands. Flecks of metal raked across his hauberk and laid open needle-thin cuts across his face. Still screaming, Asho tripped and fell to his knees, catching himself with an outstretched hand as he threw his suddenly white-hot sword hilt away with the other hand.

His eyes snapped open. He was alive. Around him lay the glowing shards of his blade, each one cherry-red and darkening even as he watched. He looked up at the Sin Caster, whose face mirrored Asho's shock.

"That's not possible," said the man. "Perhaps because you're Bythian? But no. That makes no sense."

Asho drew his dagger and threw it, a wild, underhand toss. It spun through the air and buried itself in the Sin Caster's stomach.

The man grunted and stepped back. He looked down and touched the circular pommel, traced the Ascendant's Triangle that was inscribed there and then let out a low hiss. "Kill him," he said.

Asho looked from the Sin Caster to the Agerastian soldiers. Their battle line was twenty deep, with those at the front holding kite-shaped shields and stabbing short blades.

"Gate me," said Asho as he rose to his feet.

The closest ten soldiers from the second line threw their spears. Asho threw himself into a dive, tumbled, heard spears thunking into the dirt around him, and felt one cut a line of fire down his back but not punch home. Then he was up and running, a score of soldiers at his heels.

From somewhere someone yelled, "Hold the line! Damn you, hold the line!" Glancing back, he saw his pursuers falter, curse, and return. Wild laughter erupted from his lips, a sense of euphoria and disbelief making him giddy, and then he tripped and fell hard onto the sod.

A whinny sounded above him. Asho raised his face to see Crook came cantering up as if he were at the paddock back home and hoping for an apple.

"Idiot horse!" Asho grabbed the hanging reins and pulled himself up, then threw them back over Crook's head. "You should have run while you had the chance!"

Crook shoved his damp, soft nose against. Asho's neck. Asho froze when he looked past the horse at the madness that was befalling the second wave just below. The black fire had reduced the glorious charge to a shambles. Still the Empire's knights struggled on, driven by honor and outrage. Dusk was falling, and the ebon bolts of flame shot through with crimson glowed like witchfire in the gloom as they fell again and again. It was terrible, a punishment unceasing. Asho moaned in horror. Such death. Such a massacre. There was no glory here. Nothing but destruction.

And yet. The black fire was growing markedly weaker, with fewer bolts in each attack. Scanning the Agerastian lines, Asho saw a Sin Caster collapse to her knees, head lowered as she coughed up blood. Only three yet stood on their feet, one of whom was supported by a soldier. Even as Asho watched, that man hurled a single slender bolt and slid to the ground.

The Sin Casters were done.

The remnants of the Ascendant's army screamed their defiance and urged their horses on. Lathered and foaming at the mouth, the mighty war mounts struggled up the last few blood-drenched yards. As they did so, the Agerastians sounded their own trumpets for the first time.

Asho swung up onto Crook's back as the Agerastian infantry let out a roar and parted, allowing their own lightly armored knights to race forth from between the units and charge toward him and the struggling knights. Asho cursed and wheeled Crook around. "Go! Go!" He dug his heels in and Crook took off, racing downhill, the massed might of the enemy right behind him.

It was the most reckless gallop of his life. Asho tried to guide Crook but quickly gave up and just tried to remain saddled. Crook leaped the dead and dying horses, veered sharply left and right, and nearly collided with a knot of obdurate knights who refused to turn. Behind him Asho heard the familiar crash of lance on shield, the ring of sword on plate. He thought of turning and fighting, but looking over his shoulder he saw the Agerastian charge overwhelming the remnants with ease. They kept coming, destroying everything in their path. Theirs was a charge to be envied. Racing downhill, faced with broken groups of soldiers who turned to run as much as stand and fight, the Agerastian knights were destroying all resistance with ease.

Crook stretched out his stride and hit the valley floor at full gallop. Evening was giving way to dusk, and the slumped-over kragh that lay beside butchered horses and the knights of the first wave looked like shadowed mounds. Right behind him came a dozen enemy knights. Ahead and up the opposite slope were the remnants of the Ascendant's army. Large but disorganized regiments of foot soldiers, most of them barely arrived at the battlefield, were now panicking and melting away before the oncoming tide. With the setting of the sun Asho's vision was improving, and his eyes widened as he made out the Ascendant's Grace himself, resplendent before his pavilion in his white enameled armor, his cloak of the purest ivory. He was sitting astride the largest destrier Asho had ever seen, and ringed around him were the Seven Virtues, the greatest of knights from the floating city of Aletheia itself.

Somehow, despite the death that followed at Asho's heels, the Grace and his Virtues weren't retreating. Crook, slowing once more, struggled up the slope toward them.

Asho looked back over his shoulder. The entire Agerastian army seemed to be flowing down the hill right behind him. Hundreds of Agerastian knights were punching through the last of the second wave, and behind them came a thousand or more foot soldiers.

"Your Grace! Run!" Asho knew that his voice would be drowned out by the chaos of the battlefield, but he still yelled, hoarse though he was. "Run!"

He pulled back on his reins and turned Crook around. He felt a desperate determination to hold, no matter how much his fear assailed him. Here he would stand and, if need be, here he would fall. He would not let a single Agerastian reach the Grace while he yet breathed.

Crook was snorting, his round sides heaving. What Asho wouldn't have done for a lance! Instead he raised his sword and kissed the Ascendant's Triangle embossed on the pommel.

The Agerastian knights were slowing as they powered up the hill. Still, they were but moments away. Asho could make out their saturnine faces, their pointed black beards, their blue, knee-length tunics worn under their alien scale mail.

So many of them, he thought. He took a deep breath. *My soul to the White Gate. I failed Shaya. At the very least I can die for the Ascendant's Grace!*

The mass of Ascendant infantry was melting away on all sides. Their terror was contagious. There were still several thousand men on this slope who had promised to fight for the Ascendant, but the tide of battle had turned, and now they cared nothing for numbers. They could see only the ruin on the far slope, and the charging knights, and as the first man turned and ran, they all trembled, hesitated, and then turned tail.

A horse stepped up to stand on Asho's right, a beautiful steed, mightier than even Lord Kyferin's destrier, clad in impeccable white enameled barding. Its head was encased in a helm shaped like a dragon. Astride its back was a slender knight in beautiful armor enameled a pearlescent white and fluted with silver, a single rune inscribed across his chest. *Makaria*, Asho read, and he felt light-headed as he realized beside whom he would fight. Makaria of the harbor city of Zoe, one of the Seven Virtues, the knight of Happiness himself.

Another knight rode up on his left. His mount was a beast, almost more bull than horse, and his armor had no elegance to it, formed of thick plates of iron, his greathelm horned and the rune on his chest overlaid in black metal. *Akinetos*. The Immovable, the Ennoian Virtue.

Asho tried to swallow and found that he could not. He had stepped from brutal and gruesome battle into a dream, a song of greatness such as he had only heard while sitting in Lord Kyferin's great hall, chin resting on his palm, listening to the bard tell tales of old.

Makaria lifted his visor, revealing a face dark like that of all Zoeians and handsome to the point of beauty. He smiled at Asho, his teeth bright in the light of dusk. "Your bravery is noted, young squire. Who is your Lord?"

Didn't he care that Asho was from Bythos? That twenty Agerastian knights were thundering up the hill toward them? Asho blinked, and then bowed as best he could from the waist. "Ser Kyferin, my Lord."

Makaria nodded. "The Black Wolf. Welcome. Let your sword sing his praises." He lowered his visor just as two other Virtues nudged their horses into place, so that somehow Asho formed the point, with two legendary knights on either side. The other two? Asho had no time to check. The Agerastians were upon them.

Chaos erupted. Lances splintered on shields. Asho, seized by a feral desire to not die quietly, spurred Crook forward at the last moment so that he leaped at the enemy just before they could collide. His enemy's lance cut a furrow through Asho's upper arm, and then his horse was next to Crook. Asho yelled and swung his blade down, only to find his blow blocked by the knight's kite shield. Again Asho swung, guiding Crook with his knees and hearing the ghost of Brocuff's voice yelling instructions at him, telling him to *move*, to press the attack, to keep the man off-balance. The enemy knight was skilled, however, and recovered quickly, drawing his curved Agerastian cavalry blade in time to parry once more.

Steel clanged on steel, horses reared and screamed, but past the madness that had engulfed him Asho saw more Agerastians swarming up the slope toward them. He sensed Makaria and Akinetos pulling away, each fighting two or three knights of his own. He caught a glimpse of Akinetos shearing a sword in half and taking off a man's head with the same blow. He wanted to watch, but nearly died as his opponent thrust at his face. Gasping, he dodged aside, but more blows came right after. The man was truly skilled, his curved blade as swift as a snake's tongue, and twice its edge skittered across Asho's mail but failed to penetrate.

Desperate, Asho launched himself out from his saddle right into his opponent, bull-rushing the man to the ground. The other man's foot remained stuck in his stirrup. Asho rose, gasping, and thrust his blade into the man's exposed neck.

Crook shied away, and then there were enemy knights everywhere. Shadows lengthened and merged into each other. Swords flashed, catching the last of the sunset's fiery glow. Asho stumbled back, waving his sword before him with aching arms, trying to ward off blows. The Virtues were being pressed back by sheer weight of numbers. Though the dead littered the ground at their feet, they were harried on all sides. Even as Asho watched, a Virtue leaped some twenty feet into the air, sailing impossibly high with his cloak streaming behind him, to come crashing down upon a knot of Agerastians and send them sprawling. Another Virtue swung a massive chain at whose end was affixed a sphere of spiked steel the size of a head. It sheared through the ranks of enemies with devastating effect. Yet there there were simply too many enemy knights. Numbers was proving greater than inhuman skill.

Asho staggered back, retreating and nearly falling. He turned to look for the Grace. There... The second purest man in the Empire was besieged on all sides by the enemy. Asho saw the sole Virtue left by the Grace's side dragged from his saddle, two lances embedded in his chest, infantry clutching at his legs and waist. He roared as he fell, and cut a man down before crashing into the dark.

Asho took a deep breath. The back of his throat was thick with sour spit. His lungs burned. He could barely raise his right arm. He wanted to fall to his knees. But before him the Grace was fighting for his very life. The enemy were ignoring him, seeing him as a mere Bythian, and focusing their attention on the Virtues. He had but one chance.

Taking a deep breath, stabbing and cutting to the sides as he went, Asho forced his way up the hill until he stepped into the open space before the Grace, whose sword and rearing mount were keeping the enemy at bay. Asho hesitated, looking for an opportunity to strike, and then an arrow came whistling out of the dark and plunged into the neck of the Grace's horse. It screamed and reared violently. The Grace yelled, a surprisingly human sound, and fell to the earth.

Three Agerastians leaped from their horses, blades raised. "His head! Cut off his head!"

Asho hurled himself toward them, shouldering the first into the second and slapping down the third's blade. It was less of a skilled attack than a mad collision, and when the first knight turned on him Asho stomped his boot into the inside of the man's knee, causing the joint to buckle outward with a snap. The man went down, but it wasn't enough. The second knight ran past Asho at the Grace. Asho turned to tackle him, but the third knight cracked his gloved fist into Asho's face, knocking him aside. Asho cried out and on instinct raised his blade just in time to block what would have been a killing blow.

The sun had dipped behind the hill. The sky was growing dark behind his foe. Asho could barely make out the man's sword. He blocked more on instinct than anything else. Once, twice, and then he riposted, a wild guess, and felt his blade hit home. The man grunted and stepped in for a head butt, but Asho saw the move coming. At the last moment he sidestepped and kicked the man's feet out from under him. The man went down and Asho stomped his neck, then hacked down once, twice, until the man cried out and moved no more.

"Your Grace!" Asho wheeled and stumbled up the hill. Battle was all around. There—the white armor. The Grace was on one knee, sword held aloft, parrying blow after blow that the large soldier was raining down on him. Asho struggled to run, but even with all the desperation in the world he could barely move faster than a tortured jog.

He reached the pair just as an arrow fell down blindly from the dark and punched into the Grace's side, causing him to drop his sword. The Agerastian soldier brought his sword down where the Grace's neck met his shoulder just as Asho stabbed him in the small of his back.

Both men screamed and went down. Asho lost his sword.

"No." He dropped to his knees next to the Grace. The man's helm was beautiful, molded in the gloom to appear like an angel, the white horsehair muddied now. Asho went to pull the helm free but two men in Aletheian white shoved him aside.

The Virtues were still fighting, their ferocity and skill finally pushing the Agerastians back. Asho knew he should join them, but he couldn't rise from his knees. He watched as the two men tended to the Grace. The wounds were mortal. There was no saving him. *Even the holy die*, he thought. The Grace was the second purest man in all the Empire. His soul would pass through the White Gate and return nevermore. *Even in sorrow we must rejoice.* And yet, in his heart, Asho felt a crushing sense of responsibility, ridiculous for a Bythian. *If only he'd moved a little quicker. Been stronger.*

Tears ran down his cheeks. So many dead, and now the Grace himself. All was lost. What did this mean for the Empire? His own Lord was dead, and every Black Wolf with him.

Complete destruction. Utter ruin.

"Your Grace," said one of the two men, a vulpine man in white robes. "There is still time. Give me the signal. Just nod your head."

The Grace's head was resting on the man's lap. He was only in his twenties, Asho saw with dull surprise, his features striking, his blond hair cut close to the scalp. An arrogant, handsome face, pale now and cut deep with pain.

"Your Grace," said the man again. "You have but moments. You have so much left to give. Don't do this. Give me a sign! I have the elixir here. This is your last chance!"

A ragged scream rang out to their left. Trumpets sounded somewhere in the valley below. Asho stared, mute, and saw the Grace nod his head. Immediately the man beside him hissed with triumph and uncorked a vial of black liquid. He placed it to the Grace's lips and raised it gently. The Grace drank, coughing as he did so.

Asho blinked. Should he intervene? A moment passed, and then the Grace seemed to relax, and with a sigh he closed his eyes. Had he died? No. His eyes snapped open, and he took the vial and drained it. Then he tossed it aside and rose with the other man's help to his feet.

Asho thought himself beyond shock. Thought himself inured to further horror. But this? It couldn't be. The Grace had cheated death.

Somehow. Had rejected passage through the White Gate.

"Your Grace!" A Virtue rode up. In the dark Asho couldn't make out his rune. Autophues? "We've cleared a space. We have to flee. We have but moments!"

"Very well," said the Grace, taking his helm from the white-robed man and sliding it down over his head. "Bring me another mount." He paused as he noticed Asho. "What are you doing here, Bythian?"

Asho's mouth was bone-dry. He couldn't speak.

"He's a squire of Lord Kyferin," said a blood-streaked Virtue, stepping into view. *Makaria.*

"A squire?" Despite everything, there was amusement and disbelief in the Grace's voice. "Kyferin will be squiring dogs next. Still, you have earned your spurs. Kyferin shall not fault me. Come. Kneel."

"We must leave, your Grace!" the first Virtue's steed was prancing, and the knight was reining him in left and right to keep him in place.

"Kneel!"

Asho rose to his feet and, reeling like a drunkard, he stepped forth and fell to his knees before the second most powerful man in the Empire. *But not the second most pure.*

The Grace took up his blade and touched it to Asho's left shoulder. "For your deeds done in battle I dub you a knight. Your name?"

The screams of the dying all around them were a pyre on which Asho burned. "Asho."

"For your service to my person, I, Grace to the Ascendant himself, name you Ser Asho, no doubt the first of your kind." He touched his blade to Asho's other shoulder. "In the dark times to come, I shall have need of brave and loyal men such as yourself, regardless of your origin. Will you come with me, Ser Asho, and enter my service?"

A third Virtue rode up, massively armored, a spare horse held by the reins. *Akinetos.* "Here. We must ride." His voice was deep and calm. "Now, or we ride not at all."

Asho rose to his feet. What had happened here?

Something wrong. Something evil. Something that flew in the face of Ascendancy like nothing he had heard of before. "You honor me, your Grace." He could barely choke out the words. "But I cannot abandon my Lady." His voice felt insubstantial, a wisp of smoke before the gaze of the man before him. "Lord Kyferin is dead. I must ride to her and ensure her safety."

The Grace stood frozen, as if he had not heard, and then his face stiffened as if he had been slapped and he nodded stiffly. "Your loyalty behooves you, Bythian. May the White Gate welcome you when your time comes." He took up a broken banner that lay to one side and tore free the white cloth that had hung from it. "Here. For when the world mocks your claim." He then climbed up onto his mount as Agerastian war cries sounded just downslope. "Where to, Makaria?"

"This way, your Grace," said the Virtue, and with a touch of his heels his mount leaped forward. Five other Virtues rode forth, the Grace at their center. One of their august number had fallen.

Asho watched them disappear into the darkness, riding toward the nearby forest. He felt drained, depleted beyond all measure. What had just happened? What had he witnessed?

He was a knight. *A knight.* He'd known in his bones that Lord Kyferin had no intention of ever granting him knighthood. Yet here he was, knighted by the Ascendant's Grace himself—and never would he have believed that he'd be left so sickened and confused should it occur. Slowly he unfurled the white cloth. It was the Ascendant's own war banner, the Everflame.

Something nudged his shoulder from behind. Asho wheeled and swung a sword he no longer held through Crook's head. He stepped in and hugged his horse, and then pulled himself painfully up into the saddle. Around him men were running, some fleeing, some chasing. Victorious trumpet notes were floating through the darkness.

Turning Crook around, Asho dug his heels into his horse's flanks. It was time to quit the field. He had to head home, had to return to Castle Kyferin and tell his Lady that she was now a widow, and he her only remaining knight.

CHAPTER THREE

kethe

Kethe slipped out the keep's front door as quickly and lithely as she could. The trick with the massive old monster was to open it just shy of the spot where the iron hinges let out their terrible shriek, and then catch it as it closed but an inch from the jamb. If that was done just right, one could sneak out onto the keep stairs as sly as a ghost with nobody the wiser. The door shut with nary a sound, and Kethe straightened with a smile. It might take minutes before Hessa, her lady-in-waiting, noticed that she was gone. By then it would be far too late.

The keep was the highest point of the entire castle, mounted atop its own steep hill. From here Kethe could gaze out over the castle curtain wall to where the sleepy village of Emmond lay nestled hard by Greening Wood. She raised her chin and smoothed down her dove-gray kirtle. Two sentries were watching her from atop the twin drum towers that rose from the top of the barbican. She recognized one as Beartha by his wispy beard. He slouched against a crenellation and grinned at her, revealing his stained and mostly missing teeth.

Trying to exude as much disdain as possible, she began to descend the broad slate steps, raising her dress just enough that she wouldn't trip and tumble head over heels down to the tower arch. Beartha would love that. If he called out to her, she swore to herself, she'd fetch an iron bar from the smithy and break his arm, but he stayed mercifully silent. The steps descended steeply to the arch that led into the barbican. Normally two more soldiers would guard this portal, but they were undermanned due to her father's expedition. No matter. The fewer eyes that marked her passage, the better.

It was hard to maintain her anger at the guard when she was this excited. She almost broke into a run once she was inside, ignoring the countless murder holes and the slits in the ceiling through which three separate portcullises could be dropped. The barbican was a formidable line of defense, a squat building whose entire purpose was to kill those who sought to assault the keep. The wall torches cast flickering shadows, and she heard laughter from the soldiers on the far side of the passage wall. Playing cards, no doubt. She couldn't blame them—Kyferin Castle hadn't been attacked since before she was born.

She took the left turn in the corridor's elbow and hurried back out into the sunlight. Below her spread the bailey itself, the vast yard enclosed within the curtain walls where the daily life of the castle played out for the servants, cooks, stable boys, farriers, smiths, Bythian slaves and everyone else that made the castle a vital and living entity. She loved the bailey; it pulsed with life, was filled with a tapestry of sounds and smells. Hessa always made a face when she was forced to descend from the keep to where the 'commoners' labored, but that was because she was a shallow prig who forgot that she was an Ennoian like the rest of them.

Kethe strode over the last drawbridge that connected the barbican to the stone ramp and fairly skipped down to the dirt floor.

It being late afternoon, half of the bailey was already in shadow, the great curtain wall rising up to cut into the sunlight, its base crowded with buildings that were built against it and around the open center. The cart of a bonded merchant was rolling in through the gatehouse, laden with fresh fish and no doubt come from the harbor city of Zoe through the Sun Portal in Ennoia. Trutwin the gardener and his three young helpers were standing by with wheelbarrows, waiting as the stable boys mucked out the stables, filling the air with the sickly sweet stench of manure. Four old Bythian men staggered past, their white hair slicked to their brows with sweat, bowed over under the piles of wood lashed to their backs and heading toward the massive woodpile stacked against the kitchen building's wall. A young boy sprinted out of the bakery, hooting and juggling a hot cross bun, and Aythe chased him out the door before giving up and yelling after him. Kethe spun around the urchin as he almost collided with her, grinned, and then shrugged apologetically to the baker. Everywhere she looked people were busy: creating barrels, sharpening blades at the grinding stone, crossing from one doorway to the next. The bailey was the polar opposite of the tomb-like keep; here was life and action and excitement.

Slipping through the crowd, smiling as different folk nodded respectfully to her, Kethe made for the chapel. It was beautifully convenient that the entrance to the smith lay through the most respectful destination for the Lord's daughter, a quirk of the castle's construction that she adored, no matter how much the high priest objected. As a result, she'd garnered a reputation for devoutness that allayed her mother's suspicions, and Simeon the priest was kind enough to not dispel any assumptions as to where Kethe spent her time.

She stepped through the door, then hurried along the chapel's back wall, pausing as always to curtsy to the great silver triangle that stood on the far altar, illuminated by the requisite ten candles. It was a sign of her father's wealth that the candles were fine beeswax and not tallow, each as thick and tall as her forearm and always lit. Still, she'd not come to ponder the mysteries of Ascension; with barely a guilty twinge she hurried to the smithy entrance and stepped through into the gloom.

When she was younger, entering the smithy had made her imagine she was passing through the Black Gate itself. The soft glow of the chapel candles would be replaced by the fitful illumination of the forge fires, the air acrid with smoke and the tang of scalded metal. Elon had seemed like an ogre, more massive than even an armored knight, and the hissing of quenched metal and the white and cherry-red glow of malleable steel had seemed to her to be instruments of torture. Now the smithy was her secret home, where she yearned to be when she wasn't in the Greening Wood or riding Lady along the hills. She grinned as Tongs, Elon's ebon firecat, flew up to land on her shoulders and curl about her neck just as Elon turned to regard her; she'd even managed to evade her younger brother Roddick, who thought it hilarious to race back to the keep and report her to their mother. She had at least a half hour before she was truly missed.

"You're pressing your luck, don't you think?" Elon's voice was a rumble more akin to boulders shifting in the depths of the earth than any normal person's voice. Now that she was older he no longer seemed like an ogre; he was a friend, or at the very least an accomplice. His black hair thinning, his beard cropped short, the smith's features were ruddy from a life spent bent over scorching heat. As always, he was wearing only a sleeveless tunic and his heavy leather apron. Kethe wagered that Elon could arm-wrestle any of the Black Wolves into submission without much effort—not that a knight would ever deign to contest with a peasant.

"Yes, well, I'm almost done." Kethe grinned and plucked Tongs from her shoulders, dropped him in his favorite spot by the furnace, and hurried to the back of the smithy. "Besides. Have you seen my needlework? Atrocious. Even my mother can't find the words to compliment it."

"Be that as it may," said Elon, watching her as she rummaged under a pile of empty hemp sacks. "You were nearly caught yesterday, and the day before that I came close to lying to Berthold when he came asking after you. What's going on? Is there some crisis you haven't told me about?"

"Yes," said Kethe, almost to herself. She grasped her treasure and pulled it out, then held it up to examine it in the light of the forge. It glimmered beautifully, like fish scales or a dream of silver under the moon. It was a hauberk, made slowly over the past year, each ring, each rivet, each and every piece tailored to her own body. "I need this finished. For me. Not for anybody else. For me."

She walked over to a trestle table and laid the hauberk down. Two more lines of rings were all that remained to be done before she would declare it complete. Then she'd edge it with leather—or perhaps calfskin, but that might not prove as durable—and then, finally, she'd be able to take it out to Greening Wood.

Elon set down his tongs and hammer and stepped up beside her. He rubbed his jaw. "It's not bad, I suppose."

"Not bad?" She wheeled on him. "It's better than anything *you've* ever made, what with those big sausage fingers of yours." She cut off at the sight of his grin. "I mean, yes. Not bad, I suppose."

Elon picked it up. "I still think you've meshed these rings too tightly together. Fine work, fit for jewelry, but you need flexibility as well."

Kethe bit her lower lip. "Maybe."

The smith set the hauberk back down. "Though it's all academic, isn't it? Like one of Magister Audsley's theories about the Age of Wonders." His words were soft as he regarded her, his eyes gleaming under his heavy brows. "Do you truly expect to wear this in battle, Kethe?"

She stepped over to his scrap pile and took up two heavy bars, one in each hand. A year ago they'd been too heavy for her to lift. Staring fixedly at the stone wall, she raised both bars till her arms were level with the floor. Within moments her shoulders began to burn with the effort.

"Yes," she said. The bars began to tremble. "You heard Esson, that bard who came through with Lord Gysel six months ago." It was hard to speak smoothly when she wanted to clench her stomach and lock her breath in her throat. "Women can be knights. There's a female order far to the south, the Order of the Ax." Her hands were starting to dip, and she forced herself to not lean back so as to compensate. "And Lady Otheria was a knight."

"Lady Otheria," said Elon, stepping up to where she stood, "may not have even existed." He stood in silence for another minute until her arms began to tremble wildly, and only then did he take the weights from her.

Kethe let out a sharp breath as she dropped her arms, then shook them out and rubbed her shoulders. "Even if she didn't, the idea of her is enough." This was a familiar argument, one that Elon had indulged her in many times over the past year, but something had changed. Perhaps it was the near-completion of the chainmail.

He dropped the bars into the scrap pile and then turned back to his anvil, rubbing the back of his head. "I'm just a simple smith. It's my own limitation, not understanding why a pretty young noble lady like yourself would want to get into vicious battles with full-grown men."

Kethe blew a strand of her auburn hair out of her face. "That's all right. When they're singing songs about me, then maybe you'll understand."

He laughed. "Songs? My, the young lady has some real ambition. Though it points her in a terrible direction. I know all too well what the weapons I craft can do to flesh and bone."

Kethe assumed an innocent expression. "As my mother says, women make, men break. I'm simply creating a hauberk, Elon."

"Oh? You plan to run into battle with no weapons, then?"

"Well, maybe a sword. If a man tries to break what I've created, do I not have the right to defend myself?"

Elon crossed his arms over his chest and rocked back on his heels. "I'd like to meet the knight who would strike a lady. I'd stave in his helmet with my hammer."

Kethe grinned. "If I didn't do him in first. And what would *you* be doing out on a battlefield?"

The smith scowled. "Chasing after you, no doubt, and still arguing till the last moment against your folly. Now. Are you going to finish those links? I've set the wire out for you over there."

Her mother, Lady Iskra Kyferin, had lectured her on the value of mindless tasks such as needlework. Letting your hands work allowed your mind to drift, she said, and it was during these moments of reverie that insights and ideas would come. Kethe put on her apron, pulled out the wooden stool and sat at the work station, then pulled the length of thick wire over and grabbed her rod. Tongs padded over and twined himself between her boots, his black feathered wings bumping against the undersides of her thighs. She began to wrap the wire around and around the rod, doing so with slow and methodical care. Some women enjoyed distracting themselves with needlework. She loved creating chainmail. Once the wire was completely wrapped, she'd snip circles from its coiled form, and then these she'd interweave with the unfinished hem of her hauberk and weld them shut. Quiet work. Delicate, repetitive work that allowed her to dream, to let slip her mind from the smoky confines of the smithy and out to wonder on her hopes and aspirations.

She'd never managed to convey to Elon why she wanted to dress in armor and wield a sword. Elon was a practical man; he understood the world in terms of what he could shape and handle with his powerful hands. To him weaponry meant blood and injuries and dirt and campaigning and death. Which was all true. Kethe knew that being a warrior was not a glamorous business, not like they sang about in the epics. She knew that all too well. But simply being a woman was just as dangerous and brutal in its own way.

Three years later, it was still too easy to summon the terror, the bitter, galling sense of helplessness. To remember his face as he came at her with his sword, his eyes blank with his determination to kill her. It had been three years, but she could still vividly recall the tearing pain in her throat as she'd screamed. Screamed, because she'd been unable to defend herself. Screamed, because she was weak and had to summon others to save her.

Kethe pursed her lips and stared down at the wire. Having a sword at her hip would mean never feeling that way again, never letting an animal like that knight terrorize her to the point of having nightmares for a year afterwards. She would be like her father, feared and respected for his strength. Nobody intimidated him. Nobody took advantage of him. He was the strongest, most capable man she knew. Kethe bit her lip as she wove the wire around and around the rod. Elon's hammer began to ring out anew. Methodical, rhythmic.

But becoming a knight had become more than simple self-defense. Over the past few years the blade had come to symbolize the ability to forge her own destiny. Choose her own path. Cut through the layers and layers of strangling expectations, and stand tall and proud and free. A foolish dream, no doubt. There had been many times when she'd felt desolate and alone, and had nearly thrown her coat of mail into Elon's forge. Moments when she'd felt foolish and pathetic, a child indulging in fantasies. But she hadn't given up. Coming to the smith—escaping the stifling confines of the keep whenever she could—was the only true pleasure that was hers and hers alone. Even riding Lady was stilted, accompanied as she always was by Hessa and two guards.

Shouts disturbed her thoughts. She turned to Elon, who stopped, hammer raised above his head. Both then turned to the smithy door. The cries weren't of fear or panic, but rather excitement tinged with alarm.

"A visitor?" Elon set his hammer down and wiped his hands with a dirty cloth.

"News from Father?" Kethe stood and threw a cloth sack over her mail.

Lord Kyferin had been gone two months, along with every Black Wolf and all the squires. Two months was a long time to campaign, but not unusually so; word had reached them intermittently that the Agerastian force had been avoiding pitched battle for weeks now, burning its way across the countryside as it avoided the Ascendant's forces.

More shouts. Kethe hurried through the door into the chapel just as Father Simeon came walking down the aisle with his chaplain at his heels. He was a tall, stern man, with a high forehead, severe cheekbones, and the rich bronzed skin of a Noussian born. "What's going on?"

"I don't know," Kethe said, and stepped outside into the bailey.

Everybody was emerging from their respective buildings to crowd around the gatehouse. Kethe stepped forth, people parting for her with the usual respectful nods. A young man was riding over the castle drawbridge. His white hair and skin as pale as milk marked him for a Bythian, though why he was mounted she couldn't fathom... Wait. Asho? He looked like he'd been dragged backwards by his horse through a field filled with thorns. Half his face was discolored with bruising, and his long hair was spiky with dried sweat and dirt. His horse looked blown, with its head hanging low and its hooves almost dragging across the boards.

The young man's expression was haunted, and Kethe felt the crowd harden around her. Almost every castle servant here was an Ennoian, and none of them appreciated the sight of the upstart Bythian squire.

Asho rode through the gatehouse, the sound of his horse's hooves echoing loudly in the silence until he emerged once more into the weak afternoon sunlight.

"It's Lord Kyferin's squire," muttered somebody to her left.

Asho gazed about the quiet crowd with his pale silver-green eyes, unabashed and disconcertingly direct for a Bythian. As always she felt that prick of annoyance that was just shy of anger at his insolence. He'd not the wit to realize how a little natural deference would ameliorate the anger his arrogance provoked. Still, she couldn't help but feel a pang. His delicate, almost elfin features were terribly aged. The last she'd seen of him he'd appeared but fourteen years old, a fresh-faced youth with large silver eyes and a quiet manner. Now he looked almost a man, harrowed by some experience she couldn't guess at.

Asho slid from the saddle. He was so exhausted his knees buckled as he landed, and were it not for his grip on pommel he might have fallen. Nobody moved forward to assist him, though murmurs of alarm flickered through the crowd. Raising her chin and pushing back her shoulders, Kethe stepped forth, fearing his news but knowing in her core that there was no hiding from the bleakness in his eyes.

"My Lady," said Asho, his voice barely more than a whisper. He straightened with a wince, and she realized he was not only exhausted but wounded too; his hauberk was torn along his ribs, and dirt was deeply ingrained in the links over his shoulder as if he'd fallen hard to the ground.

"Squire Asho." Her nerves made her speak more coldly than she'd meant to.

"I bring grave news, my Lady." He spoke as if they were standing alone, a terrible kindness in his eyes that she wanted to dash away with a slap. He hesitated, the moment come. The moment, Kethe realized, that he must have been dreading even as he fought to get here with all his might. "We were defeated in battle. Lord Kyferin and all his Black Wolves are dead."

The crowd erupted into exclamations of horror, and Kethe closed her eyes and rocked back on her heels, feeling her whole body grow numb. With those words her world had suddenly and irrevocably changed. People were calling out angrily, shouting questions, but when she managed to open her eyes again she saw that Asho was standing silently, ignoring everyone but her.

She had to do something. Control the crowd. Give commands. But all she could do was hold Asho's gaze. No words came to her lips. No thoughts beyond the one terrible and impossible fact: her father was dead. What would she tell Roddick?

"Yet you survived." Her voice came from a far distance. She could barely hear herself over the rushing in her ears. She wanted to hurt him. How dare he look at her with pity? "Did you flee the battle?"

"No," Asho said. He was holding on to the saddle as if it were a branch that was keeping him from drowning. "I only left after the Ascendant's Grace and his Virtues quit the field."

"Then come," she said. "The Lady Kyferin will want to hear your news at once."

The curtain walls seemed impossibly high, the barbican receding into the distance. She felt a moment of vertigo as she turned away, and tears pricked her eyes. She'd show him no weakness. She was Lord Enderl Kyferin's daughter. She would show him only strength. Almost blind with tears she refused to wipe away, she wheeled and strode toward the barbican, sending people scattering as they stumbled out of her way. She didn't care. Memory guided her footsteps. She strode up the stone ramp to the drawbridge, passed quickly over it, and only once she had stepped into the darkness of the barbican did she shudder, a deep soul quake that almost undid her knees. She pressed her hand to the wall and paused, another pang causing her lungs and heart to spasm. She gasped for breath, the sound loud in the corridor. It felt like somebody had punched her right in the solar plexus.

Father was dead. The strongest man she had ever known was

gone. It was like learning that a mountain had suddenly disappeared. And all his Black Wolves with him? Thirty-three knights. Brutal, cruel men who had at once scared her and ensured her safety. Each with his own manse or fort in the countryside about the castle, each a minor lord of his own staff and servants. Dead. All of them. She stared blindly at a wall torch as names tumbled through her mind. Her mind reeled, and then she pushed away from the wall. She took a deep breath. Held it. If she was to be a knight, that she had to accustom herself to pain and loss. She had to be strong. Roddick would be looking to her for comfort. And yet the floor felt like it was slipping out from beneath her. Before more tears could come, she strode forth down the hall and turned right at the elbow. Out the gate and onto the second drawbridge, moving swiftly, head lowered.

She passed through the drum towers and out onto the keep stairs. Lifting her dress, she ran up the steps, not caring for decorum, not caring who saw. She flitted up to the keep door and hauled it open. She turned quickly away from the large kitchen, ignoring the puzzled looks of the servants, and ran up the intramural staircase to the third floor.

While the Great Hall down in the bailey could seat over a hundred and often did, the Lord's Hall here on the third floor of the keep was more intimate, and her father tended to use it as an audience chamber in which to receive distinguished guests. A dais was set against the back wall, with her mother's pale oaken seat set next to her father's massive and beautifully carved cherry wood throne. Two long trestle tables ran down the length of the circular room, whose walls were hung with tapestries depicting her father's favorite pastimes: war and the hunt. Wall candles complemented the light that filtered through the arrow slit windows.

Their bard, Menczel, was sitting to one side, idly plucking a quiet melody from his lute and singing of the legendary trials of the Virtue Theletos. Her mother was seated on her pale chair, with the steward and his assistant standing before her.

Kethe rushed into the hall and then caught herself and stopped, took a breath and pushed her shoulders back. Her mother had been leaning back in her chair, chin resting delicately on an extended finger, listening to Bertchold as he recounted some issue regarding their stocks. At Kethe's entrance, however, her mother sat up, and both Menczel and Bertchold fell silent, turning to regard her.

"Kethe?"

Her mother was the most intelligent person she knew, and the most perceptive by far. Kethe's whole life had been one long struggle to find privacy, to shield her thoughts, to not give everything away to her mother without realizing it. She had no hopes of doing so now.

Lady Kyferin rose gracefully to her feet. In her mid-thirties, she was still a strikingly beautiful woman, her eyes the blue of stark winter midday skies, her skin as pale as fresh milk and her mien effortlessly noble. It was from her that Kethe had inherited her own auburn hair, a dark brown that the right angle of sunlight could set to smoldering like fireplace coals; but while Kethe tended to wear her hair in a rough braid thrown over one shoulder, her mother's mane was luxurious and intricately braided. Born and raised in the august mountain peak cities of Sige, Lady Iskra Kyferin's descent to Ennoia and her presence in the castle and by his side had been a source of great pride to Kethe's father. Dressed today in white accented with gold, Lady Iskra stared at her daughter, and her eyes grew wide.

Kethe fought back her tears anew. As realization dawned on her mother's face, she stepped forward, unsure what to do with her hands, what to say, where to stand.

"Father is dead," she managed at last, and at this the tears finally spilled.

CHAPTER FOUR

Asho

Asho had yearned for and dreaded this moment in equal measure since quitting the battlefield a week ago. His weary mind had played out a thousand scenarios as he'd ridden south amongst the flood of demoralized soldiers and peasants, hunched over Crook's back but refusing to rest. At times he'd imagined the blowing of trumpets as he rode up to Kyferin Castle's gatehouse, the sunlight golden, the castle folk and Lady Kyferin turning out to grant him a hero's reception. Other times he despaired and could only imagine being received as a traitor and coward, castigated by the Lady for not having died by her husband's side, his weapons and arms taken from him before he was hurled out the postern gate if not dropped into the Wolf Tower dungeon itself.

Despite his despair, he'd ridden for the great city of Ennoia, which gave its name to all those born on this plane of existence, the roads growing more choked with every passing mile. How different this journey was. It had been only a month since he had ridden along this same road as part of Lord Kyferin's proud retinue, head held defiantly high and convinced that he would return, if not covered in glory, then at least part of a victorious band.

Instead he rode alone and turned east just before reaching Ennoia's vast walls. Covered in mud, body aching and wounded, Crook nearly lame from how hard he'd been ridden, Asho had persevered, ignoring the groups of soldiers who eyed him and wondered if he was an escaped slave. The days had merged with nights spent sleeping in dense thickets and behind hedges, until finally he had reached the Flint Road and turned his horse north for the final day's ride to Lady Kyferin.

Voices murmured around him. Asho blinked. He'd nearly fallen asleep, hand still on Crook's pommel, leaning against his weary beast. Pushing away, he wiped vigorously at his face and nodded as Nenker, one of the stable boys, stepped up to take Crook's reins.

Familiar faces were all around him, glaring at him as if he were to blame. He could feel the crowd simmering, waiting for some provocation to step forward and accost him with angry questions that could quickly turn to violence. He saw a flash of pale hair at the back. It was Chikko, one of the other Bythians, watching with muted pity and no intention of helping. Asho took a deep breath. He was used to being disdained, but this open hatred he saw on people's faces was new. He looked past them and saw Kethe disappear into the barbican. His throat tightened. There had been many times over the years that he'd quietly seethed at her thoughtless arrogance, but the way her eyes had flashed with pain as he'd delivered his news had cut him to the quick. Her face had grown pale, her thick freckles stark and her lips bloodless, and he'd wished for something comforting to say. Anything. But her glare had forbidden it and reminded him that while their worlds had shattered, some rules would never be broken.

A heavy hand clapped him on the shoulder and he turned to see Brocuff by his side. The castle constable was a short man, level with Asho, but stocky and built like a bear. Grim at the best of times, prone to frowning even when receiving a gift, he'd nevertheless been one of the few on the castle staff to treat Asho with a gruff directness that was free of malice.

"Come on, lad," said the constable. "Let's bring your news to the Lady. I'll walk up with you. Save her from having to summon me right after."

I'm a knight, thought Asho. *Not a lad.* But he couldn't be bothered to correct the constable. He simply nodded and began walking toward the barbican.

"Hold up," said Brocuff. Asho turned. "You're injured."

He'd grown so used to the pain and the awful stiffness that he'd almost forgotten. The cut down his back was more messy than grave, but he knew it had soaked his aketon and caused it to stick to his chain. Only extreme exhaustion kept him from hissing when the ruptured links of his hauberk caught in the wound. "Oh. Yes. But it can wait."

"Can it, now?" Brocuff sounded skeptical. "I've seen men die of lesser wounds due to infection. You should go straight to Father Simeon."

"It can wait," said Asho again. The stubbornness that had seen him through the last week was all that was keeping him on his feet. If he should turn from his purpose, he'd collapse and never rise again. "After I've done my duty, then I'll find the Father."

"Fair enough." Brocuff studied him as if seeing him anew. "Lead the way then, good squire."

Not a squire, thought Asho again, but he simply turned and plodded up the stone ramp. How strange it all looked! The great curtain wall, the bulwark of the barbican, the drawbridges and drum towers, all of them guarding the impregnable keep. Before the battle Asho had thought it overdone; he couldn't imagine a force that could pierce the outer wall, much less the interior defenses. But how well would stone hold up against magic?

Shivering, he entered the barbican. Word had preceded him, and he saw faces at the murder holes, and the iron door leading into the guts of the barbican was open. A number of guards stood there, men-at-arms he didn't recognize. They watched him approach, and one with rotten teeth and the look of a drowned rat stepped forward to block his way.

"Where are the others, then? You a runner? Tell the truth now, Byth-grub."

Asho stopped, swaying where he stood, and stared straight through the man. He'd learned that answering only led to more insults and then shoves and even kicks. Unless he drew his blade to defend himself, and then he'd be hauled before the Lord and asked to explain why he was attacking the castle guards.

Luckily he wasn't alone. Brocuff stepped up behind him. "Back to your posts, men." The constable's growl was soft but brooked no questioning. Brocuff was in charge of castle security while Lord Kyferin and his Black Wolves were away. For all that he was not nobly born, he was respected by his men. The guards melted back into the darkness, and Asho strode past them, putting them out of mind.

The steps up through the drum towers to the keep door were interminable, and the rich smells coming from the ground floor kitchen set his mouth to watering and almost made his knees buckle. When had he eaten last? *What* had he eaten? He didn't want to remember. Turning, he climbed the stairs to the Lord's Hall and stopped just shy of the doorway on the third floor. He could hear voices within. Kethe's voice, broken and tearful. This was it. The moment he'd been fighting to reach.

Slowly, painfully, Asho straightened. He pulled his tabard down and hissed as cloth tore away from dried blood. There was no chance of making himself presentable. He was what he was: a man returned direct from war.

"I'm right behind you," whispered Brocuff. In the close dark he smelled of leather and pipe smoke. "Just deliver your news, then you can rest."

Asho nodded and stepped out into the light. The sight of Lady Kyferin caused his stomach to clench. Oh, she was beautiful, impossibly so, and now, having heard the news from her trembling daughter, she was standing before her raised seat like a marble statue, untouchable and remote, regal and elegant beyond measure. She was wearing a form-fitting white dress that was delicately embroidered with gold, with a broad golden belt hanging about her hips. Her pale hair was intricately tressed, and her eyes were locked on him as if he was bringing death and not merely news of it into her hall.

"My Lady," he said, voice faltering, and stopped a good five yards from her dais, falling to one knee. There were others already gathered here: the steward, his assistant, and the bard. He ignored them all. "My Lady, I bring terrible news."

His words hung in the silence, and he stared at the wood grain beside his right foot. *Don't fall*, he told himself as he felt his balance rock. *Just a little longer.*

"Rise, squire." Lady Kyferin's voice was impressively controlled, rich and soft, with the strange accents of Sige. "Tell me your tidings."

Asho took a deep breath and looked up. He'd not risk rising just yet. Kethe was standing behind and to one side of her mother's chair, face pale, eyes glassy. Swallowing, he met Lady Kyferin's striking blue eyes. "For three weeks we chased the Agerastians across the fields and farms north and west of Ennoia. We thought they might escape and reach the coast, but the Grace drove us hard, and we finally forced them into a confrontation a week ago."

Asho paused, trying to decide how best to select his words. To criticize the Grace was unimaginable—and yet… "They took a stand on top of a hill between a copse and the village of Utrect. Our forces arrived and positioned themselves on the lower slopes of a facing hill. Lord Kyferin was confident that we could wait till morning to attack, giving our men the chance to rest and allowing the entirety of the Grace's army to gather—at least half the infantry were still strung out behind us on the roads. But the Grace was forced to give the order to attack when one of his lords broke rank and led others down the slope. Lord Kyferin took the vanguard, along with his Black Wolves, and we charged the enemy line."

Everybody was listening, spellbound. Menczel the bard stood with furrowed brow, memorizing every word. Lady Kyferin was staring right through him; she knew how this tale turned out. All that remained to learn were the details.

"Magic, my lady." Asho's voice sounded raw in his own ears. Even now he couldn't believe what had happened. "The Agerastians had a dozen Sin Casters with them. They threw black fire, and the Grace's army was destroyed."

"Magic?" Bertchold's voice was sharp with indignation. He was an older man, well into his fifties, with the beginnings of jowls and a square, stocky frame, clad in black furs with his chain of office hanging thickly around his neck. "Impossible. There have been no Sin Casters in over two centuries."

"I swear it. I saw the flames engulf Lord Kyferin and his men. I was only spared because I was riding at the back with the other squires."

Asho saw the scene again, heard the hissing sound of ebon flame scorching flesh and iron alike.

"Nonsense!" Bertchold's voice dipped into scorn. "I'd hoped for an honest account, but if you're going to twist the tale with your debased imaginings—"

"You saw my Lord husband fall?" Lady Kyferin didn't raise her voice, but Bertchold immediately fell silent.

Asho nodded. "I did, my Lady." Years of anger and revulsion wrestled with his conscience. Here was a chance for him to strike a blow against his former Lord, twist his memory with a lie nobody could contest. But Lady Kyferin was watching him. Asho grimaced. "He died facing the enemy, running at one of the Sin Casters. He died bravely."

Lady Kyferin closed her eyes and sat slowly on her chair. A knot arose in Asho's throat. Of all the people in the castle, she was the only one who had suffered as much as he and Shaya had at Lord Kyferin's hands. Her shock was genuine, but he would bet his life that deep down she had to be feeling a wild song of unbelieving joy.

Father Simeon hurried into the hall. He had taken the time to don his robes of pure white, his silver triangle hanging prominently on his narrow chest. As one of the only two Noussians in the castle, he exuded a benevolent contempt for everybody but the noble family, but held Lady Kyferin in special regard for her being a Sigean and thus one step above him in Ascension. "I am sorry for your loss, my Lady." His voice was sonorous, rich with compassion and redolent with the authority of his office. "Yet even in sorrow we must rejoice. Know that your Lord husband is now one step closer to Ascension. He travels before us to the peak of the Triangle. Scant comfort, I know, but our grief is but the stepping stone to joy."

These last words were murmured by everyone but the Lady and Asho. Even Kethe whispered them silently to herself.

Lady Kyferin opened her eyes and smiled. "Thank you, Father."

He bowed. "Shall I prepare the chapel for tonight's Mourning?"

Lady Kyferin nodded. "Yes, though Kethe and I shall hold the vigil in my chapel upstairs."

Father Simeon hesitated, as if about to protest, and then bowed again. "As you wish."

"A week," said Lady Kyferin, turning back to Asho. "Seven days since my Lord husband and his Black Wolves perished. Tell me, were either Lord Laur or Lord Lenherd at this battle?"

Asho shook his head. "No, my Lady. Lord Kyferin thought that his brothers were still on the road behind us when the order to attack was given. I never saw them."

"So, their forces remain intact." She leaned back in her seat, her smooth brow marred by a slight frown.

Brocuff cleared his throat and stepped up next to Asho. "My Lady, when news reaches the families of the Black Wolves, they'll no doubt ask that their men stationed here at the castle be sent back to their homes."

Each Black Wolf had been a landed noble with enough wealth to arm himself and answer Lord Kyferin's call with retainers and soldiers of his own. Their families and properties formed the quilt that was Lord Kyferin's land; their simultaneous deaths would throw the entire countryside into chaos, as brothers and uncles and sons began to contest for the now empty seats of power. The next few weeks would see numerous deaths take place, as the less scrupulous and more ambitious relatives ensured that they would gain the title by any means necessary.

Kethe stepped forth. "Surely we don't have to release them."

"No," said Brocuff, rubbing his jaw. "You've the right of that. We could order each man to stay at his post. But there would be consequences. The families that demand the return of their men would be gravely offended. They're going to want as much strength as possible over the next few weeks as they fight off rivals and seek to consolidate their power. They'll remember our leaving them undermanned at this crucial time, and harbor resentment."

Bertchold scowled. "They owe their loyalty to Lady Kyferin in hard times as well as good. We can't strip the battlements of our men and send them home."

"How many soldiers do we have right now?" Lady Kyferin's voice remained quiet, almost calm.

Brocuff didn't have to think. "We've sixty-two men, all told. The vast majority of our forces rode out with our Lord."

Lady Kyferin watched her constable with half-lidded eyes. "How many of these might we expect to be recalled?"

"Thirty, most like." Brocuff nodded. "Replacements may straggle in as they return from the war, and some requests might take longer to reach us than others."

"This is not a time to be generous," said Bertchold, smacking his fist into the palm of his other hand. "We've no knights—"

"That's not true," said Asho.

Bertchold faltered and then turned to him. "You said the Black Wolves died with Lord Kyferin to a man."

"They did." Asho felt his heart begin to hammer. "But I was knighted after the fighting."

Everyone stared at him. Lady Kyferin raised an eyebrow.

"Knighted? By whom?"

Asho swallowed. "By the Grace himself, my Lady."

Bertchold snorted and Father Simeon smiled. Brocuff frowned at him, and Menczel strummed his lute with a mocking flourish.

Asho took a deep breath and held his Lady's eye. "I swear it, my Lady. He knighted me before quitting the field. He asked that I enter his service, but I told him my loyalty lay with you."

"Oh, come on," said Bertchold. "You expect us to believe this nonsense? Next you'll be telling us that the First Ascendant himself descended through the White Gate to gild you with lightning. If you can't keep your fantasies in your head and your tongue in your mouth—"

Asho opened the satchel that hung by his side with stiff fingers, never looking away from Lady Kyferin. His fingers fumbled with the clasp, and then he drew forth a folded square of white cloth. Bertchold fell silent as Asho unfolded the war banner.

"The Everflame," whispered Menczel, stepping in closer.

The Grace's banner was torn and muddied, but there was no mistaking it. Asho held it out to Lady Kyferin, who reached down as if in a dream and took it.

"His Grace gave me his banner to honor my service to him." Asho's voice felt hoarse. "I fought beside his Virtues and saved his life. He knighted me in gratitude."

Kethe was staring wide-eyed at him, and even Brocuff looked taken aback. Nobody moved. The Everflame lay in Lady Kyferin's hands like a tongue of silver fire.

"My Lady," said Asho, stepping forward to kneel once more. "I ask that you let me serve you as your knight. I know your Lord regretted bringing my sister and me out of Bythos, and had no intention of letting me ever have the honor. But I'm a knight now, regardless, and I swear to dedicate my every breath and thought to guarding your family and your honor. I may be a Bythian, but I swear that I shall do my utmost to protect you. If you will have me, I will be your knight."

"Sweetly said," murmured Menczel, and the notes he strummed on his lute were soft and reverential.

Lady Kyferin glanced down at the Everflame, and then extended it back to Asho. A spike of panic arose within him. Was she turning him down?

"I accept your most gracious offer, Ser Knight. The Everflame is a testament to your valor. Keep it, and know that I am honored to have your service."

Asho's panic evaporated along with his exhaustion. In that moment he felt as if he could leap walls, fight down a hundred men, and march for a month if it would earn Lady Kyferin's favor. He rose and took the Everflame, and then bowed low. "Thank you, my Lady."

"Fine," said Bertchold. "We have *one* knight. But as soon as word gets out as to how weak we are, we can expect to be tested. We can't release the men."

Silence. Everyone watched Lady Kyferin, who was studying Brocuff. "How long could we withstand a determined siege with sixty men, Constable?"

"Well, that's a hard question to answer. With so small a force, I'd advise pulling back to the barbican and the keep. We've enough food and water stocked to last a good six months. Though if the enemy were large enough, we'd be hard-pressed to withstand simultaneous assaults. With a force that small, I honestly can't say."

"We'd sacrifice the bailey and the curtain wall," murmured Lady Kyferin.

Brocuff nodded, looking uncomfortable. "Yes, my Lady."

"Bertchold, send out messengers to the homes of the former Black Wolves. Extend our condolences, and thank them for their service. Tell them that our need is now greater than ever. If they can send us a fully armored relative to serve as a new Black Wolf, along with as many men as they can spare, we shall abey taxes for the entirety of the next year."

Bertchold spluttered, "A whole year?"

Lady Kyferin continued firmly, "Any soldiers who receive requests to return home after these messages are delivered are to be granted permission to do so."

Brocuff nodded, and Asho saw approval in his features. "As you command, my Lady."

Bertchold coughed and then puffed out his chest. "My Lady, I served your Lord husband for over twenty years. I have some small measure of experience in the practice of governance and administration. We cannot cut taxes for a year. We cannot let our soldiers return home. I understand that you are traumatized by your loss, but please, listen to my advice. Now is the time to show strength. Make demands. Tighten your fist!"

Lady Kyferin didn't answer at first. She simply sat, relaxed, until Bertchold wilted before her gaze. "I thank you for your advice, Master Bertchold. However, one thing is clear. Our only hope of weathering the coming storm lies with my Lord husband's family. Which is why we shall reach out to Lords Laur and Lenherd, and invite them to come honor the passage of their brother."

Father Simeon nodded. "Most wise, most wise."

Asho blinked. He felt lightheaded. Menczel was saying something, but he couldn't quite catch the words.

"If you'll be excusing us," said Brocuff, closing a hand around Asho's arm. "I'd best be seeing to my guards. Ser Asho, will you join me? With your permission, my Lady?"

Asho tried to straighten. He should bow. Say something. He couldn't quite focus on Lady Kyferin, but he heard her voice as she said something.

"Here we go," said Brocuff, voice low as he turned Asho around and ushered him out of the Lord's Hall.

"I'm fine," said Asho, voice thick.

"You were bleeding on Her Ladyship's floor," said Brocuff. "She hates it when people do that."

"Oh," said Asho. The door came swaying at him as if looking to avoid his approach, and then they were through it and standing in the darkness. "I didn't mean to."

"No, I'm sure you didn't," said Brocuff. "Easy, easy. Here. Put your arm over my shoulders. Hell, you don't weigh more than a feather. Come on. I'll get you down to the kitchen at the very least."

"The kitchen would be nice," said Asho. Everything was going away. "Hot soup. Dumplings."

Brocuff chuckled, but it sounded like he was disappearing up a chimney. Asho tried to follow him, but he couldn't get his feet to work. Everything was growing faint and distant. Darkness came swirling down into his eyes, and Asho finally fell into the nothingness.

CHAPTER FIVE

ṫhaʀok

The mountain kragh stumbled but did not fall. His roughshod boot slipped off the ice-wrapped river rock and plunged into the black water, forcing him to lunge forward and palm the next stone as he fought for balance. For a precarious moment he swayed, thick tendons standing out on his forearm. The great muscles of his legs had ceased burning and were now numb with fatigue; it was only through sheer will that he was able to wrest his foot free and place it heavily on the treacherous rock.

With a grunt he straightened and turned to sight down the curve of the mountain river. Fresh snow blanketed everything six inches deep and smothered the trees that covered the gorge's steep black slopes. There was no movement, no sign of pursuit, but the kragh could sense that they were close. With a growl that resonated deep in his chest he turned and clambered heavily across the few remaining large rocks and gained the far side of the river.

There was no chance for survival. There were a dozen of the lowland kragh, and they were compensating for their lack of tracking skills with a score of great hounds. Tharok knew that if he were to simply remain where he stood, knee-deep in the snow, he could meet his pursuers here by the river, could fight them before the sun dipped behind the tallest peaks and most likely kill a third of them before he fell face-down in the snow. His blood would run down into the black water and flow into the valleys far below. It would not be a bad death, but neither would it be a glorious one.

Turning, he considered the path he was pursuing. The river curved out of sight ahead, a shoulder of the gorge reaching down to block the eye, but he knew its path. It would rise, following the raw mountain slopes, leaving the tree line behind as it became a series of waterfalls garlanded in ice. From there it would ascend higher and farther until he reached the holy lake known as the Dragon's Tear. That was as far as he'd ever climbed. He knew none who had gone farther. For there began the Dragon's Breath, the great ice road that threaded its way down from the very peaks of the mountains, down from the Valley of the Dead and the home of the gods.

Tharok took a deep breath, inhaling the painfully cold air, and shook his head to clear his thoughts. His great tribe was shattered. His brothers and uncles had either been murdered alongside his father or were being hunted down like him. Their Women's Council would have been broken, the women taken away and forced to join other tribes.

He'd been running for three days now. The time was drawing close for a confrontation. Time for blood, his or theirs, but for that he would need the best ground.

Through the frigid air came the distant call of a hound. They had picked up his scent again. These were to be his final hours. Well, he would show the Tragon scum who were following him what it meant to hunt a highland kragh in his home.

He began to run, adopting the long-limbed lope of the wolf, one hand steadying his great horn bow where it was strapped to his back. He moved up the side of the gorge until he gained the trees and then ran parallel to the river, the snow thinner beneath the canopy. There were three hours of daylight left, three hours till the air grew cold enough to shatter trees. He would gain the Dragon's Tear before nightfall, would run around its shore so as to set foot on the Dragon's Breath beneath the light of the moon, and if he was lucky, if he was sure of foot and strong, he would gain that ground before they fell upon him. Legend was that one could only safely reach the Dragon's Breath by the moon's double-horned light. Never had he thought to test the tale himself, but tonight, tonight he would see.

He ran, cresting the occasional bank of snow. A flock of stone-gray doves exploded from the trees as he passed beneath, and he cursed, his presence marked by their flight, but perhaps the lowland kragh would fail to understand their import. The river twisted and grew increasing rock-choked and narrow until the throat of the gorge closed at last and Tharok came upon the first waterfall, a plume of white water that cascaded some seventy yards down as it roared its delight to the world.

He was halfway up the face of the cliff when the first arrow struck to his left. He let out a snarl of rage and looked down over his shoulder to see the lowland kragh arrayed beside the waterfall's bowl, their dogs leaping and tugging at their leashes, their barks drowned by the roar of the waterfall. They were bending their shortbows and sighting up at him, and he almost let go so as to fall on them and crush them from this great height. Then reason asserted itself and he turned and latched on to the next handhold. If they hit him, they hit him. There was no point in worrying.

An arrow whistled past him and bounced off an elbow of rock, spinning back out into the void. Another clattered across the rocks below his feet. Tharok forced himself higher. The massive slabs of muscle across his back were on fire now, and his hands were numb, the cold having penetrated even through his thick calluses, but on he climbed. A few more arrows were essayed, but he had passed beyond the reach of the lowlanders' meager bows.

The final third of the ascent was easy. Deep fissures in the cliff face presented him with plenty of room to scramble up within them without difficulty. He gained the top and turned to look back down. The Tragon kragh had begun their own ascent, hounds hoisted up on slings, their small, bright green faces staring up at him as he considered tossing down rocks or stringing his bow. But the idea of doing so rankled; that was no way to defeat an opponent. Tharok snorted savagely and resumed following the course of the river.

So it went as the evening grew colder and the shadows longer, the layer of ice over the snow thickening beneath the calks of his boots. Sweat ran easily over his thick hide and he ran with his mouth open, breath visible as it rasped past the large tusks of his lower jaw. Another waterfall, a second and third. Now only fir trees crowded the gorge, growing in clumps and swathes about him, black and dense and releasing exhalations of cold from their centers as he shouldered past their branches. He was growing reluctantly impressed with the tenacity of the Tragon. Few highland kragh ventured this high, braved these harsh slopes, yet on they came, lowland kragh, plump herders, soft degenerates, keeping apace with him. He wondered if they knew into what land he was leading them, into the dangers posed by the wyverns. Did any of them yet remember the old legends from the time before they had descended to the valleys, the old tales that spoke of the heart of the mountains and the home of the spirits? Would they even care if they did? Did they yet hold to any part of the old ways? He thought not. They'd have turned back long ago in terror if they had.

The gorge was a knife wound between two mountain slopes, the fir trees that grew on either side standing so close that they seemed to form a continuous forest despite the sharp canyon between them. The sun had almost set. Tharok ran in near darkness, moving more by instinct and intuition than sight or smell, avoiding boulders, finding handholds, stepping where the rock and shale was stable. Up he went, and the urge to sing his death song began to grow strong, swelling his chest and seeking to escape and reverberate from the great mountain walls, a dirge to quell the joy that the kragh behind him were taking from the hunt.

He heard a scrape from behind and turned to see a dark-furred shape hurtling across the rocks toward him. Finally. Time for blood. He drew his curved hunting blade and fell into a crouch, shifting his feet for better footing as the hound bounded up the side of the gorge, a lithe bolt of baying brown muscle and fangs. It gained a boulder above him and then leaped to fall upon his upturned face. Tharok reached out and closed his fingers about the hound's neck as he fell back, driving his knife deep into its gut. The hound's howl turned guttural and wounded, golden eyes flashing in the gloom as it sought to lock its maw upon him, to sink its fangs deep into his face.

But the hound wasn't the only one with fangs. With a roar Tharok bit into the hound's neck even as it whipped its muscular, lithe body from side to side, claws scoring deep tracks in his chest. Tharok bit down, the massive tusks of his lower jaw puncturing hide and muscle to sink deep into the dog's windpipe and arteries. Hot, fresh blood filled Tharok's mouth, and the hound let loose a terrible whine. It whiplashed and thrashed in its attempt to get away, but the highland kragh held on. Only death would cause him to open his jaws now. Tharok's head was wrenched from side to side, but he continued to dig his dagger over and over into the hound's gut until the dog let loose one final cry and went limp.

Tharok opened his mouth and cast the dog to the ground, turned his head and spat its blood upon the white-covered rocks. Crimson flowers bloomed all about him. Wiping his forearm across his mouth, Tharok turned and stared down the gorge,. Other shapes were racing toward him. If more than two hounds came at him at once, he was finished. Desperate, he turned and ran, cursing the fate that had him fleeing dogs. He stopped cursing when he gained the final cliff face and picked a route up through the boulders and rocks, using fir trunks to haul himself up quicker until he tumbled over the edge and out onto the shallow valley that held the Dragon's Tear.

The moon was rising. The world was cast in melancholy blues and silver, and the snow gleamed with the unearthly beauty that made the mountains his only possible home. The rock was so dark and black where it emerged through the mantle of the snow that it appeared to be holes into Hell. The Dragon's Tear dominated the valley floor. Its black waters stood so still that they appeared frozen into the most perfect sheet of ice, yet no reflection of the Five Peaks showed on its surface.

Tharok had been here once before in his brief life. His sister had been brought here to be consecrated as a shaman. Her eyes had been put out after a torturous ceremony, and she'd been left to spend two weeks in vigil by the water's edge, left to survive two weeks alone amidst the ghosts and spirits that thronged the edges of the Tear. When Tharok and the others had returned two weeks later, there had been no sign of Loruka. She'd been deemed lost, consumed by the night and the ice and the hungry ghosts, and their father had raged for days at the insult to his honor.

Rising now, Tharok gazed once more upon the Dragon's Tear. It was said to be bottomless, was famous for never freezing. Nothing lived in its icy fastness. The spirits of fallen kragh who could not ascend to the Valley of the Dead were said to dance along its edge for eternity, broken and gibbering and hating the living. This was no place for the living. Nobody ventured here without the shamans to guide them, and even they hesitated before coming to the Tear.

Tharok took a deep breath and strode forward. He was in no mood for piety.

He scrabbled down the great rocks that hemmed in the lake's broad waters and began to follow its shore, running with fierce determination. The ghosts could go hang. He'd gain the far tapering point before the hounds caught up with him, and there take his stand. He came to the broad fan of rocks upon which the ceremony had been performed, then loped past the great obsidian rock on whose surface his sister had been bound and blinded. Old history of a now-dead tribe. Anger curdled in his gut. He ran on.

A howl split the silence and Tharok glanced over his shoulder to see three hounds come surging over the rocks at the far end of the lake. Their Tragon masters would be hard behind them, close enough that if he stopped to fight the hounds he'd soon find himself fighting all twelve lowland kragh as well. Lowering his head, Tharok summoned his reserves and truly ran. He consigned his fate to Dead Sister Moon and didn't even look at where his feet were falling amidst the rocks and snow, but simply sprinting, chest heaving for breath, his sight growing blurry as he raced around the curvature of the lake.

The sound of yelps and strangled cries came from behind him. Tharok slowed and looked back. The hounds had stopped their pursuit. They paced back and forth as if behind an invisible wall, midway along the length of the lake, whined and chuffed and came no closer. Then they began to dance back, tails between their legs, as if invisible whips were lashing them. Tharok grinned. Human-raised hounds had no place at the Tear. Let the ghosts scourge the hides from their bodies.

Tharok narrowed his eyes and saw lowland kragh at last. Slender, bald, and as green as untried mountain kragh children, they were coming fast on their bandy legs along the shoreline. Let them figure it out, he thought, and with a deep breath forced himself to begin running once more. His legs were trembling, his strength spent, but he staggered on, the lake growing ever narrower, the cliffs drawing closer, till he finally reached the Tear's far point. He stopped beside a massive, jagged boulder that had been spat out by the Dragon's Breath. It was twice his height, but he growled and climbed it through sheer force of will. When he reached the top he inhaled deeply, massive chest expanding as if he'd breathe in the world, then let his breath out in a deep, rumbling groan and turned to face his pursuers.

He unshouldered his grandfather's horn longbow, dug one end into a cleft in the rock and strung the other end with a massive bunching of the muscles of his arm. He tied it off smoothly, his taloned fingers moving with a calmness that belied the tension that coursed like fire through his veins. The band of hunters was closing around the far sweep of the lake, dark shadows that ran, short swords and bows in hand, coming in to seal his doom.

Rising, he drew a red arrow from the quiver slung over his back, the last of three. Each arrow was three feet long, as thick as his thumb and headed by a bolt of black iron, wickedly sharp and forged in the human lands. He set the arrow to the string, took a deep breath and drew. No other in his tribe could draw this bow, not even his father, and weak as he was, he worried that he too would fail to bend it. The horn groaned, the arrow drew back, he sighted down its length and released.

It was gone, blessed by Dead Sister Moon, not arcing high to fall upon his opponents but shooting straight, a bolt of fury that punched into the lead kragh. It knocked him clean off his feet, arresting his momentum as if he had run into a stone wall. The others split around their fallen comrade, coming still, and Tharok drew his second and last red arrow. Only his death arrow remained.

Tharok took a second, steadying breath. The trembling might of his body was near exhausted. He growled deep in the back of his throat, a coarse rumble of bestial fury, and then he roared and drew and fired the second great bolt in one rapid heave. It whistled out through the moonlight and missed his target. The Tragon were bunched so close, though, that it didn't matter. The bolt hit the one right behind him, slammed into his gut, passed through him as it spun him around and lodged deep into the thigh of a third.

Tharok grunted his pleasure.

He drew his last arrow. His black-fletched death arrow. He'd carried it with him since he'd learned to draw the bow. It was only to be shot when he knew he was about to die. That time had come. Now, where was the Tragon leader? There, in the middle of the pack. Cunning old wolf. One-eyed, he'd led the hunt for three days with discipline and ferocity that would have done a highland kragh proud. It was time to end his life.

Tharok took a final breath, deep into his cavernous chest, and pulled one more time at his grandfather's bow. The horn creaked, the string quivered, and he felt his hands weaken, his forearms tremble, the muscles in his shoulder and back burn and writhe. It was like trying to heave a boulder right out from the frozen ground. His lips writhed back from his fangs, his snarl turned silent as he saw red, and then he felt his ancestor's strength course through him. He hauled the arrow back. His final arrow, his death arrow, the last arrow he would ever shoot. He drew the string back farther and farther. Never had he drawn the old bow so far. He pulled it back till the wicked arrowhead was flush with the bow's curvature, drew back till it felt as if the string was going to slice through his fingers and the bow explode in his hands, and only then released.

His death arrow hit the one-eyed lowland kragh right in the face. It punched through his cheekbone with bone-shattering power and exploded out the back of his skull. Down crashed the old wolf, and Tharok lurched to his feet, a roar of defiance tearing from his throat. He cast his horn bow aside and drew his axe, the great curved blade gleaming like ice hewn from the heart of a glacier. Eight kragh were closing in on him. Their bloodlust was upon them. They cared nothing for their felled comrades. Their numbers were great, they had hunted him for three days without rest or good food, and now was the time to end it.

Tharok wanted to laugh. He wanted there to be more. He wanted an ocean of lowland kragh to dive into, the entire bloody Tragon tribe for him to attack. His own blood fury was rising. Did they think they knew what battle rage felt like? It was time for them to learn.

Tharok lowered himself into a crouch. They were almost upon him. He drew his heavy curved dagger. He felt nothing but rage and scorn. None of them were even half his height. He roared and raced forward, three great strides across the curving top of the boulder, and launched himself into the night air, right arm scything down and throwing the curved dagger so that it whipped forward, tip over pommel, right at the lead kragh. It connected hilt first, but had been thrown so hard that the kragh dropped and tripped the one directly behind him. Tharok fell amongst their charging mass, axe swinging, and all was rage and blood.

Tharok felt the berserker fury descend upon him. It swept the fatigue, the cold, and all thoughts from his mind. Like a crescendo of scouring fire, a storm of crimson, it drowned his mind in rage and he felt as if he could lift mountains, crack open boulders, tear down Dead Sister Moon with his own ragged claws.

His fall dropped three of them, his bulk and weight crushing one directly down into the rocks as the other two were swept off their feet by his outstretched arms. Tharok went down hard, but he tucked his head and left shoulder into a roll and came up running. He swept his axe in a howling arc around and behind him as he broke free of their number, only to wheel and drop into a deep crouch. He'd severed a foot. That kragh was down screaming. Only three were still standing, another three regaining their feet. The moon shone on their bald pates and glinted on the gold earrings in their ears. Their eyes burned red as their own feeble rage fueled them. Tharok opened his great maw and screamed his fury at them, ropes of spittle flying forward. Not waiting for their charge, he attacked, leaping into the madness of their blades.

One went down, a blade bit deep into his side, and he slammed the base of his palm against the face of another. Something ricocheted off his shoulder; he ducked and slammed his shoulder against a gut, staggered back as a blow cracked his temple, shook his head and bellowed once more. Another blade dug into his back, tried to penetrate the thick hide armor, but failed.

Tharok reared back and buried his axe deep in the head of the kragh before him, reached out and wrapped his fingers around the neck of another and brought it in close enough to tear its throat out with his tusks. He threw the suddenly limp body at another, ducked under a swung blade, and roared his joy. He began to roar as the enemy fell and failed to kill him.

A blade sliced deep into his left arm. Pain flared and was ignored as his arm dropped uselessly by his side. He ducked his head and rammed it to the side, wrenching it across and up so that his tusks dug tore open a stomach. Lowland kragh had no tusks. Small-toothed and pathetic, they disdained them. Here and now, Tharok would show them the meaning and power behind them.

He staggered back, turning to find a new foe. One of the lowland kragh was trying to crawl away. The others lay still. Heaving for breath, reeling, he stumbled over to it and smashed his foot down on the nape of its neck. It crunched and the kragh went still.

Silence now but for his heaving breath. He didn't know where his axe was. Blood covered his left arm, was running down his side. The pain had yet to hit him, held back by his berserker rage, but that was sluicing from him now that the battle was over. Weakness began to encroach.

Moving with clumsy haste, he knelt down by one of the corpses and tore free its shirt, then wrapped it around the wound in his left arm and tied it off tight. He bit the cloth and yanked till it bit cruelly into his arm. He took another shirt, balled it up and held it against the wound in his side. Gasping and shivering, he then took two belts, forged one from them both, and cinched it tight over the balled bandage, pulling it in against the wound.

It wouldn't be enough, not in the long run, but for now, it just might allow him to ascend to the Dragon's Breath. Why the Hell not? If he didn't bleed out, he might even reach the Valley of the Dead.

Tharok left the Dragon's Tear behind, the bodies of the Tragon kragh, the whimpering of the hounds. He began to climb, following the narrow waterfall that trickled from the base of the Breath high above to form the Tear, the water so cold it could freeze a hand solid if one were foolish enough to plunge it in. Black rock, harsh edges, hands clasping and muscles contracting as he pulled himself up. Thoughts of those behind him receded and were gone. The moon sailed overhead, crescent and casting a serene light over the mountains. Above him, calling him on, were the Five Peaks, the sacred home of the gods and where legend had it the kragh had been birthed. Only dying shamans, blind and wizened, would dare climb this high when they knew their death was upon them. As far as he knew, he was the first to attempt this climb alone and without the blessings of the spirits. He didn't care. Let them kill him if they were offended.

Soon he was high up above the Tear, which gleamed below him like an ax blade before a fire. He paused to survey the world spread out at his feet, swaying with fatigue and pain. Beyond the lake the dark crevice that was the gorge fell away into the depths, while across from him and all around surged the ragged peaks of the mountains, caped in snow and as harsh and unyielding as life itself. He saw the flitting silhouette of a lone wyvern, high up on one of the peaks. He was far above the tree line now, having left the last of the stunted firs behind, and the air this high was so thin that he had to breathe deep just to walk, just to place one booted foot before the other.

Tharok took one last look at the world. He thought of his tribe, his dead relatives, thought of the wrongs that would not be righted, of the wars and battles he would never fight, and then turned his back to it all and faced the glacier known only as the Dragon's Breath.

Its face was a shattered wall of ice, splintered cracks cutting deep into its body, a crown of warped ice spokes and slivers emerging from its upper edge. From beneath its body came the cold water that fed the world.

Tharok took a deep breath, reached out, and grasped hold of a spar of ice, hiked a boot up and dug it into a gap, and then hauled his body up. Another handhold; he kicked his other boot deep into another crack, and then he was moving, ignoring the penetrating freeze that entered his hands, moving up and up until he reached the summit and crawled out onto the Dragon's Breath itself.

Legend had it that at the end of his life, Ogri the Uniter, the kragh who had gathered all the tribes to his banner and forged the Ur-

Tribe, had ridden his dragon mount Jaermungdr high into the Five Peaks. He had returned to the home of the gods from whence he had come, had landed Jaermungdr and died, falling into the snow of the Valley of the Dead. Jaermungdr had roared its grief, and with every roar had let loose a blast of ice, a gout of pure cold so powerful that they had become the Ice Roads. It had reared up high one last time, its old hide scored by countless scars from countless battles, and then fallen and died next to its master. From the Valley of the Dead the three Ice Roads had ever since descended, with the Dragon's Breath being the greatest and reaching the farthest down below. To ascend the Dragon's Breath was to ascend grief made manifest, to walk alongside the ghosts and spirits of every kragh who had passed away and were returning to the Valley of the Dead. With Ogri's death the Ur-Tribe had split, fragmented, and never since had the kragh been of any consequence in the known world.

By the light of Dead Sister Moon Tharok stood and gazed up the sweeping curve of the great glacier. It was a great, sinuous snake whose ragged and broken surface was hidden beneath a mantle of snow. From here it looked as smooth a road to ascend as one could desire, but Tharok knew that climbing it would kill him. He had crossed glaciers before, smaller Ice Roads in other valleys, off other mountains. He knew the peril of the sudden crack that heralded a drop into the blue heart-ice deep within, how easily an ankle could twist and snap, how shards of ice could puncture and pierce. It would not be the ghosts or spirits or gods that would kill him for his effrontery; it would be the very fact that he was climbing the road itself that would do him in, if his body did not give out first.

Still, there were worse ways to die. Climbing to the Valley of the Dead on foot was as good a way as any. His death arrow had flown. There was no returning once he set foot on the greatest Ice Road in the world.

Finding some small measure of peace with his own death, finally casting away his last regrets, fears and doubts, Tharok took his first step upon the Dragon's Breath and began to climb.

CHAPTER SIX

ISKRA

Iskra Kyferin hesitated at the entrance to her chamber, her hand stopping but an inch from the heavy wooden door. The bell would soon toll to summon the castle to Mourning. She had to dress, prepare herself, assume the calm and confident mien that would convince everyone from her lowliest stable boy to Father Simeon himself that Kyferin Castle was not without a ruler. And yet, her heart fluttered in her chest like a panicked dove. She hesitated a moment longer, and then pressed her palm to the door and pushed it open.

The first time she'd entered this room had been in Enderl's arms. She'd been fifteen, and he'd been drunk. The entire castle had rung with their wedding celebration, a thousand torches banishing the night, and raucous catcalls had followed them each step of the way from the great hall to the top of the keep. Enderl had breathed deeply but never flagged. His strength had always been prodigious. He'd smelled of spiced Zoeian wine, the anointing oils from their ritual, and a deep, masculine scent that had unnerved and excited her.

Iskra paused in the doorway and smiled with bitter pity for her younger self. How little she'd known. She'd been a child. A foolish, naive child. Twenty years had passed since that awful night. An entire life. And now Enderl was dead and gone and she was alone. She raised her candle so that its soft glow spread over the furnishings, dimly outlining the huge bed on which he'd stripped away her virginity and so much more. It didn't take much effort to bring back the memory of her cries. Her pleading. The sobbing that she'd tried to bury in her pillow for fear of awakening him.

She moved from wall sconce to wall sconce, lighting each candle in turn, till the whole silent room was bathed in a delicate white glow. Enderl had always preferred the roar and dance of the hearth fire, not caring if the room filled with smoke and the illumination was poor. She never lit the fireplace when he was gone, no matter how cold it got.

The thick stone walls seemed to ache with his memory. She'd never again hear his bellow of laughter. The high ceiling would never echo with his snores, his sighs and muttered curses of as he forced himself to read through Bertchold's reports. This was his room. His tapestries hung on the walls. His weapons gleamed on their hooks. His armature stood by the fire. Twenty years she had slept here, but still it was his chamber.

Iskra moved to one of the narrow windows and gazed out into the night. Doors were opening in her mind, memories tumbling free now that she was alone. Enderl was dead. She thought of him as he'd held Kethe for the first time, his massive hands awkward, his expression tentative and then transforming into one of delight. How seven years later he'd raised Roddick in one hand over his head and bellowed, "This is my son! This is my son!" His beaming pride had warmed her even as she'd begged him to lower the babe back to her arms.

Goosebumps raced down her arms. She'd lived her life in opposition to him. Now that he was gone, she felt as she were suddenly stumbling. She didn't have to plan for his return. Steel herself against the whispers. Compose her face in just the right away to avoid arousing his ire or interest. She didn't have to hide the castle accounts. Didn't have to plan his favorite meals. Didn't have to sit by his side each night, or worse yet, sit alone when he'd left on his supposed errands. Didn't have to gaze at him and hide her true feelings from his searching eyes. Reassure him when he doubted. Fight the warmth she felt when he dreamed of a future for their children. Dread the fury that might break forth at any moment and ravage the world.

Tears brimmed in her eyes, then ran down her cheeks. A certain man was rotting in the dungeon cell beneath the Wolf Tower, placed there by husband for reasons both good and foul. She'd have to deal with that man sooner or later.

The bell began to toll. It was time to descend and pray that Enderl's soul had Ascended. She'd always considered herself superior to him in every way: more educated, more self-aware, more compassionate, a Sigean where he was but an Ennoian. Yet on a basic level he'd always been more alive than she, more vital, more entrenched in each and every moment, whereas she'd been frozen, fighting always to repress her true self, her every instinct. Now he was gone, and she hated this feeling of loss, of bewilderment, of fear.

Turning, she wiped her cheeks with her palms. Phye had left her dress laid out. Custom demanded that the Lady of the castle be tended and pampered at every opportunity by numerous ladies-in-waiting, but that was one of the few customs she'd insisted on breaking when she'd first arrived here. She'd not abandon the simplicity of her Sigean upbringing; having another woman comb her hair and dress her as if she were a child was intolerable.

The dress was monochromatic and stark, black at the hem and then gradating up through the grays to become white just shy of her chest. An allegory for Ascension, of course. She dressed quickly. The bell was still tolling.

Drying her face, she stopped at the door to cast one last look over the room. The furnishings stood mute. They were not to blame for what had transpired here over the years, but she decided then and there that she would have everything dragged away and burned.

The chapel was already full when she arrived with Kethe and little Roddick in tow. Almost a hundred members of the castle staff were in attendance, packed into the pews and wearing their Mourning clothes. The thick candles at the front had been newly replaced, and what seemed like a hundred more were burning along the walls. Father Simeon was standing at the front before the great gleaming Ascendant Triangle, and he nodded when he saw her. Heads turned and the murmurings ceased as she stepped forward, chin raised, eyes locked above the Father's head. She led her children to the very front and dipped one knee to the Triangle. Kethe did the same, her movements neat, while Roddick simply stared at everyone and had to be urged to comply.

There were no Aletheians in attendance, so she had the honor of sitting at the very front. Magister Audsley, as the only Noussian other than the Father, had the entire row behind her to himself, and then came the Ennoians, who composed the vast bulk of the gathering. A few Zoeians were behind them, with the Bythian slaves at the very back. Everything was as it should be. Iskra watched Father Simeon as he nodded to himself and then raised his hands to gather their attention.

"We are gathered here tonight to mark the passing of Lord Enderl Kyferin, an Ennoian of good standing who died but seven days ago in defense of the Ascendant Empire and its ideals. That he died fighting the Agerastian is a further testament to his devoutness; if death in defense of the Empire is the highest goal of an Ennoian, then dying while fighting the heretics is the most perfect expression of that ideal."

Kethe was staring fixedly at Father Simeon, her face pale and intent. Iskra saw her nod slightly at his words, and felt her old conflict arise anew within her. She had decided soon after Kethe's birth to shield her daughter from the worst of her father's nature; at the time that had seemed the most loving and kindest course. Now, seeing the fevered intensity in her daughter's eyes, she wondered again if that had been the right course of action.

"We cannot, of course, be sure, but I believe that a week ago an infant was born in Nous whose cry echoed with the might and command of our fallen lord. Somewhere even now, at this very moment, the spirit of Lord Enderl Kyferin is housed within the fresh and innocent body of a newborn babe. Shorn of his memories, he begins the next stage of his Ascension with every blessing, coming one step closer to passing through the White Gate and into eternal bliss."

Iskra looked down at her hands. Everything in her soul rebelled against that idea. No, not Nous. Not even Ennoia. If the Ascendant had any wisdom or sense of justice, then Enderl would have been hurled down to Zoe. Perhaps somewhere in that great port city he now lay, swaddled and dark-skinned. Or perhaps Agerastos. Or even Bythos. What justice that would be. Enderl Kyferin, a Bythian slave.

"Tonight," continued Father Simeon, "We mark and mourn his departure from our lives. We shall recount his great deeds, and any who wish to speak fondly of him may step to the fore and do so. Allow your grief to flood through you. Let go of all grudges and petty resentments. The man you once knew is no more. He is gone, his soul fled to wherever the Ascendant has deemed right, and that judgment is greater and more righteous than any emotion we might have."

The silence lay heavy over the crowd. Had Enderl's Black Wolves been present, then Iskra was sure there would have been a contingent who would have fiercely mourned the death of their master. But few here had any reason to feel fondness for her late Lord husband. She could feel their gazes behind her, stony and hard and as pitiless as the sun.

"Tomorrow morning at dawn, we shall gather to rejoice his passage and celebrate the glory of ascension. From the lowest Bythian slave to the most august Aletheian, all are fated to rise and fall through the seven stations of being, until one day we either pass through the White Gate into glory, or are cast down forever through the Black Gate into eternal perdition. Tomorrow we shall rejoice, but tonight we give vent to our sorrow. Lady Kyferin, would you care to speak first?"

Iskra blinked and stood automatically. Father Simeon was smiling benignly at her with false commiseration, and she suddenly felt a clear and cool hatred for his hypocrisy. He knew the truth of her relationship with Enderl, yet still he played his part. Stepping forward, she smiled tightly at him. But hadn't she done the same all these years?

Turning, she regarded the crowd. She knew all of their faces and most of their names. From the steward to the constable, from the magister to the marshal, and down through the carpenters, gardeners, smiths, grooms, cooks, butlers, porters, pages and slaves. Familiar faces, their attention focused on her. Curious, no doubt, to see what she might say. How she might choose to mourn the death of their Lord.

Iskra took a deep breath. She had nothing to say. Her mind was blank. The candle flames flickered, and soft, velvety shadows danced across the vaulted ceiling. She could see the Bythians at the very back, their pale faces luminous, their eyes occasionally turning red as their irises reflected the light in that disturbing manner of theirs. *Shaya*, thought Iskra, and almost started. She'd not allowed herself to think that name in years. Flustered, she looked away from the Bythians to her daughter, and in Kethe's eyes she found her words.

"It has been over twenty years since I first met my Lord. He was being feted for his great victory over the Agerastians, for his capture of Agerastos and for bringing the heretics back into the Empire, and his visit to Sige was a precursor to his tour of Aletheia. I remember that night well. Lord Enderl stood taller than any other man, and his strength and nobility were evident for all to see. That night he shone as if the Ascendant himself had marked him as special, and I knew, young as I was, that his would not be a common life."

The crowd stared at her, drinking in her words. Even Father Simeon was rapt. Talk of Sige and Aletheia was fascinating to them. How little they knew.

"In some ways, I would like to remember him as I saw him then. Young. Confident. Handsome. Talented. Brave. Strong. The twenty years that followed were to prove to all that his great victories had not been a fluke, but rather the first of many." Iskra paused. She knew that Mournings were meant to be long and detailed, filled with plaintive declarations of love and loss. But she would not lie. She would not gild his memory. "I have never regretted my decision to leave Sige and live here by his side." Doing so had brought her beloved children into her life. "It is because of him that I have shared my life with you all. It is because of him that I am now your Lady, and it is because of him that our fates are now intertwined. Kyferin Castle and my own life are forever inextricably linked. That is a gift I shall forever treasure."

Iskra lowered her head, considered, and then nodded to Father Simeon. He blinked, caught by surprise, and then stepped forward as she sat. Her heart was racing. There was so much she could have said, so many ugly truths that had fought to pass her lips. Her stomach felt sour from the effort it had taken to swallow them back down, but when Kethe sought out her hand and squeezed it tight, Iskra felt a wave of gladness and knew that she had done right.

"Lord Kyferin had two brave and beautiful children. Kethe Kyferin, would you say words of Mourning for your father?"

Kethe stood without hesitation. She strode to the front of the room and turned to face the chapel. Her face was pale, her lips pursed, and Iskra realized with a pang how much she had grown. Seeing her now preparing to Mourn her father, she recognized that her daughter was no longer a child. She was a woman grown. She was, Iskra realized, as old as Iskra herself had been when she'd first seen Enderl smile at her from across the golden hall.

"My father was the strongest and bravest man I have ever met." Kethe threw out her words as a challenge. "His Black Wolves were feared across all of Ennoia, and he was called numerous times to fight battles that other men could not win. I know he was not loved, but he was never challenged, either. Not once has this castle been besieged. No one ever insulted him without paying the price. He taught me the value of strength, and I was proud of him, more proud than I can say." Tears filled her eyes, and wiped them away angrily with the black hem of her sleeve. "My mother may be from Sige, but my father and brother and I are Ennoian. We were born into this realm to fight for the Ascendant, and no one can say my father did not fight. He fought, and he won, over and over and over again. His rule brought stability to the land, peace to our neighbors, and prosperity to our people."

Kethe's fists, Iskra saw, were clenched so tightly her knuckles were white. Her eyes searched the crowd as if daring someone to contradict her. "His memory is an example to us all. He died for us. He died fighting the heretics, and that makes him a hero. I am going to do everything I can to follow his example." She stopped suddenly, as if she wanted to continue but did not know what else to say. She bit her lower lip, suddenly self-conscious, and then nodded to Father Simeon and sat beside Iskra, gripped the edge of her seat and leaned forward to stare at the floor. She was trembling, Iskra saw.

Oh, my daughter, she thought. *What have I done?* Iskra looked up at the silver triangle. Had she thought herself free of Enderl?

"And young Master Roddick?" Father Simeon smiled kindly at her son. "Do you have anything you wish to say?"

Roddick turned to her, eyes wide, his thick brown hair an unruly mop despite being combed only minutes before their arrival. He had Enderl's broad cheeks, his strong chin and broad nose, but his eyes were a mirror of her own.

Iskra smiled and nodded. "If you want, Roddick." She pitched her voice low. "Only if you want."

He nodded, frightened, and stood. He pulled on the black hem of his shirt and then turned where he stood, forgetting that he should step up beside Father Simeon. "I loved my father," he said, voice high-pitched. "He was a big man, and he made me feel safe even though sometimes he scared me." His lower lip began to tremble, though Iskra didn't know if that was from grief or the intensity of being stared at by so many people. "I don't want him to be dead. I know I should be happy he's Ascending, but I want him back."

Roddick sat quickly and buried his face against her side. Iskra wrapped an arm around his shoulders and held him close. A moment later Roddick pulled away, however, wiped his nose, and scowled at nothing. Good. He was only four, but he had to be strong.

Father Simeon smiled kindly. A little heresy from a four-year-old was not worth challenging. "Thank you, Roddick. We all miss your father, but he has moved on, as is right. Now, Lady Kyferin will be holding her vigil in her chapel for the rest of the night with her children. My Lady."

Iskra stood, her hand on Roddick's shoulder, and turned to walk down the center aisle. Kethe strode stiffly behind her. Iskra didn't meet anybody's eyes; she kept her gaze on the door to the bailey. As she passed the Bythians, she saw to her surprise that Asho was standing amongst their number. He met her gaze, and then raised his voice.

"I would Mourn Lord Kyferin."

There was a stir as everybody turned to the back to see which Bythian had spoken with such presumption. At the sight of Ser Asho stepping forth, almost all of them turned their gazes to Iskra. The question hung in the air. Would she allow this upstart slave to speak?

Iskra watched Asho's narrow back as he moved gracefully to the front. Her instincts urged her to speak out, to call him back, but she stayed quiet. He was her knight. He need not have placed himself amongst the slaves, though doing so had no doubt ameliorated the criticisms he would have received had he dared to sit any farther forward. She crossed her hands before her and waited, and by her presence gave him the space in which to speak.

Ignoring Father Simeon, who glared at him, Ser Asho turned to face the assembled host of the castle. His pale, narrow face as always betrayed nothing of his emotions. It was an alien visage, devoid of emotion, his silver-green eyes and white hair stamping him with the powerful Bysian imprimatur of slave. That he stood so boldly, shoulders back, daring their criticism, was almost bewildering. It was as if a horse had raised itself on two legs and dared call for a mount.

Iskra frowned. She thought of his sister and bit her tongue.

"Lord Enderl Kyferin raised my sister and me from the depths of Bythos to his very own keep." Asho's words were liquid and smoothly spoken. "He brought us here of his own free will, having sworn a vow to our father that he would take care of us and raise me to be a knight and my sister to be a lady-in-waiting." These were facts, but the crowd stirred uneasily, resenting Asho's bringing up their lord's folly so baldly during his Mourning. "Lord Kyferin was serving his year in Bythos. His Black

Year. The Black Gate stayed sealed, but he nearly died while exploring remote caverns. My father saved his life and nearly died in doing so. Lord Kyferin was young. His star was climbing. He made his vow in the heat of the moment, feeling gratitude that broke all rules, and thus were our lives forever changed."

Ser Asho stared about the crowd. Waiting. Defying anybody to shout at him, to hiss in disapproval. Instead, Iskra received another battery of looks, some angry, some haughty, most imploring her to intervene.

She stayed silent.

"My sister and I did not ask to be brought here. We did not ask to be taken from Bythos. But we were, by Lord Kyferin's honor. Once he gave his vow, our course was set in stone. It is that honor that I mourn. It is that resolve that I admired in him." The rest hung unsaid in the air: *and nothing more.*

Again Asho stood silent, daring, defying. Everyone knew that his sister had killed herself only two years ago. Nobody spoke of it. This was the first time Asho himself had mentioned her, and Iskra noted that he had not said her name.

"I pray that the Ascendant give Lord Kyferin exactly what he deserves." Asho nodded, then began to walk down the aisle once more. This time people did hiss, some rising to their feet as he passed them, but nobody interfered. When Asho reached the back, he held Iskra's gaze for a beat and then looked forward. The whole time he had shown no emotion, only a studied neutrality. The other Bythians, Iskra noted, did not stand close to him. If anything, they recoiled.

"Come," she whispered to her daughter and son. This was a problem she could not deal with tonight.

When she finally stepped out into the cold night, she felt a wash of relief. She'd survived—but this trial was not over. So much depended on her performance over these next few days. Up until now she had ruled the castle in Enderl's absence as Enderl's surrogate, his authority empowering her. That was true no longer. She stood alone now. She had to compel obedience on her own. Her ability to quell the crowd and so allow Asho to speak had been a sign of her authority. She only hoped that she hadn't poisoned it already.

Walking across the bailey with two guards trailing behind her and her children with torches raised, she gazed about the interior of the castle and realized quietly, calmly, and with complete certainty that she meant to rule in Enderl's place. She would take no new Lord. She would never cede power to another man and call him her master. The thought was thrilling, terrifying, and completely right.

She caught her breath at the enormity of her resolution, and then reached out and drew Kethe and Roddick to her side. Holding her children tightly, she looked up at the great keep and shivered as hope and joy flooded her soul for the first time in decades.

CHAPTER SEVEN

kethe

Kethe fought to control her breathing. Nostrils flaring, she stepped carefully out to the side, her slender sword held out before her. Elon has made it specially for her, a castle-forged blade with a hand and a half hilt so that she could swing with all her strength. No matter how much she exercised, ten minutes into combat practice her blade felt like a greatsword. Sweat trickled down her temple, and a lock of hair fell across her face. She blew it away without taking her eyes from her opponent.

Brocuff stood at ease, the tip of his sword pointed at the loam. He hadn't even broken a sweat. She knew he was alert, however, his casual stance meant to provoke her into a rash attack—but those days were long past. She grinned, her heart beating fast, excited. Oh, no, she'd not rush at him just yet.

"Widen your stance a little," he said. "You'll trip over yourself if I run at you."

"Maybe I want you to run at me," Kethe said, though she did as she was bid. A cool breeze blew through the canopy overhead, causing the coin-sized beech leaves to rustle and whisper as if commenting on the scene below. "Maybe I'm lulling you into a sense of over-confidence."

"Ha!" Brocuff slapped the side of his thigh with his blade. "If so, you're doing an excellent job. Mind that root."

Kethe flicked her gaze down to the forest floor and regretted it immediately. Brocuff burst forward, bringing his sword around with the speed that always surprised her. She didn't have time to adjust her feet; instead, she threw herself backward, her sword coming up barely in time to deflect his blow. Another lesson she'd learned early on: it was better to deflect than to simply block attacks from stronger men.

Brocuff didn't let up. As his blade slid off her own with a metallic slither, he stepped into her space, hitting her upraised sword arm with his shoulder. Kethe's stagger turned into a stumble and she nearly fell onto her rear. Gritting her teeth, she dropped into a crouch, placed one hand on the ground and spun away, wincing in anticipation of the blow that would fall across her back.

It never came. She skitter-stepped out of his reach, panting, and brought her sword up before her, holding it with both hands now.

Brocuff was all smiles. "C'mon, my lady. You can do better than that. Stop fighting like a milkmaid."

His goading was obvious; clearly, he expected her to hold back as a result. Instead, Kethe immediately attacked. Without warning she ran at him, swinging her blade in a series of 'X' strokes with both arms, driving him back. It was a feint. If she kept at it, he'd trap her blade, but she didn't plan to give him the time. Just as he detected her pattern she leveled a vicious blow at his head, swinging her slender sword parallel with the ground. Brocuff swayed back as she'd known he would, surprisingly limber for such a stocky man, and then moved in for his counterattack. She'd not give him the chance.

Instead of checking her swing for a return stroke, Kethe followed it around and down into a spinning crouch. She heard the sound of his blade passing over her head along with his surprised grunt. Trees blurred as she pivoted on her heel, all the way around, and slammed the flat of her blade against his thigh.

Brocuff cursed and then laughed. Kethe beamed up at him just as she felt the tap of his sword's edge against her neck. Her smile slipped. "Damn. I thought I had you."

"Almost did." Brocuff offered his calloused hand, then helped her up. "No, let's be fair. That move would have taken off my leg. I'd have bled out a couple of minutes after you. Where'd you learn that fancy spinning move?"

Kethe wiped the sweat from her brow and laughed. "The ballroom floor, I think. I'm not sure. I'm not often asked to dance."

"With moves like that, I'm not surprised. But you're spinning too much." Brocuff walked over to where a waterskin nestled among the roots of a tree beside his gear. "That first one was fine, if a bit desperate. But if you start spinning every time you get in trouble, people will figure you out and you'll get a sword in the back."

"True enough." Kethe caught the waterskin one-handed and took a swig. The water was cool and tasted faintly of wine. "But this time it worked."

It had been over a week since her father's Mourning, and she was surprised to find that she didn't actually miss him; instead, his memory had impelled her to work even harder. Her mail coat was finished. A little more training with Brocuff, and then she might reach out and seize her dream.

Brocuff grunted and wiped his mouth with the back of his hand. " And you're still relying too much on your eyes. I told you, in a real battle, you won't be able to keep everyone in sight. You're bound to get surrounded. Enemies on all sides. You need to relax. Sense 'em. If we could, I'd bring a half dozen of the boys down here and arm them with sticks. Let 'em have a go at you. You'd see what I mean soon enough."

"Yes, well." Kethe tried not to let his words sting her. "I'm afraid that might ruin the 'secret' aspect of my training."

Brocuff grinned, showing all his yellow teeth. "Right. Which is why I'm right proud of my alternative. Here." He pulled out a kitchen rag.

Kethe raised an eyebrow. "You want me to clean some tree trunks?"

Brocuff snorted. "That'd be a first. No. Tie this around your eyes." He bunched up the rag in his fist and tossed it to her.

She tossed him the waterskin at the same time so the two crossed paths in midair, and caught the rag in her free hand. It was clean enough. "A blindfold?"

Brocuff nodded. "Trust me."

Kethe sighed. "Fine. Though if you spin me around three times and tell me to pin a tail on a donkey, I'll come after you." She trapped her sword between her knees and pulled the rag about her eyes, knotted it closely behind her head, and then straightened, taking up her sword.

"Now you can't see me, so don't bother trying to. I want you to relax. I ain't going nowhere." And then Brocuff went quiet.

Kethe stood stiffly. She expected a blow at any moment, but resisted the urge to lift her sword. A breeze blew past once more, and she heard the branches sighing overhead. It felt good against her brow. She forced herself to lower her shoulders and took a deep breath. Held it. It was so hard to relax.

Silence. No, not silence; Greening Wood was never truly quiet. A branch fell somewhere in the far distance and she started. She thought she could hear Lady whicker in the near distance where Hessa was waiting, but that might have been her imagination. She became very aware of her own body. Her heartbeat. The burn in her shoulders and arms. The tension in her calves. The ground through the soles of her feet. Despite her having just taken a drink, her mouth was dry.

"Now. I'm going to walk around you in a circle. Try to track me."

Kethe closed her eyes beneath the cloth and focused. She heard steps, but from where? She turned her head to one side, then the other. To her left? She started to turn.

"No, stay still. Just follow."

She stilled. She heard the faint crack of a branch. The soft tread of his boots on the loam. A crackle of leaves. Then silence. He was right behind her.

"What you're doing right now, this using your other senses, it's purposeful. You're putting your mind to it. But you need to get to where you're doing it all the time. In the keep. In the bailey. Start feeling people all around you. Tracking 'em. Exercise this skill. Always know where people are, even if you can't see them. You lose track of somebody, they might run up behind you with a knife. A trained soldier—a good one, at any rate—is always alert. You never know where an attack might come from."

Kethe nodded. It seemed obvious, but she'd never thought about it. Training meant sneaking away to Greening Wood. But she should always be training—while doing her needlework, or sneaking down to the kitchen for fresh cream.

"That's enough. You can take it off now."

She did so. The gloom under the canopy seemed extra bright, and she blinked before tossing the rag back to Brocuff. "I understand."

"No, you only think you do." Brocuff grinned again. His smile could be so annoying sometimes. "Listen, and listen good. I've seen some real killers in my time. Men to whom fighting was as natural as breathing. You can mark 'em out in a battle when you know what to look for. When everybody is gasping like fish out of water, leaping around and waving their swords like fools, these men are as calm as you please. They're in control of themselves. And as a result, they're *aware*. They're masters of the battle. What you felt there for a moment with that blindfold on? They've got that going on all the time."

Brocuff paused, watching her. Watching to see if his words were sinking in. "First you master your fear. That done, you work on getting past being excited. Then you swallow your pride and kill the urge to show off. In the end, your final challenge will be to subdue your anger. Only when you're calm and clear and collected, with all those emotions passing through you like the wind through these branches, only then will you be on your way to being a real fighter. Master yourself, girl. Stop thinking so much. Calm down. Be in your skin, and open your mind to the world around you. Odds are you'll still die screaming, but until then, you'll fight hard and you'll fight true."

This time it was Kethe's turn to snort. "Great. That's a rousing note to end on. For a moment I was almost inspired."

"I'm a constable, not a bard. Now, let's do the three-chop against your favorite tree. Five minutes. Neck, chest, knee, then the other side. One-handed. And in the other," he said, moving back to gear, "you get to hold this lovely shield."

Kethe refrained from groaning. Groaning meant double the time spent hacking at a tree trunk. She took the shield with her left hand, heavy boards rimmed with iron. Great. Taking a deep breath, she stepped up to the scarred beech tree. It probably hated her to no end, unable to fathom why she attacked it every few days.

"All right," said Brocuff, sitting down and leaning back against another tree. He kicked his legs out in front of him and sighed contentedly. "Let's see some spirit. Start!"

Kethe fell into her fighting stance and chopped at the tree at neck height. The blade bit into the wood and she immediately hauled it free only to slice it back in. She fought back a grimace and put all her focus into the blows, over and over, until she forgot about the passage of the seconds and the world narrowed to her elbow, wrist, her knees, the strength coming from her hips, the blade dancing and flickering, over and over and over again.

The tree disappeared and she saw the knight approaching. His dense, bristly black beard. Face like a shovel blade, hooked nose, eyes blank with murderous hatred. Broad shoulders, narrow waist. One of her father's best Wolves. Her blade thunked harder against the tree, sending a jarring vibration up her arms that felt right. The knight was closing on her, lips pulled back in a snarl. It was his eyes that had terrified her so. He wanted to kill her. Was willing to charge an armed caravan to cut her open. She heard her screams again, knew that she would not get away. He was massive. He loomed like a monster, blotting out the sun.

Kethe tightened her grip and cut faster. Each blow slammed into the knight's body. Neck. Chest. Knee. Still he came, unstoppable, death incarnate. She put more weight behind each blow. The blade sank deeper with each cut, but she wrenched it out all the quicker. Over and over again, she poured her fear and anger into the strikes. Nobody would find her helpless again. Nobody would take advantage of her. Nobody would tell her what to do. Tell her who she was. Hold her life in their hands. Make her scream. Make her fear.

Faster. Harder. Her blade was thunking into the tree so quickly now that the blows were becoming a drumming tattoo, hard to tell apart. Kethe felt something blossom within her. Felt something open, like the petals of a morning glory opening to meet the sun. She was snarling, she realized. Something was wrong with her sword. Brocuff was calling her name. *No.* She dropped her shield and grabbed the hilt with both hands. *Thunk-thunk-thunk.* Switch sides. Sweat was flying from her brow.

She felt something burning in her shoulders, her breath scorching her throat. *Faster.* Strength flowed through her. She could do this forever. The knight's face blotted out the sky, lined and cruel and driven mad by hatred. No matter how fast she attacked, he still came after her. *Faster.* Each blow was digging several inches into the tree. Wood chips were flying.

His blade was coming down toward her face. Death. Death. *Death.*

Kethe screamed and struck the tree as hard as she could. Her blade shattered. Half of it remained embedded six inches into the trunk. The rest went spinning across the ground.

Kethe stared at her hand. Blood was welling from the creases of her palm. She could barely hear over the ringing in her head. She looked over at where Brocuff was standing, his eyes so wide she could see the whites all the way around his irises. She followed his gaze to the tree. Three massive wounds had been dealt to the old giant on each side, as if a pair of woodsmen had attacked it with great axes for an hour. She'd cut deep grooves right into the heartwood.

"By the Ascendant," whispered Brocuff.

She straightened and stared at the constable. "Not a word," she said, voice low. "This stays between us."

"As you command, my Lady." His voice was almost fearful. "But what exactly is 'this'?"

Kethe looked at the half of her blade that remained buried deep in the tree. The image of the blossoming flower faded from her mind, that exhilarating sense of strength and limitless power. She sagged, suddenly exhausted. "I don't know." She hesitated, and suddenly felt drained beyond belief. She'd never be able to pull the shard of her blade out.

She looked down at her bloody palm, and then slowly squeezed it into a fist. Blood ran down her wrist and soaked into the hem of her sleeve. "But whatever it is, I welcome it."

~~~

Half an hour later the three of them rode out of Greening Wood. The wind was developing some bite, and Hessa pulled her bright yellow cloak with crimson tassels tightly about her chin.

"Your calluses are going to give you away, you know." She could barely keep the disdain from her voice. "Your hands are starting to look like those of a stable boy."

Kethe frowned down at her palms. It was true. A ridge of calluses had formed at the top of her palm and the base of her thumb. "Well, I'll wear gloves."

"To dinner?" Hessa sniffed. "And, look, I've been meaning to tell you." She turned in her saddle to fix Kethe with her gaze. "Your dresses. Honestly. That green velvet one? I thought you were going to burst the seams when you reached for your third plate of ham last night."

Kethe felt her face burn. She searched for a sharp retort, but couldn't find one. She couldn't fit into half her gowns any longer. Her shoulders had grown. Thank goodness her thighs and calves were hidden by her skirts. If she wore leggings like Menczel, her mother would faint.

"Yes, well, in case you hadn't noticed, a certain amount of strength is needed to wield a blade." As retorts went, it was pretty weak.

Hessa shook her head and turned back on her saddle. "Given the way you look, who couldn't help but notice? You do realize that you're starting to become so muscular that you look like a man, don't you? Is that what you really want? Really?"

Kethe set her jaw and stared ahead at the narrow trail. She was barely able to keep Hessa quiet about her training, and she'd yet to find a way to stop her mouth altogether.

"Kethe. Seriously. You can't keep doing this." Hessa stopped her horse, and a genuine note of plaintiveness entered her voice. "These three years that I've been assigned to you as your lady-in-waiting are going to be interminable for both of us if I can't help guide you the way I should. I've tried subtle hints, I've tried forbearance, I've tried everything I can think of, but you seem more intent on escaping me than paying attention to what I have to say. Please. Listen. We're meant to be like sisters, so take these next words to heart: with the shape your House is in, you're going to need to wed, and soon. You are your mother's greatest asset. A wise marriage right now could bring in a strong ally and shore up your weaknesses. But if you keep disappearing into the smithy—yes, I know about that—and hiding in the woods to chop down trees, what man is going to want you? You can't sing, you don't care to dance, you don't play any instruments, you brood at the table and don't laugh at Menczel's witticisms. All you think about is fighting and killing and pretending to be a knight. This can't go on. If you really want to help your family, stop this foolishness and start playing your part. The great Winter Shriving is coming up in two months. Have you even picked your dress? Your mask? If you don't start preparing, you'll have no choice but to go looking like a dancing bear."

Dull anger beat at her temples. Kethe pulled on her reins and Lady came to a stop as well. Brocuff, she noticed, was keeping a wise distance.

"Look." She'd tried explaining in the past, but each time had failed to make Hessa understand. "Everyone has a path they wish to walk. Mostly life sets your path, but sometimes, if you're lucky and you try really hard, you can pick a different one. That's what I'm trying to do." She stared down at her hands. She could make out the veins on their backs. They were nothing like a true maiden's hands. "I know you don't understand. I know you think beautiful gowns and feasts and gossip and courtly love and a fine marriage are the most important things in the world. And that's fine. I don't judge you. You can have them." Kethe looked over to her companion. "But I don't. I don't want any of it. Just accept that I want to walk my own path."

Hessa sat still, and for a moment, Kethe thought she'd reached her. Then her companion sighed and shook her head. "The world is full of wonders. Very well. You can walk this path, but I tell you true: it's unnatural, and the world will punish you for it. But enough. I've finally spoken my piece. From now on I'll leave you well alone. Just don't come to me crying when it all comes crashing down around your head."

Kethe felt a sharp pain like broken glass in her chest. Not that she cared for Hessa. They'd sized each other up on the day that Hessa had come to stay at the castle a year ago, and known they were two very different creatures. But Hessa's words, Hessa's thoughts—they were everything she fought against.

"Don't you worry," she said, nudging Lady back into a canter. "I won't come running to you. That you can count on."

The forest path wound its way around the end of Greening Wood and then broke into view of the castle. It was monstrously large. Fearsome. Its walls were unscalable, and the great keep rose on its private hill, daring any army to break itself against its walls. Kyferin Castle. Her home.

Up ahead on the main road she saw two men riding up to the gatehouse. One was clearly a knight, clad in gleaming armor, a lance held upright by his side, a pennant fluttering in the wind. Kethe studied the man, then slowed to allow Brocuff to catch her. "Who might that be?"

Brocuff shielded his eyes against the sun and studied the distant figure. "A black wolf on a field of azure. That's Ser Wyland's coat of arms." The constable smiled and ran his hand over his hair with excitement. "Ser Wyland. The Ascendant be praised! Now, that's a stroke of luck!"

"Are you sure?" Kethe rose in her stirrups and laughed. "It is! Come on! Hurry!" She kicked her heels into Lady's flanks and crouched in the saddle. Lady needed no urging; she burst forward into a gallop, and Kethe laughed anew, giving the mare her head. She pounded down the narrow trail and out onto the road, then turned and surged up the hill toward the distant gate.

Looking back, she saw that Hessa had refused to go any faster, forcing Brocuff to lag behind so as to not abandon her. No matter. The guards were accustomed to seeing Kethe come racing up to the gate in a most unladylike manner. Up ahead she saw Ser Wyland and his squire reach the massive drawbridge and cross over. A trumpet sounded, announcing his arrival, and Wyland lifted an arm in greeting. The portcullis rose, and the knight rode into the tunnel beyond.

Moments later Kethe reached the drawbridge herself and crossed at a canter, the wood resonating with each thud of Lady's delicate hooves. The portcullis had remained raised, and she passed under its heavy teeth and into shadow. Up ahead she could see Ser Wyland dismounting in the bailey. Guards were spilling out of the base of the gatehouse, a couple of them laughing and cheering as they approached.

Kethe slid off her saddle as she emerged back into the sunshine, handing Lady's reins without looking to one of the stable boys. Ser Wyland was surrounded by soldiers now, but he stood taller than all of them. Reaching up, he removed his greathelm and handed it to his squire Ryck. He grinned, and Kethe felt a thrill of joy. Her father had been served by a wide variety of men, but all had been marked by a certain lethal brutality. Lord Kyferin's Black Wolves were feared as much for their skill in arms as their merciless nature, yet amongst that company Wyland had stood apart.

"Ser Wyland!" She waved, and he turned and on catching sight of her smiled broadly.

"Lady Kethe!" His voice was a rich baritone, the kind that with little effort could be projected across a battlefield. The soldiers parted and Ser Wyland approached. He looked every inch the perfect knight, his armor gleaming, his cloak the same peerless azure as his banner. Dark brown hair was cut close to his scalp and grew in a thick beard along his jaw and upper lip. Handsome, kind, and prone to laughter, Ser Wyland had easily been her favorite amongst the Black Wolves, and the sight of him standing once again within the bailey gave her a surge of joy and nervousness.

"My, one season away from the castle and you've grown an inch." He beamed down at her. "And you've grown into a beautiful maiden as well. I see I'm going to be kept busy from now on, repelling all sorts of bothersome suitors."

Kethe laughed. For a moment the world returned to some semblance of normal; she could almost imagine her father in the stable with a handful of his other Wolves, a feast set in the great hall to welcome the men home, and her mother descending from the keep to welcome and toast them in their latest victory.

Ser Wyland glanced about the inside of the bailey and up at the keep. "How is your Lord father? I've not heard from him since his summons to join the campaign. The Solar Portals are a riot of confusion, and I could barely pass through to Ennoia from Sige."

Kethe swallowed, and like that, the moment passed. Even Ser Wyland couldn't bring back the past. "He died fighting the Agerastians." Her chest felt as if it had turned into two blocks of wood, and her voice was the strained groan that would be made by grinding them together. "With all the Black Wolves. Two weeks ago now."

Ser Wyland's eyes widened in shock and his jaw clenched. He looked as if she'd slid her sword smoothly into his chest. He didn't say a word as he searched her face and then slowly lifted his head to stare past her blankly at the far wall. "Two weeks ago." His voice was hollow. Kethe watched him, heart racing, feeling anew her pain and sorrow. Before her eyes she saw Ser Wyland master himself, absorb this news, internalize it, and then look back down to her. "I'm so sorry." She saw pain in his dark eyes. "You have my sincerest condolences, my Lady."

Kethe felt strangely adult and grave. Was it wrong to feel so thrilled at having Ser Wyland focus so intently on her? If only she weren't coming from a training bout in the woods, but rather were clad in an elegant gown. She tried for a sorrowful smile. "I'm so glad that you've returned to us, Ser Wyland. We feared you dead with the other Wolves. Your presence has been sorely missed."

Ser Wyland nodded gravely. "I was on a pilgrimage in Sige. Too far out in the mountains for word to reach me in time. I'll never forgive myself for not being by your father's side. But perhaps I can still honor his memory by doing your Lady mother what service I can render."

Kethe nodded mutely. At that point Brocuff and Hessa rode in through the gatehouse. Ser Wyland looked up, and a wry smile returned to his face. "Constable!"

"All right, you men. You want the castle to fall while you're out here mooning like fools? You've seen a real knight before. Back to your posts!" Brocuff's bark sent the soldiers scrambling, though a number of them called out final welcomes to the knight before they ran away.

A groom helped Hessa dismount, but Brocuff simply slid from his saddle and strode over, a big smile on his square face. "Ser Wyland! I never thought I'd be so happy to see your offensively handsome face."

Ser Wyland laughed and clapped Brocuff on the shoulder so hard the constable stumbled. "Watch yourself, Constable, or I'll give you a hug that will snap your spine."

"Just you try it," said Brocuff, grinning. "I've not bathed in weeks in anticipation of just such an attack."

Ser Wyland raised his gauntlets in mock surrender. "I yield! You're a master of defense. No wonder Lord Kyferin handed the defenses of the castle to your capable armpits."

Brocuff guffawed. "Where are you coming in from?"

"My pilgrimage to Ethering Woods." The knight smiled sadly. "There'll be time to catch up once I've presented myself to Lady Kyferin."

"Aye, fair enough. She'll be glad to see you." Brocuff tugged on his ear. "We're in dire straits. It's good to have you with us."

Ser Wyland nodded and looked up to the keep. "Thank you, Brocuff." He took a deep breath, then sighed. "Lady Kethe? Will you escort me to your mother?"

"Of course." *Curses.* She'd wanted to wash up first. Ser Wyland might be too gentlemanly to remark on her disheveled and unladylike appearance, but her mother would notice right away. She'd have to stay back by the door and slip away as soon as she could.

"Lady Hessa," said Ser Wyland, turning as her companion emerged from the stables. "I'm glad to see that you still grace Kyferin Castle."

Hessa simpered and curtseyed, then threw in a giggle for good measure. "Oh, Ser Wyland, having you back is like finally seeing sunlight after an interminable night. We've all been so afraid, haven't we, Kethe?"

Kethe's smile froze, but she forced herself to nod. "Oh, yes. Some of us have been terrified."

Ser Wyland raised an eyebrow, but he gave no further sign of noticing the change in their tone. "You're too kind. Now, shall we ascend? I must pay my respects."

Hessa smiled, took a step forward, and tripped artfully right into Ser Wyland's arms. He caught her smoothly, but found that she'd taken a strong grip of his arm and was now beaming up at him. Ser Wyland paused, raised an eyebrow in amusement, then smiled and began to escort her up to the barbican. Kethe shook her head and followed a few paces behind, listening as Hessa giggled and complimented Ser Wyland and asked an endless stream of questions.

They passed through the barbican and up past the drum towers to the keep. Kethe's mind turned to practical details. Brocuff would take care of the remnants of her sword, stashing them in Elon's smithy along with her leather training clothes. She hoped Elon wouldn't investigate the blade too closely—the constable had agreed to claim she'd struck a rock, but she knew Elon was too sharp to fall for that lie if he did more than glance at the sword.

When they reached the entrance to the Lord's Hall, Hessa stepped reluctantly away to make room for Kethe, who took Ser

Wyland's arm with a nervous smile. It felt surprisingly good to stand by his side, to feel lithe and feminine. Was this what Hessa was urging her to embrace? A life spent with a man just like this, tall and strong and wonderfully handsome?

She raised her chin as they stepped forth into the light.

CHAPTER EIGHT

Audsley

Magister Audsley stepped into his tower room and closed the door behind him. He pressed it firmly into the jamb, then turned and leaned back against it with a sigh. Eyes closed, he inhaled the scent of his private domain, allowing the familiar smells to sink into his being and soothe away the stress: sandalwood incense, the mellifluous complexity of a thousand parchments and papers, old leather, the ghost of coal smoke, spices and his own familiar scent. Ah, now this was bliss, to have a corner of one's own. Everyone else in the castle lived atop one another, sleeping like logs in the woodpile, stepping over each other when they had to leave the great hall to relieve themselves, rubbing elbows and hearing every biological eruption, eructation and ejection of effluvium. Not Audsley King, however; as a Noussian and the castle's resident expert on all things literary, cosmological, alchemical and mythological, he'd earned himself an entire level of the Ferret Tower.

With a sigh he opened his eyes, adjusted his precious spectacles, and pushed away from the door with his ample arse. The Ferret Tower had been one of the last built, and unlike the cruder, square towers such as the Wolf and Stag, his was circular so as to not provide a besieging enemy with a convenient corner to bombard with catapult stones. This was an advancement that he was most pleased to take advantage of, because the circularity of his chamber provided him with all manner of philosophical metaphors. It was lamentably true that there was no fireplace to be had, much to his firecat Aedelbert's dismay, and this, alas, was the large room's true failing; during the winter months his rich brown skin grew ashy and he could see his breath plume before him as he turned his pages with fingers made numb despite his quite expensive calfskin gloves—but it was his, all his, and he wouldn't have traded it for the choicest spot before the great hall's fire and all the lamb crackling in the world.

"Aedelbert?" he called, and stepped lightly across his rug, rounded his central table and stopped at the far side of the room. He'd covered this section of the wall's curvature with a storage system whose design was his own: a wooden honeycomb that reached to the ceiling, within which he kept his smaller scrolls and maps. It had taken the carpenter two months to carve and assemble. Now, where was that map?

He held up his hands as he hesitated, fingers rippling, then took out an old, faded green scroll case. He undid the copper clasp, popped it open, and with great care drew out the heavy vellum roll within. Was this it? Ah, yes. Ah, yes, indeed.

He turned back to his table and hummed as he cleared a space, moving aside a pile of precious books, a number of rocks he was trying to categorize, the deformed skull of a calf, then unrolled the scroll with great care.

"Ah," he sighed. "Beautiful." And it was. Regardless of the precious information it contained, the scroll itself was a work of art. Deep cobalt blues were inked smoothly onto its surface, while small stoneclouds were carefully delineated everywhere, their orbits marked by dotted lines of gold ink. Fine calligraphy identified each stonecloud, its nature and history, while unique glyphs along the orbiting line marked where it would appear during which month. His master's master, the Magister Plune, had acquired it in Aletheia itself, the largest floating stonecloud by far in the Empire. He'd paid three ingots of gold for it, but that had been a symbolic exchange. There was no putting a price on such beauty and information.

"Aedelbert? You're missing out. Come see." He heard a sleepy chirp from somewhere under the voluminous covers piled up high on his bed. "Very well, your loss. Now," said Audsley, leaning forward over the table and placing his finger just above one of the stoneclouds. "You. You, I say! Reveal yourself unto me!" He squinted down at the cramped writing, humming lightly as he took in the information, then moved his finger, never actually touching the vellum, to follow the accused stonecloud's orbiting line. Out and over, till he reached the glyph for their current month. Beneath that lay the sign for Ennoia, followed by a notation that marked the stonecloud as moving over Kyferin Castle's domain. "Yes, yes," he muttered. "Indeed! And quoth, verily, and poom poom pah!"

He carefully laid a heavy book on each of the map's corners and then hurried over to another section of wall, where a large, plain wooden board hung, truncating the curvature of the wall. Reaching out, Audsley opened a vertical container affixed to the board's left edge, and with great care unfurled a map across the board, then clipped it to the far side. He took a moment to smooth out the heavy vellum, then linked his hands behind his back and considered the expanse of the Empire.

The map was more beautiful than Lady Kyferin, though not by much. The seven realms of the empire were depicted in their order of Ascension, from chthonic Bythos in its dark and oppressive caverns up to Aletheia's empyreal might. This portrayal was little more than a pious conceit, for only Ennoia and Agerastos could reach each other without the aid of a gate.

As always, Audsley's gaze lingered on his home city of Nous, painted just below the peaks of Sige. The conical city emerged from the azure waters of the Illimitable Ocean, and he blinked as old memories arose to assail him. Inhaling briskly, he turned sternly to the realm in which he was destined to spend the last of his days. "Ennoia, three days ago." He picked up a long, thin wand and pointed imperiously at where the city was marked. "Given its trajectory and speed..." He did the sums quickly in his head. "That should place the stonecloud about... here." He moved his wand hesitantly up and to the right, then tapped where a small symbol was marked 'Kyferin Castle'. "Not an exact pass. Oh, no, let it be noted that I'm making no definitive statements! But... from the top of the keep, it should be eminently visible! Indeed, indeed."

He chewed his lower lip as he studied the map a moment longer, then his eyes strayed as if by their own account to the island of the heretics, just off the southern coast of the Ennoian mainland. He frowned. The island looked perpetually poised to attack, its splintered, circular coastline sweeping together to form the bristling flanks of an invading host, perforated only by the straits of Bohesus which allowed entrance to the great inland sea on whose shore the city of Agerastos stood.

Audsley tapped his lips with his wand. To think! What gall, what hubris, to destroy their Solar Gate and remove themselves so decisively from the Ascendant Empire! They'd practically demanded the invasions that had followed, the last of which had been led by Lord Kyferin himself. Enderl had captured Agerastos and returned victorious, but the Empire's grip of the island had slipped and been cast off only a decade later. Such a pity!

Audsley sighed and turned to his shelving, where he drew down a massive tome with great difficulty. This he set down on a broad book stand and absent-mindedly turned the pages. He could lose hours browsing this Stonecloud Atlas, but this time his mind remained on Agerastos and the destruction of its Gate. He'd been but a boy when word had shaken the Empire. Thirty years? And now the land was besieged by war, death, and a future so uncertain he hated to think of it. Blasted heretics. They'd earned their centuries-long punishment twice over.

Sighing, he opened the atlas to the right stonecloud's page. A talented artist had rendered it in charcoal shades long ago, down to the craggy edges, the teardrop underbelly, the flattened top with its undergrowth single abbey, the mass of twisted trees and their trailing roots. Beautifully done. If only all the stoneclouds were so portrayed. Some were little more than blobs or vague sketches; they had not been seen in centuries and were thought to perhaps have broken free of their orbits to wander off the edge of the world or crash into the ocean or mountains without anyone being the wiser. Ah! To be a stonecloud hunter, filling the blanks using monocular, mathematics, and sheer determination to track his floating prey! To be the man that, say, located Starkadr, the lost stonecloud of the Sin Casters themselves! In his next life, perhaps.

Audsley sighed and squinted down at the annotations. This one was but a small body of rock, only a quarter of a mile in diameter, and devoid of water. Slight vegetation. A small abbey had been built upon it almost two centuries ago by Nethys, the famous sister of the Third Ascendant, only to be abandoned a few years after her death and then inhabited intermittently by bandits and hermits. Audsley's gaze dropped to the last entry, written in his own hand seven years ago.

The Stonecloud of Nethys passed a half mile west of Kyferin Castle at an estimated altitude of one hundred feet, having lost several hundred feet since its last sighting. Momentum was smooth, with a constant speed of fifteen miles per hour. Its dimensions remained constant with the last measuring, and I espied no movement or life upon its surface. It would seem that the bandit Tycsco has quit it since last it passed us by. Its loss in speed and height is of concern. If it continues to lose height in such manner, we may only see it one or two more times before it crashes to the ground.

Audsley pursed his lips. That had been his first entry in this great tome. He remembered the day clearly. The light had been poor, but he'd also been crying. Magister Yeon had passed away the night before, his wasting disease finally claiming his last breath and ushering him into Ascendance. Audsley had barricaded himself in here, his master's room, bereft and gutted, and had spent the entire night taking down scrolls and opening books, not reading but deriving a simple comfort from the feel of the paper beneath his fingertips, the scent of ink and the mystery of the painted metals. At dawn he'd resumed his duties in a rote manner, his limbs heavy, his mind numb, only to realize that the stonecloud was to pass by within a few hours. He'd notified Lord Kyferin as to the stonecloud's imminent passage, his voice shaking in the great hall, and then climbed to the keep's roof to take his observations even as the castle went on alert in case Tycsco should attempt a raid. None had been forthcoming, and Audsley had retired to his master's room to make his annotations, the Kyferin's mocking thanks still ringing in his ears. That was when he'd discovered Aedelbert, smoky gray and no larger than a kitten, lost and fierce and too weak to fly back out through the window. He'd scooped him up and sat down to cry, hugging the hissing little firecat tight even as he'd realized that this room was now his own, a final gift from a master he'd come to love.

He sighed. Old memories. He closed the tome, took up his satchel, checked that it had parchment, quill and ink, then hunted around behind his bed until he found his white-oak traveling case. Breathing lightly, he set it on his bed and sprung the catches, opening it to examine his leather-bound monocular. This alone was worth more than the orbital map and the skycloud atlas combined. Such treasures were entrusted to his care! He shook his head, marveling. To think! And nobody else in the castle, except for perhaps Father Simeon and Lady Kyferin, appreciated how valuable these items were. What a world.

He snapped the case closed, then pulled on his heaviest cloak, slung the satchel over his shoulder, and took up his monocular case. "I'm going out, all right?"

A sleepy chirp was his only response. He hesitated at the door, eying the satchel's strap. It had nearly worn through. He'd have to fix it soon. Fingering the frayed leather, he surveyed his quarters. Had he forgotten anything? He did a quick review, and then nodded decisively. All ready. He shook out his shoulders, cast a last look around his room, and then departed.

~~~

Half an hour later he reached the top of the keep. Panting for breath, sweat running down his back, face flushed, he stopped just below the heavy trapdoor. Damn it. He'd hoped it would be open. He steadied his breath, placed one shoulder against the boards and pushed. The trapdoor rose an inch and then stuck.

Audsley grunted and considered putting down his monocular case, then gritted his teeth and shoved harder. The door rose another inch, then another. Suddenly it lifted easily and disappeared, and he let out a cry and almost fell, stumbling up the steps and into the cold air.

"There, there, ser." A gruff voice, and somebody steadied him by the shoulder. "No need to get into a lather."

"Oh, well, I—thank you. Most opportune, indeed." Audsley squinted at the figure, then pushed his spectacles up his nose and tried for a smile. The guardsman was a grizzled older man with the face of a bloodhound and the flat eyes of a veteran. Just the kind of man he could never make a conversation with. "How is everything? Brisk morning, isn't it? Bracing."

The man raised both eyebrows, as if he'd never thought about it. "Could be," he allowed.

"Ah, yes." Audsley fought to keep his smile and then bobbed his head. "Well, if you'll excuse me." He glanced over at his pigeon coop, eyed the gaunt Raven's Gate standing tall and ominous in the center of the roof, then hurried to the battlement on the keep's western side and set his case on a merlon. Holding it tightly, he squinted at the horizon.

To his annoyance, the guardsman stepped up next to him. "Looking for some aught?"

"I—ah—yes, in fact. Um. A stonecloud. Do you see one?" Audsley shot a quick glance up at the sun. "It should be coming into view right about there." He pointed at the sun, glanced at a worn compass etching on the merlon's top, and then dropped his finger to point roughly south by southwest.

"One of them flying islands, hey?" The man placed both gloved hands on the merlon next to Audsley's and leaned forward, peering at the horizon. "Aye, there's something over there. A fleck of some kind. If it were any closer, I'd warrant it a big bird."

Audsley beamed at the man. "No wonder they've got you on sentry duty, my good man!" His excitement made him feel ebullient. "Sharp eyes, sharp eyes. Now, let me show you something. This is a true wonder." He unfastened the case and went to open it, but a vivid image of the case, monocular and all, toppling over the battlement to crash below seized him and he quickly moved it to the floor. Crouching beside it, he pried the long, bulky object from its cavity and grinned at the soldier.

"What's that, then?" The man leaned in close, smelling of smoke, sweat, and halitosis. "A leather sausage?"

"No, it most certainly is not a leather sausage," said Audsley, clambering back up to his feet. "This is a treasure. Here. You sight in through this little hole, and wonder of wonders, the larger end magnifies the world..." He looked through it at the distant stonecloud. "And... there. Oh, beautiful. Perhaps only thirty feet off the ground? And moving in fits and starts, it seems. That's odd."

"Here, give us a look, then." The guard edged in closer.

Audsley detected strong undercurrents of onion to his smell. Lovely. He tried to turn his grimace into a smile. "Well, all right, but do be careful. Yes, through that end. Now point it at the stonecloud..." He waited, half-expecting the man to start, to let out a superstitious oath and drop the monocular, but instead the guard simply smiled in pleasure.

"Well, this is nice." He examined the stonecloud for a bit, then slowly swung the scope across the whole of the countryside. He lowered it and grinned, revealing strong yellow teeth like those of an old pony. "A sight better than a dried sausage, if you'll pardon the pun. How come we sentries don't have one up here to keep watch with?"

Audsley took it back gladly. "Because they're delicate, rarer than hen's teeth, and worth more than everything in this castle combined." He fought the urge to wipe the eyepiece. "Now, I'm going to have to take some measurements. If Nethys' Isle is really coming in close, I'm going to have to warn our Lady."

The guard nodded sagely, then both men turned to watch as a pigeon flew up from below to flutter around the empty arch of the Raven's Gate and hover around the coop and then disappear inside through one of the holes.

"Magister Audsley!" A young boy emerged, holding the pigeon between his hands. "Look! A message!"

"Indeed, Master Roddick. So I see." Audsley smiled at the young lord, glanced at the stonecloud, then set his monocular back in its case and hurried over. "Who is it from?"

The young boy emerged fully from the coop, a few small downy feathers in his black hair, and frowned as he studied at the little case attached to the pigeon's leg. "Well, this color metal means family. I think?"

"Very good, very good. Now." Audsley reached him and took the pigeon carefully from Roddick's clasped hands. The bird was warm and surprisingly bony beneath its soft cloud of feathers; Audsley held it expertly in one hand and unclipped the message with the other. "Here. Now, let's put this little fellow back in his coop. He's flown a long way to reach us. From... Laur Castle, it would seem." He smiled at Roddick, who eagerly took the pigeon back and disappeared into the coop. When the young lord reappeared, Audsley squatted carefully and held out the case. "See here? Bronze case for the Kyferin family, and here? Two slashes. Second son, which would mean Lord Laur. An important message, I'll wager."

Roddick nodded, his expression solemn. "Uncle Mertyn. He'll be writing about Father's death."

"Yes, most likely. Now, let us see." Audsley unclipped the casing and pulled free a tiny scroll. Adjusting his spectacles, he held the paper up to the light. Fine lettering spelled out a concise message. "Ah. Well, now. That *is* news. I'll have to hurry downstairs to tell your mother."

"What's it say?" Roddick peered vainly up at the little scroll.

"You'll have to wait for your mother to share that information with me, my good man. I'm allowed to read these messages so as to send them on to their correct destinations, but share them with all and sundry? The horror!"

Roddick scowled. "I'm not sundry. I'm Roddick."

Audsley stood, knees popping, and grinned down at the boy. "And a very fine Roddick you are. Now, if you like, you can come down with me to the Lord's Hall and see what this is all about, or you can stay up here with the pigeons. What will it be?"

Roddick tongued the inside of his cheek, considering. "Pigeons," he said at last. "I'm counting how many we've got. They're almost all gone. When are we going to get more back? I think the ones left must be lonely in there by themselves."

"Soon, I hope." Audsley hesitated and looked toward the southwest. Did he have time to measure the approaching stonecloud's trajectory? It was still hours away, he decided. It would keep. Tucking the message in a small pocket, he ruffled Roddick's hair with his free hand, then hurried to the trapdoor. "Please watch my belongings!" The veteran nodded, and Audsley made his way back below.

He moved down the stairs past the Lady's solarium to the third floor where she seemed to live these days, holding court and brooding over the fate of her family and their castle. Audsley paused at the entrance, took a deep breath, held it so as to slow his heart, and then let out a sigh. Him a Noussian and still hesitant about stepping forth to execute his duties. When would he grow that careless confidence he so admired in others? Adopting a grave expression, he rounded the corner and stepped into the warm candlelight.

A massive knight was standing before Lady Kyferin, his armor gleaming, a deep azure cloak falling richly to his calves. Squire Asho—no, *Ser* Asho—was standing to one side, looking much mended. Lady Kyferin herself was seated on her chair above them all on the dais. All of them turned to regard him as he entered, and despite his best efforts he felt his face flush.

"I—I'm most sorry to intrude, my Lady, and I shall endeavor to make my message quick, but... Ser Wyland?"

Ser Wyland smiled, though the expression didn't touch his eyes. He'd no doubt just learned of their tragedy. "Magister Audsley."

"You're alive! I thought all the Black Wolves dead, dead and gone, but here you stand... How?"

Ser Wyland's smile turned tight. "I was away when Lord Kyferin's call to arms was issued, on pilgrimage on the borders of the Black Forest. I received the message too late to join with him, so I rode here as quickly as I could. My fastest, it seems, was still far too slow."

"Oh," said Audsley. "That's both terrible and most fortunate for us." He paused, unsure whether to beam with relief or frown in commiseration, and then caught sight of Lady Kyferin and realized the pause had stretched out for too long. "Oh! My pardon. Yes, a message from your brother-in-law, my Lady. It just arrived." He hurried over and handed it to her.

Stepping back, he linked his hands behind his back and tried to look solemn and grave. He was the Magister. His was an important calling. Still, even after all these years, he wasn't sure if he was pulling it off. Lord Kyferin had never seemed really convinced. Audsley frowned and tried to stand straighter, then focused again on the Lady who was reading the cramped script on the message paper.

"It seems we should soon expect a visit from Lord Laur," she said dryly, lowering the tiny scroll to her lap.

Ser Asho stirred as if to speak, but frowned instead. Audsley felt a pang of commiseration. The poor Bythian probably was still settling into his new role.

Ser Wyland, however, had no qualms. "How soon, my Lady?"

"Within a week. He sent this message this morning as he marched out from Castle Laur."

"Giving us as little time as possible to prepare. Any details on his retinue?"

"Scant. He said he comes with his personal guard to pay homage to his dead brother and offer me consolation in this time of need." She lifted the message again and reread a portion. "He urges me not to fret, as he shall apparently provide the solution to all our troubles."

Audsley frowned. "Well, that would be nice of him. Perhaps he means to loan us knights?"

"Only if it's to his advantage," said Lady Kyferin. "I know Lord Mertyn Laur better than I would like. A more political and conniving animal was never born. He sees our weakness as opportunity. The question is how hard a bargain he'll try to drive. Ser Wyland, you've dealt with him before, by my Lord husband's side. Your thoughts?"

Ser Wyland frowned. "Lord Kyferin never gave him the chance to speak or strike deals. He rode roughshod over him every time they met, much to Lord Laur's chagrin. Still, I've campaigned alongside him twice. He's as ruthless as our Lord was, if not more so. A very pragmatic man. Whatever he offers us will only be to serve his own interests. No doubt he'll seek to frighten us with the Agerastian victory to his benefit."

Audsley blinked. "And shouldn't we be frightened? After such a conclusive victory, might they not threaten Ennoia itself?"

79

"Not really." Ser Wyland's smile was cold. "An army marches on its stomach. Ser Asho has told me that the Ascendant's forces chased the Agerastians for weeks before forcing them to battle. Even though they won, the Agerastians will be half-starved, without arrows, and in dire need of reinforcements and supplies. I'll wager they'll head for the coast in hopes of meeting up with the Agerastian fleet."

Ser Asho frowned. "But they have a clear line of attack on Ennoia. If they take the capital, they'll gain access to the Solar Gates. They'll be able to strike at every corner of the empire - at Aletheia itself! They can't pass that up."

Ser Wyland shook his head. "They might take it, but they'd never hold it. Mark my words. They need provisions. They need reinforcements. If the Agerastian general is anything short of a fool, he'll withdraw to the coast."

Ser Asho nodded, then took a step forward. "My Lady. I know I'm newly knighted, but if I may?"

Lady Kyferin nodded.

"We need all the strength we can muster to resist him. Perhaps Lord Wyland and I could ride to some of your more remote holdings and urge the families of the fallen Black Wolves to send men, if only while Lord Laur visits?"

Audsley nodded. The suggestion was wise. If Asho went alone, he would risk being laughed at by the Black Wolves, or insulting them. What would they think of Lady Kyferin sending a Bythian with such a summons? But with Ser Wyland leading the mission...

Ser Wyland eyed Ser Asho. Clearly the squire's elevation was taking some getting used to. "A good idea, but it would project our weakness most clearly."

"You have a suggestion, Ser Wyland?" asked Lady Kyferin.

"As a matter of fact, I do." Ser Wyland's smile was just shy of roguish. "Hold a tourney the day Lord Laur is due to arrive. We have twenty-five families' worth of unproven sons and brothers. While they might balk at simply lending you their strength, they will leap at the chance to prove their skill in arms and demonstrate their right to lead their families. You could even say the tourney is being held to commemorate your late Lord husband's passion for combat. None could gainsay you."

Audsley felt a squiggle of delight worm its way through him. "A brilliant idea! Lord Laur will ride into a surprising display of military might, and seeing him, these new knights will naturally feel beholden to you and lend you their arms. Brilliant!"

Ser Wyland sketched a gently mocking bow. "I am glad

Magister Audsley approves."

Audsley flushed but decided he wasn't really being mocked, only gently teased. Ser Asho, however, had stepped back, his pale face neutral. Ah, his first suggestion, and it had been squelched.

"I approve, Ser Wyland. Lord Laur will take at least a week to arrive. Let's spread the word." Lady Kyferin looked to the doorway, where a page was standing. "Please summon Marshal Thiemo and Master Bertchold." The boy nodded and took off.

Ser Wyland hesitated. "My Lady? There is another option open to us. I would not have suggested it were your Lord alive, but with him gone and us in dire straits…"

"Yes, Ser Wyland?"

"There is a man being held beneath the Wolf Tower. He's been there three years now."

Lady Kyferin stiffened. "You're speaking of Ser Tiron."

Ser Wyland nodded uneasily. "I know his case is not a simple one." He hesitated. "But before your Lord husband gave him… cause to go mad, he was as loyal and dangerous a man as could be found amongst the Black Wolves. If you could convince him to put the past behind him and serve you in exchange for his freedom, he would make a mighty addition to your forces."

"He is in that dungeon for a reason, Ser Wyland." Lady Kyferin's voice was cold. "I don't think he's forgotten his grievances. Nor have I mine."

"Well I know it." Ser Wyland shrugged. "But the past is past. I merely make the suggestion. Regardless of how successful our tourney is, we will still have only greenhorn knights on hand. Ser Tiron is a brutal, seasoned, and ferocious warrior. I know he's no longer the man we once knew—how could he be? But whatever is left of him in that dungeon cell is still worth ten untried sons."

In the silence that followed, Audsley looked for something to hide behind. The look on Lady Kyferin's face was one he wished never to have directed at him. Her cheekbones seemed to have become more prominent, her eyes as hard as water under a winter sky.

Finally, she nodded. "I will think on it. Thank you, ser knights."

Both men nodded, stepped back, then turned to quit the Lord's Hall. Audsley nodded as he watched them leave, then realized that Lady Kyferin was looking at him expectantly.

"Is there anything else, Master Audsley?"

"What? I mean, my pardon, my Lady? Oh! No, nothing. Not yet. Soon? A stonecloud floats our way. I'll just go take the measurements, and then I'll return, that is, if the measurements urge me to do so?"

A flicker of amusement passed across Lady Kyferin's face, but it didn't linger. "Very well. Please keep me apprised."

"Yes, I will. Right now, in fact. If you'll excuse me?" Blushing ever more fiercely, Audsley turned and hurried out of the room, turned up the steps and paused once he was out of sight. He leaned against the wall. One day he'd have the poise and grace of Ser Wyland, and would be effortlessly courteous and controlled. But not yet.

In the meantime, however, the Nethys Stonecloud awaited him. Buoyed up by this prospect, he smiled in the darkness, tugged down on his tunic, and hurried back up to the keep's roof.

CHAPTER NINE

Asho

Asho followed Ser Wyland down the dark keep stairs and out into the sunlight. The sight of the large man's back filled him with troubled doubts. This was a real knight, a true Black Wolf, a man trusted by Lord Kyferin and proven in dozens of battles. Where Asho barely stood over five feet tall, Ser Wyland towered over six. Each of the knight's steps was a powerful thud that was accompanied by the ring of his heavy armor. Asho ghosted down behind him, feeling insubstantial and inconsequential. Ser Wyland had greeted him politely enough in the Lord's Hall, but made no move to speak to him now that they had left it. He opened his mouth several times to address the man, but each time closed it with a sense of futility. What would he say? *Here I am*? *Acknowledge me a knight*?

They stepped out onto the bailey. While life continued apace, there was a tension to the air that betrayed everyone's fear. Nobody laughed, and even the children were subdued. Asho hesitated. With nobody to guide him, he'd taken Ser Eckel's room in the Stag Tower, though the experience had been unpleasant. He'd lain awake each night in the bannerman's large bed, unable to sleep, feeling like an imposter, expecting at any moment to be rousted from under the covers and thrown out on his ear. Just before dawn on that first night he'd risen, irresolute. He couldn't return to his old spot beside the fireplace in the great hall, but he could not sleep in the Stag Tower. Instead, he'd stolen down to the stables and up into the hayloft past the sleeping grooms, and bedded down at the very back. Each night since then he'd snuck back, but he knew it couldn't last.

Should he march brazenly back into the Stag Tower as if he belonged there?

Ser Wyland took a half dozen paces and then stopped, turned and stared at Asho. "Come on, then." He nodded to the tower and resumed striding toward it.

Asho swallowed. An invitation? A threat? He hurried after.

People smiled at the newly arrived knight. Trutwin the gardener called out a greeting, and then looked past Ser Wyland to Asho. His smile flattened and he turned away. Asho kept his expression blank, and was glad when the darkness of the tower claimed him.

Ser Wyland climbed to the very top, up four flights, and then out onto the roof. There was no guard. Asho stepped out after him. A cinder of three firecats glared at them for intruding, then spread their feathered wings and dove through the crenellations to glide down into the bailey. The wind plucked at Asho's hair, pulled a lock free and blew it across his face. Asho ignored it and instead watched the other man. Ser Wyland moved to a merlon, placed his hands on its top and studied the land, then turned to regard Asho.

"Tell me of the battle. Leave nothing out."

Asho nodded and stepped up beside him. They stood shoulder to shoulder, staring out over the land while Asho told the knight everything. It felt good to tell him the tale. He left nothing out, and Ser Wyland proved a good listener, asking only clarifying questions and nodding. Asho spoke for half an hour, recounting everything from the procession through the city of Ennoia at the start of the campaign right up to their doomed charge up the hill. The only things he left out were how he'd survived the Sin Caster's attack, and the wounding and healing of the Grace. When he had finished, Ser Wyland looked down at him, eyes narrowed.

"So. You saw the Virtues in combat. I've had the honor but once. Believe me when I say there is no greater privilege than to witness their powers in action." Wyland paused, gaze distant for a moment, then shook his head as if to clear old memories away. "And knighted by the Grace himself. An honor usually reserved for heroes."

Did he imagine that tone of reproof? Asho nodded and looked away. "I didn't ask for it."

"Lord Kyferin had no intention of knighting you." Ser Wyland's words were flat. "He intended to drive you so hard that you would ask to return to Bythos and release him from his vow."

"I know." Asho looked down at his pale hands. "I figured that out two years ago."

"Then why did you stay?"

He thought of that night. The rain slicing down from the black sky. The flash of lightning. Shaya turning to him, huddled on her pony. Her wounded, irrevocably broken smile. The guard waiting to ride out and take her to Ennoia to leave him. Abandon him forever. Pain rose within him, that pain that he could sometimes now forget, but which never truly went away. He hoped it never would.

He took a deep breath. "To defy him."

He saw Wyland nod out of the corner of his eye. "I can understand that. But why?"

Asho gripped the rough merlon tight. A thousand memories

assailed him. Slights and injuries, mockery and insults. Beatings that had only stopped when he'd forced Kyferin to raise him from page to squire by defeating the older squires and winning the Ebon Cup. The haunting isolation ever since Shaya had abandoned him. The loneliness. The knowledge that it would never get any better, not so long as Lord Kyferin lived.

"Why?" Perhaps it was Ser Wyland's calm words. His directness. Perhaps it was the fact that Kyferin was now dead. Whatever it was, something in his breast snapped, and he turned to glare up at the larger knight. "Because I loathed him. I loathed him with every ounce of my soul. And if he wanted me to give up so as to get rid of me, then I would never give up, never give him the satisfaction. I'd rather have died than grant him his wish."

Ser Wyland studied him. He showed no reaction to Asho's words. "You're a Bythian. By all rights you should be a slave, cleaning out the latrines or worse. Lord Kyferin granted you and your sister an unheard-of honor by raising you to his staff, an unnatural promotion that could only harm everybody involved." There was no rancor to his words; he spoke with measured calm. "Erland's mistake was to raise you up from the pit. I can understand hating him for that initial act of misguided kindness. But to hate him for the life that followed? That seems ungrateful."

Asho laughed, a bitter bark that he cut short. "Ungrateful? Yes, perhaps I am. You're right. My sister and I didn't ask for his charity. My father didn't expect it when he saved Kyferin's life during his Black Year in Bythos. But, no, that's not why I hated him."

"Enderl was a hard man. Cruel, even. I don't condone much of what he did, but he was an Ennoian warlord. The Ascendant has judged him and he is now living his penance or celebrating his Ascension." Ser Wyland shook his head. "I know your life has not been easy. But you could have returned to Bythos at any point and removed yourself from this situation. Don't you think your stubbornness is partly to blame for the hardship you've endured?"

A black and terrible anger began to throb deep in Asho's soul, the anger he never let himself feel. It was fed each and every day, but he repressed it with all his might lest it ever break free and destroy him. But Wyland's calm certitude, his ignorance, his Ennoian superiority and false rationality were driving Asho past the point of control. He should look away, back down, remove himself from this situation. Do as he had always done, and bow his head.

But he was a knight now. If that title was ever to mean something, then he had to stop running, had to stand up for himself, or else he might as well turn over his blade and return to Bythos tonight.

"Lord Kyferin's cruelty broke my sister. It drove her back to Bythos, to a life of slavery and abuse." He was trembling with fury. "Do you know what it takes to prefer a lifetime of slavery and an early death in the mines over an existence in this castle? He gave us the sky, this life, only to change his mind and force us back underground. She vowed to resist him no matter what, and then he broke her. He promised to keep breaking her until she fled and—"

Asho stopped and took a deep, trembling breath. Wyland paled in shock. He hadn't known. Of course he hadn't. "I almost killed him afterwards. I dreamt about it for months and months: slipping into his chamber with a knife and opening his neck while he slept. He had me watched, but that wouldn't have stopped me."

It felt terrible to speak these words, to reveal this truth at long last. It was terrible and liberating at the same time, even as Asho knew it would damn him. But he was past caring. Wyland listened intently as Asho went on. "But I didn't. You know why? Because killing him would have achieved nothing. It would just set him free. No." Asho's voice was thick with hatred. "I wanted to force him to knight me. I wanted to shove his charity down his throat till he choked on it, humiliate him and show him that I wouldn't break, that he couldn't break me. And when he finally did so? I would challenge him to a duel, and only then cut his throat in front of everybody."

Asho felt sick. Bringing forth this poison that had lain deep in his soul was almost more than he could bear. He stood there with his whole frame shaking, not caring for once in his life what somebody might think. He felt naked, brazen, bold, past redemption. Let Wyland tell the world. He was a knight now. He'd challenge anybody who came for him, and die at their blade if need be. He didn't care.

Wyland frowned but did not look away. "I didn't know. We were told your sister came to her senses and chose freely to return to her native element. We believed it. It made sense to us."

Again Asho felt that bitter urge to laugh. He bit it down. "That was true. She couldn't adjust to the life Kyferin gave her."

Wyland exhaled. "I admire you for not trying to kill him."

Asho's eyes stung with tears, and he turned away to look out over the countryside. "I regret it now. I never got to avenge Shaya. Kyferin got the glorious death he wanted." He closed his eyes tight and grimaced as pain lanced through his heart. "I should have killed him."

"Do you really regret it?" Wyland asked.

Asho sighed. "I—no. I don't know." He felt exhausted. "Maybe not."

"No," agreed Wyland. "And you did avenge your sister. You're a knight, against all odds. You're standing here in service to Lady Kyferin while her husband is gone."

Asho smiled bitterly. "A knight. It hasn't changed anything. I'm still despised. I'm still ignored. Still a Bythian."

Ser Wyland's blow took him completely by surprise. Asho stumbled and crashed to the stone floor, head ringing. Wyland stepped over him. "If you truly believe that, stay down."

Asho pushed himself up to sitting, tasting blood. He climbed to his feet and drew his sword just in time to block a cut from Ser Wyland, who had drawn his own sword with startling speed. Backing away, Asho gripped his blade with both hands, eyes wide.

"Knighting a man does not make him a knight," said Ser Wyland, advancing. "Nor does armor, a sword, or power." He glided forward and slammed his sword down once, twice, three times, the strength of his blows causing Asho to grit his teeth and fall back each time. Ser Wyland's voice was implacable. "A true knight remains such even if he loses everything. His name. His reputation. His wealth. His weapons. His friends." Each statement was accompanied by another blow. Asho had to keep backing away, circling around the inside of the battlements.

Ser Wyland paused, then asked, "Are you a true knight?"

Asho hesitated. Ser Wyland shook his head and surged forward, and for the next ten seconds Asho fought for his life, backing away again and again as he desperately parried the bigger man's blows.

Ser Wyland paused, not even out of breath, and pointed at Asho with his leveled sword. "Nobody can answer that question but you. Nobody can make you a knight. Not even the Grace himself. Nobody can take it away. When you refrained from murdering Lord Kyferin, you proved yourself noble. So I ask you again: Do you still have that strength within you?"

Asho felt a surge of anger. "What do you know about being a true knight? You followed Lord Kyferin. You were a Black Wolf. You call them true knights?"

Ser Wyland lowered his blade. "No. I don't."

"Then why did you fight with them?"

Ser Wyland hesitated. "I've wrestled with that question for years. Was it better to stay home and refuse to fight for Lord Kyferin? Preserve my honor and shut myself away from the world? Or go out amongst their number and do what I could to help others? Offer counsel that might sway his actions toward justice, seek to provide an example that might influence the other men? I chose to do what I could, no matter how hard the road."

Asho wanted to lash back out at him. Handsome, strong, lauded and privileged, what right did Wyland have to lecture him on hardship? "You're an Ennoian. Nobody has ever hated you for being born in the wrong cycle of Ascension. What do you know about hard roads?"

"More than you may think." Ser Wyland raised his blade again. "Now, Lady Kyferin has only two knights left in her service. Will you let go of your anger, put your past behind you, and serve her as a true knight?"

Asho smiled bitterly. "How do you think I've managed to get this far? It's been my anger that's kept me on my feet, my hatred of Lord Kyferin that refused to let him break me. You want me to play the part of a good Bythian slave and thank my masters for their abuse? No." He raised his sword. "I'm a knight now. I don't need anybody to like me. I don't need people to admire me. All I need is my sword and my will to serve Lady Kyferin. The rest can go hang."

Ser Wyland straightened. His expression grew hard. "I'm sorry to hear that. You've a hard road ahead of you, Asho, if you think a blade is all it takes to be a knight."

Asho struggled with his desire to impress Wyland. He thought of Shaya; thought of Trutwin's scowl just moments before, and the thousands that had preceded it. "I cannot forget the life that has made me who I am." His words felt like hammer blows on his soul. "You're right. I don't know how hard your road has been. But I do know you were born an Ennoian lord." Asho fought to keep the scorn from his voice. "You've lived a life of luxury and had everything handed to you. I've had to claw my way to this position from the depths of Bythos itself. You can't understand me. You can't understand what I've been through, or what it takes to keep standing."

His heart was thudding. His words sounded overly loud to his own ears as he spoke truths he'd never before dared voice to an Ennoian so baldly. "So, no. I won't give up who I am, or what has made me strong. I won't pretend to be a gracious Ennoian knight. I'm Bythian. I'm Asho. And I will serve my Lady with every ounce of my being while never forgetting where I came from."

Ser Wyland sighed and sheathed his blade. "Very well. That is my answer, then. We are bound to fight together in our service of Lady Kyferin." He paused and studied Asho, his dark eyes pensive and almost sorrowful. "I fear that your trials are just beginning, ser knight. But I see you, and mark you as my brother. I shall be here for you if you ever wish to talk. I will be here to help you stand if ever you should fall. My shield shall always be at your back, and my sword at your side. We are Black

Wolves. We live and die for the Kyferins."

Asho felt a chill run through him. The Black Wolf oath. Should he repeat it? No, he was no Black Wolf. He was no part of any brotherhood. Instead, he bowed stiffly. "Thank you, Ser Wyland. I swear to you that I shall do my best to serve Lady Kyferin with all my heart and soul."

Ser Wyland sighed and clasped Asho's forearm in a warrior's grip. "I know you will, lad. Of that I have no doubt. Now, come. There's much for us to see to."

He marched to the trapdoor and turned to descend down the ladder and out of sight.

Asho hesitated and stepped to the battlement and gazed out over the countryside. He felt his emotions roiling, a confluence of excitement and doubt, regret and determination. Was he right in his beliefs? Could Asho the Bythian become someone else—Asho the knight?

He thought of Shaya, turning away from him to ride to Ennoia's solar gate, and felt again his heartbreak and despair. No, he wouldn't forget her, wouldn't forget his past, wouldn't turn his back on his past and pretend he was other than he was. It had gotten him this far.

"I swear to you, Lady Kyferin. I shall be your bravest and truest knight."

The wind tore his words from his lips, and drowned them in its soft wail.

CHAPTER TEN

ᴛһᴀʀᴏᴋ

Delirious, blood frozen black in the numerous cuts and gashes that had been opened in his dark hide, his roughshod boots near split and broken, reeling and exhausted, Tharok looked up and saw that he had navigated the perilous maze of shattered ice to reach the mouth of the great glacier. How long he had climbed, he knew not. How he had avoid the pitfalls and chasms, he couldn't explain. No one but Ogri had even been so high, the very roof of the world, for no longer did the peaks and tops of mountains soar above him. Now he stood in their midst, each peak but a jagged rise to one side, the point of a crown into whose heart the Dragon's Breath swept.

The silence resonated, vast and spellbinding, the great sweep of the highest plateau in the world terrible in its soundless splendor. Never had the sky been so open above him, dark with night and glorious with the iridescent shimmer of countless constellations. Tharok fell to his knees and gazed at where the buckled surface of the glacier fanned open into the Valley of the Dead, a sight more beautiful and terrible than any he had imagined.

Ghosts had tormented him, shades of kragh he had never known, faces to which he could not put names. Great chieftains of eras past, foul shamans who gibbered and danced about him as they howled their incantations into the night. He had heard chants that had not been sung by living throats for centuries, had ignored voices that spoke with accents so thick that the meaning of their words could not be divined. He had walked amongst legends and given them no mind, for by his side he had caught glimpses of his father, climbing with him to the Valley of the Dead. Together for the last time they had climbed, but now his father's ghost had disappeared. Now Tharok was alone.

With effort Tharok arose once more. He would walk into the heart of the Valley, and there lie down and let the cold steal his heart's heat from him. The ice beneath his boots had grown compact, so with increasing confidence he moved forward, stumbling only because of his extreme fatigue and the pervasive numbness that now filled his body, up the final rise of the glacier—and then his boots crunched the snow of the Valley itself. Tharok stepped out onto the land of the dead.

About him, invisible but sensed in the way that a hand plunged into a quiet stream can sense the turbulence of the flowing current, surged the spirits of his ancestors. They did not call to him, did not heed him, but they were there, illimitable and present in the ecstasy of death. Tharok moved through them, walked out step by dragging step into the cupped valley, and only then did he begin to sing his dirge, his song of death. From the depths of his chest he sang, his voice low and reverberating, using his avalanche voice such that the night air resonated like a struck bell. He sang in the old manner, introducing himself, telling of his deeds; sang of his ancestors, sang of the joy of summer and spring, the sorrow of autumn and the death that came in winter. He struggled forward, the snow deepening, eyes closing for stretches of time as he waded into the center of his own death.

Ahead lay a great mound standing tall in the center of the valley. Tharok moved toward it. It wouldn't be long now. Only the very tips of the Five Peaks were closer to the Sky Father than he was. Perhaps he would climb a peak himself and from there leap upward and be taken into the sky.

He gained the mound. It was as big as a lowland house. He reached out to take hold of the rock so that he might pull himself up and then froze as his hand closed on scales beneath the snow. He brushed snow aside in great sweeps of his hand and revealed a patch of blue, the color of the soul of a glacier, a great hide with scales as large as his palm. He reeled, then, with an energy he thought had been expended long ago, he swept the snow from the flank of the dead dragon.

He uncovered most of its side before he abandoned the task and surged toward the front where the mound tapered and narrowed down to the ground. There he uncovered a great and sinuous neck, massive horned scales rising along the central ridge all the way down to the head. With reverence he swept the snow from vast horns, the bony ridges over the eyes, the heavy muscles of the jaw. The dragon's eyes were closed, and when he was done and stepped back, it seemed as if Jaermungdr was asleep, peaceful in the grip of an eternal winter. Tharok knew awe such as he had never felt before, staring upon true legend made flesh, the grandest tale of the kragh, the mount of the greatest leader they had ever known.

With a cry he roused himself, shook off the cold, and gazed about at the snow. If Jaermungdr lay here, then so did the Uniter. Clumsily he began to cast about, moving in circles about Jaermungdr's body, weaving drunkenly beneath the cruel stars. He had begun to despair when he tripped and fell, hands plunging into the snow as he toppled and then lay still.

It was hard to breathe, to get enough air into his lungs. He felt a terrible comfort, a languor that was more delicious then red flesh, more enticing than the open thighs of a female or the deepest softness of a bed of furs. He lay still and knew that he was sinking at long last, the vital fire that burned within him finally guttering. With a great effort of will he turned onto his back and looked up at the stars. He would never join them, had not done anything sufficient to merit such an honor, but lying here was honor enough. To have found Jaermungdr, to have been permitted entry to the Valley of the Dead, to gaze upon these sights with living eyes—that was, he decided, honor enough.

Reaching up, he brushed a flurry of snow from his eyes and then allowed his arm to collapse by his side. His forearm fell across a hard object, something sharp and unnatural in the snow. Dim curiosity pricked him. Turning his head, he gazed at the bank of snow into which his arm had fallen and dug deeper, probing with numb fingers until his hand closed around a shard of metal. Gritting his teeth, he wrenched it free and saw that it was a blade, a great scimitar made of black metal, broad and fell and strangely light. The crossguard was made of crimson metal, and the hilt was of black sable, frozen solid and twined with metal wire.

Ogri's blade.

Tharok dropped it onto the snow so as to grasp it by the hilt. Strength rushed into him; heat caused his muscles and skin to prickle viciously enough that he gasped in pain. His heart surged, began to pound in his chest, and with a choking cry he sat up, the pain receding from his wounds, new energy surging into him. It was as if his body were dry tinder and the blade a living brand; its fire swept through him, dispelling the cold and gifting him with a new grasp on living. Knuckles white, he brought the blade before his face, then gazed down its length, marveling.

It was Ogri's blade, known as World Breaker, the blade that had led countless charges, that had severed thousands of heads, that had bathed in more blood than the valleys below had stream water. Despite its size it felt light in his hand, the metal of the blade appearing almost akin to obsidian, the edge so sharp that it seemed to disappear into the air and never quite end. Breathing deeply, Tharok blinked away the lethargy and began to sweep at the snowy bank with his right fist, his left arm still useless, reluctant to release the blade. He sent great flurries flying, and then, deeper down, found the great war leader himself.

It was with great care and reverence that Tharok uncovered the body of the greatest kragh chieftain who had ever lived. For untold hundreds of years he had lain here, preserved in the cold, lying as if in state in his armor, a heavy lance fallen by his side, thickly plated black iron scales clothing his form with the same grace and strength as

Jaermungdr. Ogri had been huge, and with a grunt of pleasure Tharok saw that he had indeed been a highland kragh: the same thick tusks, the breadth of shoulder, skin so dark it was almost black, not the bright green of fresh grass and weeds of their lowland cousins. Tharok had never seen a larger or darker kragh. A shiver of awe passed through him. Ogri had been beyond formidable. He must have been unstoppable.

Around the dead chieftain's brow lay a circlet of iron. Tharok tried to recall it from the legends, but could only remember tales of Ogri's great golden crown, inset with black fire opals and gleaming with more light than all the constellations together. Perhaps the crown had fallen somewhere in the snow. Tharok considered searching for it but desisted; the strength that World Breaker imparted had him back on his feet, but the thought of scouring the snow and ice for a missing crown was more than his ravaged body could bear.

What company to die in. He must have done something right during his fifteen years of life to merit such an ending. On impulse, Tharok reached down and took the iron circlet from Ogri's weathered brow. It came off after a brief tug and he held it up to the starlight. A perfect circle, with no mark or seam to indicate how it had been forged. Common iron, without adornment, without rune or glyph. For a moment Tharok hesitated, and then, obeying the impulse of instinct, he slipped it onto his head.

Time stopped. A key turned. He heard every voice and word that had ever been spoken to him all at once in a roar. Saw every scene from his life blur before his eyes, gone before he could grasp them. A deep pain split his skull as if an ax had been plunged into his mind, a gash as bright and awful as lightning. He screamed and released World Breaker, set his hands to his temples as he fought to keep his head from bursting, a thousand voices roaring in his mind, a thousand songs and faces, the peaks spinning about him. The stars were falling, the world was ending, and he passed out, fell into darkness and knew no more.

When he awoke, the stars had returned to the great bowl of the sky above him. He lay in the web of pain that was his body, but felt detached from it, aloof to the aches and sobs and grinding agony that suffused his flesh and bones.

For a long while he thought of nothing and simply gazed at the stars. He knew their names now, knew each and every one, names coming to him as he looked at them. The Falling Axe, the Troll, Ogri's Foot, the Little Peak, the Dawn Stars. They were the same, but now he saw them with a new awareness, understood the interplay between their appearance and the seasons: that The Falling Ax would sink ever closer to the horizon until they disappeared, heralding the beginning of spring, while the Dawn Stars had once been known as the Stars of Deepest Dark, and ages before that, the Dusk Stars. He lay still, gazing up from the bed of snow and pain, and then took a deep breath and sat up.

He didn't have to die here. It wasn't ordained. Only now did he realize that he could have whittled the lowland kraghs' numbers down one by one with carefully placed ambushes and traps. Or, more easily, he could have challenged their one-eyed leader in direct combat, using words and phrases that would have forced his hand, such that the leadership of the group would have gone to the victor, invoking lowland customs that they would not have dared defy. He didn't need to have killed them all, could even now be leading them if he had thought quicker in the moment.

Still, had he done so, he would not be here now, with Ogri's circlet on his brow and World Breaker at hand. He would not be sitting here, half-dead but for the mystic power that sustained him, aware of so much, suddenly seeing the connections and patterns between people, tribes, the world and nature that had never been evident to him before.

Looking down, he studied Ogri. Had he too had to contend with so much awareness and rapidity of thought? Of course he had, and now his sudden rise to power, his meteoric ascension through the tribes, could be understood in a new light. Where had Ogri found this circlet, and who had he been before it?

Reaching up, Tharok took hold of the iron ring and pulled it free. The universe went silent, his mind crashed into the mud, his thoughts slowed, the meaning of words vanished from him, and with a roar the darkness came rushing back in. What had he understood about the women's councils? What was that truth he had glimpsed about the right of raiding? The names of all the stars fell from his eyes, and suddenly the Valley of the Dead seemed vast and final. Shivering, he placed the ring once more atop his head, and his mind opened up to the cosmos again.

Tharok heaved himself to his feet and took stock. There would be time for reflection later, but for now time was of the essence. He had no food, was low on blood and strength, was far from the closest habitation, was no doubt already suffering from frostbite and hypothermia, and soon even World Breaker's strength would be insufficient to keep him going. He would need first and foremost heat, then sustenance, then a means to move down the mountains, and finally a place to recover his strength. He forced himself to circle to where Ogri's body lay, his reverence evaporating before his need, and located the dead chieftain's pack. The canvas was frozen, but he tore it open and spilled out the contents into the snow. His own flint and steel had been lost on the second day, but Ogri's would suffice. He then climbed up onto

Jaermungdr's foreleg and swept World Breaker back and forth, dislodging snow and ice until the blade thunked into the war saddle. Gritting his teeth, Tharok brought the legendary blade crashing down once, twice, and the third time the ancient saddle, frozen as hard as rock, splintered and smashed free of the straps that tied it to the dragon's shoulders.

Cursing his useless arm, Tharok gathered the planks of wood and canvas, all of it frozen solid, and tossed it down into a pile below. He then leaped down and nearly passed out from the effort. Only the steadily pulsing waves of heat from the blade kept him on his feet. Growling obstinately in his chest, he moved around to Jaermungdr's head and gazed upon the ferocious visage, the wicked horns, the serrated brows, the great beaked mouth. Casting all piety to the wind, he took up World Breaker and smote as hard a blow as he could across the dragon's snout. The wicked blade dug deep, far deeper than any other blade ever would, parting the ancient and frozen scales as if they were but wooden slats, shattering bone and carving a huge crack into the dragon's face.

Again and again he hewed at the dragon's muzzle, until with a few final sweeps and several kicks he knocked the remnants of its mutilated head away and exposed the great tongue where it lay between the cruel fangs. He did not question how he knew, but reaching down he found the tongue still soft and spongy despite the cold, as long as his arm and deeply socketed within the dragon's throat. It was grim, awful work, but after much hacking and levering, he pried the tongue free, and with it tossed over his shoulder he made his way back to the broken remnants of the saddle.

There he knelt and coiled the tongue into a great fleshy snail shell, atop which he piled the remnants of the saddle, wood carved deep with scrollwork and sigils, the crimson leather now faded to the lightest of pinks and stiff with the cold. Shaking, losing the ability to move properly, he took the flint and steel and crouched down so that his face was practically in the pile and tried to strike a spark.

He was forced to use his left arm, and the effort caused him to moan gently each time he struck the flint against the steel. His hands felt as if they were encased in huge gloves, there was no sensation in this fingers, and for having relinquished World Breaker he felt his energy leaving him faster. Gritting his jaw, curbing the impatience and anger within him, fighting the urge to simply rest his forehead on the ground and close his eyes, he struck once, twice, thrice, and finally the sparks leapt free.

The tongue caught fire with an audible WHOOMP, blue and green flames exploding forth from the coiled mass, immediately thawing out the wood and setting it ablaze. Tharok pushed himself away from the sudden violent heat and took up World Breaker once more. For a moment he was tempted to enjoy the warmth, to banish the numbness, but there was no time. Rising, he turned to Jaermungdr and stepped to his side, up to the great bunching of the thigh, and with a cry of pain he brought World Breaker down in a massive overhead swing so that it sliced cleanly through scale and muscle and came out the other side, thunking into the snow. He raised the scimitar, aimed carefully, and brought it down once more, the black metal sliding through the frozen flesh with ease, making a cut that was parallel to the first. Then, by inserting the blade's tip and working it around, he forced the wedge of flesh to crack, shiver free, and tumble to the ground.

The wedge of flesh was triangular and deep purple, almost black, the skin and scales thick and crusted along one edge. Taking the flesh, he turned back to where the fire was burning bright and tall against the night sky and without ceremony cast the steak into the flames. He was having trouble keeping his eyes open, so he allowed himself a moment in front of the fire, standing close enough that it felt as if his skin would burn and blacken to cinders, allowing the dancing tongues of fire to caress and cook him as much as they did the dragon meat which was already beginning to sizzle.

Then, with a cry, he tamed his desires and turned back to the Jaermungdr's thigh, where he hewed another and then a third great slice of flesh, which he also cast into the fire. He gazed up at the night sky, turning his back to the fire so that he could see better in the darkness, and scoured the Five Peaks. No movement yet. Would they come?

He moved with purpose back to Ogri's body and drew forth the dagger from the sheath at his side. He held the blade before the firelight and then plunged it into the heart of the fire, sliding the metal deep into the tongue itself, which was already greatly diminished. The hilt began to char in the heat. Darting his hand in and seized the dagger. The metal had not heated enough to glow white, but a faint blush of rose could be detected along its outer edges. Hot enough. With a grunt he tore free the bandage that was wrapped across the wound on his arm. Blood began to pulse forth once more. Tharok clenched his jaw and laid the blade across the clean slice and pressed hard. He couldn't help it; he threw back his head and roared, thick veins and tendons standing out in his neck. He pulled the knife free after a few seconds, not wishing it to stick to his flesh, and then adjusted his grip and pressed it again, and again, until the wound was thoroughly cauterized. Weak, he sank to the snow and plunged the knife once more into the fire. He waited another thirty seconds, then drew it forth and treated the deep gash in his side, biting down on his scream as he molded the wound shut, sealing it closed with his own burnt and smeared flesh.

When he was finished, he flung the knife away and turned back to the fire with a gasp. His head was spinning, but he knew there was no time to waste. He had heat, he had cauterized the wounds, now he had to gain strength. He plunged the tip of World Breaker into the first steak and drew it forth. He dropped the blade, clasped the meat with one hand, and sank his fangs into it. The outside was blackened and charred, the center still frozen, but between those two layers the flesh had begun to sizzle and was cooked to perfection, so hot and salubrious that he found himself groaning with pleasure, choking down great raw chunks in his haste to eat. The meat was incredibly stringy, the taste appalling, but Tharok did not care. He wolfed down the entirety of the steak, even the outer charred edges, pausing to spit out chunks of scale, and then, with the heat of the cooked flesh warming his belly and new strength already flowing into his arms, he stood before the fire, absorbing as much heat as he could, rubbing at his muscles with the blade of his hand and sighting up into the night sky.

It all came down to this. Either his conjectures would prove correct and he still had a fighting chance of leaving the Valley of Death, or he would stand here and freeze once the fire had died out. The flames crackled behind him, breaking the echoing silence of the Valley, and the twin steaks sizzled and spat as they cooked and burned over the dragon's own tongue. His great body was a continuous laceration of pain, awakened now by the heat, that beguiling numbness gone, and he felt that a strong wind might knock him down. But with World Breaker in his hand he knew that he could stand, would stand, until long after the fire had burned to ashes.

He turned, looking about in the darkness. He stabbed World Breaker through one and then the second steak, took up the lance with effort with his left hand, and backed away from the fire, toward the raw flank of the frozen dragon. There he stood still, listening for the sound of wings, trying to gauge their direction. The steaks hissed and sizzled before him, slowly sliding down the length of the black blade. The air above the flames suddenly manifested wings, the whip of a great tail, a hide dirt-brown and heavily armored, and then there was darkness once more. Tharok peered futilely into the darkness, trying to gauge its approach by where it blotted out the stars. It had to land, or else all was for naught.

There was another flash of wings, heavy and awkward, and then with a crunch of flattened snow and broken ice the wyvern landed but ten paces from Jaermungdr, balancing on its heavy rear legs, wings fanning the fire so that the flames whipped and leaped and almost went out. It turned its great shovel head, eyes piss-yellow cruel and its great fanged mouth smacking open and closed as it tasted the night air, tasted the scent of cooking flesh. It was small, no true dragon this, perhaps a quarter of the size of Jaermungdr, without forelegs and ungainly in flight. But it was one of the most terrible predators of the mountain peaks, and Tharok had only ever seen them from afar, circling the higher cliffs as they hunted mountain goats and errant kragh. Here, now, brown and bronze scales gleaming and glinting in the blue and green fire, it was vast and primal and his only hope for survival.

He set the lance against the dragon's side and pulled free the first steak. It was hot and badly charred, but rich juices ran down his forearm even as he tossed it forward, aiming carefully so that it landed five yards from him, sinking out of sight as it fell into the snow bank. Then, without pausing, Tharok turned and scrabbled up the dragon's flank, ignoring the pain thanks to the fire that raged in his blood, plunged World Breaker deep into Jaermungdr's side so as to provide a handhold, and then hefted himself up onto the knee, and from there up the ridge onto its great armored back. Reaching down, he pulled free the sword, hauled up the lance, and turned to watch.

The wyvern hopped forward, wings partially opened for balance, great splayed talons giving it purchase on the ice and snow. It darted its head forward once, twice, snapping its maw, the clack of teeth loud and startling. Around the fire it came, thick tail weaving from side to side, until it stood close enough to the hole in the snow to give one last wary glance up at Tharok before abandoning caution to plunge its head down after the meat.

Tharok leaped. He turned as he jumped, arms and legs wide, so that he spun in the air and landed athwart the wyvern's shoulders, crashing down on the dull bone horns that ran the length of its back, clamping tight as hard as he could, resisting the urge to plunge World Breaker into the wyvern's hide for purchase, lance almost tearing free from his hand as the wyvern screeched its outrage and fury and began to sweep its wings back and forth with unstoppable power, spinning in place and leaping up into the air, almost gaining flight before crashing down again. It reached its head around to snap at him, fangs flashing close to his face, and blank whiteness surged before Tharok's eyes, pain and fatigue almost causing him to black out, but he held on, gritted his teeth, legs wrapped around the wyvern's great neck where it met the barrel chest, and then it was racing, running and leaping in its ungainly manner, till with a final surge and great pump of its wings it was aloft, shaking and heaving in its effort to dislodge him.

Up into the air they soared, rising with great swoops as each powerful wing beat forced the wyvern higher. Tharok pressed his cheek against the leather hide, hugged as tightly as he could so that the wyvern couldn't reach him, its thick neck too short for complete flexibility. Up they flew, and then the wyvern banked hard to the left, falling and losing almost all of its gained height as it sought to dislodge him. He roared, felt himself begin to slip free, and clutched tighter, squeezing as hard as he could with his legs. At the last moment the wyvern righted itself, one wing's edge catching the ground as it struggled for air once more, and up they went, rising and fighting for altitude. The fire was already falling behind them, a speck of blue light in that awful white valley, and up they went, the wyvern shrieking its fury as it fought for height.

Tharok moved. He couldn't allow it to keep ascending to the point where he would no longer be able to breathe, to match its great lungs. He didn't know if it was consciously trying to knock him free by knocking him out, but he wasn't going to give it the chance. He allowed the lance to droop through his hand until there were only a couple of feet left before the tip, and then impaled the steak onto its cruel point and pulled World Breaker free. That done, he threw the lance up a couple of times, each time latching his hand lower and lower until he held it by the hilt. Then, carefully, minding the flapping wings and the great, heavy neck, he swung the steak through the night air so that it hung before the wyvern's great broad head.

It immediately lunged forward to bite at the meat, jaws clacking shut but a foot from where it hung steaming in the night air. Tharok laughed and lowered the lance's point, causing the wyvern to follow, losing altitude as it continued to burst forward, throwing itself through the air after its ever-retreating prey. Down they flew, and Tharok narrowed his eyes as he gazed past the lance's tip at the mountains beyond. He swung the lance wide to the left, and the wyvern followed, screeching now in frustration, eager and furious, and the Five Peaks rotated about them, the stars wheeling overhead. They flew to the left and then straight, so that they were pointed at the mouth of the Dragon's Breath, then down and out of the Valley of the Dead, out from the home of the gods, to return, sky-borne and bearing the blade and circlet of Ogri himself, down from the highest peaks to the world of the living once more.

CHAPTER ELEVEN

ISKRA

It was gone past midnight. Lady Iskra Kyferin lay awake atop her bed, her auburn hair undone and strewn across her pillow and covers. The cold night air blew in through the open window. It caused the candle she'd set on the lintel to flare, but it never went out. She lay still, listening to the sound of Otilge, her lady-in-waiting, sleeping in her cot at the foot of the bed. Listening to and feeling the texture of silence that enveloped her pushed her down, oppressed her as never before.

There had been many nights over the course of her marriage when she'd slept alone in their great bed, lost in its ocean of covers and furs. Nights when she'd lain thinking of her husband, wandering where his campaigns had taken him, to which field or manor house. Whether he was lying alone as she did, or had sought the company of others. Enderl had often preferred to go on extended hunting trips rather than staying home, preferring to bed in an inn or local manse rather than ride all the way back to the castle. All the way back to her.

And now she was truly alone. He wasn't out there, larger than life, clad in mail and leather or wrapped in the arms of another woman. He was dead, stinking and merging with the soil if he'd not been buried. Most war dead weren't; they were left out for the crows and foxes, for beaks and clever milk-white teeth. It was almost impossible to imagine her mighty husband shriveling and rotting away, his basso profundo voice stilled, the strength gone from his hands. It had been years since he'd left his mark on her flesh, but she could remember it still, how he'd grip her upper arm to shake her, how he'd send her stumbling with a push. He'd considered himself a gentleman because he never used his fist. Perhaps he had been.

Otilge's breath caught, went silent, and then smoothed back out into her steady, husky breathing.

Iskra turned her head on her pillow, trying for an angle where she might catch sight of the moon. No luck. She was alone, and suddenly the world was no longer divided between her husband, wherever he might be out there, and herself holding the castle in his name; now she was surrounded by an ocean of night without end, and the castle would stand or fall by her own wit and wisdom. Her daughter and son would live or die by the agility of her mind. There were far too many pieces in motion for her to seek to understand them all, far too many unknown elements. The Agerastians. The Ascendant's Grace and his Seven Virtues. Who knew how Aletheia would react to its terrible loss?

There was too much she couldn't control—so she wouldn't try. She would take one step at a time, as her father used to say. Take a problem, break it down to the smallest pieces, each irreducible. Then take the first and solve it. Then the next. Don't look at the whole. Focus on the space before your feet and take that step. That step taken, take the next, and if you proceed in such manner, you shall one day look up, surprised, to see that you have succeeded.

Iskra sat up. She swung her legs over the edge of her bed and stood, her gossamer gown barely keeping the cold away. Moving silently past Otilge, she took her heavy fur cloak from where it hung on a hook and wrapped it around her shoulders, then stepped up to the window and craned down to look up and out. There it was, the moon, pockmarked and mysterious, waxing toward full, the source of mystery and magic. Iskra stared for ten heartbeats, taking her blessing, and then blew out the candle and slipped from her room.

The fourth floor of the keep was hers and her family's alone. Four slender towers were affixed around the keep, three containing bedrooms, the fourth their private chapel. The central room was the family solarium, where they could retreat from public view when duty allowed. Lord Kyferin had made of it a gallery of his victories, and she'd yet to take the trophies down; walls were covered with the mounted heads of beasts, including a massive mountain kragh that Enderl had slain alone. Another wall was drenched in iron and steel weaponry. The tapestries were dedicated to the hunt, so that she felt the room was a hunter's lodge more than a family space. Tomorrow, she vowed. This all comes down tomorrow.

She slipped out into the stairwell as quietly as a wraith and hurried past the Lord's Hall, past the guard floor, to the kitchens and servants' rooms. Pulling her cloak tightly about her neck, she pushed open the keep door just enough that the iron hinge wouldn't scream, then caught it an inch from the jamb so it wouldn't slam. Then she turned and looked up at the moon in the depths of the black night sky, so bright it drowned out the stars. The air was cold, so she didn't linger; she hurried down the steps, her footfalls so soft and silent that the sentries atop the drum towers didn't mark her passage. She continued through the arch and out onto the drawbridge, through the barbican, unnoticed by the men in the guard room beyond the murder holes.

Was it this easy to traverse the castle at night? She would bring the matter to Brocuff's attention. Two soldiers were posted at the other drawbridge, standing guard at the barbican's entrance. She slowed in the tunnel and studied them. They were still as statues, each holding a spear. Not talking. Not leaning against the wall. Good men.

"Soldiers," she said, pitching her voice to carry. They both stiffened and turned, and she saw their eyes widen at the sight of her. Before they could speak, she swept out past them onto the drawbridge. "Stay at your posts."

The bailey was abandoned. The men and women who ran the castle were sleeping off the day's toil in anticipation of a lifetime's more to come. She trod down the stone ramp, then turned toward the Wolf Tower. The soft dirt of the bailey floor was frozen into iron ridges that radiated cold through her slippers. Moving quickly, she traversed the bailey to the tower door. To her left she could hear the soft whicker of a horse in the stable. The stable boys would be asleep in the loft above, buried down in the hay like so many dormice. For a moment she envied them their lack of responsibilities and care, and then chided herself for her assumptions. What did she know of a stable boy's woes?

The black tower door was shut fast against the night. She considered rapping her knuckles on the planks but simply pushed it open instead. The hinges groaned in protest, but then she was through and inside. She closed the door quickly and turned blindly to the interior. It was pitch dark. No torch was burning on the ground floor, and no gaoler was sitting watch. It was a barren room, the flagstones bare. She knew through memory that a staircase wound up along the inside of the wall to the second floor, where soldiers would be asleep, and then up again to the third, where military supplies lay in wait for some future attack. One more flight of stairs would bring her to the curtain wall parapet and the sentries who paced its length.

But her business was here in the dark depths of the Wolf Tower. She stepped forward to the center of the room where the iron grate was buried in the stone and lowered herself into a crouch to listen.

Silence came from below.

She knew that the prisoner was fed. Three years he'd lived in that square room below. Her Lord husband had sworn that the man would die down there, would rot away until he was forgotten, until only his bones, hair, and teeth remained to be thrown over the wall into the moat. She knew Ser Tiron was alive, or else the soldiers would have told her. But that silence… There was no sound of soft sleep. No snores, gentle or otherwise. It was an active silence, aching in its acuity. The ground floor was as dark as a tomb, but the space between the iron bars might as well have led through the Black Gate. She couldn't make out a thing.

"Ser Tiron?" Her voice was a breathless whisper, and she felt herself again a little girl in her father's palace, so unimaginably far away. A young girl, scared of the dark, and for that very reason determined to face it.

A sound came up from below. A shift on stone. She heard a croak, a rough cough, then a hoarse voice. "Iskra. What do you want?"

She shivered. The cruel familiarity in his voice was unnerving. She should correct him, demand that he call her Lady Kyferin, but after what they had been through, to do so felt petty. She imagined Ser Tiron's hard face looking up at her. His black beard and hair would have grown wild over the past three years, and his face would be pale, but those black eyes—she knew they would not have lost their glimmer.

"My Lord is dead," she whispered, not knowing why she was volunteering that information.

"So I heard." His voice was growing stronger, more sure, as if he were becoming familiar with it once more. "It's rare that I hear such good news."

She opened her mouth to retort, then bit her lower lip. She stared down at the dark, down to where he must be looking up at her. Could he make out her outline in the gloom? His eyes must have grown terribly sharp after so many years of darkness.

"The Black Wolves died with him—all but Ser Wyland. Kyferin Castle stands undefended."

He grunted. "There were some good men amongst the Wolves." He paused. "I'm sorry to hear of their deaths. Some of them."

Iskra hesitated. Her need was there, but the words would not come.

"What do you want, Iskra?" His voice was harsh, almost amused. "Why have you come down here to tell me this?"

"I want you to serve me," she said, "I want your oath. For you to swear on your honor to protect me and mine."

Ser Tiron laughed, a grinding, gravely sound. "Do you, now? So, tonight's entertainment is to be a comedy?"

"You will rot down there if you do not," she hissed. "Don't doubt it."

"Oh, I made my peace with my fate the night Enderl broke Sarah's neck." It was if he had drawn a blade. "Don't you worry about that."

Iskra felt his words in her gut like a blow. "He was wrong." Her words were but a whisper.

"What was that?" She heard him shift again. His tone was cruel. "Did you say something?"

"He was wrong," she said again, louder. She sat straighter, hands in her lap, not looking down; instead, she looked blankly at one of the invisible walls. "He was wrong in what he did."

"Was he, now? It's taken you three years to come to that decision? Three years to decide that he was wrong in raping my wife and killing my son?" There was a long pause. "That's quite generous of you."

"You attacked him. You attacked me. You tried to kill my daughter." Her words were steel.

"Yes, and it's my sincere regret that I wasn't able to bring him the same pain he brought me. Not that I think he would have minded as much. I truly loved my Sarah. Do you think Lord Kyferin loved you?"

Iskra began to rise. She shouldn't have come here. What had she expected? Then she stopped, thinking of her daughter, of her son. Pride was a luxury she could no longer afford, so she sank back down. "No. He didn't. You know that. I know that. It's why he did what he did."

There was silence from below. He seemed to be considering her words. "True. That, and he was an inhuman monster. I hate him, Iskra. By the Ascendant, no man should be able to feel as much hatred as I do. You don't know what it does to you. How it consumes you. Destroys you." His voice had grown raw. He stopped. She listened, waiting. "Did he suffer, at the end? I've not heard how he died. Was it badly?"

"Magic," she said, voice hollow. "The Agerastians fielded Sin Casters. They destroyed the Grace's army."

"Magic?" For the first time she heard surprise in Ser Tiron's voice, and it came from closer, as if he'd stood.

"Magic," she said again. "The world is changing, ser knight. Faster perhaps than I can understand. My castle is undefended. Lord Kyferin is dead. Danger rides to greet me within the week. I need good men at my side. You were once one such. If there is anything left of that man I once so admired, I need him by my side. I need your oath. I won't waste you down here any longer. Swear to me. Put the past behind, just as I am doing. Swear to me, and step back into the light."

Silence again. Iskra sat still, hands clutched together. She stared into the dark so fiercely she thought she might pierce it.

"You call me a good man."

"I do. I understand why you did what you did." It was hard to pry the words from her throat. That they were true made it only marginally easier. "I might have tried the same in your position."

"I'm not a good man, Iskra." The voice was hard. Cruel. "What goodness I might have had in me died with Sarah. You pull me out of this hole, you'll be bringing a beast into the world."

Iskra nodded mutely. Her hands were tightly locked. "You were always a man of honor. Is that gone too?"

"My honor died when I attacked Lord Kyferin. You know that."

She didn't know what to say. The silence unspooled between them. She could hear her heart beat. Her mouth was ashen. She'd admired him greatly, once. It felt like a lifetime ago. She had watched him covertly whenever he came to the castle, had secretly cheered for him in the many tournaments her husband had held. Ser Tiron had been Enderl's most dangerous Wolf. Dark and intense, he had simmered with a violence that was barely restrained by his chivalric code. He had been everything she had once thought Enderl to be, back when she had been a naive young girl in Sige, for more than anything, he had loved his wife and son.

And one night, Enderl had noticed her admiration.

"You've known pain I can't understand." Her voice faltered, and she took a deep breath and tried again. "It's your pain, and I don't want any part in it. But you've also known love. You had your time with Sarah. You had light and laughter and the Ascendant knows what else, because I don't. I've never had any of that. I've never known that kind of happiness, that love. I've only ever known Lord Enderl Kyferin, his ways and his habits. His... desires. The first years were the worst, but once I became pregnant I managed to keep him away. But that only drove him to other women. Does it make me evil to say I was glad they suffered instead of me? Maybe. But after I bore him a daughter, he came back. He'd not grown any gentler. Eventually I was blessed with Roddick, and again he left me alone. All this time, I've had to live with him. Respect him. Treat him as my Lord, each and every day since I arrived at this damn castle over twenty years ago."

She stopped. She realized she was leaning over the grating, clutching its iron bars with both hands. She was shaking. She pulled away, took a shivering breath and closed her eyes. "We've both suffered because of him. But he's dead now. He's gone, so I'm asking you: Put your pain aside. Please. Come back. Be a knight once more."

Iskra felt spent. Hollow. She'd never spoken those words to anybody. Never admitted them. She'd held them pent up within her soul for almost two decades. To unburden herself like this, to confess to this dark hole, had drained her more than she could have guessed. She felt as light and frail as an autumn leaf. She lowered her head and pressed her face into her hands.

"All right." His voice was low and rough and ugly. "I'll come out of this hole. I'll fight for you. But on one condition."

"What is it?"

"I choose when to announce myself. You don't breathe a word of my release until I do."

Iskra paused. It was a dangerous request. "Why?"

He was silent long enough that she thought he would not answer. Then, quietly, he said, "I want time alone at my former home. I want as much time as I need to say my goodbyes."

Iskra exhaled. "Done. But you have at most a week. There's to be a tournament in Enderl's honor. We're holding it when Lord Laur is due to arrive with his men. I will expect you there."

"Agreed. Did—" He cut off, as if afraid to ask his question. A beat, then he tried again, his voice a rough rasp. "What did your husband do with my blade?"

"It's hanging on his trophy wall." She said the words coldly, not wanting to feel anything, trying to separate herself from that fact.

"Have it brought to me." His voice was a low snarl.

She felt no triumph, no burst of victory. Just a sad and weary acceptance. "I will. Thank you."

"Don't thank me. Enderl broke me. I don't know who I am, what I've become. I make no promises. You may yet live to regret freeing me."

"I'll take that risk." She rose to her feet. She wanted nothing more than to collapse into her bed and sleep and think no more. "You shall be released immediately. Good night, Ser Tiron."

Shivering, she stepped back to the door. She'd order the barbican guards to see to it that he was released.

She pulled the door open and stepped out into the light of the moon. *Thank you*, she whispered, looking up. *Thank you for giving me strength. Please, don't fail me now. I'm only getting started.*

CHAPTER TWELVE

Asho

Asho stepped into the silence of the bailey chapel. Elon and his journeymen had moved their smithy down to the tournament field for emergency repairs, and the majority of the castle staff was down there as well, putting the finishing touches on the stands, pavilions and organizing the market stalls. The silence here was in sharp contrast to the tourney grounds. He unbuckled his sword but carried it with him to the front of the chapel, where the great Triangle of Ascension stood, its silver surface intricately filigreed and reflecting the golden candlelight.

Father Simeon was not in evidence, for which Asho was glad. He'd not come to chapel since the Mourning, choosing not to attend the dawn Rejoicing. He'd avoided thinking of Ascension as much as possible—but he could put it off no longer. He lowered himself to his knees and laid his sword beside him on the stone floor. For the first time in years he truly saw the Path of Ascension where it was painted on the back wall, scrutinizing the familiar images with an interrogatory stare.

A Bythian slave stood humbly before the Black Gate at the far left, eyes cast down, his hair pale and alabaster skin. The same man then stood defiantly a step beyond him, but now his hair was black, his skin bronzed, his mouth curved in disdain: the Bythian had risen to become an Agerastian heretic. The same man passed in quick order through the following stations of Ascension: the Zoeian sensate, the Ennoian warrior, the Noussian scholar, the Sigean holy servant, and finally the Aletheian perfecti who faced the White Gate with arms raised. Simple. Elegant. The ineluctable truth of the spiritual world. And yet.

Asho scowled and formed the triangle with his thumbs and forefingers. He reined in his thoughts and lowered his head, closed his eyes, took a deep breath, and then slowly exhaled.

He was to fight in the melee today. Ser Wyland had promised it would be a small, provincial affair, not like some of the great tournaments where hundreds of foreign knights competed for glory and riches before a screaming crowd. And yet, despite the modesty of the tournament's size, it was his first. He would ride before Lady Kyferin and would fight for her honor. Normally such a prospect would have thrilled him, but not today.

Asho frowned. A prickly memory he'd fought to forget pushed

its way to the fore. He saw again the Grace dying in his Aletheian advisor's arms and the Virtues heroically keeping the Agerastians at bay; heard the distant din of battle all around. The Grace had been on the point of dying. There was no doubt that he had been mortally wounded. His august soul had journeyed through seven virtuous lives to reach this very moment where it would abandon his body and pass through the White Gate into Eternity, never to be reborn again, his trials over, his holiness rewarded at long last.

And yet, the Grace had accepted the black vial. Who had that advisor been? What did it mean for the second holiest man in the Empire to turn away from his professed reward? There was no doubt that he was a righteous man, for his soul had been rewarded for all its previous acts by being born into the Aletheian body who would become the Grace. But why would he turn away from Ascension? What had been in that vial that could cure a dying man?

Asho sighed and sat back on his heels, hands on his thighs. He would fight today, strive to fulfill the role of an honorable knight—but for what? So that when he died, he could do so with the knowledge that his soul would come one step closer to Ascension? But why should he strive so if the Grace himself had turned away from the White Gate?

Asho had no answers. He stared up at the triangle. How far along his path was he? As a Bythian, he was at the very bottom of the cycle, but he was also a knight; did that mean he would be born in the next life as a Noussian, like all good Ennoians? Father Simeon had scowled at him in the past when he'd asked him these questions and had chased him out of the chapel, cursing him for his irreverence. Asho thought the good Father simply didn't know. And what in turn did that mean?

His gaze turned from the Triangle to the flame of a candle, and he lost himself in there, old memories resurfacing, old thoughts, new fears. When the trumpets sounded from outside, he started. Snatching up his blade, he leaped to his feet and rushed out of the chapel into the bailey.

Lady Kyferin's retinue was descending to the tourney field. Hurrying forth, he stepped up next to Ser Wyland, who gave him a wry smile. "I was beginning to think you weren't going to come."

"Just praying to the Ascendant," he said quietly.

Their group was a small one, barely twenty strong, and they mounted the steeds the stable hands were holding for them: Lady Kyferin, her lady-in-waiting Otilge, Hessa, Master Bertchold the steward, Marshall Thiemo, Magister Audsley, Brocuff, and a dozen soldiers.

"Have you seen Lady Kethe?" Ser Wyland was scanning the

group. "She's been missing all morning."

"Oh?" Asho rose in his stirrups and looked around. "Trouble?"

Ser Wyland shrugged. "The girl's lost her father. Perhaps she wants nothing to do with violence. I wouldn't blame her."

Another trumpet sounded, and Ser Wyland nudged his horse forward, Crook falling into step naturally by his side. As the only knights in Lady Kyferin's retinue, Wyland and Asho took the lead, passed over the main drawbridge and rode down to the Southern Field. It took but five minutes to descend, but their elevation afforded Asho a good view of the proceedings. It was indeed a small tournament, with one stand for local viewers and a second for visitors on the other side. A small crowd was milling around the market stalls, and vendors were walking to and fro with trays hanging from straps around their necks. A half-dozen small tents of different colors had been pitched at one end of the field, where servants were busy with armor and weaponry and tending to horses. The summoned knights, Asho guessed. Six, perhaps seven of them? Not a horde, but better than nothing.

"Right on time," Ser Wyland murmured, and nodded to the right.

Asho looked over and saw a large group riding down toward the field from the main road. His breath caught. Two massive, flowing banners showed a gray wolf on a black background, Lord Laur's personal emblem. A group of twenty knights was riding at the fore, their armor shining and resplendent, with another fifty soldiers following behind. A baggage train trailed behind them, but Asho's eyes were drawn to one figure at the front and center: Lord Laur. He wasn't as massive as Lord Kyferin had been, but he was sitting on a great black destrier, his armor enameled a beautiful blue, with a heavy cloak of white fur falling from his shoulders.

"Seventy men," whispered Asho to Ser Wyland. "Is that appropriate for a personal guard?"

Ser Wyland's face was grave. "Depends on your definition of personal, I suppose. Prepare yourself, Ser Asho. Today is going to be challenging."

They rode down and out onto the tourney field and both parties met in the center. Lord Laur motioned for the bulk of his men to remain at the field's edge and rode forward with only five knights and their squires behind him. Lady Kyferin rode forth with Asho and Ser Wyland alone.

They stopped ten yards from each other. Lord Laur dismounted, his armor clanking as he stepped down onto the grass. Asho slipped off Crook and stepped up next to Lady Kyferin, whom he helped dismount in turn.

Asho strove to keep calm. Ser Wyland looked completely at ease, competent and strong and imposing all at once. Asho adopted his normal blank expression and ignored the amused and contemptuous looks the other knights gave him.

Lord Laur removed his greathelm, handed it back to his squire, and then stepped forward to bow deeply at the waist. "Lady Kyferin. I came as quickly as I could. I may have lost a cherished brother, but you have lost your Lord husband."

Asho had never stood this close to Lord Laur. He was the middle brother, but seemed older than Kyferin; a weak chin stopped him from being handsome, but he had Kyferin's dark eyes, thick hair, and broad nose. There was something inscrutable about him, something inherently duplicitous in how easily he smiled without any light entering his eyes. His voice, however, was rich and cultured, and he used it to good effect; all could hear him without trouble.

"Lord Laur, be welcomed to Kyferin Castle. Your arrival gladdens my heart." Lady Kyferin was clad in a gown of soft blue that darkened beautifully to gray at the hem; it hugged her figure, and her sleeves were wide and hung down nearly to her waist. With her auburn hair done up and with jewels flashing at her throat and wrists, she looked every inch a ruling lady. "I can only imagine how our loss has wounded you. You have my deepest condolences."

Lord Laur smiled tightly and bowed again. "Thank you, my Lady."

Turning, Lady Kyferin took his arm in her own and began to lead him toward the stands. "Your arrival is most fortuitous, for I'm holding a tournament to celebrate and honor my husband's memory. You of course remember how much he loved these affairs." She smiled sadly.

Ser Wyland fell in behind them, as did Ser Laur's five knights. Asho studied them curiously. One was a monster of a man, as tall as Ser Wyland but twice as wide, with a chest deeper than a bull's and with ram's horns curling from the sides of his greathelm. His armor was painted a forest green, and he had a battle-ax of fearsome size slung over his shoulder. That would be Ser Bero, famed for cutting a horse in half the year before on a wager.

Beside him walked two brothers, slender as saplings and as elegant as the first man seemed brutish; they were carrying their bascinet helms under their arms, and wore their blond hair long. Their features were delicate, their eyes mocking and cruel. They weren't exactly identical, but close enough that Asho had to stop himself from staring openly at them to figure out the differences. Ser Cunot and Ser Cunad, known as the Golden Vipers. Asho remembered stories of their cruelty.

They would have fit in well with the Black Wolves.

The fourth man was the eldest, his hair silvered at the temples. He had numerous nicks and small scars across his face, and his left ear was altogether gone. He moved well for his age, and his armor was cunningly wrought, embossed and filigreed along the edges. Ser Olbrecht, thought Asho.

But it was the fifth knight who truly drew the eye. His armor was enameled blue like his father's, and his great shield bore a crimson wolf emblazoned on his tabard; a memory clicked in Asho's mind, and he realized that this had to be Lord Laur's vaunted son, Ser Kitan Laur.

Ser Wyland walked easily behind them, speaking with Ser Olbrecht, but Asho made no move to socialize. He knew any attempt to do so would result in either laughter or insults, so he stared straight ahead, ignoring their pointed stares, and watched Lady Kyferin as she made small talk with Lord Laur. When they reached the stands, the pair climbed to the best seats and sat under the extended canopy.

"Come," said Ser Wyland, touching Asho's shoulder and nodding toward their tents. "We'll leave Lord Laur to our Lady's tender ministrations. She's safe enough out here in the open. We'd best prepare for the introductions."

Asho nodded, mouth dry. Lord Laur's knights had peeled away and were moving toward the quarter of the field his retinue had staked out for themselves, while servants and squires were tending the Lord and Lady.

"Do you think his knights will enter the tourney?"

Ser Wyland nodded. "You can count on it." They strode over the already torn grass toward where Ser Wyland's tent had been erected; his squire Ryck was waiting patiently by the tent flap. "The question is how many he'll enter. He'd not insult Lady Kyferin by crushing our tournament under the weight of his twenty knights, and entering just his best man might see his knight wounded or beaten, no matter how skilled. Five men? Ten? The number will tell us much about his intentions and confidence."

Ryck held open the large tent's flap and both men stepped inside. The interior was barren but for two armor trees on which their polished plate hung. Outside Asho could hear the sound of Elon's hammer, banging away rhythmically at his anvil.

Asho felt the first stirrings of fear and moved to crush them. "How many visiting knights did you count?"

"Eight," said Ser Wyland, lifting one foot so that Reck could push his iron sabaton on, and then the other. "Though who knows if they're any good." Reck then set about attaching Ser Wyland's greaves about his legs. "With a little luck, none of them will embarrass us by falling on his sword."

Not having a squire, Asho set to putting on his armor. It was an old suit of Ser Merboth's that Elon had reworked as best he could. Merboth had been the smallest of the Black Wolves, but even his armor had been too large. Asho had worn it but twice, and both times had felt a strange combination of euphoria and claustrophobia. Still, he'd buckled Lord Kyferin himself into his plate for years as his squire, and his fingers worked nimbly as he pulled on his own sabatons and greaves, then stood to assemble the rest.

Ryck darted over to help him with the back plate and some of the more troublesome buckles. Asho hesitated, unsure of how to accept his help, but nodded stiffly when Ryck moved away. Soon he was ready, weighted down by almost thirty pounds of steel. He swung his arms around experimentally, then tried twisting at the waist. Not perfect, but not too bad either.

A clarion call sounded, and then a small cheer.

"All right," said Ser Wyland, grinning wolfishly. "Are you ready? We're going out there to represent our Lady, to represent the honor of her family, which is more valuable than our own, to fight and suffer and if necessary, to die for her. Ready?"

Asho nodded, feeling a sour sensation in his stomach. The idea of riding out before the entire crowd was terrifying. What if they all started to hiss and throw fruit?

Ser Wyland grabbed him by the shoulder and shook him. "Ser Asho? Are you ready?"

"Yes, ser." Asho took a deep breath. An image came to him, of fiery rain slicing men in half. "Yes. I am."

"Good." Ser Wyland clapped him on the back, the metal ringing out loudly, then pulled on his greathelm. His voice took on a muffled quality. "Then let's go."

Asho followed him out of the tent to where their horses were tied and with some difficulty climbed up onto Crook's saddle. Turning her around, he followed Ser Wyland as the knight led them to the edge of their tents. As the resident knights, they would be introduced first, the others gathering behind them to await their turn.

Asho swallowed. Eight of Lord Laur's knights had gathered already, along with another eight local knights who had arrived earlier that morning. Some of these wore glittering armor and sat on beautiful horses. Others were less impressive. One man in particular seemed to have recovered his armor from the scrap heap; the iron was rusted and dented, but he wore it well enough. His mount was a familiar-looking destrier.

A horn blew, and Ser Wyland touched his heels to his horse's flanks and rode forth.

Asho watched carefully. He'd seen this a dozen times as Lord Kyferin's squire, but always on foot by the tent, ready to supply a new lance or rush forward with a fresh blade; never on horseback, never before the crowd, ready to introduce himself. It made a world of difference.

There were some two hundred people gathered in the stands, almost a third of them Lord Laur's people, and they cheered warmly as Ser Wyland stopped before Lady Kyferin and Lord Laur.

Menczel cried out Ser Wyland's name, then began listing his honors. They were numerous. He'd won nine major tournaments, had fought in seven battles, taken part in five sieges, and earned the coveted title of Black Wolf. The applause was enthusiastic, and Ser Wyland bowed at the waist to Lady Kyferin, who smiled and nodded in turn.

The trumpet blew again, and Ser Asho's heart leaped even as his stomach gurgled uneasily. He urged Crook forward. Crook turned to eye him, then lowered his head to crop the grass. Blushing furiously, grateful for his helm, he kicked Crook's flanks again, but was studiously ignored. One of the knights behind him laughed.

The trumpet sounded once more, and now laughter filtered from the stands. Asho leaned down. "Look, either you go forward or—"

Crook suddenly set forth at a canter, and Asho had to grab on as he nearly overbalanced. Gritting his teeth, he straightened as smoothly as he could. "You're going to get nothing but old pinecones for a month," he growled, and then he was sitting in front of the stands. Taking a deep breath, he removed his helm and stared up at his Lady as the Menczel called out his name.

Silence followed. He had no accomplishments, so he simply bowed as Ser Wyland had done. The silence was deafening. Then laughter rang out from several quarters, and a few people yelled out crude demands that he come and clean different parts of their anatomy. Lady Kyferin nodded gravely to him, giving him the confidence he needed to continue sitting tall. Lord Laur was watching him with his glittering eyes, and leaned over to ask a question as Asho turned Crook to ride over to where Ser Wyland was sitting on his destrier, helm and gauntlets removed.

"Interesting approach," said Ser Wyland mildly, watching as the next knight approached the stands.

Asho fought the urge to scowl. Only a lifetime of dealing with such humiliations allowed him to maintain his poise. "I wish I could say

I'm not used to such treatment."

"Let's both pretend you were being purposefully cunning," said Ser Wyland. "I think you've succeeded admirably in convincing everybody that you're not a threat. Well done."

"Thank you." Asho squirmed in his saddle. The trumpet blew again, and another knight rode forth. "Bythians are nothing if not unwittingly devious."

Ser Wyland laughed. "I approve. But when they sound the charge, let's exchange deviousness for lethal boldness, shall we?"

"Just you watch. They'll underestimate me at their peril." Asho placed his helm back on and finally allowed himself to scowl.

The eight visiting knights were introduced in short order, none having any accomplishments to their name, all having assumed the position of a fallen Black Wolf. Asho saw one banner after another displaying all manner of heraldry, their names familiar though their faces weren't.

Ser Wyland shook his head. "I can't believe we lost every Black Wolf." He was watching the new lords with a hard expression. "Twenty-five of the greatest warriors, wiped out of existence just like that." He snapped his fingers. "Damned Sin Casters. These children and uncles won't come close to replacing them."

The eighth knight rode up. He was the man in the battered armor. There was something about him, thought Asho, though he couldn't put his finger on it. He should have been laughable in his ancient suit of banged-up plate, but nobody was smiling. There was an intensity to him; he projected a wicked sense of competence simply in the manner in which he rode his mount. He had no banner, no emblem, and the Menczel looked at him in confusion before turning to the stands.

"This knight has offered no name or coat of arms. He asks only to be known as the Black Knight, and seeks our Lady's permission to enter the tournament as such."

Whispers filled the stands. One of the newly arrived local knights called out, "Black Knight? Rusted Kettle, more like." Laughter rippled through the crowd, but it was uneasy.

Lady Kyferin studied the Black Knight and nodded. The man dipped his helm, then turned his destier and rode calmly to the side.

"Black Knight?" asked Asho, leaning over to Ser Wyland.

Ser Wyland didn't seem fazed. "It happens. Men will sometimes seek to hide their identity so as to be judged by their skill at arms. The Virtues themselves are said to roam the land during times of peace, entering tournaments anonymously. Knights who would not dare raise a weapon against them thus give them a fair fight."

Asho stared at the Black Knight, who was sitting calmly on his mount off to the left. "He doesn't look like one of the Virtues to me."

"No," said Ser Wyland. "To me either. Still, the more knights on our side, the better."

"Ser Laur," called Menczel as Lord Laur's son rode forth. His armor was almost a work of art, so beautifully enameled that it gleamed with a slick, nacreous sheen. Menczel called out his accomplishments, and they were impressive; he was undefeated in battle, having won each of the six major tournaments that he had entered, including the Great Ennoian tourney that was held only once every five years.

"No real combat, however," said Ser Wyland out of the corner of his mouth. "Interesting."

Then came the older knight, Ser Olbrecht, whose list of accomplishments were second only to Ser Wyland's. He was followed by the twins Ser Cunot and Ser Cunad, and finally the massive, ram-horned knight Ser Bero. Three other knights from Lord Laur's retinue were introduced, but Asho barely heard their names, so intent was he on examining the first five.

"His best knights. He's held nothing back in reserve."

Ser Wyland nodded. "Eight men. He's clearly playing a strong hand. He wishes to win, but not embarrass Lady Kyferin too badly. He's asserting himself as the greatest power present."

Asho felt restless, energy rising within him like a fire beginning to race through a dry forest. "It will be a pity to disappoint him."

"Oh?" Ser Wyland turned to him. "You aim to defeat them all?"

"What? No. But if I take two, you'll take the rest, won't you?"

Ser Wyland arched an eyebrow, then laughed loudly. It was a confident laugh, and it set Asho at ease. "But of course! I like your confidence in me, Ser Asho. You take two, and I'll take care of the other six. Sounds just about right."

Menczel stepped out to face the stands. "All the knights are present and ready to do battle in order to earn your favor, Lady Kyferin."

The crowd stirred as if a wind had passed through it, voices rising in anticipation. Several of the knights' steeds picked up on the tension and nickered, side-stepping and fighting their reins.

Lady Kyferin rose so that Menczel might announce the tourney prize. Asho's heart began to beat faster. His mouth was dry. It might be just a tournament, but he knew that much more was at stake. Soon he would be put to his first great test.

"Wait!" A voice rang out through the brisk morning air. Everyone stopped, heads turning toward the tents. Slender and clad in a strange combination of shining mail, leather, and plate, a knight came cantering forth without banner or coat of arms. Asho bolted upright in the saddle, disbelief, horror, and astonishment seizing him by the throat.

Though the slender knight was covered from head to toe in armor, he knew immediately who it was.

CHAPTER THIRTEEN

kethe

Kethe took a deep breath and fought the urge to run. It wasn't too late. She could hear the crowd as it took the stands, the words and catcalls, the shouts and laughter. There was still time to slink out the back of her tent, to make her way up the slope and slip back into the castle like whipped dog.

No.

She closed her eyes, pressed both hands over her mouth and held her breath, willing her heart to still. This was the moment she'd been waiting for all her life. Her moment of truth, when she would prove to herself and the world that the past few years had not been just idle fantasy, had not been a series of games and make-believe.

She opened her eyes and stared at the canvas side of her tent. Elon had erected it first thing that dawn as he'd set up his smithy, ostensibly to house his materials and gear. He'd also brought down a specific bundle that she'd entrusted to him the night before. He'd been unwilling, reluctant, but she'd used every tool at her disposal. Begging. Wheedling. Flattering. Commanding. He'd stood immovable, aghast, until at last she'd taken his massive paw of a hand and held it with both of hers, looking up at him with mute appeal. He'd sighed and hung his head, and she knew she'd won.

Now here she was. There were real knights out there. She'd spied Lord Laur's arrival through a seam and knew that he'd brought a dangerous retinue with him. Her own uncle—not that she'd ever liked him much. He'd always teased her when she was little, and had made wagers with her that he'd refused to honor when she won. Would he protest? Would he sway her mother to deny her request? Possibly. But she'd not let him. She'd not let anybody.

Turning, she unrolled her bundle. Metal gleamed. Suddenly exhilarated, she stripped off her gown and pulled on her thin woolen undershirt and leggings. She had to struggle into them, so tightly did they fit. Then she picked up her leather jerkin, tailor-made by a man in Emmond to her exact specifications. She slipped her arms into the sleeves, then exhaled and sucked in her stomach so she could wrap the front right side around to where the buttons ran up the length of her left ribs. The leather was cured and stiff, tough enough to turn a blade. She pulled on a pair of leather breaches and grinned.

Next came her hauberk, her pride and joy. Again she struggled, swimming into it as she pulled it on over her head and fought to get her arms through the sleeves. Her leather armor caught numerous times, but she worked steadily and patiently until at last it fell down to her thighs. She shrugged, windmilled her arms, and twisted about until it was settled in place.

Then she took up her chest plate. She'd had Elon customize it to her demands. Instead of covering her from abdomen to neck, it only covered her from clavicles to her lower ribs, leaving her torso free. Her back plate was of the same design, and it took ten minutes of swinging it around and trying to catch the straps before she was able to lock them both in place. She cinched them tight and then pulled on a leather gorget that swooped up her neck and came right up to her jaw.

She spent another five minutes buckling on her steel pauldrons over her shoulders, each of which had overlapping plates that ran down to her elbows. Then she buckled on her belt, scabbard hanging low over her left hip, and took up her metal gauntlets that reached up to cover her forearms.

When each had been pulled on tight, she paused. She was encased, yet eminently flexible. She'd seen her father's men fight all her life. Trapped in their suits, they relied on the impenetrable nature of their plate armor to compensate for their clumsy stiffness. Not her. The last thing she wanted was to feel trapped. With her helm, half-cuirass, pauldrons and gauntlets, she'd still be resolutely shielded. Her hauberk would protect the rest, with her leather beneath to provide a final protective measure.

Best of all, she could still move. She fell into a crouch, then leaped up into the air, twisted, reached for the top of the tent, and swung her arms around. Perfect. She took up her helm, forged in the modern barbute manner, smooth and circular all around but for a Y-faced slit in the front that would allow her to see and breathe easily while protecting her nose.

She could hear the knights being introduced outside. This was it. This was her moment. It was now or never.

Kethe pulled the barbute down over her head and onto her braided hair which she had coiled atop her crown so as to provide extra cushioning. Fully armored, she slid her new blade into her scabbard, took a deep breath, and stepped outside.

Elon was waiting for her, arms crossed, and she studied his expression carefully. "Well?"

He smiled reluctantly. "You look good. If I didn't know better,

I'd say you were some kind of knight."

"Just wait," she said. "You'll find out exactly what kind soon enough."

"Here," said Elon. "I'll help you up."

"No need." She stepped up to the destrier confidently. With all the Black Wolves gone, there had been a surplus of these great beasts waiting unclaimed in the stables. While she'd been riding all her life, she'd only taken to practicing on these massive animals these past few months. Mexus, a former destrier of Ser Merboth, had been the smallest in the stable, but still it towered over her at fifteen hands. She eyed the saddle. It seemed to float high above her. Grabbing the pommel, she leaped up and swung her leg over the cantle. Mexus didn't even register her slight weight.

Elon held up her lance. She'd had little time to practice with it, but she'd known there would never be enough time.

"Last chance," said Elon softly. "It's not too late to stop this madness now."

"I'll never forget your role in all this," she promised him.

"That's what I'm worried about," he sighed, and then despite himself he smiled. "I'll be watching. Send them through the Black Gate, my Lady. Show them no mercy."

"I won't." A shiver ran through her, and she saw Menczel step out onto the field to announce the tourney prize. She urged Mexus forward, digging her heels in so that he broke out into a canter. "Wait!"

Hundreds of people turned to stare at her as she rode out into open view. She knew she cut a strange sight, her custom armor completely unlike the great beetle plates of the others. She didn't care. She rode, head high, right up to the stands, supremely aware of her every movement, the weight of the chain, how her leather vest constricted her breathing, how her sword bounced against her thigh as Mexus cantered.

Her mother was lowering herself into her seat, face guarded. Her uncle was watching her with open curiosity and amusement. Neither had recognized her yet. She pulled lightly on Mexus' rein, leaning back in the saddle, and he stopped before them all.

"I wish to enter the tourney," she said, suddenly breathless.

Recognition dawned on her mother's face, followed closely by alarm. She bolted to her feet. "What is this?"

Kethe felt madness seize her. Madness and anger and determination so pure nothing could stop her. She reached up and pulled the barbute free. She heard the gasps but ignored them. Her eyes were locked on her mother's. "I demand the right to serve as one of your knights."

"This is preposterous," said Lady Kyferin. "Kethe, have you lost your mind?"

"No," she said. "The exact opposite. I want this. I will have it. I will serve you with my sword."

Snickers and laughter came from the audience, but just as many hissed at them to be silent.

Lord Laur stirred in his seat. "Niece. It's a pleasure to see you, though I must admit to being somewhat... surprised."

"Lord Uncle," she said, bowing her head. Then she turned back to her mother, who had grown pale. "You cannot deny me this. You've always told me that women are the equal of men in all matters. That we need but the courage to seize the moment, to believe in ourselves, and that there is nothing we can't do. Well, I am taking you at your word. I want this. I will have it."

Lady Kyferin shook her head softly. "You can't stand against these knights, Kethe."

Kethe smiled, fighting the tears that threatened to come from the sheer intensity of her emotion. "I can, and I will. Give me this chance. I know what I'm doing. By the Ascendant and my hope for the White Gate, I swear it. Mother, let me fight."

Silence ached between them. Lord Laur went to speak, saw Lady Kyferin's expression, and fell still. The moment dragged out, but Kethe never flinched, never looked away. She held her mother's gaze with a steadiness and resolution that she had never managed before, and finally her mother looked over to Lord Laur.

"Will your men allow a woman to contest them?"

Lord Laur considered the question, then shrugged. "That is up to them. I suppose there are legendary precedents. It is said that centuries ago women did indeed fight alongside men." He paused, calculating. "But you are our host, my Lady. Order it, and I shall see it done. For better or worse, they will treat my dear niece as they would any other knight."

Lady Kyferin looked back to Kethe. "Is this truly what you wish?"

Kethe's desire was so strong that she found she couldn't speak. She simply nodded.

Something in her mother gave way. "So be it," said Lady Kyferin. "Lord Laur, tell your men to withhold nothing. My daughter will enter the melee as a knight of Kyferin Castle."

Kethe wanted to cry, to grin, to give an ebullient whoop, but she controlled herself and did none of those things. This had been the easiest part. As she turned to consider the eighteen other mounted knights, she found her confidence wilting. They were massive, their armor ponderous and heavy, their destriers huge, and they were all staring at her. She could read their minds: Incredulity. Disdain. Mockery. Except for Asho, she saw. His customary expression of neutrality had given way to the slightest of grins. Kethe restrained the urge to smile back, and instead placed her helm back over her head. "My Lady. By your leave."

Lady Kyferin nodded weakly, and Kethe rode over to Asho and Ser Wyland.

"Do you know what you're doing?" Asho didn't sound incredulous, much to her relief. Merely incredibly dubious.

"Of course I do." Mexus was massive between her legs, a world of difference compared to Lady. No matter. He was as highly trained as destriers came. He'd do what she bid. "I think."

Ser Wyland was staring at her, his expression inscrutable. She wanted to pretend that his words and opinion wouldn't matter any more than Asho's, but that would be a lie. She watched him carefully out of the corner of her eye.

Finally he rubbed his face with both hands. "By the White Gate. Stay close to me. I'll do what I can to protect you."

Anger was followed quickly by bitter self-control. She bit down her retort. "Thank you, Ser Wyland. I'll do my best to watch your back as well."

Ser Kitan Laur guided his horse over, riding with an enviable ease in his expertly crafted plate. He stopped before her and pushed up his visor's helm. She'd last seen him four years ago at one of their family's rare reunions. He'd been a lean young man at that time, barely out of his teens, face petulant, his thin lips always pressed in displeasure. She'd hated being caught alone with him, because he'd always tried to corner her and kiss her hair. He'd filled out, she saw, his frame now muscled though not nearly as broad as Ser Wyland's. His eyes, though— they retained their mocking amusement.

"Cousin," he said. "This is unexpected. Do you seriously mean to ride against us?"

Kethe met his eyes with a flat stare of her own. "That and more."

Kitan leaned back in his saddle, both hands resting on his pommel. "You'll ruin this contest, Kethe. Nobody will strike against you in earnest. Instead, we'll all be reduced to fumbling over ourselves as we seek to avoid you and not fall over laughing at the same time. Come. Withdraw. Let the men do the fighting."

Kethe felt her fear leave her. Into its place stole a solid, impenetrable anger as heavy and flat as Elon's anvil. "Watch yourself, Kitan. I'll be coming for you."

He sneered. "I've faced the greatest knights in the realm and never been defeated. What chance do you really think you have against me?"

The other knights were all watching. She felt the weight of their eyes. Her leather armor creaked as she leaned forward. "Watch your back, Kitan. I'm taking you out. And when you're lying on the mud with my foot on your face, I'll remind you of this exchange."

Ser Wyland gave a low whistle, and Kitan snapped his visor down. "You'll rue those words, sweet Kethe. Once the signal has been given, I'll forget you're family and a woman. You want to play at war? Then come at me. I'm more than willing to play."

He turned his horse and rode back to the other Laur knights.

"Well," said Ser Wyland, gazing out over the field. "That's one way to make sure you have an easy first fight."

"I don't want easy," snapped Kethe.

"Clearly not," said Asho. He grinned at her, and she realized that she'd never seen him smile like that. It brought life to his normally dour and sullen features. "Just leave some for the rest of us, will you? I promised Ser Wyland at least six of them."

Kethe couldn't help but smile back. "Fine. I'll see what I can do."

In the stands, Lady Kyferin was speaking with Lord Laur. She finally seemed to agree to something and rose to her feet. The crowd silenced as everyone turned to her. She spoke to Menczel, who rose up and called out in his rich voice so that all could hear.

"The prize for today's melee is a golden cup, blessed by the Ascendant and brought from Sige by the Lady Kyferin herself."

Whispers of excitement flickered through the throng, and several of the knights sat up straighter, each as attentive as a hunting hound waiting for the signal to spring.

"Lady Kyferin has accepted Lord Laur's suggestion that his knights face the rest combined. As such, will his knights please ride to the far side of the field. This is to be a contest in the classic manner, held in honor of the late Lord Kyferin; both sides are to ride against each other three times, and then those who are still mounted are to dismount and engage the opposition on foot. Combat shall continue until one side has surrendered completely. The greatest knight shall receive the cup, and the winning side an equal measure in gold coin."

Kitan's mount sprang forward and the other seven knights followed him to canter across the field, where they turned and lined up. They looked glorious, the sunlight gleaming on their armor, their brightly colored tabards and high-spirited mounts giving them a romantic and dashing air. Were Kethe still in the stands, she might have favored them. They were clearly the better armed, most united, and professional company here.

Looking at her companions, she resisted the urge to wince. There were ten of them, an advantage that she was sure would quickly evaporate after the first charge. Ser Wyland took the center of the line, Kethe to his left, Asho to his right. The other newly arrived knights flanked them, with the Black Knight at the far left. They were a mismatched company, some wearing armor too large for them, their armorers not having had time to make adjustments, while others were holding their lances awkwardly. Young knights. Untested, unproven, and with who knew how much training.

"All right, my brothers and sisters, listen up." Ser Wyland sat large and confident in their center. Everyone stilled and turned to him. "This is going to happen fast and rough. We're strangers to each other, but before us lies our enemy, and for the next hour we are family. Ride hard, and when you reach the far side of the field, turn and wait my mark."

Ser Wyland's voice sent a thrill down Kethe's spine. She nodded, eager to show that she understood, and saw that many of the other knights did as well. Ser Wyland smiled broadly, his eyes shining. "Look for me. Line up beside me, and wait till I give the order to charge for the second pass. Order and control are worth more here than individual skill. Save your heroics for when you hit the ground. While mounted, you are mine, you are part of this line, you are the hammer and every ugly face looking at us from over there is your personal anvil. Do you hear me?"

A number of the knights shouted their agreement, their horses shying and pawing at the air with their hooves.

"Any moment now." Ser Wyland pulled on his helm and his voice became muffled. "Ride slow to begin with. Nobody pass me. Save the gallop for the very last second. I'll set the pace. Don't let excitement or fear get to your head. Slow and steady, right up till the last, then we knock them on their fat arses and turn to mop up the rest. Clear?"

Menczel had stepped up to where the trumpeters were watching Lady Kyferin for the signal. Squires were racing into position with extra lances. Everyone in the crowd was on their feet. It seemed as if the entire world were holding its breath.

Brocuff had given Kethe several months' worth of lance training, but he'd told her up front that he was no knight. Her pulse was pounding in her ears. She could barely breathe, couldn't swallow. All she could remember was how over and over again she'd failed to put her lance through the small ring Brocuff had hung from a branch, and that with riding at it at only a canter. The lance towered above her, eight feet long and made of beautiful and supple ash. She yearned to draw her sword instead.

"Here we go," said Ser Wyland, and the trumpets blew.

Kethe almost dug her heels into Mexus' flanks, almost urged him into an explosive gallop. She barely managed to check the impulse and instead simply clucked him forward. Ser Wyland led the line, moving at an easy trot, lance held erect. Before them the eight Laur knights did the same, their line perfect, their legs almost touching, so close were they riding to each other.

"Easy," called Ser Wyland, his voice powerful and carrying even with his helm on. "Stay close. Now, a little faster, shall we?" He urged his mount into a canter, moving ahead so that they formed a very shallow 'V'.

Kethe felt like a child atop Mexus, suddenly clumsy as fear swamped her anew. The Laur knights were moving steadily toward them, and the crowd was screaming, a shrill, surreal sound that made the acid burning her stomach all the worse. She couldn't breathe. Her whole body felt numb. What had she been thinking?

"All right!" bellowed Ser Wyland over the drumming of their hooves. "Lower lances! Send them to the Black Gate, men! Charge!"

Madness erupted. Kethe did as she was bid, the tip of her lance weaving down through the sky to point at the great knight before her. She leaned forward, digging her knees into Mexus, and he responded by opening up into a gallop. It was like riding an avalanche. She raised her shield with the other arm, lance tucked against her ribs, and stared at her opponent. It was the massive brute, Ser Bero, astride what looked to be a plow horse, a moving wall of flesh and green steel. His antlers gleamed, their points shod in iron, and his lance was an oak tree, as thick as her arm.

The thunder became a crescendo. She was yelling at the top of her voice, her whole body tensed, the world reduced to one small point, and then the lines collided. She heard screams, the shattering of lances, the resounding clash of metal, dirt clods flying everywhere.

Kethe took Beros' lance full on her shield, and tried to twist at the last moment so as to deflect it at an angle. It was like galloping into a wall. Her own lance shattered, though she had no idea where it had hit, and then the world became a bright smear. The earth and sky flipped, then again, then everything went white as she smashed to the ground, hitting the field so hard that she bounced, rolled, and came to a stop in a crumpled heap.

Roars, cheers, and screams filled the air around her. She felt like puking. Her lungs no longer worked. She lay on her side, mouth gaping like a landed fish's. She couldn't even wheeze. Reflex more than anything else had her roll onto her front and push up onto her knees.

Suddenly her lungs opened and she gasped, tears springing into her eyes. Her whole left side was throbbing, every bone wrenched. The world was doubled, her vision blurred. With a cry of anger she forced her feet under herself and stood, though doing so nearly made her sick. The world swayed, but she managed to keep her feet.

People were yelling her name. Reaching up, she adjusted her helm, settling it back into place, and finally took in the grounds around her.

The Laur knights were wheeling, taking up fresh lances from their squires, forming a new line. Kethe counted. Six remained mounted. She turned and saw that only four of their own knights were turning to form up again. Ice flooded her veins. Ser Wyland, Asho, the Black Knight, and a young knight with a crimson surcoat emblazoned with a white lily.

They'd dropped two of the enemy and lost five of their own. Not good. Looking around, she saw the two fallen Laur knights gaining their feet, drawing their blades and backing away. Kethe cursed, drew her own sword, and immediately she felt better with the blade in her hand. This, she knew. This, she could control.

Three of the fallen knights from her side weren't moving. The other one rose, his left arm hanging loosely by his side.

"Come on!" She beckoned to him. "Get out of the way!"

He jogged over just as the trumpets sounded and the two lines charged each other again. Kethe watched, her heart in her mouth. The distance between them was much shorter this time, and both sides immediately threw themselves into a full gallop, lances leveled. The other knight hurried over to stand beside her and they watched as the knights collided.

The sound was terrible. Splinters of wood flew. Knights fell, their horses rearing, and the survivors rode on to turn again. Kethe's hopes sank. Only Ser Wyland and the Black Knight made it to the far side. Two more of Laur's nights had fallen, including the massive Ser Bero, unhorsed by the Black Knight.

"Two against four," said her companion, voice bitter. "Ser Laur, the Golden Vipers, and Ser Olbrecht. Damn them!"

Asho was lying on his side in the dirt. Kethe cursed and ran out into the center to crouch by his side. He was groaning, but sat up as she reached him.

"Asho! Get up!"

"Who said being a knight was a good idea?" He took her hand, however, and hauled himself up.

The other two knights were also standing, and just in time—the trumpets sounded. The horses began to gallop. Kethe wanted to scream in frustration. Two against four. Impossible.

Ser Wyland and the Black Knight lowered their lances and galloped fiercely toward the enemy. They collided for a third and final time, and the Black Knight unhorsed Ser Olbrecht, who smashed down to the earth. Ser Wyland drove his lance straight into Kitan, whose own lance shattered on Ser Wyland's shield even as one of the twins caught him in the side. Ser Wyland reeled in his saddle, almost sliding right off the back, but somehow managed to hold on, gripping his pommel and hauling himself erect through sheer bloody strength and determination.

Kethe screamed with a savage pride and joy—they'd kept two men up! The Golden Vipers and Kitan turned and stared as Ser Wyland drew his sword and pointed at Kitan, then down at the tourney floor. The crowd was deafening as it cheered and roared. The riding was over. Lord Laur's men had won the jousting, but only barely. The bloodiest, hardest work was yet to come.

Kethe shook out her arms and swung her blade back and forth in a vicious figure eight. "All right, boys," she said, and realized that she was grinning. "It's time to show them what we can do."

CHAPTER FOURTEEN

ƮIRON

Ser Tiron's breath was a harsh rasp within his battered helm. He threw his shattered lance contemptuously down onto the ground, but resisted the urge to pluck his helm free too. His armor wasn't worth a cup of mule's piss, rusted and battered as it was. Once it had been worth a fortune, but Lord Kyferin had spared no effort to insult him; for three long years it had been strapped to the tilting dummy for the knights to practice on. He'd laughed at the sight of it the night he had been released and had almost thrown it on the refuse heap, but pride, bitter pride, had made him take it down. He'd left the castle and ridden for two days to reach the ruins of his family home. It was there that he'd worked on the armor, managing to restore it to some semblance of functionality. That it had lasted three rounds of the joust was a bloody miracle.

He swung his leg over the pommel of his borrowed horse and slid to the ground. The sensation jarred him his bones. Three years he'd rotted in an underground cell. He'd lost much of his strength and vitality. But no matter. While his body might be failing, his will was yet unbroken.

"Well done," said Ser Wyland, stepping up beside him. "Your name, ser knight? I would know beside whom I fought."

"Piss off, Jander." Ser Tiron drew his blade. "Watch yourself, because I won't."

His family sword gleamed in the sun. This at least Ser Kyferin hadn't ruined; instead, he'd hung it on his wall as a trophy. The blade was freshly oiled and sharp enough to shave with, and its hilt felt as familiar in his palm as Sarah's own hand had once done.

The Laur knights had already engaged those who had fallen during the first two passes. Oaths, yells, and the clangor of battle filled the air. Ser Tiron swirled his blade around in a vicious arc, his body awakening to years upon years of training for war. An old hunger stirred within him. For too long he'd been cooped up like an animal. For too long his rage had built without release.

It was time to unleash it.

Tiron loped out to the side like a wolf tracking prey along the edge of a wood. He circled the melee, in no hurry to close. The winner would be the last man standing, not the first to fall.

127

The action in the center was getting serious. That fool girl was fighting back to back with the Bythian. Around them men were squaring off, swords clashing, some forcing their way forward, others giving ground. Ser Tiron studied the combat, moving easily, searching for prey. For weakness. Where to strike?

There was a bellow as Ser Wyland charged straight into the center of the fray. "For the Black Wolves! For Lady Kyferin!" That turned heads. Good. Ser Tiron marked where the giant Ser Bero was hammering at a young knight half his size, each blow battering at the man's blade, driving him back and down to one knee. Beyond him the twins were fighting as a pair, each holding two blades, a short sword and a slaughter seax, spinning with impressive speed and skill. Kitan Laur was standing at the back, waiting, longsword resting on his shoulder, watching as Jander Wyland engaged a nameless Laur knight.

Well, then. Tiron grinned mirthlessly. Time for blood.

In the old days he might have roared a battle cry himself and charged his enemy from the front. That man was gone. Instead, he darted in soundlessly and came at Ser Bero from the flank. The massive man held his great ax high, ready to shatter his opponent's blade once and for all. Gripping his family blade with both hands, Tiron leaped up with a grunt and brought it whistling down on the ax's haft. He sheared clear through it, the massive moon blades falling to the dirt behind Bero as the great man staggered and nearly fell, unbalanced.

"Idiot. Who brings a wooden weapon to man's fight?" Tiron moved in before Bero could regain his balance, planted his foot square on Bero's hip and shoved. The massive knight roared in anger and toppled over onto his side with a resounding crash. "There," said Tiron to the stunned knight who was still kneeling on the ground, notched sword held before him. "Even you should be able to handle him now."

A rushing sensation, a blur of movement out of the corner of his eye, and Tiron wheeled, swinging his sword around in time to ward off a blow that would have taken off his head. Ser Olbrecht had lost his helm, and his gray hair hung wild about his shoulders; his smile was chilling.

"Bad move, old man," said Ser Tiron. He rushed Olbrecht, attacking with a series of brutal overhead chops. Olbrecht moved with surprising agility for his age, deflecting the blow with clever parries, giving ground before Tiron's strength—a strength that quickly began to fade. Tiron grimaced within his helm. He'd still not recovered. Where before he might have hammered Olbrecht into the ground, now his lungs were already burning, his muscles screaming in protest.

Tiron stepped back, gasping for breath, and Olbrecht grinned. "Tired already, Rusted Kettle? For shame. To think you're going to lose to an old man."

Tiron scowled. Olbrecht was good. Perhaps too good. In his prime he'd have bested any man here, but even now, in the twilight of his career, he was sufficiently skilled to outfight Tiron in his current state.

"To the Black Gate with you," said Tiron, and hurled his sword at Olbrecht's head.

The old man's eyes widened in shock and he flinched to one side, Tiron's blade crashing off his armored shoulder. He recovered quickly, but it was too late. Tiron slammed his gauntlet across Olbrecht's jaw with everything he had, rose up onto one foot so that he could come down with all his weight, turning from his hips to bring his metal fist down onto the man's face.

Olbrecht spun, blood and teeth spraying into the air, and crashed to the ground. Tiron fell after him, sinking down to one knee, and hissed through clenched teeth at the stitch that burned in his side and the way his vision was blurring. This wasted body. He snatched up his sword and stood, turning and quickly backpedaling away from any oncoming opponents.

There were none. The number of contestants had dropped sharply. Bero had somehow gained his feet; the young knight was lying face-down in the dirt. The twins were going toe-to-toe with the girl and the squire, and in the center Jander and Kitan were circling each other, blades raised, doing a slow sideways shuffle as each sought an opening.

One of the Laur knights was getting back up to his feet. Tiron walked over and slammed the pommel of his blade into the back of his head and the man fell to the dirt again.

Tiron's breath was burning in his raw throat. *Damn.* He was as weak as a lamb. His whole body was shaking.

Jander and Kitan leaped at each other, blades ringing out.

"Hey!" Tiron began to run forward. "You! The idiot!"

Bero had been closing in on Ser Wyland's flank, but he stopped and turned. He was holding the fallen knight's sword in one massive fist, making it look like a child's blade. A deep, bestial growl sounded from within his antlered helm. "Kettle Knight."

"Yeah, yeah," muttered Tiron. "Heard it before."

He put on a burst of speed and ran in, blade held overhead as if for a downward swing. Bero raised his own sword to parry, but at the last moment Tiron checked his blow, pulled it and ducked down under the huge knight's sword. He darted past the other man and cut down and behind at his calf as he went.

His blade connected, but Bero's thick greaves blocked the blow. The antlered knight turned, but not as quickly as Tiron, who spun and laid a massive strike against his back. His armor rang out like a bell.

Tiron gripped his sword with both hands. An image came to him: Sarah's face, a flickerflash of her joy as she laughed in the high meadow, golden with the light of the setting sun and fresh and beautiful forever. Then, her face as he'd seen it last, swollen and purple in the darkness of their ruined home, her head listing unnaturally to one side. Tiron roared, the sound coming from his very depths. Rage infused him, rushing up sick and ravaging from his core. Bero raised his blade but it didn't matter.

Tiron swung. His sword was weightless. Growling and barking with hatred, he wanted one thing and one thing only: blood. He would crack this monster's shell, shatter his breastplate through force alone. Bero was clearly not used to being assaulted straight-on. He couldn't catch his balance. He took as many blows on the shoulder and chest as he did on the blade.

"Die!" Tiron stepped in, and stepped in again. He could see only Bero's wide eyes through the slits of his helm. His family blade struck down again and again, and each time it left a dent in the heavy armor, chipping away the green paint and revealing dull iron beneath. He sheared off an antler horn. Smashed the helm in the side. Cracked Bero's gorget.

His anger was febrile. He felt the black madness start to pull him down. He fought it, felt the exhaustion and weakness clutch at him with claws and haul him back into the pit, but he wouldn't go. He smashed aside Bero's blade. It flew and fell to the ground. Bero raised his arms and sank down to one knee. Tiron shattered a gauntlet, kicked the man in the chest and drove him onto his back.

Was that roaring sound the crowd or his own blood? He stood over the fallen knight and pounded at his helm, crushing it, disfiguring it, over and over. Bero was bellowing, yelling something, but Tiron couldn't hear him. Finally the huge knight stopped moving. Tiron stared at the man's dead eyes then staggered away, almost sobbing in his attempt to breathe, blade falling from his hands.

He couldn't breathe. Couldn't stand.

The rage left him. Sarah was still dead. His years wasted in a pit were still gone. There was nothing he could do to change that. He was powerless. Fate had crushed him.

The world was swimming. He growled. He wouldn't fall. He wouldn't surrender. Never again. Never.

CHAPTER FIFTEEN

Asho

Asho had never held a blade until he was eleven years old. Brought up from Bythos, he had stood alone amongst the other pages in Kyferin Castle's bailey, and held his wooden training sword as if it were a fork. The others had laughed. Brocuff had corrected his stance, given him basic instructions, and then set him to train against Alardo—who had beaten him mercilessly until Brocuff intervened. Ever since that day, the sword had been his only means of protecting himself from other such beatings, so he had trained hard. He had vowed to humiliate them all at their own game, and four years later had won the Ebon Cup, beating all the other pages in the three-day competition. Because of that, Kyferin had grudgingly made him a squire. Asho had exulted and trained all the harder. He had started to think he was talented with the blade. Plus he had survived the battle with the Agerastians, where all others had died. Perhaps he was gifted. Meant for great things.

But, backing away rapidly from Ser Cunot, desperately keeping his guard up and trying not to trip, he realized just how much he still had to learn. The Golden Viper was smiling, advancing with gliding steps, his sword a flickering needle, almost unreadable, striking as quickly as lightning. Asho was soaked in sweat. His arm was burning from effort, his armor weighing him down. The worst of it was that he knew Ser Cunot wasn't even exerting himself. He was toying with Asho, stealing some glory and honor away from Lady Kyferin by humiliating one of her sole two knights.

In the periphery of his vision he saw Kethe desperately fighting the other Golden Viper. Her swordplay was impressive, but she too was giving ground. He thought of Ser Wyland's words: *My shield will always be at your back, my sword by your side.* Would she agree to fight alongside him? Would they stand a greater chance of defeating the Vipers if they did so?

No. He could only rely on himself.

Asho let out a yell and threw himself forward, spearing his sword toward Ser Cunot's face. The other knight batted his blade away and crouched low so as to take the impact of Asho's charge on his shoulder. Their armor clashed as they collided, and then Ser Cunot shoved hard. Asho staggered, his charge neatly caught and rebuffed.

There was no time to think. He parried a slice, then tried for a riposte, but abandoned it quickly in favor of another parry. His hand was numb from the shiver that ran down his sword each time he blocked. The crowd was screaming. Ser Cunot delivered an overhand chop, which Asho took on his shield and immediately sliced at Ser Cunot's flank. The other man spun neatly away, and somehow stepped behind him.

Asho's stomach dropped. This man was brilliant with the blade, surefooted, agile and fast beyond belief. He tried to spin, but knew it was too late. He felt Ser Cunot's sabaton stomp his calf and drive him down to one knee. Twisting, he dropped his shield and caught himself on the ground, his sword raised just in time to catch the strike that would have brained him from behind.

Ser Cunot smiled at him with vulpine delight, his eyes slitted behind the gap in his helm. "Yield, slave, or I'll dismember you before your Lady."

Sweat stung in Asho's eyes, and just then he heard a surprised cry of pain. Kethe toppled to the ground, sword falling from her hand as Ser Cunad stumbled through the swing that had connected with her head. *No.* He couldn't yield. Maybe Ser Wyland could keep Ser Cunad and Ser Laur at bay, but he would be doomed if Ser Cunot joined the fight. Gritting his teeth, he shoved Ser Cunot's sword away and tried to rise, only to receive a kick in the chest that sent him sprawling onto his back.

"Yield," said Ser Cunot, still smiling sweetly. Asho swung his blade up, but Ser Cunot struck his hand with the flat of his sword and knocked it flying. Then the twin placed his sabaton on Asho's chest and pressed his blade into the joint of his shoulder, driving the tip against the links of his hauberk. "Yield!"

"Go to the Black Gate," hissed Asho, and grasped Ser Cunot's naked blade with his gauntlet. He gripped tight, trying to arrest its descent, but there were almost three hundred pounds of metal and man behind it. Leaning forward, Ser Cunot drove the sword slowly into his shoulder. Asho arched his back in pain, and then lashed out with his foot at Ser Cunot's legs, hoping to knock him sprawling. The Viper danced aside, avoiding the blow and leaving his sword embedded in Asho's shoulder. With a grunt Asho sat up and pulled the blade free, fumbling it so that it fell to the mud.

In the near distance he heard a roar. Ser Cunad was charging the Black Knight, who stood unarmed. The Black Knight took off his helm and threw it at the Viper, who dodged easily and smacked the flat of his blade across the older man's forehead. The Black Knight dropped.

Damn. Asho reached down for Cunot's blade, only to receive a thrusting kick to the shoulder that knocked him onto his back. With cruel precision Cunad embedded the tip of his murder seax into the same wound in Asho's shoulder. Asho screamed, but the other man simply leaned in and pushed it even deeper.

"That's good, you Bythian whoreson," said Ser Cunot again. "Keep fighting me. Give me the excuse I need to take off your arm."

The pain was excruciating, beyond anything Asho had ever known. He could hear Ser Wyland's grunts and the rapid ring of metal as he fended off both attackers. Asho couldn't yield. Wouldn't. He closed his eyes, desperately trying to think of some stratagem, any ploy that might grant him reprieve, and then the weight behind the blade suddenly disappeared.

Asho opened his eyes. Ser Cunot was staring down at him with a dazed expression. Then he toppled over sideways, and Asho saw Kethe standing behind him, blood running down one side of her face. Her blue eyes were wide with what was either shock or cold determination.

"Kethe!" Asho went to rise, but pain stabbed through his shoulder and his guts churned greasily. Kethe stared at where Ser Cunot had fallen, and then turned to look over at where Ser Wyland was fighting on, backing away rapidly as he sought to keep both men before him. Asho felt a fierce frustration, and extended his arm to her. "Help me up!"

Kethe looked down at him and shook her head. Hefting her slender sword, she turned and began to run toward the last three combatants.

The stands were going wild. Asho gritted his teeth and pushed himself up to watch. Ser Cunad saw Kethe approaching and peeled away, a look of sufferance in his expression as he moved to intercept her.

Asho tried to rise. He pushed himself up to one knee, and then managed a crouch. Casting around, he saw his longsword and picked it up. With a cry he stood, and saw Kethe engage Ser Cunad.

The second twin was just as fast—if not faster—than the first. He fought with his blade and murder seax, and came at Kethe whipping both before him in an intertwined pattern of glittering steel. Kethe didn't hesitate. She timed her thrust just right, stepping in to engage Cunad while he was mid-stride, and caught his seax at the right angle. It slid halfway down, and then she flicked her sword around sharply and sent his long knife flying through the air.

His sword, however, caught her across the shoulder and rang out loudly as it crashed into her pauldron. The force of the blow sent her staggering to one side, but she went with it and fell into a roll, then came back up smoothly on her feet in a way no man in full plate would ever have been able to do. Cunad was after her quicker than a thought, but

Kethe danced back, her blade a snake's tongue, catching and meeting Cunad's every stroke faster than Asho could follow. She fell back again and again, and then slowly seemed to catch her stride. She stopped retreating, held her place, and then forced Cunad back a step.

Asho yelled in exhilaration and disbelief and ran forward. Cunad's swordplay was turning desperate. Kethe's blows were gaining strength while his were growing weaker. Their blows rang louder and louder, Cunad's blade leaping away from each block, his skill tested to its limit, until at last he was barely moving it from side to side, almost hugging himself in an attempt to keep away from her attacks.

Asho slowed in amazement. He'd never seen anybody move so fast. Kethe grabbed her sword with both hands and brought it down in a powerful arc as if hewing right through the side of a tree. Cunad's sword was smacked aside, and she followed through, spinning around, her blade swinging up and then coming down with terrible power to smash into Cunad's chest.

The sound was akin to Elon bringing his mightiest hammer down on a piece of white-hot metal. Cunad's cuirass was stoved in, and the man fell to the ground in a heap.

Ser Wyland disengaged from Ser Laur, who glanced toward Kethe, looked away, and then looked right back in amazement. Ser Wyland staggered and fell to his knees. His armor was battered and rent, his time spent dueling both enemies having taken a bitter toll.

For a moment no one fought. Silence fell across the stands. Everyone stood waiting and watching as noble cousin faced noble cousin.

Kethe stepped forth, her blade held down and to one side. Her tight braid was in disarray, her freckled face made all the paler by the shocking blood that caked one side of it, but she stood tall and seemed to radiate with a barely restrained power.

Ser Laur was breathing heavily, but he was unharmed; his enameled armor looked as spotless as when he had first arrived. He lifted his visor and stared at her in disbelief. "What is this?"

"I warned you," said Kethe. She raised her blade and pointed its tip at him. "It's time to start begging."

Asho limped up, sword in hand, and stood next to her. Ser Laur's gaze flicked over to him, and when Ser Wyland also rose to his feet and walked over, he took a step back.

"Three against one," said Ser Wyland, his voice weary and almost apologetic.

"I've fought against greater odds," said Ser Laur, casting about the battlefield for any of his allies who might yet come to his aid. None rose.

Asho knew he was the weakest of the group, but he had to press their advantage. He started to circle around Ser Laur, becoming the far point of the triangle that would crush him. Was the knight mad enough to insist on combat? He was staring at Kethe, whose gaze was blank and cold. There was death in the depths of her eyes, a promise of no quarter or mercy. Despite himself, Asho shivered. He'd never seen her like this, had never guessed she possessed such strength.

Laur spread his arms out wide as if offering to embrace her, and then reversed his blade and drove its point deep into the earth. He removed his helm and set it on the pommel, and then began to applaud, turning to the stands and gesturing that the crowd join him. Cheers broke out, and Laur grinned, gesturing to Kethe, urging the crowd on. "It pleases me to concede to Lord Kyferin's own daughter at a tourney held in his honor," he cried. "What better way to pay respects to my uncle than to allow his daughter to take the victory? A knight in truth! Honor to Lady Kethe!"

The crowd roared, and Laur turned back to her, his smile as warm as a knife cut. "Enjoy this, cousin. The next time I'll beat you so badly you'll bleed from all your holes for a week." Then he bowed, clapped his hands again in mock applause, and stalked off to see to his fallen companions.

Asho's shoulders slumped, and he almost dropped his blade. Instead he sheathed it shakily and walked over to where Ser Wyland had joined Kethe. She was blinking in shock, and when he drew close, Asho saw that she was trembling violently.

"Easy," said Ser Wyland. "Deep breaths. Knights older than Ser Olbrecht have broken down after a good fight. Breathe deep. It's over." Then he laughed, half in amazement, and turned to survey the field. Squires were running forth to tend to their lords; servants were carrying out refreshments and chasing down horses. "It's over, and by the Ascendant we still stand. A miracle. I can scarce believe it." He shook his head, grinned wolfishly, and turned back to Kethe. "I've never seen the like. How long have you been training?"

Kethe shook herself and looked up at him. "Training? Two and a half years."

"That's it?" Asho removed his helm and placed it under one arm. "Two and a half years?"

Kethe nodded woodenly. "Brocuff's been teaching me. In Greening Wood. Once a week."

"Once a week?" Ser Wyland whistled. "I'm going to have to ask Brocuff for lessons, then. Impossible. A miracle, in truth. Perhaps a greater hand than your own guided your blade today. Or perhaps not. Still, you saved the hour, Lady Kyferin." He pulled his helm off, revealing his short, thick, dark hair, which was matted with sweat. "I could have held Laur and Cunad off another minute, perhaps, but beat them both? Not likely."

"I saw you fall," Asho said to Kethe. "You took a blow to the side of the head that would have felled an ox. How are you still standing?"

Kethe touched the wound at the side of her head, then pulled her hand away and looked at her red fingertips. "I don't know. I just got back up."

Trumpets sounded and cheers broke out all over again. Ser Wyland bowed low to Kethe. "Come. There are rewards to be collected. Shall we?"

For the first time she smiled, and some semblance of the Kethe that Asho recognized appeared on her face once more. "Yes." Then she laughed and covered her mouth with both hands. "We won."

"Against all the odds. Yes, we did. Now, come!"

Ser Wyland started striding toward the stands in which Lady Kyferin and Lord Laur stood, the other knights limping and hobbling their way there too so as to form a crowd. Some required several squires to help them stand, but only one was carried off the field: the massive form of Ser Bero.

When all had been assembled, Lady Kyferin stepped forth, Lord Laur by her side, his face inscrutable. "Honorable knights, you have all performed most bravely on this field of battle. You have shown the gathered populace deeds of daring and skill that shall live on in tales and song. All of you displayed admirable courage and tenacity, and all of you did honor my late Lord husband as a result. Would that I could reward you all equal to your measure, but to do so would beggar the land. As such, it is my great pleasure to recognize the winning knights. Please step forth as you are named."

Menczel nodded to the trumpeters, who gave a brief call and named the first visiting knight. One by one the men stepped forward to bow low as Lady Kyferin lay a white sash over their shoulders and praised them full and long. Each of the visiting knights was named, and then the trumpets sounded for a seventh time and Menczel called out clearly, "All honor to Ser Tiron, late Lord of Tiron Hall."

Asho turned in shock and saw the Black Knight step forward. His helm was missing, and only now did Asho catch sight of his face. It was a hard visage, carved as if by the elements from granite, with a dense, shortly cropped black beard and roughly cut hair. One eye was swollen closed, his temple bruised and purple, but his other eye was sharp as light reflected from the heart of a ridge of ice. It was a harsh face, striking and fierce.

Ashe felt someone grip his forearm, and looked down to see Kethe's gauntlet. He glanced up her arm and saw that she had turned so pale he thought she would faint. She was breathing rapidly and shallowly, eyes locked on the Black Knight.

Asho watched as the man stepped forward and bowed as the white sash was laid over his shoulders.

Lord Laur stared, mouth agape. "Lady Kyferin. Ser Tiron? Ser *Tiron*? The man who nearly slew your daughter three years ago?"

Lady Kyferin turned to him serenely. "The very same. I've forgiven him. Ascension preaches that we pardon our enemies, so that both they and ourselves may Ascend. I have seen fit to do so."

"I—but—as you will, my Lady," said Lord Laur, schooling his features into a frown so as to hide his shock.

"No," whispered Kethe. "No no no." She took a step back, then a second, then turned and ran back to the tents, fleet of foot in her light armor, clearly not caring for the curious stares that trailed after her.

Asho glanced up at Lady Kyferin, doing his best not to gape, and saw pain and uncertainty flash across her face before she regained her poise once more.

"Ser Asho of Kyferin Castle," called Menczel, and as the trumpets sounded, Asho stepped up to receive his first honors. Despite everything, despite his scorn for these tournaments and all those who entered them, he felt his heart soar. The air was crisp, the pain in his shoulder remote, and for a moment he set aside all his doubts and misgivings and fought hard not to grin.

Lady Kyferin smiled. "You do my House much honor with your victory, valiant knight. My blessings upon you and your sword."

Asho bowed his head and felt her sleeves brush his cheeks as she laid the sash upon his pauldrons. He straightened, inhaled till he felt his chest would burst, and then stepped back.

"Ser Wyland, Black Wolf and Lord of the Autumn Fort."

The trumpets blared, and Asho couldn't help but clap along with everyone else. The big knight made no attempt at dignity, but stepped forward with a wide smile on his face. He had to bow very low to receive the sash, and then he turned and extended his hand to where Lady Kethe had stood. He hesitated, realizing she was gone, and then recovered quickly to step back with a final wave.

Menczel glanced at Lady Kyferin, saw her nod, and cried, "Lady Kethe, of House Kyferin and Kyferin Castle!"

The trumpets cried their sweet song to the heavens, and despite her absence applause rang out. People cheered from both stands, and Asho stared after her, wishing he'd seen into which tent she'd escaped.

Lady Kyferin held up a hand for silence, and when the crowd had finally quieted, she spoke clearly for all to hear. "My daughter has retired to her tent to deal with her wounds. She has not only brought great glory to our House, and honor to Lord Kyferin, but has shown us all what a strong woman can do. She has shown us that there are no limits, that we each may forge our own destiny, that within each of us lies the potential for greatness. I name her in truth a knight of House Kyferin, and look forward with great pride to bestowing upon her the winner's sash."

The applause was mixed, with many people whispering amongst themselves. Lord Laur, Asho saw, did not look pleased.

"Now," said Lady Kyferin, "as is customary, the golden cup will be awarded to the greatest knight of this battle." Silence fell. "As your host and Lady of Kyferin Castle, it is my right to award it to the knight who performed with the most bravery on the field, and who exemplified the knightly code of chivalry. As such, I call forth Ser Laur to receive this highest of accolades."

Asho gasped. He stared incredulously as Ser Laur stepped forth, smiling with what had to be false modesty. "What?" Asho looked up to Ser Wyland. "But why?"

Ser Wyland was smiling and clapping, though his smile was just as false as Ser Laur's. "Politics, Ser Asho. There is far more at play here than a mere tourney."

Asho frowned and turned back to where Ser Laur was kneeling before Lady Kyferin. She held aloft the golden cup, which gleamed as if with its own inner ruddy light. "Ser Laur, you performed admirably on horseback, lasting through all three jousts with great skill. You then fought beautifully in the melee, never receiving a serious blow, but better yet, when the odds were clearly too high for any mortal man to overcome, you displayed the grace and humility of a true knight, and surrendered with honor rather than ruin the moment with desperate defiance. For such chivalry, awesome skill at arms, and wisdom, it is my great pleasure to declare you the greatest knight of this tourney, and award you this blessed cup."

The crowd cheered, but the sound was muted in Asho's ears. Ser Laur rose and took the cup, then raised it high overhead. His fellow knights and camp followers roared their approval, and Ser Laur shot Asho and Ser Wyland a look of sublime smugness before turning to walk toward his camp.

"Well, we not only survived," said Ser Wyland, turning to face Asho, "but we actually won. Come. The best part of any tournament is when you get to take off your armor."

Asho watched Ser Laur as he entered the crowd of his men, receiving their hails and approbation with a raised fist. "This isn't over, is it? The danger we're in?"

Ser Wyland followed Asho's gaze and then looked over to Lord Laur, who was escorting Lady Kyferin down from the stand. "Oh, no. Not by a long shot. The real danger is just beginning."

CHAPTER SIXTEEN

ϑΛROK

Tharok groaned and turned his head. He was lying on hard-packed dirt, and pain was warring with weakness for his attention. He fluttered open his eyes and saw the sky above him, a pale morning sky of the kind of porcelain blue you only saw from the mid-slopes of the mountains. He felt as if his body were a great sheet of metal that a hundred apprentices had used for smithing practice. Dull fire smoldered in his shoulder and deep in his side, and just sitting up took almost all of his energy. A thick collar of metal was banded around his neck; with a growl he pulled at it, digging his fingers in beneath the iron and hauling to no avail. Ignoring his surroundings and the sound of voices, he turned and grabbed the heavy links of chain with both hands and hauled at them, trying with panic and fury to tear them apart, but they held firm, tying him to the bole of a great tree.

Only after his vision threatened to blank out did he release the chains and slump over, turning to regard the camp. It was a women's permanent camp, female kragh sitting before their huts, children screeching as they raced about, the smell of campfires close by. There was a calm air to it all, as if this were but another day and he was not chained up in the camp's center like a slave.

Tharok froze. Tried to think. The circlet was gone, the sword. Everything but his tunic and pants. The last he remembered, he had been hugging the wyvern, flying ever lower into the familiar valleys, vision blurring, growing double, the lance almost slipping from his hands. He had been trying desperately to direct the wyvern to where the women of the Grey Smoke tribe had last made camp.

After that, there was nothing. He must have fallen from the wyvern's back, close enough to be found and then brought to this camp. From the number of males he saw sitting around campfires and walking around, it had to be this tribe's mating season. Four times a year the roving male packs would be drawn to their women's camp to celebrate the passing of the season, renew the bonds of the tribe, and to compete for the chance to mate. But which tribe was this? From where he was sitting, he couldn't see any banners or familiar faces.

Tharok closed his eyes. It was hard to think, to string his thoughts together. Last night with the circlet on his brow it had been easy to figure out what should be done. One efficient step had followed another, their logic obvious. There had been no doubt in his mind, no hesitation. He had been able to gaze at the vast tapestry of being and understand its weft and weave. Now that was gone and he was left with his hunger, his pain, his rage. He wanted to trick somebody into coming close enough to him so that he could wrap the chain around their neck and choke them to death. It didn't matter who. He wanted to roar and throw himself against the chain until it broke.

He was a slave. All of last night's victories and now this, sitting near-naked and collared and without a tribe to barter for his freedom or raid for forceful liberation.

Footsteps approached. Tharok opened his eyes and saw that a small group had assembled before him. His heart sank at the sight of gray-haired Wrok, warlord of the Red River tribe and his father's primary rival for power in the area. Wrok was old, nearing thirty summers, his once-large body wracked by age so that now he was but a shadow of his former self. His skin might have been as dark as any warlord's, but his authority rested on the support of his three younger brothers. Together they buttressed his authority, keeping back contenders in a style that Tharok's father had claimed was more lowlander than true kragh. But what he lacked in body he made up in mind, and his small black eyes glittered like the depths of the night sky.

By his side was his brother Krol, in his prime, his black hair pulled back in a glossy ponytail braided with bones, his barrel chest and shoulders as large as Tharok's. He was as powerful as a mountain goat and just as stupid, his skin a shade lighter than Wrok's. Next to him were the one-armed weapons master, Barok, almost as old as Wrok, and Toad, the misshapen tale-teller of the tribe, his skin nearly as light as a Tragon's, his curved spine and gash of a mouth reason enough for his name.

But his gaze curved from these men and turned instead to the red-haired kragh woman who was standing to one side. Powerfully built, even for a kragh, she had her arms crossed over her broad bosom, forearms as thick as tree branches and heavily veined. She was wearing a great mantle about her shoulders, but her midriff and legs were uncovered, so that even in his state Tharok could admire the cut of her long muscles, their tone and strength. But it was her eyes, flat and evaluating, that gave him pause. She was Maur, the wise woman, the leader of the women's circle and the heart of the Red River tribe. While Wrok would lead the males to war, he could do so only with the blessings of the wise woman and her council.

"You're finally awake," said Wrok. "It took you long enough."

Tharok glared at him, and then saw that he had World Breaker strapped to his side. "Give that to me," he said. "It's mine."

"This?" asked Wrok, looking down at World Breaker in surprise. "Yours? Krol."

The huge kragh stepped forward, swift and sure, and before Tharok could do more than half-rise, he thundered a backhand across Tharok's jaw, snapping his head to the side so that he fell heavily to the ground. Growling, Tharok surged back up, instinct making him whip his head to the side so as to dig his tusks into Krol's thigh, only to receive a knee directly to the face.

He blinked. He was on his back. Blood was hot on his face. With a groan that was only part growl, he rolled to his side and pushed himself back up. The others were still standing there. Good. He had only blacked out for a moment.

"Where did you get this blade?" asked Barok, the swordsmaster, his voice quiet, intent.

"None of your damn business," he growled.

Krol stepped forward once more, but Wrok stopped him with a wave of his hand. "We need him awake if he's to tell us anything. Answer the weapons master, slave. Or we'll get our answers through other means."

Tharok rose to his full height and pushed back his shoulders. None of them was wearing the circlet. That meant they'd not discovered its true value. Good. "I pulled it out of your mother's ass," he said, staring Wrok full in the eye. "Slowly. She doesn't like it when I rush."

Toad brayed laughter, slapping his knees, and Krol's face flushed dark. Not waiting for Wrok's command, he surged forward and drew his hand back to smash in Tharok's face—which was exactly what Tharok had known he'd do. Stupid Krol. With difficulty he ducked under the punch and drew the chain around the kragh's body as he kicked his feet out from under him. He got the chain up and around Krol's massive neck and turned to make his demands…

Only to feel the point of a blade against the side of his neck. Tharok froze and turned to look up the length of naked steel at where Barok was standing. How Barok had moved fast enough to get behind him, he had no idea. He'd have sworn it was impossible, but there he stood, the weapons master's eyes like pinpoints as he stared down at Tharok, his brow furrowed with focus.

"Release him, you stinking pile of filth!" roared Wrok, and having no option, the cruel tip of the blade pushing into his neck, Tharok did so, unwinding the chain so that Krol jerked away, coughing and cursing.

"Now, it looks like you need a lesson in your new station. Drop him, and then string him up." Barok nodded, and before the chained kragh could move, brained him with a lightning blow with the pommel of his sword.

Tharok fell. The last thing he saw was Maur's flat, contemplative gaze.

The world was rocking slowly back and forth. Tharok's head felt swollen to twice its normal size, the skin taut over his cheeks and forehead, so tender he felt it might split open. Groaning, he opened his eyes and saw that the world was upside down. No, he was hanging from his feet. He was on the outskirts of the camp and his body was pasted with rotten fruit, which also lay about his head. He'd been used for sport, and with that realization he growled, unable to control his ever-ready rage. But he was too tired, in too much pain to hold on to his anger for long, and with a groan he allowed his head to drop and his eyes to close.

Wrok had World Breaker. He would use it to his own ends, cement his leadership over the Red River tribe, and with his new power would draw other clans in the area to join his. Tharok's father, Grakor, had been Wrok's only true opposition. Grakor had led too many successful raids into the lowlands for Wrok, old and unable to fight, to contest. For years Wrok had watched and waited for his chance to exert his dominance. Tharok's father had been powerful but feared. No one would help the sole survivor of the Gray Smoke tribe now that he was gone. Tharok was on his own.

"Would it help if I stood on my own head?" Tharok opened his eyes to see Toad standing before him. "We could then at least pretend that the whole world had gone mad and only you and I stayed sane."

"What do you want, Toad?"

"Me? What, more than a tale or two? You know my role, my obligations. I must keep them entertained or they'll cast me off a cliff and save the food for someone worthier. So, come, have a heart. Tell me how you came upon the sword. Did you venture up to the Valley of the Dead, where Ogri is said to sleep?"

"Go screw yourself, Toad, and tell Wrok where he can shove it too."

Toad frowned, pantomiming sadness. "Tharok, Tharok, your harsh words will get you killed. You're already a slave, and I think your skin is already lightening. If you keep this up, Wrok will sell you to the Tragon, and they'll either torture you to death or sell you to the humans. And what do you think they would do with such a mighty highland kragh? Hmm?"

Tharok closed his eyes. He hadn't expected to come this far. He was strung up, still badly hurt, without friend or ally. It was as grim, if not worse a situation than the one he had escaped from the night before. If only he had the circlet, he might be able to think of something. But as it was…

"You want a tale?" He opened his eyes. "I'll tell you how I got the sword, by my clan's honor, if you do me one favor."

"What kind of favor is that, mighty Tharok?" asked Toad, sidling closer but carefully staying out of arm's reach.

"Bring me something. It was my family's. It would give me comfort."

"Bring you something? A joke! You might as well ask that I free you and slit my own throat while I'm at it."

"Fine," said Tharok, closing his eyes once more. "I'll tell the tale to Maur. I'm sure she'd appreciate the knowledge."

"Maur?" Toad sounded outraged. "And throw a perfectly great tale away? She would butcher it in the telling. She'd ruin it all. No, no no no. Tell me, tell me. I'll tell it so that you are a hero, and perhaps it will buy you some favor amongst the tribe. Tell me, Tharok, not that meddling wise woman."

Tharok opened one eye. "Bring me my trinket and I'll tell all."

"Trinket. What trinket? What is it, then?"

"What I was wearing when they found me." Suddenly Tharok stiffened with fear. What if it had fallen off as he fell? What if it was lost in the mountains somewhere? "Bring me the iron circle I was wearing on my head. It was my mother's. Bring it to me and I'll tell you everything."

Toad pursed his wide mouth, closed one eye and squinted at Tharok. "Metal circle. Well, you can't do much with that. Can't kill somebody with it. I suppose you could break it in two and jab someone with the point. Hmm. I'll tell you what: I'll go take a look, see if I can find it. If it seems harmless, I'll bring it. Agreed?"

Again Tharok bit his tongue. What if the damn Toad put it on? He was already too clever by half. Give him that clarity of thought and Tharok would have no chance. He almost told Toad to not wear it, almost ordered him to promise to not put it on his head, but some low cunning saved him. Ordering Toad to not wear it was as good a way as any to guarantee that he would. So, instead, he just closed his eyes and nodded. "Fine, but hurry. I've a mind to tell Maur if she passes by."

Toad hissed and ran away. Tharok watched him go, disappearing behind the first hut. He had no idea what the circlet might tell him to do, but it was better than waiting for Wrok and Krol to come back for more answers.

Half an hour passed. Tharok blacked out several times, only to awaken with his head pounding with the worst headache he'd ever suffered. His tongue was swollen to the point where he couldn't swallow, and it was only belatedly that he realized he couldn't feel anything below his knees. He hung there, hands two feet from the ground, and wondered if he could climb the chain to the branch overhead. Looking up, he saw that it was some ten yards up to the branch. Right now he couldn't even curl up to touch his feet.

He heard the sound of footsteps, and he looked up, expecting Toad. Instead, he saw Maur approaching, her aunt Krilla behind her. Their red hair glinted like the embers of a dying fire, and their square jaws and flat eyes set his pulse to racing. These were the real leaders of the tribe, the wise women who saw through the mysteries and advised Wrok as to what the proper course of action should be.

"Maur-krya," he said, choosing the honorific. It wouldn't hurt, and anyway, thinking of the circlet had put him in a crafty mood.

"Tharok," she said, stopping some five paces from him and crossing her arms. Krilla stopped a merciful eight paces away. She was as ugly as a drowned goat that had been left to bloat in the sun—and she was the only woman Tharok had ever seen best Krol in an arm-wrestling match.

"You've come to ask about the sword," he said, not liking the silence.

Maur studied him, generous lips pursed, the nubs of her feminine tusks barely breaking past her lips. "No. It doesn't matter where you found it, not now that Wrok possesses it. What I want to know is your version of what happened in the Jorin Valley when your clan was attacked. I've heard from Wrok, from Krol, even from several Tragon kragh themselves. But you're the first of the White Smoke tribe I've had a chance to speak to, and the women's circle would know your side of the tale."

Tharok closed his eyes and snorted. "My father always said that the winners write history. My tribe is lost. What does it matter now what happened?"

"It matters, fool, because the truth has weight, and we don't like how Wrok is dancing to the Tragons' song. So, speak up, or Krilla will tear off your manhood and feed it to you."

"I've heard that's her usual way of mating." Tharok grinned and opened one eye. Krilla, however, did not charge forward, as he had thought she might. "You're smarter than Krol; I'll give you that."

"That's not saying much," said Krilla. "You males are all equally dumb."

Tharok shrugged. "I won't argue that. But, fine, I'll tell you what happened if you cut me down."

"Tell me what happened, or I'll cut you until you do."

Tharok stared into Maur's gray eyes and knew that she would.

"Alright. Here is the truth of what happened. My father received word that the Tragon kragh wanted our entire tribe and the Red River tribe to join them in a raid to the north. They promised a good cut of the animals and foods from a wealthy caravan that was making its way through the Saragan Pass."

Tharok closed his eyes and tried to quiet the pounding headache. "My father was suspicious, allied as he is—was—to the Orlokor tribe to the south, but he thought it worth investigating. He took our clan to meet with the Tragon, but we were ambushed on the neutral meeting ground, and though some escaped, most of my family were killed." Tharok paused, examining the words. So much pain expressed in so simple a manner. "I escaped. The Tragon launched attacks on the other Gray Smoke clans and seized the women's camp. My tribe was destroyed."

Maur stood silently in thought, one arm laid beneath her breasts, the other hand stroking her chin as she gazed at nothing.

"Wrok has given us a large batch of shaman stone," said Krilla in a deep rumble.

"And now a fancy new sword to match his ambitions," said Maur, shaking her head. "I sense war on the horizon."

Tharok opened his mouth to ask them about the shaman stone, but they had already turned their backs and begun to walk away. He needed to escape. He needed a way out of this mess, to escape and head down to the lowland Orlokor tribe that infested the southern slopes of the mountain range, lowland kragh that they were. His father had sworn himself blood brother to their warlord, a squat, thick-bellied kragh by the name of Porloc who ruled over the endless thousands of Orlokor. They were the mightiest tribe there was, ever since his father had helped Porloc smash the Hrakar to the east so many years ago. If he could escape and make his way down to the Orlokor, he could present them with his grievance, and then… But that was as far as his plan went. He couldn't envision more than that.

Frustration made his headache pulse. He needed the circlet.

Another span of time passed, and for a while he drifted on an ocean of turbulent pain, barely aware of the world. Something tickled his nose—a fly landing on it—and he clumsily swept a hand past his face. It was tickled again and he opened one eye to see Toad standing just before him, a feather in his hand. With a roar he swiped at the light-skinned runt, but Toad laughed and fell back, landing on his back and clapping his feet together in glee.

"Human clap, human clap, this is how the humans clap!"

Tharok growled and flexed his hands with a savage yearning to snap Toad's neck, but the little kragh seemed unaffected. He sat up, looking at Tharok from one eye and then the other. "Are you mad at me, mighty Tharok? Has Toad offended you? Well, perhaps you can find a way to forgive me." And he drew the iron circlet from behind his back.

Tharok went still. "Give it to me."

"For the tale, the full tale, with every detail that belongs within the tale," said Toad, climbing back awkwardly to his feet.

"Everything," said Tharok. "I'll tell all. Every detail you want. Now give it."

Toad held it out, teasingly close, and then drew it back. "I saw you speaking with Maur. You wouldn't have gone and told her already, would you?"

Tharok laughed. "She doesn't give a damn for the sword. She wanted to hear my father's end."

"As do I! I want it all. Give me your blood word that you will tell me everything I desire to know, and I'll hand this metal band to you right now."

"My word, on my blood."

Toad nodded, well-pleased, and held out the circlet. Tharok reached out, took it carefully, and then pulled it onto his brow.

The world spun, laughter and voices played all at once in his mind, he saw a thousand different views of the mountains overlaid, and a clear picture emerged of the powers in play. He closed his eyes, digesting it all, allowing the image to grow definite as a course of action emerged.

"Come on," said Toad, impatience in his voice. "You swore."

"I did swear," Tharok said, and his voice was calm now, quiet, confident. The anger was gone. In its place came certainty and deliberation. He discarded immediately the plan to escape, to flee to the Orlokor Tribe. Such a move, if effected, would only result in Porloc offering shallow condolences and a place amongst his soldiers, nothing more. Porloc would not march into the high mountain valleys to administer justice to a highland kragh tribe, even if it had belonged to his blood brother. No, Porloc would instead accept the news that Wrok had risen in power and begin courting him, seeking to replace his father with the old kragh.

"I'll begin at the beginning, and you will tell me if you are well-satisfied with the tale. Agreed?"

Toad nodded suspiciously and lowered himself into a crouch.

"A vision of Ogri the Uniter came to my father. Mounted on his great dragon, Jaermungdr, Ogri told my father that the time had come for the highland kragh to unite, for the many small clans to become one, a great tribe at last, and that my father would lead the highland kragh down into the world, uniting the Tragon to the North, the Orlokor to the South, even the Hrakar to the East. That it was time for the kragh to unite once more. Ogri's blood ran in my father's veins, and my father would be the one to lead us."

Tharok paused, gauging the effect of his words on Toad. The little kragh sat enthralled, whispering the words even as Tharok said them, committing them to memory.

He realized that he was being watched and nodded impatiently. "Go on."

"My father was proud. You know this to be true." Indeed, his father had called Toad a goblin and not a real kragh when last they had met, and had urged that he be killed and put out of his misery. "Though Ogri ordered him to collect World Breaker first, Grakor decided that this opportunity to meet with the Tragon would be the first step in uniting us all. He sent me instead, since I am his son, to collect the blade from the Valley of Death, while he went down with words of fellowship for the Tragon.

"I bid him wait, but he refused. So he descended into the valleys and I went up to the Dragon's Tear, where I meditated and tried to decide on my next course of action. I knew my father was to be ambushed, even if he refused to see it. Should I follow him, to fight at his side, or should I ascend further and retrieve the blade if I was able?"

Toad scooted closer a few inches, nodding his head, eyes unfocused as he pictured the scene. Tharok repressed a smile. "It was there that the Tragon kragh fell upon me. A score of them, with hounds. They had expected my father to expect an ambush and flee, and sent a group out to catch him if he did. But once they had killed him, they realized I was missing, so they came after me instead. I thought myself dead, but Ogri came to me, he filled my arm with strength, and I slew them all."

Toad let out a low whistle. "You killed a score of Tragons? Even though they were lowland kragh, that's a bit hard to believe."

"Not with Ogri guiding my blade. The bodies still lie by the lake. If anyone doubts me, they can climb up there and see for themselves."

Toad shrugged, allowing the point to pass. "Go on."

"Ogri spoke to me then, told me that my father was dead and that I had to collect World Breaker for myself. That just as his blood had run in my father, it ran in me. So I gathered myself and climbed the Dragon's Breath, climbed till I gained the Valley of the Dead, and there between the Five Peaks I found Jaermungdr frozen with Ogri's body by his side, looking but asleep, covered by the thinnest layer of snow. I stood before them beneath the stars and there I found World Breaker, clutched still in Ogri's hand. With reverence I took it, prayed to the Sky Father, and then Ogri sent a wyvern for me to ride down into the valleys below."

"He sent you a wyvern?"

"Yes. He did. I rode its shoulders all the way down, but my injuries were too many, and I fell from its back. That's how I was able to get down here so fast."

Toad sat back on his heels, chewing the insides of his lips. "So you're descended from Ogri, who helped you in a fight and told you to get World Breaker, because with it you would unite all the tribes."

Tharok nodded. "That's the short of it."

"Well, if Ogri said that's your destiny, what are you doing naked and upside down?"

Tharok grinned at him, baring his tusks. "I'm not dead yet. My fate is not yet sealed."

Toad nodded slowly, rubbing at the underside of his chin. "Well, what proof do you have of all this? Barring somebody climbing all the way up to the Dragon's Tear to look for Tragon bodies?"

"The blade itself," whispered Tharok. "World Breaker has returned to us out of legend. It's been hidden for who knows how many years. Do you think it an accident that I should find it? No, Ogri guided my hand. It was my destiny to find the blade, Toad. Fate. These are the words of the hour."

Toad nodded again, absorbing all this, eyelids lowering. "Ogri's blood. It has a good ring to it. The blade is indeed here. Still, I don't know."

Tharok took a deep breath. "You're wise to have doubt. But I'll give you one more piece of proof. Let it slip to Wrok that you've heard from a stranger who just passed by—say he's a member of the Little Spider tribe—that a hunting party of Tragon kragh have been found dead in the high slopes, but a survivor is being brought down to the Red River camp to tell all that happened. Watch his face. He'll not welcome the news. Watch him panic. He'll send Krol with some kragh to intercept the Tragon. You know why he'll do this, Toad?"

Toad shook his head, mystified.

"Because he will want that Tragon killed. He can't afford to allow it to reach our camp. Because then it would speak of Wrok taking the Tragon shaman stone to set up my father's death, and will reveal him to be a Tragon lackey, no true highland leader."

"How do you know this?"

"Ogri's blood flows in my veins, little Toad. I know many things. Run my test, and watch Wrok's face. See if it is the face of a noble chieftain or a panicked lickspittle."

Toad rose to his feet. "And if he does what you say, what will that prove?"

"It will prove, my good friend, that there was indeed a Tragon hunting party in the high slopes. That Wrok knew of them, and that they hunted me. That he was in on my father's murder, and that my tale is true."

Toad thought that over some more, taking a few steps away, muttering to himself. "The Tragon. Your father. Wrok. A hunting party chasing you, which you killed. Ogri giving you the blade, World Breaker itself, here today amongst us. You, a descendent of Ogri." He tapped his chin and looked cautiously at Tharok. "If this is true, then, well, I'm sorry about tickling your nose with the feather."

Tharok relaxed, allowing himself to smile, "It's nothing, Toad. Now go, run my test. See what Wrok does. Tonight is the mating feast, is it not?"

"Yes." Toad looked glum. "The greatest of the Red River kragh will impress the women and take them to mate. We're also celebrating Wrok's claiming of the sword."

"Then tonight, if Wrok fails my test, tell my story to all the Red River kragh just as I told it to you."

Toad ran that through his mind and grinned. "You're a sly one, Tharok, you are. I always thought you as dumb as Krol, but if I do that, if I tell them all your tale, then things will get interesting."

"I told you," said Tharok, closing his eyes once more. "My fate is not yet sealed."

CHAPTER SEVENTEEN

ISKRA

The night was growing late. The feast in the great hall had lasted for many hours, but now at long last the toasting and innumerable courses were over. The notables from Emmonds had ridden home, the knights and their squires had retired to their tents, and only the servants now remained, cleaning and scrubbing and undoing all signs of the evening's festivities.

Iskra stepped into the Lord's Hall with a sigh. If only her night were done. What she wouldn't do to escape to her chambers, to fall into her great bed and pull the covers over herself, to close her eyes and drift away into sleep...

She'd seen no sign of Kethe since leaving the tourney field. Trapped by her responsibilities as the hostess, she had sent Hessa to search for her daughter, but to no avail. That look of terror she'd seen in Kethe's eyes when Tiron had taken off his helm had struck her to the quick. Should she have refused to swear that oath of silence to Tiron? Or simply broken it? Erland would have sworn that oath and not cared how much it hurt anyone if it garnered him an important advantage. Was that the sign of a strong leader, then? A willingness to hurt others for the greater good? These questions and others swarmed in Iskra's mind like bees around a disturbed nest. She wanted to find Kethe, sit with her, take her hands and explain why she had done what she had done. Make her understand. Ask her forgiveness.

Others followed her into the hall as she mounted the dais and sat on her white oaken chair. Lord Laur stopped just below her, dressed in a formal black outfit trimmed with gold. Ser Kitan Laur was there as well, dressed all in white with a half-robe falling rakishly just shy of his hips. The twin knights, Ser Cunot and Ser Cunad, and Lord Laur's priest, Father Elisio, were standing to one side. Her contingent was composed of Ser Wyland, the wounded yet adamant Ser Asho, and Master Bertchold.

Iskra set a sweet smile on her face and leaned forward. "Well, my good Lord. The hour is late, and our brave knights are no doubt wearied by their full day. What matter needed so urgently to be discussed tonight?"

Lord Laur smiled and spread his hands. "Please, Lord Laur is too formal. Call me Mertyn." He waited for Iskra to incline her head. "These are dangerous times, my dear Iskra. Every hour is precious. A terrible foe stalks our lands, wielding illicit magics. I've heard that even now the Agerastians are besieging the coastal city of Otran, but word is that the Grace disbanded his forces upon reaching Ennoia and retreated through the Solar Gate to Aletheia, only to change his mind and issue a summons for a new host with which to alleviate the siege. Our losses were so grave, however, that I've heard that precious few are flocking to his banner."

Mertyn paused, as if hesitating over continuing a distasteful line of conversation. "Should Otran fall, the Agerastians will gain a foothold on the mainland and cease to be a mere band of roving marauders." He began to pull off his black leather gloves, one finger at a time. "They shall gain a permanent foothold from which to launch future attacks." He glanced up at her almost idly. "Otran is not far from Castle Kyferin, is it? I wonder where their first attack shall fall? Surely you understand why I press for haste?"

Iskra inclined her head. "You are wise to the ways of the world, and I agree. These are perilous times. All the more reason for me to rejoice in our alliance. Family must stand together. With your and Lord Lenherd's support, I know that my lands are safe."

Mertyn nodded and stepped forward. "I couldn't have spoken truer words, dear Iskra. The closer we stand, the stronger we are. That is why I raced here upon receiving word of my dear, dear brother's passing. Without his Black Wolves, you are... terribly vulnerable. I've seen no more than fifty soldiers guarding your walls. You have—what—a half-dozen knights? Most of whom are now injured due to today's tourney?"

Iskra felt a cold pool of dread coalesce in the bottom of her stomach, and though she allowed her smile to fade, she kept her expression amicable. "You perhaps underestimate our strength, but near enough. No doubt you now understand the value of our alliance."

"Oh, to be sure." Mertyn smiled and stepped closer again. "Were these other times, I would approach my proposition with greater tact and discretion. Some might think it unseemly, given how recently bereaved you are, but as I said, these are dangerous times, and we must look to the safety of our families, our children, our wards."

The pool of cold hardened into ice, and Iskra stiffened. She willed him to stop. To speak no more. Instead, he smiled and reached up to take her hand.

"Dear Iskra. Long have I admired you from afar. You are wise, courageous, and surpassingly beautiful. You wield great wealth, but have not the means to defend your holdings. I, on the other hand, have that force, and in plenty. The twenty knights whom I have brought here with me are but a token of the might I can assemble. Together we can unite our lands, restore order and soothe all doubts. Together we will be the strongest couple in the land, and all shall tremble at our passing."

His smile never reached his eyes. "Before those gathered here, I ask that you unite your life with mine, that we both seek Ascendancy together as man and wife, to support and ennoble each other, to the betterment of the land and our people." He paused, then raised her hand farther, as if to kiss its back. "Will you be my wife?"

Iskra sat frozen. She felt like an image caught in glass. The slightest motion would cause everything to shatter. She stared down at Mertyn's face and felt nothing but repulsion. As much as she'd despised Erland, his younger brother Mertyn would be infinitely worse. There was a darkness to him that she couldn't fathom, a cruelty that she had only seen hints of.

Slowly, with great care, she drew her hand from his own. "I am sorry, Lord Laur. This proposal comes too soon. I must ask that you give me time to grieve for my late husband and your brother."

Mertyn hesitated, then gave a small shrug and stepped back. "A most honorable request."

Iskra allowed herself to relax for but a moment. If she could buy time, she could perhaps string him along for a season, enough time perhaps for her to regain her strength...

"Unfortunately, I need an answer tonight." He smiled sweetly. "Hence my insistence on this meeting. So. Yes? Or no?"

Ser Wyland took a step forward. "My Lord, you overstep yourself. Nobody gives my Lady orders within her own castle."

Mertyn didn't even turn; he kept his gaze on Iskra. They locked eyes. She saw in his own a resolution that chilled her. To say yes would be awful. But to say no? What would that portend?

Everybody was watching her. She saw Kethe standing in the shadows of the doorway, eyes wide with horror. She forced herself to think of her lands, her distant properties, the amount of time it would take to raise an armed force, the proximity of the city of Otranto, her duty to safeguard her people, what it would feel like to be kissed and caressed by her brother-in-law.

"No, Lord Laur." She stood. "I will not take you as a husband. I find your demands insulting and verging on extortion. Shame on you."

Mertyn sighed. "As I feared. Still, it was worth the attempt. My Lady, it is with sincere regret that I must inform you that Lord Lenherd and the rest of my family are deeply concerned with your son's wellbeing during these dangerous times. We have all agreed that you are not fit to protect him from danger, and thus it is with great reluctance that I have agreed to make him my ward until he comes of age."

Iskra felt anger flare up within her. "Your ward? By what right? I don't care what you and the rest of your family believe, he is my son! He shall remain safe here at Kyferin Castle. How dare you! I knew you to be ambitious, but you presume too much!" She felt enraged, alive, regal and alarmed. "I must ask that you and your men quit the castle immediately. You are no longer welcome here."

Mertyn's smile never disappeared. He drew off his second glove, tugging neatly at each fingertip. "My, but you are a little slow. Perhaps you've had too much wine? No matter. Why on earth would I ever quit Kyferin Castle? I take my duty to your son most seriously. My men are fully prepared to defend him, even now, at any cost."

Ser Wyland drew his blade, only to be matched immediately by Ser Laur and the twins.

Iskra threw up a hand. "Stop! What madness is this? What are you saying, Mertyn?"

"What I am saying, my dear Iskra, is that the situation has changed." He stepped up onto the dais. "I have twenty knights and over forty loyal soldiers within your walls. They are all in position and are prepared to do violence to defend your son." He rounded the great cherry wood throne and sat. "Effective at this moment, I am the new Lord of Kyferin Castle." He leaned back, testing the chair, then turned to smile at her again. "It is, I am sure you will agree, for the best."

"You bastard," whispered Iskra. It galled her how neatly she'd been duped. Her mistake had been to underestimate how brazen Mertyn could be. "I will appeal to the Ascendant's Grace. I shall return with his Seven Virtues at the head of a new army and destroy you."

"Oh, come, come. I have already sent a messenger to the Grace promising him knights, funds, and whatever else he might need from both your lands and mine. Do you really think he will waste his energies on removing me, with the Agerastian threat so dire? Of course not. He will thank me and most likely reward me for my generosity." He sighed and waved his hand. "Please, spare us all the theatrics. This is done. You have no hand to play. Of course, you could order your knights to their deaths, but that would make you a traitor and I would have to hang you come morning in front of your son. You wouldn't want to force me to do that, would you? Make him watch as you danced and urinated on yourself at the end of a rope?"

"You make me sick," said Iskra.

"Of course, it's not too late to accept my offer." Lord Laur's smile turned dark. "Though now you're going to have to beg."

"Never." She resisted the urge to spit in his face. She turned to Ser Wyland and Ser Asho, both of whom had their blades out. "Sheath your weapons." They hesitated, but then Ser Wyland grimaced and did as he was told, followed moments later by a reluctant Asho.

"Disarm them," said Mertyn with a lazy wave of his hand. "Let's remove all temptation for folly, yes?"

"You know I'll never serve you," said Iskra. "Nor will my men. What do you intend to do with us? Keep us in a dungeon until my son turns of age?"

"No, that would be tiresome and bad for my image. You are now a Lady Dowager. It is only proper that you retire with dignity to a distant property. Perhaps you could take up a new hobby. Find a way to pass the time."

Iskra snorted. "You're a fool as well as a madman."

Mertyn examined his nails. "Well, I thought it a generous offer. Of course, I get to pick which property you'll retire to. No sense in placing you where you'll cause mischief, is there? Which is why I've hit upon the perfect solution. An ancient and respected holding of your family, rich with history and character. A little isolated, but that's not so bad. Of course, you'll have to leave tonight. An abrupt departure, but I would hate to waste a month."

Iskra had thought herself inured to further shock. "You wouldn't dare."

"No?" He sat up. "You can't really be surprised. Look at it from my point of view. Tell me it's not a perfect solution."

"Mythgræfen Hold is a ruin."

Mertyn sighed. "Well, I'm sure you will spend no small amount of energy in changing that, won't you? Think of it as a project. The very hobby I mentioned before."

Iskra took a step toward him, and Ser Laur's blade flicked up in alarm. She looked at him in disgust and he lowered his blade. Slowly, she turned back to Mertyn. "You know the legends that surround those stones. You know it's dangerous. Your sending us there is a death sentence."

Impatience flickered across Mertyn's face, and he scowled. "Enough. I said no dramatics. Yes, it is in poor condition, and yes, it's never been successfully held for long, but you shall change that history with determination and lack of options. Now, I am not a cruel man. I'll let you take whomever will agree to go with you, along with what furnishings and food supplies you can carry. You have until midnight to prepare. The Lunar Gate will remain open for only five minutes. Anything or anyone that gets left behind will find gainful usage at my hands. Am I clear?"

Iskra stared down at him and tears filled her vision. The reality of what was happening hit her like a slap. He was taking her sweet boy. "Please. Don't do this. Don't take my son."

"Enough!" He stood and turned away. "You have less than an hour. Gather your people and belongings. Kitan, follow me. We're going to secure the boy." He turned back sharply. "I have been more than civil. Any nonsense from here on out will be punished with the blade. Am I absolutely clear?"

Iskra felt gutted. Tears ran down her face, but she refused to let her expression crumple with the grief she was feeling. "Oh, yes. More than clear." She stared at him, feeling impotent and furious. A great and terrible certainty arose within her. "This is not the end, Mertyn. You're making the gravest mistake of your life. By my hope of Ascension, I swear it. You'll rue this day."

Mertyn shook his head and gestured. His son hurried after him, but both froze at the whisper of a sword being drawn. Kethe stepped out to block the stairs. "You'll lay hands on Roddick over my dead body."

Kitan immediately stepped in front of his father, his own blade rising to stop an inch from her own. His smile was grim.

"Stop this foolishness, niece." Mertyn's voice was sharp. "Do you think you can defeat every single knight and soldier in the castle before they can start killing your servants and friends?"

"You sick, twisted bastard," said Kethe, her voice low.

"Yes, yes, get it out of your system. Then step aside. Otherwise I'll send Ser Cunad to give a certain signal, and the killing will begin. How many deaths will it take before you lay down your blade? Five? Ten? Twenty? I'll have them bring in the heads if you don't believe me."

Kethe grimaced, a spasm of true pain twisting her features. "He's just a boy."

"I know." Something seemed to soften within Mertyn. "He is my nephew. My blood. I will treat him well. I swear you that." He raised his hands and stepped past Kitan, right up to her blade. "He's an innocent, and I promise he'll remain such. But lay down your blade. Don't cause more suffering. This is now inevitable."

Kethe bit her lower lip and took her sword with both hands. Iskra felt her heart come close to breaking. "Kethe," she whispered. "Please. This will only make it worse."

Kethe slowly lowered her sword and surrendered it to Kitan. He grinned—then he slammed his fist right into her solar plexus. She didn't even cry out, just crumpled to her knees, gasping.

Asho let out a cry of anger and rushed forward, unarmed, but stopped short when Kitan spun and raised his blade. "Down, Bythian dog." Kitan smiled coldly. "Or better yet, give me cause to open your stomach."

Mertyn stepped forward and backhanded Kitan across the cheek, causing his head to snap around. "She is your blood! How dare you?"

"She raised her blade to me," whispered Kitan, turning back slowly to face his father, tongue probing out to taste the blood that ran down his lip. "Nobody does that without consequences."

"Get up there," said Mertyn and shoved his son toward the steps. "Get out of my sight." He hesitated as Asho knelt by Kethe's side, face twisted in annoyance, and then turned to Iskra. "You have less than one hour. Go." Then he too began to climb the stairs.

Iskra sank back into her seat. Ser Cunad and Cunot remained, faces hard, swords drawn. She studied them, then looked at Master Bertchold. "Summon the castle staff and soldiers to the bailey. Have them assemble in the next ten minutes. I will speak with them."

Kethe finally inhaled with a shuddering gasp and sat up.

"You," said Ser Wyland, pointing at the twins, "are scum."

Both men slitted their eyes and twitched their blades.

"What?" Ser Wyland stepped forward. "Are you going to cut me down for speaking the truth? That would be fitting for cowards like you. Scum. I've shat out nobler pieces of excrement than you two." He towered over them both. "Go on." His voice was a harsh growl. "Prove yourself men."

"Enough," said Iskra, rising to her feet. "Ser Asho, help Kethe down to the bailey. Ser Wyland, gather Ser Tiron and whichever other knights are willing to listen. I'll be down shortly."

"Where are you going?" Kethe's voice was breathless.

Iskra stared up the steps. "To see my son. If Laur thinks he can keep me from him, he's going to have to cut me down. Now go."

She climbed the steps and pushed open the door to her solarium. Roddick was standing with his back to the wall, a dagger in his hand, staring at Kitan, who was smiling in amusement, sword sheathed. "Mother!"

"Put the knife down, Roddick."

Lord Laur nodded to her. "Thank goodness. Is your entire family given to hysterics? Tell him the facts of the matter. I'll give you five minutes." He stepped outside and Kitan followed, pulling the door closed behind him.

Roddick ran across the room into her arms. She knelt to hug him and held him tight, burying her face in his neck. She inhaled his scent deeply, the warm, clean smell of his hair. It went right through her, and she nearly came undone.

He gripped her tight, then pulled back. "What's happening? What did Uncle Laur mean, you're going away without me?"

She smiled at him, a broken smile, and smoothed his thick hair back. Love blossomed within her, breaking down her self-control, shattering her walls. He'd grown so fast. She could still see the baby he had been within his face, the little boy he'd been just a short while ago. That, truly, he still was. "Oh, Roddick. My darling boy. You're going to have to be brave. You're going to have to be very strong and very brave for your mother."

"Is it true?" His voice grew higher. "Are you leaving?"

She took his little hands and brought them to her lips. They were growing, losing the baby fat that had encased them and made them so delightfully pudgy. The dimples over his knuckles had finally disappeared. She turned his hands and kissed his palms, then smiled as best she could again. "Yes. I don't have a choice, but it won't be forever. I promise."

"I don't want you to go." He frowned at her, eyes growing liquid with tears. "You can't go."

"Oh, my darling boy." She pulled him in tight again. This was worse than anything; this was like tearing herself in half, ripping her body from left shoulder to right hip. Her love for him went to her core, and leaving him felt like tearing out a tree by the roots, feeling each and every tendril rip out of her soul. "Please. Be strong. I don't have a choice. Do as your uncle says. Listen to him, but remember." She pulled back and stared hard at him, giving him a soft shake. "Remember. He is not your friend. Never trust him. Do as he says, but never, ever trust him. Wait for me. I'll come for you. I promise."

"Noooo!" he said, voice rising to a wail. "I don't want you to go!"

She closed her eyes and hugged him again. She wanted to press him into her body, carry him away with her as she had once borne him for nine months. What kind of world could do this? "I love you, and you will be strong, and I will come back, and when I do you will tell me all the wonderful things you have done and seen, and we will be happy." She held his body against her own, feeling his every bone, feeling how vulnerable and defenseless he was. "Yes? Tell your mother yes."

"No." He stared at the ground. "No. No no no."

"Shh," she said. "Here." She took her pendant from around her neck and handed it to him. "Keep this somewhere secret and safe. And whenever you miss me, just look at it, and know that you are in my heart and I love you more than the world. All right?"

He blurred as the tears filled her eyes, but she saw him close his hand around the pendant. "All right."

"Good." She wiped at her face briskly with the blade of one hand. "Now, I don't have any more time. I have to go. Remember what I told you. Don't trust Uncle Laur or any of his men, but do as they say until I return." She stood and looked down at him. "Will you do that?"

"Can I still tend the pigeons?" His face was pale, a red dot on each cheek.

She laughed, a shuddering sound that was weak and tender and shot through with pain. "Yes. Of course. Now go to bed. It's late. Come on." She led him to his little cot set beside her own large bed, and laid him down, pulling his blanket over him.

"Will you tell me a story?"

"How about a song?" She crouched beside him and stroked his hair.

"The one about the clever little fox," he said.

"Yes. Just like you. My clever little fox."

So she stroked his hair and sang him his favorite lullaby, and by the time Lord Laur opened the door again, Roddick was fast asleep, his eyelashes lying on his cheeks like thick, dark snowflakes.

Iskra stood and crept away so as not to wake him, then turned to face Lord Laur. "If you harm him–if you hurt a single hair on his head—"

"You have my word as family that I shall treat him honorably." Lord Laur's face was grave. "I admit that I am taking advantage of you, but you are an adult. He is a child. I shall see to it that he is loved as if he were my own son."

"I've seen how your son turned out. Spare me that fate."

Laur's expression turned hard. "Forty minutes until the Gate opens, my Lady. You'd better run."

Iskra stepped to the door and turned back for one last look at her son. She stared at him, engraving the sight of him sleeping peacefully in her mind. Then she took a deep breath, turned, and descended quickly down the stairs.

CHAPTER EIGHTEEN

TIRON

Ser Tiron stood in his room in the Stag Tower. It was barren, containing only a cot and an armature on which his rusted armor hung. Frigid air was unspooling into the room through the arrow slit, though after his years spent in a cell that bothered him little.

He stood by the window, holding his blade across his other palm. The light of the full moon set his sword to gleaming. He turned it slowly, causing the faint ripples in the steel to shine. His ancestor had earned it on some bloody battlefield in the service of Aletheia during the Unification. His reward for his deeds that day had been to select any blade he liked from the Ascendant's private armory. Each successive Ser Tiron had wielded this sword in battle, never losing it or their honor... up until Lord Kyferin had taken it from him.

Six guards had wrestled him to the ground. He'd bellowed like a stuck bull, the sounds he made tearing his throat as he fought them. Hands on his hips, Lord Kyferin had stood watching and smiling. Six men had fought to pull Tiron down, and still he'd found the strength to take a step forward, and then another. He'd wrenched every muscle in his neck, back, thighs and hamstrings. But he'd fought on, this very sword gleaming in his hand. He'd taken a third step, and then a seventh man had piled on, and he'd been driven down to his knees. His cries had been terrible. He'd fought his way back up to both feet, had taken a fourth step, and then collapsed. He'd been pinned to the ground on his back.

Only then had Lord Kyferin approached. The sun had been bright behind his head. Hoarse shouts and sobs had come from the caravan as Kyferin stood over him, smiling. "Death's too easy an escape for traitors like you. You mark my words: I'm going to petition the Ascendant himself for the right to open the Black Gate and throw you through it. You're going straight to hell, Tiron. Until then? You'll rot." Then Kyferin had placed his boot on Tiron's wrist and pressed down until Tiron had been forced to release his sword.

Kyferin had knelt to take the blade, and in doing so brought his face close to Tiron's ear. "I strangled her even as I took her. To this day, I don't know if she died before I came."

Madness had descended. Tiron shuddered as he recalled the snap. He'd heard it, within his mind, within his soul, a sound like the sundering of a dry twig. He'd broken right there and then, had bucked and heaved and screamed. Lord Kyferin had laughed and walked away, Tiron's family blade resting over his shoulder. Moments later, someone had started punching him in the face, over and over, but it didn't seem to do any good. The pain was distant and irrelevant. Finally they'd resorted to kicks, and the world had gone black.

Ser Tiron turned the blade over and fought a shudder. After that day, the world had turned monochrome. He'd lived on with the slim hope that fate might give him a chance at revenge. It was the only thing worth living for. Honor, love, wealth, joy—all of that was ashes. All that remained was Lord Kyferin's smiling face, and a base, bestial need to crush it.

The sound of voices filtered in from the stairwell. Ser Tiron sheathed his blade and turned as his door was shoved open. Ser Kitan Laur stood there, his plate armor refulgent in the candlelight, four Laur soldiers behind him. "Ser Tiron. May I have a word with you?"

Ser Tiron kept his hand on the pommel of his sword. "No. Piss off."

Kitan smiled and stepped inside. "I see captivity has done wonders for your eloquence, but I must insist. One moment is all I ask. You'll find it worth your while."

Ser Tiron rocked back on his heels. "You're a worm, Kitan. Before I might have kept that opinion to myself, but now I see no reason not to speak my mind. You're a boot-licking, crotch-sniffing, spineless worm. Get out before I take off your head."

A vicious expression of contempt and amusement crossed Kitan's face, and he drew his own blade. "Watch yourself, old man. You might have been a threat before you were thrown in that hole, but now? Don't make me laugh."

"Let's find out, shall we?" Ser Tiron drew his sword.

"No, I'd rather not. It would be ignomious to cut you down in your own bed chamber. Of course I could challenge you for killing Ser Bero, but the man was little more than a beast. I don't think anyone will miss him. No, I'm serious about giving you a message. Or have you forgotten your dead wife so quickly?"

The lazy smile died on Ser Tiron's face, and his glove creaked as he tightened his grip on his sword. "Well, now." His voice turned soft. "Now I'm going to really enjoy this."

Kitan sighed and raised his hands. "Diplomacy has never been my strong suit, though you've made this encounter far more difficult than it should have been. Lady Kyferin has been banished. I assume you plan to go with her?"

Ser Tiron nodded slowly.

"As I thought. And I can guess why. My father and I know the truth about what happened to your late wife and son. Lord Kyferin spoke of it one night while in his cups. I'll tell you straight: Lord Laur was sickened." Kitan watched Tiron closely. "I can't imagine what you must have gone through, and I know you don't want my pity. So here's my point: you want revenge. Of course you do. Why else follow Kyferin's bitch into banishment? Any true man would want what you want—vengeance. When you kill her and her daughter too, Lord Laur will consider you a friend. You'll be welcomed into his service should you seek it, or given your own plot of land and left alone." He paused. "Am I being clear?"

Ser Tiron sneered. "Only too clear."

"There's one thing I can't figure out," said Kitan. "Why did Iskra let you out? She must know you're untrustworthy. That you'll want revenge."

Ser Tiron sheathed his blade. "Maybe she believes in redemption."

"Redemption?" Kitan considered the thought, then laughed. "Tell me she's not so naive. By the Ascendant. Women! Now, what shall I tell Lord Laur?"

The nature of Ser Tiron's stare cased Kitan to stiffen. "Tell him that I don't want or need his protection or support. What I'll do, I'll do for myself alone. Now get the hell out of here."

"Good enough," said Kitan cheerfully. "As long as you get it done." He stopped at the door. "Just don't turn soft. Remember your dead wife and son if you start feeling any sympathy for the bitch, yes?"

Tiron took a step forward. "Stupid boy. You should not have said those words." His grin was sickly and he felt feverish. "Come back in here. I've a deep yearning to kill you. I'd like to plant my boot on your chest and pull off that yapping jaw of yours, tear it free and then grind my boot in your bloody gullet. You ready?"

Kitan's smile vanished. "Watch yourself."

"No? Too scared? Then get out," said Tiron. "The sight of your face makes me sick, and that takes some doing."

Kitan glared at him. "If my father didn't want you alive—"

"You mewling, cowardly toad, GET OUT!"

In a flash Ser Tiron had his blade in hand and swung it down with all his strength at the wide-eyed Kitan, who leaped back and slammed the door closed. Tiron's sword thunked into the old ironwood and stuck there, quivering.

Tiron groaned and backed away. He pressed his knuckles into

his eyes. His head was pounding. He turned and stumbled back to his cot, where he sat heavily, fighting the throbbing waves of grief and fury that threatened to drown him. He saw Sarah's face, heard Kyferin's laughter, and all he could do was writhe impotently with no outlet for his fury. How could Kyferin be dead? How could the Ascendant have robbed him of his vengeance? He roared and stood and threw himself at the wall, crashing into it and then leaning against the cold stone, gasping as he fought back the tears he hated so much.

Any true man would want what you want. Vengeance.

Kitan's words rung in his mind like the peal of a bell. Tiron grew still, staring blindly at the stone as he pictured Iskra and Kethe. He thought of Sarah, of his son. Heard Kyferin's laughter again, and stood.

He'd vowed revenge on Lord Kyferin while rotting in his dungeon, a revenge so total and annihilating that it had animated his every breath, had driven him to go on living long after his Sarah had been lowered into the ground. Kyferin was gone, but he could still have his vengeance.

Turning, he walked slowly to the door, feet dragging, and wrapped his fingers around the hilt of his sword.

Vengeance.

With a sharp yank he tugged it free.

CHAPTER NINETEEN

AUÐSLEY

A pounding on Audsley's door awoke him with a cry. He wrestled with his sheets and blanket, kicking and struggling, and heard Aedelbert's indignant *mrhaoi* as he leaped to the floor. He reached out in the dark for his nightstand where his spectacles lay, almost knocked them over, then rose to one elbow and placed them on his nose. With the shutters pulled and thick curtains hanging over the windows, the room was muffled and dark. Sitting up, heart pounding, he called out, "Who is it?"

The door cracked open, ruddy torchlight spilling in behind the guard. "Apologies for waking you, Magister, but everyone's being summoned to the bailey. Lady Kyferin's command. Right now, like." Then he pulled the door shut and plunged Audsley back into darkness.

"Now? Wait! Are we under attack?" He scrambled out from under his covers and hurried to the window, where he yanked aside the curtains and threw open the shutters. Immediately freezing air washed over him, but he leaned out bravely to peer at the inky landscape below. No army, no torches, no catapults being readied for an assault. Mystified, he slammed the window shut and fumbled over to pick up his candle. He knelt and held it out, and a moment later a flame flared to life as Aedelbert licked the wick. Audsley set it on his bedside table and set about getting dressed.

"Summoned to the bailey, he says. No further explanations! What am I, a magister or a groom?"

"*Mrhao,*" said Aedelbert, and hopped up onto the bed to watch him intently, his eyes catching the candlelight and flaring gold.

"Yes, quite," said Audsley. "But I do hate to cause a fuss. Regardless, we shall soon see."

A few minutes later he threw on his cloak and hurried out the door, only to turn and rush back to place the candle in a lantern and hurry back out again, only to return for his satchel, into which he threw some parchment, a spare quill, a stoppered vial of ink, and his Noussian glass. Aedelbert, having expected his various returns, waited till the last to hop up onto Audsley's shoulders and settled down comfortably.

He stepped out of the Ferret Tower into bedlam. A large crowd was gathered in the bailey, most holding candles or lanterns, swaddled in sheets or huddling together in the cold. Stumbling forward, he saw soldiers everywhere, none familiar, facing the crowd with their hands on the hilts of their swords. Knights, too. Lord Laur's men, he realized, wearing hauberks and helms.

He saw Elon the smith and hurried over. "What's going on?"

Elon had his biggest hammer with him, casually resting it over his shoulder. "No idea, Magister Audsley." The smith's voice was a barely audible rumble. "But from the look of things, nothing good."

"Oh, dear," said Audsley, pushing his spectacles back up his nose.

Aythe the baker was there, the pages and stable boys, the cooper and butler. Master Bertchold was standing beside an empty cart which was clearly going to be used as a platform from which to address the crowd. Everybody was present, he saw, including a large number of their own soldiers, some of them with cuts and scrapes on their faces and none with blades in their scabbards.

"By the Black Gate," he whispered. "The castle's been taken."

"What?" Elon hunched over. "You think?"

Audsley nodded. "Quick. What should we do?" He pressed his fingertips to his lips. "Lady Kyferin called this assembly, so she's not being held prisoner. Yet she's clearly being forced to act. Do you think—"

The muttering all around him stilled as Lady Kyferin emerged from the barbican. She looked like a vision, a thick white fur robe draped around her shoulders and hanging to her heels, a gray gown of thick wool beneath. She was accompanied by Asho and Ser Wyland, with Kethe following, all of them still in their feasting finery.

"What's going on, my Lady?" yelled a soldier.

She ignored the question and took Ser Wyland's hand as he helped her step onto the cart's wheel, then up onto its back. She stood gazing out over the crowd, her face somber. Audsley felt his dread deepen and he resisted the urge to take hold of Elon's hand.

"My friends, we are undone. Lord Laur has installed himself as my son's ward against my wishes and has demanded that I remove myself at midnight through the Raven's Gate to Mythgræfen Hold."

The crowd erupted into exclamations of shock and wonder, and Audsley saw the foreign soldiers stiffen in anticipation. Aedelbert sat up in alarm, but Lady Kyferin raised her hands and the crowd stilled.

"Lord Laur has stated that any who wish to accompany me through the Gate may do so. No one here is compelled to go, and I wish to say it plainly: I do not expect any of you to come. Mythgræfen Hold is a ruin, and all of you know its reputation. You would be following me into exile and perhaps worse." She smiled then, and that smile, broken and kind and sorrowful, pierced Audsley's heart like an arrow. "You are all brave and good people. I would not wish the dangers I am to face on any of you. So please, step forth if you wish to follow me, but know that I will rejoice at the sight of each and every one of you who choose to stay. For now more than ever we must have faith in the Ascendant. His Grace shall act as soon as he hears of this, but until then we must accede to Lord Laur's demands."

Again the angry whispers sprang up, as if the canopy of a great forest were being shaken by a stern wind. Audsley couldn't swallow. Mythgræfen Hold, known as The Doomed, where countless soldiers and knights had died and disappeared. The outpost that could not be held. People were arguing with each other, most of them looking down shamefacedly, or away altogether.

Elon started forward. Audsley startled, hesitated, and then thought to himself: *be bold!* Immediately he stepped after the smith. The crowd parted before them, falling away, and in moments Audsley found himself before the cart, staring up in fear at Lady Kyferin. She looked down upon him, and her smile near cracked his heart all over again. He felt a frisson of terror and excitement. Mythgræfen Hold! Ser Wyland, Asho, and Kethe all moved around to stand with them. Brocuff the constable stepped up along with ten other soldiers, but Master Bertchold walked away to join the great crowd that was hanging back. Marshall Thiemo was staring at the ground. Audsley peered around, trying to catch sight of Father Simeon, but couldn't see him anywhere. Ser Tiron emerged from the crowd, fully armored and growling at people who didn't move aside quickly enough. A handful of other servants joined them; Audsley recognized an undercook and a baker, along with two grooms and Elon's apprentice, Edwyn.

Lady Kyferin waited a moment longer and then looked down at the twenty or so people who had stepped forward. "You don't know what your loyalty means to me. I will never be able to thank you enough, but we've precious little time. The Gate opens soon. We must be ready. Please, gather your belongings and then meet me at the keep roof as quickly as you can."

Ser Wyland helped her down, and then she was gone. The crowd erupted in a roar of outrage.

Ser Laur leaped up easily onto the cart, which creaked dangerously under his weight. "Listen up! Lord Laur was your Lord's brother. It is right that he be Roddick's guardian, and he shall discharge this duty with all honor! By what right does he take this duty? The right born of blood! He is a fair master, and he shall see your walls safe and guarded by loyal men. Your lives will not change. The only change is that your future is now assured. Now, everyone disperse. To bed! I want this bailey cleared but for those who are fleeing through the Gate. Go!"

The crowd began to break up. Audsley stood there wide-eyed until Elon clapped him on the shoulder, causing Aedelbert to flare his wings in alarm. "Hurry, my friend. We've precious little time. Do you need help with your belongings?"

Audsley pressed his fingers to his temples. His belongings? How was he to carry everything that he needed? "Yes," he whispered. "By the White Gate, yes! Brocuff!" He hurried over to the constable, who was giving his men orders. "Please! Two of your men—by all that's sacred, I need them now!"

Brocuff hesitated and then gave a curt nod. "Janderke, Ord, help Magister Audsley."

Audsley almost wilted in relief. He knew Ord from a few card games he'd joined on the sly earlier that year in the barbican—he was a man with caustic wit—but Janderke was a hulking new guard he'd only seen about the yard. "Thank you, thank you. Now, please hurry. Follow me."

He led them up the Ferret Tower stairs to his room and threw open the door, lantern held in one shaking hand. Aedelbert flew from his shoulder to the far windowsill. Moving forward, he set the lantern on the center of the table and then stopped, despair swamping him. He needed a week to pack up, not twenty minutes, and three carts, not two pairs of arms. He turned in a slow circle, wanting to pull out his hair, and then shook himself. "All right. Quick, gather those sacks. I'll place scrolls here for you to put in them, Ord. Be careful! Janderke, I'll set out cases for you to pack. Again, by your hope of Ascension, be careful with these treasures!"

Choosing which scrolls and ledgers to take was like choosing which teeth to keep. Agonizing, he drew forth one tube only to replace it and draw another, then curse and take out both. He withdrew boxes from beneath his bed, pulled down charts from his walls and rolled them up, gathered his writing materials, five large jars of ink, his blank vellum, his personal Silver Triangle, his various lenses, his runic stones. The pile on the table mounted, and both guards strove to pack everything away in the increasingly heavy bags.

"Magister, it's time." Ord placed his second sack on the table next to the first.

"But—one moment more. I know it's here somewhere. I can't leave without—"

"Sorry, but if we don't go now, we won't be going at all." Ord swung one bag over his left shoulder, and caught the second under his right arm. "I'm heading up to the keep. Janderke?"

"Ready," grunted the other man, bear-hugging a massive and unwieldy sack to his chest.

"All right, all right." Audsley threw a random assortment of clothing onto his bed, then wrapped it all up in his covers and threw the rough sausage over his shoulder. He hurried after both men to the door, then turned to stare back at his room.

His satchel! He ran back in, threw it over his neck and picked up the lantern. So many wonders left behind. So much precious knowledge.

He ran back to the door again and stopped. He'd forgotten Amethaes' Celestial Rubric. And the Genealogies of Prim. And his Ur-crystal!

Aedelbert hopped up onto his shoulder and licked his cheek. Audsley groaned, turned, and ran down after the two soldiers, cursing Lord Laur each step of the way.

Fifteen minutes later he staggered out onto the keep roof, puffing for breath and sweating profusely despite the cold. A large crowd had gathered, carrying bags, sacks, and crates, and pushing goods piled high in the ancient keep wheelbarrows. The customary full moon guard were standing to one side, faces drawn with tension. A large contingent of Lord Laur's own soldiers along with ten of his knights were also in evidence, Ser Laur standing beside Lady Kyferin, face as cold and hard as marble. Audsley drifted forward, suddenly unsure where to stand. At the front with the other dignitaries? In the back and away from attention?

The Gate Keeper was standing to attention, hand resting just above the Gate Glass, ready to turn it the moment the Gate flickered to life. Ord and Janderke were waiting for him, and he stopped by their side before patting himself.

His satchel. It was gone.

Panic surged inside him. He knew he'd grabbed it. Where had it gone? Dumping his bedroll sausage, he searched frantically about his person. Gone! "One moment," he whispered. "Aelderbert, watch our belongings." The firecat leaped down onto his bedroll, and Audsley ran back to the staircase.

"Master Audsley!" hissed Ord, but Audsley ran on, mind spinning. He had only minutes. The strap must have finally given way under the weight of everything else he'd been carrying. Holding his candle aloft, he examined each step, casting about, knowing he had to turn back, knowing that the Gate would only be open for a few minutes. "Where are you? Where?"

He descended down to the level of the Lord's Hall, and as he approached the archway he heard a murmur of voices. Seeing his satchel lying against the landing wall, he snatched it up, and then hesitated. One of the voices was clearly that of Lord Laur. Blowing out his candle, he sidled closer to the doorway and saw the Lord in an apparent disagreement with his priest, Elisio.

Audsley hesitated, then pressed as close as he dared. He was no soft-soled creep-abouter, but he could tread quietly when necessary. The Lord's Hall was dark, lit now only by a candelabra in Elias' hand. Taking advantage of the gloom, Audsley snuck farther in, his heart pounding fit to burst, not daring to breathe.

"...I understand," Lord Laur was saying. "But that's out of the question. That's my final word on it. We'll wait till the next opening."

Elisio was scowling. "You hold them in the palm of your hand. All you need do is squeeze, and this threat is finished."

"There are forms, priest." Lord Laur looked at the man in disgust. "I'll wait the month. Then we'll proceed through the Talon, and that will be the end of it."

Audsley quivered, every ounce of him riven by fear. The priest turned to glance in his direction, and that was all the impetus Audsley needed. Bursting for air, he retreated back around the corner, satchel clasped to his chest, and raced back up to the roof.

The Raven's Gate had come alive. The space within its arch now rippled as if filled with black ink, small waves undulating over its surface. The Gate Keeper was watching the sand pour through the turned Gate Glass, face fiercely focused. Men and women were already passing through, most making the sign of the Ascendant with their hands if they were able as they took a deep breath and plunged in.

Hurrying up, Audsley heaved his rolled-up covers onto his shoulder.

"Thought you'd run out on us," said Ord, staring with wide eyes at the Gate. "Wouldn't't'veblamed you."

"No, no, just fetching one last little thing."

Aedelbert twined about his legs, clearly agitated. The crowd was thinning out. More and more were stepping through the Gate, carrying all that they could. There would be no coming back for at least a month.

Audsley felt his throat close up in fear, and he turned to smile thinly at his two men. "Well, shall we? Mythgræfen Hold awaits!"

Not waiting for their response, he clucked his tongue so that Aedelbert hopped up onto his shoulder, then strode forward, feeling as if he were stepping toward a cliff's edge with every intention of throwing himself over. Elon was just ahead of him, a massive load on one shoulder, a huge pack slung over his back, a small anvil held in one fist and the other by leather straps wrapped around it. Audsley watched the smith take a deep breath and then lower his chin and step into the ink.

Only two of Brocuff's soldiers were left, along with Ord and Janderke. "Oh," whispered Audsley, stepping up close. The ink swirled before his face. He glanced at the upturned Gate Glass. Only a minute left before the Gate closed. "My soul to the White Gate," he said, and stepped forward.

There was a slight sensation of resistance, cool and smooth, like pressing one's face into a bowl of pudding, and then he was through and stumbling on rough, rocky ground, tussocks of thick grass rising in bunches to knee height. Audsley gasped in shock and heard Aedelbert hiss in displeasure and take to the air.

"Aedelbert! Not here! Come back!"

It was no use. His firecat flitted up into the darkness and was gone. Hands clasped his shoulder and pulled him away from the Gate, leading him to one side. The same moon hung in the sky above them, illuminating a bone-white castle that reared up only a dozen paces before him. It fairly glowed in the moonlight. The wilderness seemed to be trying to reclaim it, sending swathes of dark ivy up the walls, while a great knotted oak rose up before the central gate, its canopy reaching the battlements above. The arched windows gaped darkly, hinting at an empty and cavernous interior, and Audsley saw that a deep fissure ran down the side of the far tower, causing it to list and look liable to collapse at any moment.

It was a ghostly, haunted building, its pale stone made all the more ethereal by the lichen and ivy that smothered it. The teeth of the battlements were crooked or missing altogether. A cold, cutting wind was blowing in off the lake, setting the leaves to whispering and causing him to hunch his shoulders.

"Mythgræfen Hold," he said to himself. "Known as the Doomed. Oh, joy."

An owl flew out from one of the tower windows, its wings broad and white, and swept out overhead. Audsley turned to follow its passage and gasped again, a hand shooting to his mouth. They were completely surrounded by black waters; the island on which the Hold stood was even smaller than he'd imagined. The moon shone on the stark, precipitous mountains that ringed the water on all sides. Audsley's legs felt weak. The lake was cupped as if in the palm of a giant, surrounded by peaks whose summits he couldn't see, their lower slopes looking rugged and furred with thick trees, the upper masses ridged and glittering whitely with ice and snow.

"Steady, Magister," said Elon, placing a hand on his shoulder.

"Oh, my. I'd seen the maps, of course, and even read some accounts, but seeing it for one's self, it's a completely—well. An utterly different experience." He smiled tremulously up at the smith. "Not the most welcoming of locales, is it?"

Elon snorted. "It's got atmosphere. Come on. Let's see about getting ourselves situated. For better or worse, this is home for the time being."

"Yes," whispered Audsley, nodding to Ord and Janderke to follow. He wanted to call out to Aedelbert, but didn't dare disturb the tomb-like silence.

Ser Wyland and Asho had lit torches whose flames streamed fitfully with each exhalation of the lake's wind. They were stomping through the undergrowth toward the central gate, rounding the large tree, swords glittering as they used their blades to part the brush. Lady Kyferin was standing with her daughter, both of them ringed by Brocuff's guards, while the others huddled close by. Turning, Audsley felt his stomach sink; the Raven's Gate was dead, and the world could once again be seen normally through its arch.

A month. A month till the next full moon.

Elon lowered his gear to the dirt, the anvil thudding against the earth. "Edwyn, stand watch."

His apprentice, already showing the signs of the broad shoulders and massive forearms of a smith, nodded and stepped closer.

"Where are you going?" Audsley had never felt panic and curiosity at the same time.

Elon hefted his massive hammer. "Those knights might need a hand if they find something. I'll tag along."

"Oh, me too," said Audsley, dumping his covers onto the dirt and nodding to Ord and Janderke. "Could you keep watch? Thank you!"

Hurrying after Elon, he suddenly realized that he didn't have a weapon of any kind. Not even a letter opener. Still, he felt safer hurrying behind Elon than he did standing out in the open—and a wild desire to see what lay within the Hold had seized him.

The knights had reached the front gate, which their torchlight revealed was little more than an empty archway. Pushing his spectacles up his nose, he touched Elon's arm. "Fascinating. Note that the windows have lancet peaks, which is a strong build, but the main gate has a trefoil peak, a double arch, in essence. This place was built to withstand punishment. The walls must be terribly thick and heavy."

Elon grunted, hefting his hammer in both hands. The knights had turned at the sound of the their voices. Neither was wearing his helm, though both had taken the time to put on their plate. Ser Wyland nodded to Elon, and then swept his gaze past Audsley as if he were of no account. Audsley frowned and pushed out his chest. He wished that he had a small hammer or a stick to brandish.

Asho raised his torch overhead, and the Hold's entrance was lit warmly in pale oranges and yellows. The main arch was singed as if by fire, and the wreckage of a portcullis lay smashed asunder a few feet in.

"Will you look at that," said Ser Wyland softly.

"A battering ram?" asked Asho doubtfully.

"No." Ser Wyland stepped forward, his steel sabatons crunching on gravel. "This looks like it was torn asunder by huge hands. Look how the metal's warped. I've never seen the like."

Audsley shivered. A score of legends ran through his mind, myths from the Age of Wonders, tales of giants and fell beasts. Could their like still exist out here on the fringes of civilization? No, they were beyond the fringes. If ever there was a holdout for such beasts, it was here.

He bit his lower lip and followed his companions through the archway and into the Hold proper. The torches seemed to only make the shadows darker and whip them into a dance rather than anything else; he resisted the urge to crowd in behind Elon, and instead peered around his broad back.

They stepped out into a small, square internal courtyard. Ser Wyland and Asho raised their torches and they gazed upon the moonlit scene. A small grove of ash tree saplings had sprung up through the flagstones, their slender trunks silvered, their foliage reaching up to the second floor. The ground itself was covered in ferns, amongst which glinted traces of rusted metal, broken blades and the occasional bleached bone. Dark windows peered down at them, and numerous doorways led into the surrounding keep.

"Looks like a last stand was fought here," said Ser Wyland, moving forward cautiously. He toed a rusted cuirass. "A long, long time ago." He looked over at Audsley. "How long has it been since Mythgræfen was inhabited?"

Audsley patted at his pockets as if searching for the right text and then drew himself up. "As I remember, it's been over a century since the last attempt. Perhaps a century and a half."

Elon peered up at the ash trees. "Long enough for these to grow, at any rate."

"Wait," said Asho. "What's that?"

They all froze. Audsley tried to see what Asho was staring at, but couldn't pierce the far gloom. "What is it?"

"He's watching us." Asho drew his blade slowly. "In that corner. A small man. Pale like a Bythian, but—" He cut off, uncertain. "I don't think it's human."

Those words sent a frisson of terror down Audsley's back and he almost leaped behind Elon. A weapon! Anything! Searching amongst the ferns, he saw a rusted blade and plucked it free. A plain sword, now all but useless, its hilt gritty and rough in his palm.

Ser Wyland had oriented on the far corner, but it was plain he couldn't see what Asho was talking about. "What is it doing?"

"Watching us," said Asho. "Now it's stepping back. Right up against—no, it's going through—there must be a door there. It's gone!"

Torch held aloft, the young knight strode through the ash saplings into the far corner. Audsley followed alongside the others until Asho stopped. His torchlight showed that there was no door.

"Are you sure?" Ser Wyland stepped forward and frowned at the solid walls, then looked back to Asho.

"I—yes." Asho nodded fiercely. "I saw it. I swear to you. He was watching us. But—" He shook his head. "I don't know what happened."

"It would seem," said Audsley, tapping the wall with his rusted blade, "that it passed through the wall. Most interesting!" He felt something tug at his memory. "I've heard of something like this. In a book of children's fairy tales, I'm afraid, which doesn't lend your account much credence, but still. Can you describe what you saw in greater detail?"

Asho nodded and sheathed his sword. "It was small, about three feet in height. Muscled, with brawny shoulders and a very hunched back. A large head, covered in pale hair. It was quite ugly, with a huge nose and a broad mouth. I couldn't make out its clothing, but it seemed to be wearing a vest, pants, and boots."

"Sounds like a Bythian of some kind," said Ser Wyland carefully.

"No," said Asho. "It wasn't human."

Nor are Bythians, thought Audsley reflexively, and then he felt ashamed. "Well, from what I remember, these creatures are quite awful. They love honeyed apples, but if bothered with, they will creep up on the sleeping so as to drain their blood."

"That's cheering," said Elon. "How do they defeat them in the children's tale?"

"Ah, yes. Well, they don't. The farmer leaves his farm and his dead family behind in the keeping of the naugrim. It's one of those old tales where they thought entertaining children meant terrifying them."

"Come on," said Ser Wyland. "Enough. We'll deal with this creature when next we see it, and in the meantime we'll remain vigilant. Let's search the rest of the castle. The sooner we finish the sooner the Lady can rest. Stay close."

He led them into the keep, through one deserted room after another. There had originally been three stories, Audsley could see, but the wooden floors of the second and third floors were treacherous; only the dry mountain air had preserved them this long. Guard rooms flanked the entry tunnel, while the functions of other rooms could only be guessed at. Servants' quarters, a great hall, a kitchen, a small smithy.

Elon poked around the rusted remains, then shook his head. "Nothing of use left here."

They climbed the stone staircase, but Ser Wyland decided not to try the wooden floors. Instead they went up to the battlements. Audsley shivered and hugged himself tightly as he stepped out into the razor-sharp wind, his eyes watering as he peered down at the Lady's group below. The view was stunning. The moon was already drifting to the east, sinking in the sky. The lake was shaped like a diamond, he saw, tapering to two points while swelling out in the middle. Their island was tiny, and from the steepness of the mountain slopes as they plunged down to the waterline he could only imagine the depths of the black lake.

"What's this?" Asho had stopped beside a massive construct that beetled out over the gate, precariously set on the battlement. The others gathered around it. It looked like a vast crossbow, its arms thicker than Audsley's thighs, the rope rotted and torn. It was looked large enough to have shot Asho into the void if he'd dare lie in its central groove.

"A ballista," said Ser Wyland, ducking under it to gain the far side. "Or the remains of one."

Elon rapped its frame with his hammer. "Made from iron ash, however." He sounded pensive. "It's not badly rotted. The dry air up here has saved it, in large part."

Asho grinned, his teeth white in the gloom. "Salvageable?"

Elon hesitated. "If we were back home, with all my tools? Sure. Here? I'll have to examine it in the light of day."

"See that you do," said Ser Wyland. "Ser Asho, join me in a circuit of the walls. I want to inspect that fissure from up top."

Audsley watched their torches bob as the knights walked away and buried his chin against his chest. How were they going to reside here for a month? How could they make this dour pile of stones habitable? It would need an entire village's worth of craftsmen and masons to repair. Impossible.

Trying not to let despair swamp him, he placed his hands on a mangonel and gazed out over the silvered lake. "You've always wanted adventure," he whispered to himself. "Well, Audsley, my boy, you've finally got all that you could have asked for, and more. If only your friends back at Nous could see you now!"

A winged shape flew up out of the gloom at him, and Audsley almost let out a shriek before realizing it was his firecat. Aedelbert landed on the battlement, stalked quickly toward him and sat, presenting his back to the Magister to indicate his displeasure.

"Oh, I am sorry," said Audsley, reaching out to run his palms gently over Aedelbert's delicately feathered wings. He found the firecat's favorite spot, just below where his left wing connected with his shoulder, and gave it a good scritch. Aedelbert fought to remain aloof, then gave a sulky *mrkao* and turned to run up Audsley's shoulder and wrap around his neck.

"I know," Audsley said. "But we're together, which is something, and I promise to take care of you if you'll take care of me. Is it a deal?"

He stopped. In the very far distance, high above, something flitted across the face of the moon. He gripped the battlements, steadying himself as he strained to make out the shape. A bat? Not at that distance. No, it was something fell and vast. Audsley felt terror rise up within him. What had that been? Where, by the Ascendant's love for humanity, had the Raven's Gate taken them?

CHAPTER TWENTY

kethe

Kethe shouldered her pack roughly and fought the urge to shiver. The wind off the lake seemed to pierce her hauberk and leathers with no difficulty. Still, she'd rather die before showing any sign of weakness before Ser Tiron.

Ser. That title was a mockery. She watched him as he stood beside her mother, calm and sure of himself as if he belonged out here and not rotting in a hole. She'd spent the whole evening seething, waiting for a chance to corner her mother and demand an explanation, but then their world had imploded. Roddick. Kyferin Castle. Lord Laur. It was hard to believe. Her mind leaped from one thought to another, intense emotions washing through her without rhyme or reason: grief, panic, hatred, anger, fear. Exhaustion undercut it all; she'd expected a night of deep sleep after today's combat. Instead they'd been cast into perdition—with Tiron, her very own personal demon.

Flames appeared high up on the Hold's walls, and Ser Wyland called down that all seemed clear. The group stirred, grabbing packs and gear, and Kethe stalked forward. A strange sensation stopped her and she turned to eye the lake. The dark waters were still. Nothing disturbed their surface but the passage of the wind, but a different kind of shiver ran down her spine. For a moment she'd felt watched, and her skin had crawled with the sensation. Clenching her jaw and swallowing, she resisted the urge to draw her sword. There was no way she was going to appear like a foolish girl. Instead, she turned and hurried through the gate into the central courtyard. There, her mother was giving commands with quiet assurance. They would all camp together in the ruined great hall, where she had set the grooms to building a fire and tasked the undercook Jekil to heating some wine for the group.

Kethe stood to one side. As angry as she was, she had to admire her mother's calm. Outside their group had been on the verge of falling apart, and now people were moving with purpose, gathering fallen wood for the fire, clearing away the plants and weeds that had grown up through the cracks in the stone, laying out blankets, piling up their belongings.

Ser Wyland descended from above and smacked his hands together loudly as if anticipating a delicious meal. Striding forward, he beamed at everyone and stopped before the small fire. "Come on, boys, let's build this one nice and high. I think we could all use a little light tonight. And how else are we going to roast that whole boar that Magister Audsley brought us?"

Audsley, plump and diffident, gaped at Ser Wyland, and laughter broke out amongst the servants. Kethe couldn't help but smile as well, but then she thought of Roddick and her smile disappeared. She dumped her pack against the wall and hugged herself. What were they going to do? Molder here until Roddick turned eighteen?

Sparks flared up as several large planks were dumped across the fire, and the crackle and spit of the flames cheered her despite her resentment. Fire in the dark. Was there anything more primal?

The Hold's great hall was barely larger than the Lord's Hall; while one corner was now lit by a warm glow, the rest was shifting shadows, with thin beams of moonlight sliding down through chinks in the wall and gaps in the ceiling above. The cold was brutal, and she was terribly aware of the dark waters only a dozen paces from the Hold's wall outside.

Her mother was moving amongst those who had chosen to follow her, touching a shoulder here, sparing a kind word there. Kethe would be last, she knew, so she moved over to where Audsley was sitting on a roll of blankets and staring into the fire, absent-mindedly scratching behind the ears of his firecat, lips pursed. He glanced up at her in surprise, and then smiled and patted the roll next to him.

Pushing the hilt of her sword down so that its tip rose as she sat, she stared into the fire and watched as the flames licked up the desiccated boards hungrily. "Magister Audsley. Thank you for coming."

Audsley gave an awkward shrug. "Well, but of course. Where goes Lady Kyferin, there go I. Or something along those lines. And who else would see to it that you continued your lessons?" He smiled at her, then looked back at the flames.

"Mythgræfen Hold." She said the name softly, almost to herself. "To think we're actually here. There was a time when I was little that I very much wanted to escape through the Raven's Gate." She pursed her lips. "I was unhappy, I suppose. Father yelled at me. It's the one time I was truly scared of him." She paused, considering. "Well, one of the few times. I never made it through, obviously. But I came close, once."

She thought of that night, Brocuff hauling her kicking and screaming down to her father, and the month-long confinement to her room that had followed, along with the selling of her pony and the giving away of her pet hound.

"I'm glad you failed," said Audsley quietly. "To think."

Kethe nodded. "But coming through tonight, I realized that I know about the same that I did as a child. Children's tales. It's always just been here. But why? Why does the Raven's Gate lead to this island, and why did we build a castle here?"

Such basic questions. How had she settled for nursery tales and unquestioning acceptance for so long?

"Well, those are wonderful questions," said Audsley, interlacing his fingers over his stomach and leaning forward with a frown. His spectacles caught the firelight, and for a moment they flashed an opaque white. "Lunar Gates are rare and wondrous things. Their origin dates back centuries and centuries, to the Age of Wonders. Nobody knows why they were built, really. Why does one connect a cave to a stonecloud, and so forth? A fascinating if frustrating field of study."

Audsley subsided into thought. Kethe was used to his diversions, however, and waited patiently. Aedelbert scooted forward to the edge of the fire and inhaled a tongue of flame, hissing it in and then edging back, a puff of smoke emerging from its muzzle as it purred contentedly.

"Now, you assume your ancestors built the Raven's Gate to connect them to Mythgræfen Hold. A natural assumption, but is it a correct one? The records go back centuries, and I've read most of them, though the language grows stranger the further back you go. There was a time when the curtain wall was just logs with sharpened tips, and—well, never mind." He gave her an apologetic smile. "Kyferin Keep is old. Terribly old. It predates the Unification, and as far as I can tell, your family has always held it. But Mythgræfen Hold is even older. I believe your family originated here, and eventually made its way to Kyferin Castle. Why? I don't know. As for the original purpose of the Hold, well…" He shivered and hunched his shoulders. "It must have something to do with the destruction that was visited upon it each time your family tried to defend its walls. Whatever that purpose was, it's not been observed in centuries."

Kethe stared into the crackling heart of the fire and fought the urge to shiver as well. "And nobody knows? What attacks the castle and kills everyone?"

Audsley frowned and shook his head slowly. "There was a purging of your castle's accounts ninety-nine years ago, during the reign of the Seventh Ascendant. Lamentable, though fortunately not complete. Your great-great-grandfather apparently was driven mad with grief after losing the Hold. It is said that his son wore the mantle of the Virtue Akinetos and led the forces that protected the Hold. That for three nights he fought against a mysterious force that assailed the castle's walls, and despite his strength and ability to cleave the tops off mountains, he fell.

His father cursed the Hold and ordered the records cleansed of all knowledge as to its history and purpose. He intended that nobody return, and nobody ever did."

This time Kethe did shiver and hugged herself tightly. "Great. Now we're trapped here for a month, at least. And none of us can cleave the top off a hill, much less a mountain. Just wonderful."

Audsley gave her a lopsided smile. "With a little luck, whatever doom has been visited upon Mythgræfen Hold won't notice we're here. We'll stay quiet, figure out a way to get back, and slip away before anybody comes knocking. Or tearing down portcullises. Right?"

"Right," said Kethe, but without conviction. "Though I doubt Lord Laur has any interest in letting us return. And you know he'll have the Raven's Gate blockaded in case we try to force a return."

Audsley nodded morosely. "Yes, I think you're right." Suddenly he sat up again. "You know, I heard the strangest thing before we left. Actually, I should tell your mother. I've been meaning to. But, you understand, with all this change…" He stood. "Lady Kyferin?"

Her mother was talking quietly with Brocuff and Ser Wyland, but she looked over, an eyebrow raised. "Yes?"

"A word." Audsley gave an apologetic smile. "It might be important."

Lady Kyferin nodded. "In fact, we should all talk. Why don't you join me over here. Ser Wyland, Ser Asho? Brocuff, please ask Ser Tiron to join us."

"Mother." Kethe strode to her side and took her arm, her voice a hiss. "Ser Tiron? What are you thinking?"

Iskra looked pained and reluctant. "Oh, Kethe. I owe you an apology. I haven't found time to talk to you as I've wanted to since he revealed himself."

"You've had time to talk to everybody from the grooms to the undercook."

"Kethe." Her mother exhaled. "Do you understand how much danger we're in? How much we owe these people for following us out here?"

Kethe hated feeling like a sulking child, but she spoke anyway. "I can't believe I have to explain myself. I'm your daughter. He tried to kill me. Why by the Black Gate didn't you tell me?"

Iskra's eyes narrowed at the curse. "I vowed I wouldn't tell a soul till he was ready."

"You vowed? To him? But why?" Kethe felt tears sting her eyes. This was so unfair. Why was her mother discounting his obvious monstrosity and evil? Why was she talking so rationally about this, as if he were the equal of Ser Wyland?

"We need him," said her mother. "Now, more than ever. I will use every tool at my disposal to regain what we have lost. Do you mark me, Kethe? *Every* tool, including Ser Tiron. You have to understand. We need him."

Kethe released her arm as if she'd been stung. "Need him? *Him?* To do what? Butcher us in our sleep?"

Her mother gazed at her with such compassion and pity and regret that Kethe had to look away. "I will talk to you about this. There are parts of this story that you do not know, that your father and I hid from you. I do not deny your anger, but I must look to our survival. Please, Kethe. Trust me. Wait, and I will tell you as soon as I can why I have done this."

Kethe scowled and looked away. She had nothing to offer to her mother, nothing but her simmering fury.

A few minutes later they were seated in a small circle to one side, a new, albeit smaller fire burning merrily between them. Kethe steadfastly ignored Ser Tiron and kept her gaze on her mother, who was the only one to remain standing. Lady Kyferin waited till they had all settled and then took a half-step forward, which drew everyone's attention as effectively as if she'd clapped her hands.

"We are a small force," she began, voice soft. "But there can be no question of our loyalty."

Kethe wanted to scoff, but instead looked away. She felt her mother's stare but ignored it, staring down at her hands.

"None of you were compelled to follow me into exile. The fact that you did so means more to me than I can express. Know, then, that you have my deepest gratitude, and that your service and friendship will not be forgotten." She paused, allowing her words to sink in, then sighed. "Mythgræfen Hold is bleaker than I'd feared. We cannot repair it without outside help. And while we may now have all the time in the world, given Lord Laur's control of the Raven's Gate, that may matter little if the forces that have devastated the Hold in the past take notice of us. Magister Audsley, you are well-versed in history and Kyferin lore. Why don't you tell us what you know, so that we may all understand?"

Audsley coughed and stood awkwardly. "My Lady, before I delve into the multifarious and riveting history of the Hold—no, I mean that quite sincerely—I would like to share something that I heard as I was departing the keep." He blushed suddenly. "It was my satchel, you see. The strap had grown worn, and I had been meaning to fix it for some time now. But good intentions are worth a thousand fish in the sea, as they say in Nous, and none in the hand if they are not acted on."

Lady Kyferin raised an eyebrow, and Audsley coughed again. "Yes. To hew closely to the point, then. My satchel fell in the keep stairwell, so I hurried back to retrieve it. But, you see, while I was picking it up, and totally by accident, please let me assure you, because it's not my nature to snoop—"

"It's all right, Master Audsley," said Lady Kyferin. "What did you hear?"

"Lord Laur and Father Elisio in argument. Elisio seemed to desire immediate and violent action against us. But Lord Laur said that 'there were forms', and quite steadfastly refused. I was on the verge of feeling gladdened until he instead admonished his priest that he would wait a month, and then proceed through the Talon, and that would be the end of it." That last had all come out in a rush, and he paused as he let the gravity of his words sink in, nodding as he did so. "The Talon. That's the name of the only other fort in this region, isn't it? The one whose Lunar Gate connects to Lord Laur's castle?"

Lady Kyferin pinched the bridge of her nose, grimaced, and then visibly took control of herself and nodded. "Well, then. So much for all the time in the world. If the evils of this place don't get us, Lord Laur means to kill us as soon as his private Gate opens. I fear there is little time now for his Grace to come to our rescue."

Kethe bolted to her feet. "But why? What harm can we do, banished all the way out here? And if he means to kill us, why wait?"

Ser Tiron shrugged and leaned back on one elbow, completely at ease. "Like he said, girl, there are forms. Appearances to keep. He means to murder us, but quietly, out of sight. A cunning stratagem, really."

Kethe drew her blade and pointed it at him over the flames. "Go on. Call me 'girl' again. I'll have your tongue out before you can blink."

Ser Wyland leaped to his feet and Asho called out her name in alarm, but Ser Tiron only grinned, a vulpine drawing of his lips that didn't touch his flat, dead eyes. "Go on then, girl. Cut away."

Kethe's blade trembled over the leaping flames. Damn him. He was so relaxed, reclining there as if he couldn't care less. One side of his face was purpled and swollen, but his eyes... His eyes gleamed coldly, as if he welcomed this. As if he was daring her to proceed.

"Kethe." Her mother's voice was a whipcrack. "Stop this. Now."

So close. All she had to do was lunge over the flames and stab with her blade. He wouldn't move. On some level that she couldn't understand, she realized that he would take the cut.

Everybody was staring at her, even the servants from the other fire. She put up her blade. "Just because you came through the Raven's Gate doesn't make you an honorable man. You're a coward and a monster, and very soon I'm going to pay you back for what you did to me."

Ser Tiron nodded, eyes still gleaming darkly in the firelight. "You'll find me ready and waiting, girl. Don't you worry about that."

"Kethe! Enough!" Her mother was glaring at her with a fury so incandescent her eyes nearly blazed. "Sit down or leave this fire. Now."

Kethe sheathed her blade and almost walked away. Her whole body was shaking. She hadn't felt this worked up even at the tournament. She wanted nothing better than to spurn them all, but instead she took a shuddering breath and sat. Ser Wyland lowered himself as well, and Audsley patted her timidly on the arm.

"I freed Ser Tiron from the dungeon," said her mother, still staring at her, "knowing full well what he did. As I said, there is more to this tale than you know. But I have decided to enlist Ser Tiron to our cause, and while he is under my roof you will treat him with respect. If you cannot control your sword, I will have it taken from you. Am I clear?"

Kethe felt her face flush. Hadn't she won the tourney and saved their honor? Hadn't she proved herself a warrior? How dare her mother treat her like this!

She opened her mouth to retort, and then saw Ser Wyland's level gaze. Brocuff's face was craggy and hard as if carved from rock. Even Asho's pale eyes were flat and gauging her. She swallowed and raised her chin. She would have her revenge. But regardless of how unfair this was, she wouldn't act the child. "Fine," she said. "Continue."

Her mother held her gaze for a moment longer, then nodded. "All right. Magister Audsley, how long till the Talon's Gate opens?"

Audsley beamed. "Ask that of any other soul and you would receive a blank stare. But I am a resourceful man, and came prepared." He fairly bounced to his feet and hustled to his packs, where he rummaged amongst a collection of books before drawing forth a battered tome. "This," he said, turning around with a look of shy pride, "is Alistair's Lunar Almanac." He hurried back to the fire. "Many Gates are recorded here, including which moon phase they are tied to. A true treasure. So, let us see. The Talon." He rifled through the pages, frowning, then nodded. "Here it is. Preamble, unnecessary prolegomena, et cetera et cetera, a rather nicely executed illustration, and finally we have it. The half moon." He looked up with a proud smile, then he blinked. "Oh."

Kethe's mother sighed. "So, we have two weeks before Lord Laur sends men against us from the Talon." She took a deep breath, and uncertainty flickered across her face. "I am open to hearing your thoughts. How should we proceed?"

Ser Wyland rose slowly, almost with a sense of inevitability. "We've fifteen swords amongst us. Not enough to resist Lord Laur's men when they come calling, especially not with the Hold in the condition it's in. Come morning, we're going to have a lot of work to do. I suggest we do a full reconnaissance of the island, and then turn our attention outward. We know the Talon is downriver of us by what—a few days?"

"About a week's ride," said Audsley.

Ser Wyland nodded. "So, we look for help. Forge alliances. Are there others in this land?"

"There are," said Audsley. "But not many. There used to be mining operations up on the slopes, but no longer. Those were apparently abandoned centuries ago. There are a few villages, however. At least they're marked on a map I brought. Whether they're still there, who can say?"

"You brought a map?" Ser Wyland beamed at Audsley. "A Noussian after my own heart. We'll study it in the morning. Now, what else can you tell us about this Hold and the lands around it?"

Audsley replied, "Not much, unfortunately. Most of the records were destroyed almost a century ago in a lamentable purge. The Hold is fearsomely old, going back easily four centuries, maybe half a millennium or more. I believe it was built by Kyferin ancestors, who, when the ability to create Lunar Gates was discovered, opened one to the present location of Kyferin Castle, a convenient few days' ride from Ennoia. It was continuously held until around the Unification, at which point it was abandoned. We don't know why. I believe there were three different attempts to garrison it thereafter, but each ended with the disappearance of everybody who had been sent to man the Hold." He paused and glanced at Kethe. "Or woman it? Hold the Hold? No. Garrison it." He'd turned a deep shade of red again, and kept glancing at Ser Tiron, who was grinning like a wolf. He coughed loudly. "Regardless. Nobody has ever ridden from this land to any other known territory, and only a handful of villages and the Talon exist in this area. None are as high in the mountains as the Hold."

He paused. "Also, Asho saw what I believe to be a naugrim when we first entered the castle. I had thought such creatures the stuff of nurses' tales, but, well, Asho is adamant. As such, don't go about by yourself. They're small and quick and can pass through walls—and they have a predilection for drinking human blood. So—nasty. And in the tales they're never alone, but operate in packs. Like rats. I would suggest we place vigilant watches, and all sleep in the same room."

Ser Tiron raised an eyebrow. "Wait. Bloodsucking albino rats that can walk through walls? You've got to be shitting me."

"I, ah, am not, as you put it, uh—"

Brocuff shook himself as if coming awake. "Watches will of course be set. We'll not bother with the walls, and rather simply set guards around the perimeter of this hall. If these... naugrim can really walk through walls, I'll have a man at each corner of the hall, and not just the doors. We'll keep the fire burning. Good enough?"

"Yes," said Audsley. "I hope?"

Ser Wyland rose and stretched and turned to Lady Kyferin. "It's been a long day. But twelve hours ago, a third of our number fought in a brutal tournament. With my Lady's permission, I suggest we all turn in for the night. We've a long day tomorrow. We're going to need all the rest we can get."

Lady Kyferin had been staring away at nothing, and blinked as she focused on the group again. Her eyes were glassy, and Kethe knew with a terrible certainty that she was thinking of Roddick, alone with Lord Laur and his men. She had to be as exhausted as any of them, and beyond that, who knew how heavily the responsibility for their fates rested on her shoulders? Kethe's anger began to melt away, but then she forced herself to sit up straight. It was admirable for her mother to be concerned about her son. A pity she couldn't spare much time to think about her daughter.

Her mother smiled wanly and nodded. "Yes. Thank you, Brocuff. Rest. Tomorrow we'll convene and make specific plans. Thank you."

As the others dispersed, Kethe rose to her feet, resolute, and then moved over to her mother and sat beside her. Lady Kyferin rested her head against Kethe's shoulder and gazed into the fire, the warm hues flicking over the new lines that night seemed to have carved into her face. Kethe had never seen her like this. Always she had been vigilant, self-possessed, prepared to face any crisis. Even when facing her father at his worst, her mother had always seemed coiled and ready. Now, for the first time, she looked overwhelmed. Tired. At a loss. The sight tugged at Kethe in a way she had never felt before, and she suddenly had an intuition as to how her mother would always grow older, each day, each month, until her strength began to leave her, her mind growing vague, becoming thinner and more stooped till at last she was an old lady, and Kethe would have to be strong for her, take care of her, hold her hand at night and tell her that everything would be all right.

Given all that, her anger seemed childish. She hugged her mother tightly, and her mother finally smiled at her and kissed her cheek. "You should sleep," said Lady Kyferin. "You're battered and bruised from your first glorious fight today. How are you keeping your eyes open?"

Kethe shrugged, trying not to feel pleased by the compliment. "I don't know."

The others were moving to their separate places, some around the big fire, Ser Wyland and Asho helping each other with their armor. Ser Wyland's squire had been left behind, Kethe knew, to return his steed to his home. Asho had but recently been a squire, and it showed in how effectively he helped Ser Wyland with his armor, unbuckling and pulling off each piece with a methodical practice that was mesmerizing. Ser Wyland sat ignoring the process, his plain brown eyes reflecting the firelight, mouth pursed in thought.

Thank the Ascendant he's with us, thought Kethe.

"I'm sorry, Kethe. I should have told you." Her mother's voice was almost a murmur. "About Ser Tiron. It tore at me to keep my oath to him, but I gave my word. It was his condition. "

Kethe fought the urge to stiffen, to pull away. "I don't understand why you freed a man who tried to kill us. How can you trust him?"

Her mother sighed and turned Kethe's hand over to trace the lines in her palm. Her fingertips ghosted over the thick calluses. "How did I not notice these before?" Her voice was filled with a quiet, almost sad wonder. "This is the hand of a warrior." She gazed up at Kethe. "You don't know how proud I was of you today when you forced that worm Laur to surrender."

Kethe felt again a burst of pride that made her smile, but this time she wanted to protest and keep the focus on the monster her mother had loosed.

Her mother continued, "Do you know why I let you fight? When I thought—no, I was sure—that you would suffer?"

"Because..." Kethe trailed off. She could guess, but she wanted to hear it from Lady Kyferin. "No. Why?"

Her mother looked back down at Kethe's palm, and again traced the ridges. "I've known since the moment your father died that I would not be taking another husband. I would not be letting another man determine the course of my life and yours. Not due to some misguided loyalty to your father. You know that there was no love there." Her mother paused and gazed at her. "Don't you?"

Kethe ducked her head. Of course she knew. Deep down, she'd always sensed it. But she'd fought against that truth, denied it, told herself that all relationships were complex, that on some level her parents did love each other, in their own strange fashion. Now, she pursed her lips. Hearing her mother put it so bluntly hurt.

Lady Kyferin waited a moment, then continued, "I swore not to take another man as my Lord because I *could*. Because I knew I had it within me to do what was most important, which was to care for my family and my servants and be the leader I knew they needed."

Kethe opened her mouth to make the obvious response, but managed to close it just in time. Her mother noticed, of course, and her smile was touched by an element of self-mockery. "I know. Look at where that determination has got us. Banished and out-maneuvered in the blink of an eye. But I swear to you, Kethe, we're not done yet, and I mean to bend every ounce of my being toward regaining what I've lost. We women have within us a depth, a capacity for striving, that men for all their swords and wars don't comprehend. We can endure where they are brittle, we can persevere where they snap. It is our own unique form of grace. And we will endure. We will persevere." She closed Kethe's hand into a fist and cupped it with both of her own. "And one day we will return to Kyferin Castle, rescue Roddick, and retake what is ours."

Kethe couldn't breathe. She could only nod, knowing in that moment her mother was speaking from the depths of her soul with a certainty that rang like a bell. While her mind might doubt, her heart heard and resonated.

"Which is why I let you fight," said her mother, reaching up to curl a strand of hair behind Kethe's ear. "I knew it was dangerous, more dangerous that you could imagine. I've borne witness to the consequences of swordplay my whole life. Yet I saw in your eyes that same determination to take control of your destiny. How could I deny it to you, no matter my misgivings, when I was seeking the same independence?" Now her mother's smile turned fond and a love shone in her eyes that made Kethe feel a little girl again. Tears came to her eyes and she returned her mother's smile, laughing huskily under her breath. "I know Ser Tiron's attack marked you. It marked us all, more deeply than you could know. That was when the last vestiges of respect for your father died within my breast." Her mother paused. "Do you know why Ser Tiron attacked us?"

"Father insulted his honor," said Kethe. It had been a subject nobody would speak of to her, one she hadn't really wanted to shed any light on. It was so much easier to hate somebody when they could be reduced to black and white.

"Oh, yes, that he did." Her mother hesitated and looked away, frowning at the fire as she clearly fought to reach a decision. "You're old enough now to know. Circumstances demand it. Your father..." Her words broke off and she frowned, took a deep breath, and tried again, still holding Kethe's hand tightly. "Your father was a violent man. All knights are, at their core. But the code of chivalry failed to direct his violence as it should. He abused Ser Tiron's wife, and then killed her. Ser Tiron's son was there, and came at him with a knife, so your father slew him too. He then returned to Kyferin Castle and ordered Ser Tiron to quit his lands and leave."

Kethe's insides felt like they were falling to pieces. Anger flared up within her. She searched out Ser Tiron in the great hall and couldn't see him. She sat locked in place. "No."

Her mother squeezed her hands and sighed. "I'm sorry."

Kethe thought of her father, a remote and loud and frightening figure. There were a few good memories, made all the more precious by their rarity: of being tickled and screaming as he pretended to roar and chase her around the Lord's Hall when she was little. How she'd crawl atop his bulk and sleep on his chest, his belly lifting and lowering with a power her weight had no ability to affect. How his beard and mustache had tickled her cheek when he kissed her goodnight, though that had stopped a few years ago. How he had taught her to ride, and how he had bellowed with laughter as they had finally both galloped across the Southern Field, her heart given wings by his admiration and Lady's speed.

Her throat constricted, and she rose to her feet. She couldn't look at her mother. She couldn't make sense of her mother's words. Her father was a lord. A knight. A violent man, yes, but a knight. Her father...

No.

Moving quickly, she walked past the fire, picking her way over sleeping bodies, and out into the courtyard. The moon no longer shone directly on the ash saplings, which now stood in shades of pewter and charcoal. No wind disturbed their canopy. She looked up at them and felt at once numb and on the verge of collapsing into sobs. Furious at her mother without knowing why, she strode past the trees and out the front gate, passing the two guards without a word, out into the cold and dark. One of the guards called after her, but she ignored him.

The mass of Mythgræfen Hold rose above her. She tried to think of her father, and found that her mind shied away, time and again. She tried to think of Ser Tiron, and now the image of his face twisting in hatred as he came at her with a sword was all changed, and she could no longer think of that either.

She thought of Roddick at home, alone, and that image was the final plunge of the knife. She stumbled against the castle wall and slid down into a crouch, buried her face in her hands, and wept.

CHAPTER TWENTY-ONE

TIRON

Ser Tiron felt his age. He'd found a small, pebbled beach on the lee side of the castle, little more than a crescent moon of grit and branches washed smooth of their bark, a half-step down from the thick turf, with the still waters of the lake lapping up with a quiet trickling sound. Bending down, he felt a twinge in his hip. He picked up a flat stone and turned it around in his hand, wiping it clear of sand. It fit his palm nicely.

As boys, he and his brothers had loved skipping stones across Yarrow Pond. The sound of Petyr's laughter floated to him across the years, high-pitched hoots of victory as his stone skipped nine times. Tiron smiled and threw his. It skipped four times and then disappeared.

Dawn was imminent. Mist was rising off the lake in enigmatic eddies. The air was cold and moist, but he couldn't feel the wind here. The mountains rose up on all sides, savage and raw as if they'd just finished clawing their way out of the earth. He could make out the thin plume of a waterfall cascading over a cliff face and falling hundreds of feet to what had to be the head of the lake. It was far enough away that he couldn't make out its roar. It would be hours yet before the sun rose enough to shine down into this valley.

He'd not slept. Oh, he'd lain down for a score of hours, wrapped in a blanket that did nothing to dispel the cold, but he'd grown used to damp and chill in his hole over the past few years. That wasn't what bothered him. Eventually he'd risen, buckled on his sword, and stepped out to hunt. Asho had joined him at first. The young Bythian had been eager to patrol, to explore, do anything *knightly* to prove his honor. Tiron had tolerated his presence for a whole ten minutes until the boy began asking about Tiron's family blade, and wondering aloud if he'd ever be awarded one of his own. A glorious blade, silvered and razor sharp, fit for a knight in Lady Kyferin's employ.

Perhaps he should have held his tongue. Instead, he'd told Asho exactly what he thought of knighthood, of being a Black Wolf, and honor in general. Asho had stopped, face blank, bowed and walked away. It was the bow that told Tiron the boy hadn't understood a word he'd said.

After that he'd spent an hour poking around the castle, a candle held high, trying to read the lives that had once filled the Hold's hollow bones. There was little trace of it left, but what he'd really wanted was to find some sign of these naugrim—to find one and kill it, or be killed by it. There would be a neat simplicity in that, in avoiding the complex arguments in his mind by dying quietly off to one side by himself, but he had no luck. Finally, reluctantly, he'd slipped out through the massive crack in the wall so as to avoid the guards, intending to explore the island's coastline. He'd found a solitary causeway that extended like an accusing finger to point toward the head of the lake, off to one side of this small beach. With no desire to listen to the inane small talk that would inevitably take place around the breakfast fire, he'd settled down to wait and be alone.

He felt a new kind of tiredness. Not physical exhaustion, though that was graying his vision. He was used to that exhaustion, the depletion of a long campaign, of fighting and then marching and then being forced to fight once more. No knight expected a life of ease, far from it; it was privation that blessed and sanctified his violence in the eyes of the Ascendant. No, this tiredness was of the soul.

He threw his stone, whipping it from the elbow, and scored five skips. He'd never beaten Petyr's nine. Had never come close.

The mist was lightening. An occasional splash floated over the water to him as some fish disturbed the surface. The land here was beautiful in a wild, dangerous way. He missed the old yearning that his soul would once have felt at the challenge of the mountain slopes. How long might it take a well-provisioned and well-equipped team to scale those peaks? But he couldn't rouse a genuine interest. His years in the dungeon had aged him, he decided. No, they'd allowed his age to catch up with him at last. The Black Wolves had called him Ser Iron for his inexhaustible stamina and deep reservoirs of strength—a name he'd pretended to disdain, but which he had secretly taken pride in. That iron was gone now. He was an old man without a wife and son, without his hall, with nothing but memories to torment him and a future he couldn't help but ridicule.

Kethe's face came to him, her blade pointed over the flames at his throat. Oh, the life that had burned within her. The sharpness of her hatred, the fierceness of her passion. Had he once burned so brightly? That was hard to believe. He'd wanted to lean forward and urge her on, had welcomed her disgust, which made him feel all the more pathetic. Why was he bothering to tag along with this band of refugees if he couldn't even muster the will to stand up to a spoiled brat?

He sat on a rock and stared out into the mist. *Oh, Sarah*, he thought. *Would you recognize me now?* It was such sweet torment to think of her. He doubted the Black Gate could hold any torture more effective than this love that refused to die. It was too easy to summon her sharp smile, her hand on her broad hip, the curve of her back as she lay curled against him, the sweat on her golden skin. He couldn't remember her smell any longer. His memories were starting to collapse into a dozen favorite touchstones, worn smooth by repetition. She was being reduced to a series of static images: Her smile. That afternoon in the hayloft. The sight of her asleep with their son in her arms, both of them worn out, a moment of peace in the morning sunlight that had held him riveted to the spot for an hour, marveling that such beauty could enter an ugly and violent life such as his.

Ser Tiron felt his face flush, his eyes sting, and he buried his face in his hands as a silent sob wracked his frame. Then he hissed in anger and stood. How naive of Lady Kyferin to think she could ever free him. There was no escape. His pain would follow him always, like a stench.

He scooped up a large rock and hurled it with all his strength out over the lake. It disappeared into the mist and then splashed loudly. Ser Tiron panted, and as quickly as it had come, his anger left him.

"Old fool," he muttered. "Temper tantrums. What next? Talking to yourself?"

He heard the sound of someone moving through the tall grass behind him and turned to see Kethe approaching with the feral focus of a hunting cat. He almost laughed. "Come to kill me? Honestly, you might be doing me a favor."

She drew up short and blinked several times, as if awakening from a trance. Then she straightened and frowned at him, hand on the hilt of her sword. "So you admit you're filth."

Her eyes were red, he saw, her young face haggard. "I'm flattered. It's been a while since thoughts of me have kept a young woman awake all night."

Kethe stepped off the ridge and dropped neatly to land on the shingle. Her hauberk barely made any sound. Almost absently, he noted its fine construction. She'd probably paid good coin for that. Her hand never strayed from her sword's pommel. "Why did you come?" she asked. "In truth?"

Tiron turned to face her full-on, hands on his hips. She was practically vibrating with the desire to draw her sword. It wouldn't take much to provoke her to do so. Then he could claim he'd acted in self-defense. She'd attacked him by surprise, and he'd had to kill her. Tragic, but oh-so-neatly explained. "Why?" He paused, considering the question. "It's hard to explain."

"Try." There was steel in her voice—or the promise of it.

"Why?" He leaned back on his heels, making no effort to ready a defense. "You heard your mother. She trusts me. Why should I justify myself to you?"

Kethe slowly drew her sword. The calculated control of her action reminded him of a hunter drawing back a bow to shoot at an unsuspecting deer, as if moving rapidly or making a sound might dispel the moment and set him running. "Why?" Her smile was bitter. "Because of everyone here, I know who you really are. I know what you're capable of. I saw it in your eyes when you tried your best to kill me." She brought her sword forward to grasp it with both hands. "I won't let you hurt my family again."

Tiron didn't say anything. A wave of sadness passed through him, and he felt old and weary. He honestly didn't know if he had it in him to kill her. Didn't know if he could live with himself if he didn't. He thought of Sarah. His son. His gut coiled with tension at their memory. He reached down and drew his sword, the blade whispering as it came free to gleam in the dawn.

"You think you know me?" The mockery was gone from his voice. "You? A girl of seventeen, eighteen years? You think you can understand my life, what I've been through, the depth of my pain, the span of my experiences?" He shook his head. "You have no idea. All you know is fear and outrage and anger, and those only shallowly." He took a step forward, his foot grinding on the loose stones of the beach. "Have you ever killed a man, Kethe?"

The muscles of her jaw tightened. "What has that to do with anything?"

"So, no. You haven't. Have you ever been fucked?"

Her pale, freckled face flushed immediately. "How dare you?"

"So, that's another no. What *have* you done in your brief life? Other than play the part of the spoiled nobleman's daughter, ridden your pretty palfrey, swung a sword in a tournament, and felt a momentary spasm of terror when your life was threatened? You're a child. Yet you presume to judge me."

Kethe smiled, and Tiron recognized it for the predatory expression it was. So, she did have some backbone to her. "I don't need to have lived to a hundred to know filth when I see it."

Tiron took another step forward. He kept his sword down by his side. "Have you ever lost someone you loved with all your soul?"

This time she hesitated. Her brow furrowed and anger caused her eyes to narrow. "Of course I have. My father."

"Your father?" Tiron stopped. "Are you being serious?"

Her knuckles whitened. "Disrespect him at your peril."

"Enderl Kyferin? You loved him with all your soul?"

"He was my father," she grated, and tears brimmed in her eyes. Her sword never wavered. "Of course I did."

"Enderl Kyferin." Tiron shook his head. "You know, when they first threw me into that dungeon, I hated him blindly, completely, and without any discrimination. I really can't convey how much my hatred consumed me. I would howl in that hole each night with my desire to tear out his throat. Did you ever hear me? Probably not. The guards would have had to come down and beat me unconscious." Tiron shrugged. "It turns out that you can't sustain that kind of hatred for very long, no matter how good the cause. So, after a month or two of that screaming, I fell into a simmering level of insanity. I just paced and paced and talked to myself. I almost went mad. I think I might have, for a while. There are stretches that I don't remember. I lost most of my fingernails at that point." He stared down at his gloves. "I can show you, if you like. I think it was from clawing at the walls."

"Shut up," said Kethe, her voice thick with emotion. "I don't care how you suffered. No, that's not true. I'm glad. I wish you had gone insane."

"After a while, however, that madness receded. In the end it was just me, in that hole, with time to think about Kyferin. And I came to realize that he was exceptional." Tiron paused, raising an eyebrow at Kethe, but she simply glared at him. "Exceptionally violent, yes. Exceptionally cruel. Capable of hurting people in ways your mind can't encompass. But more than that. He didn't care about anything but himself. He was completely free to do what he liked, no matter the consequences. He broke all customs when he convinced your Sigean mother to abandon her lofty mountain city and descend to his level. He did it again when he elevated Asho and Shaya, bringing them up from Bythos itself to sit at his table. He was a force of nature. Is it any wonder he was so feared and respected?"

"I don't understand," said Kethe. "What are you saying? I thought you hated him."

"Oh, more than you'll ever know. If you were to throw me back in that dungeon for the rest of my life but give me Kyferin to torture every single day, I would now consider that a life well-lived. But what I'm saying to you is this, Kethe. You may have loved him, but he never loved you."

"Shut up!" Kethe flared her fingers around the hilt of her sword and gripped it tighter.

"He couldn't, you see. He was incapable of doing so. Perhaps he was fond of you, like he was of his horses, but that was all." Tiron smiled. "And the worst of it is that you know I'm telling the truth. You know in your heart that he never truly loved you. Perhaps that made you adore him all the more, in order to compensate for that lack. But when you look into that dark hole in your center—"

Kethe screamed and attacked him, whipping her sword around in a wide arc to take off his head. Tiron darted back, and her sword sliced through the air an inch from his neck. She recovered and brought her blade up and down in a vicious chop. Tiron turned quickly so as to present his profile, her sword missing him again by a hair's breath. She staggered past him with a cry and reversed her sword to crack her pommel into his face. He ducked and jumped back, stones skittering underneath his feet.

"You lie!" She was heaving for breath, sword weaving drunkenly now. "You twisted, bitter, filthy—" She launched herself at him once more, and this time he was forced to parry, over and again. He slowly gave way before her fury, moving back toward the far end of the crescent-shaped beach. The sound of their blades echoed out over the lake, flat and muffled by the mist.

Finally he stepped into her swing and blocked her sword with his own at their bases so that they stared at each other with only a foot of air between them. "I'm not lying." His words were harsh growls. "Your father was a murderer." He shoved and she fell back, stumbling on her heels as she fought for balance. Just as she caught it, he slammed his blade against her own, sending her stumbling back again. "A rapist." She fell into a crouch, caught herself with one hand and stood just in time to take another blow. "And he never loved a damn thing in his whole life but himself."

Kethe's sword flew from her hand into the tall grass and she fell back onto her ass. Her eyes were glassy with shock and pain, and her lips were trembling, and suddenly Tiron felt sickened with himself, disgusted. She was just a girl.

He reared back, breathing heavily, and lowered his blade. "You can't judge me," he said. "Not when you don't know shit about the world or about yourself."

She raised a shaking hand to her face and turned away from him, silent sobs causing her shoulders to shake. His breath rasped in his throat, and he felt a ridiculous urge to apologize to her. He clenched his jaw and restrained himself from hurling his blade out into the lake. He sheathed it instead, then turned away and looked back at her. Kethe had dragged herself into the lee of the drop from the grass to the beach, and was curled up and shaking as if she'd taken a punch to the gut.

He hung his head and rubbed his brow. He'd been a father once, something close to a good man. Clearly that was no longer the case.

"Look. You're right: I'm filth. Ignore what I said. What do I know? Believe what you want."

She didn't respond. Her sobs were pained gasps, as if each breath were a stab in her back.

Just walk away. She's not your damn daughter. You don't owe her a thing.

But he couldn't look away. Couldn't leave. Something held him. A truth, something he in all his vaunted wisdom had failed to see and appreciate. He frowned at her, and then it hit him. She'd been hurt by Kyferin, perhaps as badly as he had been. She was a fellow victim, just like him. He'd been in his dungeon for three years. She'd spent her whole life in her father's shadow, and here he was, rubbing her face in her wounds. Hurting her even more. Was this how he'd honor Sarah? Avenge himself on Kyferin?

The words clawed at his throat, crude and scabby and terrifying. *I'm sorry.*

He couldn't breathe. Kethe's gasps turned into broken weeping. *I'm sorry.* Two damn words.

He thought of Kitan. *Any true man would want what you want.* A rusted blade turned in his heart. He thought of Sarah lying on their broken bed, heard Kyferin's laughter as he walked away. *Kill her*, he thought, then stepped back. *No, kill yourself. End it. End it now.*

That old madness began to take hold of him. He needed to run, to get away. Kethe's soft cries were cutting into the fabric of his mind. He stepped back again and shook his head.

He could see Sarah asleep in the sunlight, their son cradled in her arms.

It was too much.

"I'm sorry," he whispered, then he turned and scrambled up the bluff and was gone.

CHAPTER TWENTY-TWO

Tharok

Tharok was not invited to the celebration. As night fell and the great shadow of the far mountain swept across the valley, a couple of Red River kragh let him down but then promptly chained him directly to the tree, wrapping the thick links around the trunk twice before locking them once more. Tharok didn't resist. He was too tired, his headache was bloody murder, and all he wanted to do was sleep.

He awoke when somebody kicked him, hard. The roughshod boot dug deep into his thigh, and he snapped awake, a growl tearing free from his lips. It was full dark now, the stars blistering the sky above, and in the center of the great camp a large bonfire was burning. Two kragh were standing above him, hunched and scowling. Tharok recognized them both: Olok and Urok, Wrok's youngest brothers. Both were powerfully built, though neither matched Krol in size and their tusks were only of medium length. As one they reached down to grip his arms as a third kragh unlocked the chains from his neck.

"Come on, slave," said Olok, his voice thick with disgust. "You're going to pay for your lies."

Tharok didn't bother to answer. The cold was vicious and his legs were in searing pain; his feet were swollen and the hide around his ankles had chafed them to bleeding. At least the headache was gone. The brothers hustled him forward roughly, trying to make him trip, but Tharok kept his feet as he was brought from the outskirts into the center of the camp.

There were at least two dozen great huts set up in a rough circle around the fire, thick white mountain goat fur stretched taut across the whip-like branches that had been bent down into half-globes. A few kragh were watching the perimeter, but it was in the central circle that the mass of the Red River tribe was assembled.

The Red River tribe was large, perhaps one of the largest highland tribes, though it paled in comparison to the size of the lowland kragh tribes below. Arrayed about the fires were perhaps a hundred kragh, from the most powerful of the warriors, some sixteen summers strong and dark of skin, to old and toothless males in their final years. The males only gathered like this four times a year; normally they ranged the valleys and slopes in small family clans, hunting and protecting the central camp. Only the women and children lived here throughout the season, the crones, the young females, and the women of the women's circle.

The fire leaped and danced, its thunderous reds and oranges causing hundreds of black eyes to gleam like wet stones as they turned to stare at him. He recognized a good half of them from previous meetings with his tribe. More clans had come during the evening to join Wrok's tribe, endorsing his leadership by simply being here. By sheer numbers, he was doing well.

Wrok himself, however, was not pleased. He was standing by the central fire, hands on his hips, Toad sitting bloodied and silent at his feet. The air was tense. What had once been a celebration was now a sleeping great bear, roused to the point of near-waking and massacre. All eyes turned to Tharok, who grinned, showing his tusks to full vantage. They might bring him forth bound, but he was no slave.

"You!" said Wrok, striding forward. "You've come to your death. You've filled Toad's head with nonsense, and he speaks of you, the stinking issue of your mother's foul hole, as having the blood of Ogri himself running through your veins! Ha!"

Tharok shook himself free of the twin brothers' hands and stepped forward. He raised his chin, fighting back the nausea and fatigue. "Ogri's blood flows within me, yes. How else do you think World Breaker came to my hands?"

"World Breaker is mine!"

"Only because, like any carrion crow, you took it from me as I lay unconscious. It doesn't take much bravery to rob a sleeping kragh."

The crowd hissed, gazes flipping from Wrok to Tharok, and several kragh began to pound their fists onto the dirt, creating a dull drumming sound of approval.

"Your clan and tribe are finished. The Sky Mother saw fit to have your father gutted, your brothers slain, and your womenfolk scattered. The Gray Smoke are gone, and here before everybody I am going to split you open like a lowland pig and feed you to my hounds."

The gathered kragh went silent. Wrok could not have offered greater insult. Destroying a body by either burning it or feeding it to animals would destroy the kragh's very soul.

"I carry Ogri's blood in my veins. I am of the line of the Uniter. You would use the World Breaker for your own selfish ends, and in doing so, bring ruin upon this tribe. If you would kill me, then do so in a manner befitting a warlord. Let us fight to the death!"

"You dare make demands?" roared Wrok, spraying spittle. "You are a slave! I have brought you here to kill you and show them all that this talk of Ogri is nonsense! There shall be no fight. You have been summoned to die."

"I see Krol is not here," said Tharok, looking about the crowd, a small smile carving itself across his face. "No wonder you are too scared to fight."

Again the crowd hissed, and more of their number punched the ground. Wrok snarled, drew World Breaker and strode forward. Tharok stood firm and turned to stare at Maur, who stepped out of the crowd into the space before the flames.

"Enough!" she cried. Wrok froze, fury contorting his features, but he dared not disobey the wise woman. "Enough. Wrok-krya, stay your hand. We cannot risk offending Ogri on this sacred night. The spirits that live amongst us would never forgive the insult, and our fortunes would shatter."

"Maur," said Wrok, turning and forcing his tone to remain polite. "Our fortunes rise. We have gold, we have shaman stone, we have World Breaker. I will lead us to glory. Only this fool needs die before we do even better."

"You hold World Breaker," said Maur. "Yet you deny that Ogri is involved in these events. Tharok claims Ogri's blood runs in his veins. You are bringing great honor to our tribe, but we think it wise for you to accept Tharok's challenge. After all, he has been bound for days and can barely stand. If Ogri's blood does not run in his veins, the chieftain of the Red River should have no difficulty killing him. Am I right?"

Again the assembled kragh hissed so that the air filled with the sound of a thousand snakes, and now all of them pummeled the ground, great iron knuckles shaking the earth.

Wrok glared about him as if he had been cornered, then turned to stare at Tharok, who chose that moment to let his knees buckle. Only Urok's swift hand stopped him from crashing to the ground.

Wrok pursed his lips and glared at Maur, who held his gaze with firm assurance. He looked past her at where the women's circle was standing, Krilla looming over them all, and saw no give, no deviation from Maur's request. With a growl he snapped his gaze across to where old Golden Crow was sitting, the blind shaman grinning a yellowed grin, his face so wrinkled that he looked half-mummified. The shaman was rocking back and forth, clearly enjoying himself, and for a moment it looked like Wrok would ask him his opinion, reach for the shaman's aid against the wise woman. But then he shook his head, retreating from that desperate move.

"Of course," he growled. "I have nothing to fear from this filth. His father was the true warrior of his tribe. This runt is nothing but a lying windbag. I'll slit him from throat to gizzard, and then we can resume our great celebration, turning our minds to the future, to our glory."

He raised his hands, seeking the crowd's approval, but only received a meditative murmur. They would not side with him before the fight.

Hands pushed Tharok forward. He blinked, rolled his shoulders, and began to methodically stretch out his muscles. He worked quickly through a series of movements he had never practiced before, obeying impulses alien to him but logical, so that in short order he had stretched out all the great muscles of his legs, hips, core and shoulders. Olok and Urok stared at him in confusion. Kragh warriors never stretched. They warmed their muscles in battle. Tharok ignored them. He was too sore and stiff to allow fury to warm his body.

With Krol missing, Wrok didn't dare nominate a champion. In this battle only his clan members, direct blood relatives, would agree without hesitation to represent him, but Urok and Orok were young, untested. Tharok watched him carefully, unsure of how the pressure might force him to act.

By the firelight the chieftain examined the crowd, and for a long while he stared at his twin younger brothers, both of whom bristled with eagerness to be nominated to battle. Then Wrok turned and stared at the weapons master. It had been Tharok's own father who had cut his arm from his shoulder, leaving the weapons master permanently crippled, if still lethal with the blade. The chieftain gazed into the weapons master's eyes, trying desperately to guess whether the enmity Barok felt for the father would be sufficient to pass to the son. With a deep growl, he turned away and sliced at the air with World Breaker.

"Let's end this farce! I've meat and drink to attend to and willing women to mate with! The time for blood has come!" And with those words he charged across the open space, not giving anybody time to arm Tharok or prevent him from using World Breaker in the duel.

Time slowed. Maur and the shaman both were moving forward, mouths opening to roar their protests. The great fire danced and crackled and spat like an imprisoned demon, a conflagration that lit everything in shades of hell. A sea of faces surrounded them, light green ranging to black with maws opened in excitement, eyes glinting reflections back at him. Wrok was wielding World Breaker, and its power would sustain him, give him strength and vitality far beyond what his old body could normally muster. Tharok was unarmed, brutalized and exhausted.

He smiled.

A hand pressed between his shoulder blades in the beginning of a shove. Tharok fell to one knee and reached back to grasp Orok's wrist and haul him forward. Orok overbalanced and fell into a roll, surprised by the sudden lack of resistance, and sprawled out on his back before the charging Wrok. Tharok, down on one knee, reached forward, neatly drew Orok's blade and rose even as Wrok leaped over his fallen brother and brought World Breaker swinging down at his head.

With a cry, Tharok stepped to the side, raising his blade not in a direct block, which would have shattered his sword, but in an oblique deflection so that sparks ran out down the length of his sword as World Breaker slid off it. Wrok's momentum carried him past and into the arms of his brother, Urok, who steadied him and turned him around.

Tharok glanced at his blade. The brush with World Breaker had warped it, dulling the edge completely along one side. Orok was rising to his feet, so Tharok retreated until he was standing with his back to the great fire, the heat raging and licking at his bare skin, the light bright in Wrok's eyes as he approached with greater caution. Maur was calling forth an objection, but it was too late. The males knew that the battle had been joined and that the rules and conditions could no longer be changed.

Tharok's mind spun. He was too injured, too exhausted and in too much pain to summon his battle rage. No matter. Doing so would only dull his mind and exchange intelligence and strategy for sheer force that would throw him right onto World Breaker's point. He forced his anger down and watched as Wrok approached, confident now, enjoying the power and strength that World Breaker afforded him, such power as he had not felt since his youth. It would make him arrogant, would make him eager to demonstrate his newfound prowess. That was Tharok's only advantage, and he allowed himself to look panicked, gazing from side to side as if seeking escape.

"There's nowhere to run, slave," roared Wrok, grinning mightily as he enjoyed the sight. "Bitten off more than you can chew? You should have thought twice before defying me!" He stepped forward and brought World Breaker down in an overhead slash. Tharok deflected it once more, purposefully taking more of the brunt of the blow so that his own blade was nearly knocked from his hand.

Again Wrok brought World Breaker down, eschewing a skilled assault for all-out brutality, and again, and then once more, Tharok deflected the blow, each time allowing his blade to be distorted and bent even further, so that by the fifth block not only were his right shoulder and arm on fire and his head swimming, but his sword was nearly useless, gashed and notched and nearly shattered at the hilt.

Wrok, sensing his primacy, continued to hew down as if striking at a block of wood. Tharok dropped to one knee, holding his blade directly overhead now so as to take the next strike full on, no deflection. It was clear that World Breaker would smash through and bury itself deep in his head. Wrok grasped World Breaker with both hands, and with a roar that did his old lungs proud swung World Breaker as high as he could and brought it shattering down.

But Tharok was no longer there. At the last moment he dropped his sword and threw himself at the chieftain's legs, diving forward even as the old kragh stepped in to him, taking a boot in the ribs but tripping the chieftain as his weight was thrown into his forward chop. Wrok let out a cry of fury as he stumbled over Tharok and into the great bonfire.

Head ringing, Tharok reached up to make sure the circlet was still affixed to his brow and then forced himself to stand. He picked up his mangled sword. Wrok was screeching, desperately pushing himself off the conflagration of logs, his clothing burning, his skin blistering, his iron-grey braid smoking. With a cry the old kragh heaved himself out of the fire, World Breaker still in his hands, and turned to face Tharok, eyes maddened by pain and panic. But he still stood, sustained by the sword's powers, heaving for deep breaths through his scorched lungs.

Tharok stood unsteadily, mangled blade at the ready, and knew that now was his only chance. With a roar of his own he staggered forward, desperately trying not to trip, and brought his ruined sword down upon Wrok in the same manner the chieftain had attacked him, hammering down like a smith at his anvil, only now allowing his anger to slip free of his control and his rage to shine forth.

"Die!" roared Tharok, staring at Wrok's blistered, terrified face. "Die and burn, die and burn!"

This kragh had helped kill his father, had destroyed his tribe, had tried to enslave him, was allying with the Tragon, and had almost gotten away with it. Fury fueled his blows, and he pressed the chieftain with more force of will than actual power, for World Breaker was sending chunks of metal flying from his blade even as he warded off the blows. Wrok stood, his heels to the fire, trying to regain his balance, trying to move himself forward, to seize the initiative, but before he could do so, Tharok brought his blade down one more time as hard as he could, perfectly aligning World Breaker's edge with his own so that the great sword cut through his mangled one cleanly. The tip of his mangled blade flew down into Wrok's face. The chunk of metal cut deep into his left eye, ruined his cheek, and without pause Tharok stepped back and brought the remnants of his sword sweeping crosswise through Wrok's still upheld wrists, severing both of the warlord's scrawny hands from his bird-boned arms.

Wrok's screams were lost in the roar of the crowd as black blood fountained from his stumps. Tharok stepped back, heaving for breath, and cast his ruined sword aside. Wrok, savagely burned, partially blinded and without hands, turned his one good eye upon him. Tharok growled deep in his chest and stepped forward to power a forward kick from his hips into the warlord's chest, snapping bones and sending the old kragh flying into the fire, dislodging heavy logs as he fell into the orange and crimson heart of the blaze, his scream rising to a shrill cry before suddenly cutting short.

Without pausing, on the verge of passing out, knowing that every second was critical, Tharok reached down and took up World Breaker. Strength flooded into him, he steadied, and then lifted his head as if a great weight had slipped from his shoulders. He spun and raised World Breaker so that it was between him and Orok and Urok, who had already been rushing forward, naked steel in their hands.

"You would dispute my victory?" Tharok took a step forward. Ah, the joy of strength, of pain receding, of newfound energy! He felt fevered, but the energy was hollow. He would sleep for days if he so much as sat down.

Orok and Urok snarled and then cast quick glances at the crowd, at Maur, at Golden Crow, at where Barok was standing. No one supported them, so they lowered their blades reluctantly.

"No, Tharok," said Urok, the elder of the two. "We were moving to retrieve our brother before he burned completely and lost his soul. You misunderstood our intention."

"Did I now," said Tharok, staring Urok in the eyes until the other looked away. He then locked his gaze on Orok until the other kragh did the same. Only then did he turn to the assembled clans who had all risen to their feet, faces intent as they stared at him.

"I am Tharok, son of Grakor, the last of my clan and tribe, but here, with World Breaker in my hands, with Ogri's blood in my veins and his blessing on my head and sword arm, I stand before you as the Red River's new warlord. I have proven myself in trial by combat, and I say to you now, if you follow me, I will lead you to glory, to victory heaped upon victory, so that the name of the Red River will be forever linked to the greatest deeds and riches. If you follow me, you will join me in creating new legends. We shall forge a new kragh empire! We shall rise in power and leave behind us a trail of broken bodies, defeated enemies, burned cities and ruined lands!"

Many of the kragh around him gave voice to their pleasure, stamping their broad feet and pounding their fists on their chests, shaking their heads from side to side and snapping their jaws open and closed. A third of them, however, did not. Those were the kragh most closely allied with Wrok's clan, two or three clans that had formed the core of the Red River under Wrok and supported his rule. Tharok's father's cruel leadership of the Gray Smoke tribe was fresh in their memories, and they were clearly loath to crown his son over them so soon.

Maur stepped forward, several other crimson-haired kragh of the women's circle behind her, and the clans stilled. She stood before Tharok and studied him, her broad cheekbones and flat eyes reflecting the fiery light. With a great fur wrapped around her shoulders and neck but little more than a loincloth below, she looked savage and beautiful, yet contemplative as she assessed him. Tonight was the night for mating, thought Tharok. Maur would be feeling the instinct as much as any other.

Finally, she turned to the crowd. "The women's circle finds in Tharok a worthy warlord for the Red River tribe. We support his claim, proven by blood, and by the sword he now holds in his hand."

Tharok resisted letting out a sigh of relief. Had Maur ruled against him, his followers would have easily been cut in half, leaving him wide open to a number of challenges. But with her and the women's circle behind him, his claim had become vastly more solid.

The shaman, Golden Crow, hobbled before Tharok and stared up at him. It was a disconcerting sight, looking into the shaman's withered and dry eye sockets, and the ancient kragh, older even than Wrok had been, pulled out a chunk of shaman stone and worked it between his fingers as he whispered incantations. When he deemed the moment right, he popped the shaman stone into his mouth and chewed on it while everyone waited in silence.

"Ogri has clearly blessed this warrior," he said, his tone grave and surprisingly deep for his wiry figure as he used his avalanche voice. "Whispers come to me from those who saw Tharok climb the Dragon's Breath. He speaks true! Ogri himself blesses his rise. He would not allow Tharok to stand with World Breaker in his hands were he telling anything but the truth." His words rung in the air, and the very nature of the silence changed in texture. "The spirits have blessed him, and through him the Red River tribe. They have sent forth one of Ogri's blood to lead and unite us. Tharok is the chieftain of the Red River."

The silence continued for several heartbeats more, and then, as one, the kragh began to roar and stamp their feet, the words of the wise woman and the shaman cementing what the trial by combat had already told them. Tharok lifted his arms, World Breaker gleaming in the firelight, and turned slowly so as to stare all the kragh in the face. It was clear that some were cheering with more gusto than others, that some were forcing themselves to participate, despite the overwhelming vote of confidence given to him.

Tharok lowered World Breaker. Only the vitality of the sword was keeping him on his feet now. But he needed to do one thing more.

"Kragh of the Red River, I am your chieftain. My clan is scattered, my father is dead, but I stand before you ready to rule, to lead you to greatness. My first act will be one of blood. Bring me Orok and Urok."

Several large kragh men stepped forward and gripped the twin brothers, who had already begun to fade back into the ranks, looking to make their escape. They strove to cast off the grips that held them tight, but were brought stumbling and cursing before Tharok. He looked into their faces, already darkening with their growing authority, tusks lengthening, younger images of Krol.

"Blood of Wrok, you are of his clan and share his spirit amongst you. Your fortune was tied to his. Your power came from his rule. You gave him strength, supported his plans, and benefited from his victories."

Orok and Urok stood very still and tensed.

Tharok lifted his blade. "This sword is called World Breaker, for with it Ogri broke the world. He did not cut off the tops of mountains or cut between the peaks to form deeper valleys, as is said, but with this very sword he broke the world of kragh and men. He shattered tradition, he broke rules, he remade the kragh into one grand tribe that ranged from horizon to horizon. It was called World Breaker, for before its blade the old world could not stand."

Orok let out a cry and threw himself backward, trying to rip free, but the three kragh who had hold of him held fast. They drew him back, and then one kicked out his feet from under him so that he fell to his knees. Urok had enough dignity to lower himself, though he never took his eyes from Tharok.

"Wrok's death should free you, and by tradition your clan should be allowed to leave the Red River and join whichever tribe you desire. But you killed my clan. You betrayed us to lowlanders. You helped Wrok destroy my tribe. Because of you, the Gray Smoke are no more. So with World Breaker in my hand, I say tradition ends here. Tonight."

Tharok took up World Breaker, and with one sweep took off Urok's head, severing it so cleanly that he went on kneeling for several seconds before finally toppling over and crashing to the ground.

Orok stilled and shook his head. "You can't do this."

Tharok didn't respond. Instead, he firmed his grip and backhanded the blade across Orok's throat, taking his head off as well.

The gathered clans stood still, eyes locked on him and the dead twins at his feet. He stared at the six kragh who had held them only moments ago. "When Krol returns, I want him taken and brought to me.

Do not explain why. Simply do this. You six are to watch for him. I know your faces, I know your clans, and I hold you responsible. Is that clear?"

The six kragh looked at each other, brows raised, and then as one they nodded and stepped back into the crowd.

Tharok knew he wouldn't last much longer, but he had to look strong until the end. He turned to regard the crowd. "I wield World Breaker. Mark me. We shall break worlds together. I will shatter traditions and end how things have been done. The only thing I hold sacred is uniting our tribes. All who oppose me will die."

He came to a stop in front of Golden Crow and lowered himself to one knee before the old kragh, who reached out and placed his hand on Tharok's shoulder. "I ask that your insight and knowledge of the spirits be put to great use in the service of the Red River tribe. Will you serve me, Golden Crow-krya, even as I respect you and do you honor?"

The old shaman nodded. "I will, warlord."

Tharok stood with difficulty. He turned to Maur and the women who stood with her. "I recognize the women's circle, and would meet with them tomorrow. No action may be taken without their counsel, no move made without their guidance. Would you meet with me tomorrow, all of you, so that we may discuss the future of the Red River tribe?"

Maur grimaced, but there was wry amusement in her eyes; his actions thus far undercut his words, but it had been nicely said, so she nodded her consent.

Finally Tharok turned to regard them all. "Continue the celebration, for tonight marks the birth of a new era amongst the kragh. Drink, dance, laugh and fight. Find your mates, rut hard and long, so that the women may bear us strong warriors for tomorrow's wars! The Red River tribe shall rise above them all!"

He raised World Breaker over his head, causing it to gleam and burn, and the clans let loose a cacophony of shrill cries and roars. That was all he could manage. He lowered the sword and strode away, needing darkness, a place to collapse.

Someone ran alongside him: Toad.

"Find me a hut," he said thickly to the little kragh. "Find me a place to sleep."

"Wrok's hut is currently empty," said Toad, grinning and hopping. "Follow me. It's not far."

Tharok locked his eyes on the small kragh's back and stumbled after him, passing tents, leaving the fire behind, till he reached the largest hut, smothered in the whitest goat pelts and with two braziers burning before it. Toad stepped forward to speak to a kragh of Wrok's clan who was standing before the entrance even as Tharok blundered past the hanging goat skin and into the darkness of the hut's interior.

He paused, spotted the great bed, and without word, without thought, strode over to it and collapsed face-first, World Breaker still clutched in his had, asleep before his face even hit the pillows.

CHAPTER TWENTY-THREE

ISKRA

Iskra accepted a mug of heated black tea from Jekil the undercook with a smile. The young boy blushed and quickly looked away, turning to the next in line with a slightly straighter back. Iskra moved away from the fire, holding the mug and enjoying the heat that radiated into her palms. It was a bitterly cold morning. Her people were moving lethargically, most of them wrapping their bedclothes around them as they stumbled around their small camp, talking quietly and avoiding eye contact. The mood was fragile. Nobody had slept well, and with the terror of last night's rush gone, the direness of their situation was sinking in.

What would Erland have done? She tried to imagine him here, either up glowering on the walls or brooding by the fire, nursing wine instead of beer and planning his revenge. Somehow she couldn't picture him amongst this rubble. He wouldn't have allowed Mertyn to back him into this corner. More likely Mertyn would never have dared to try such a coup. But against her he'd more than dared; he'd succeeded, and now she needed to salvage the situation with what little authority she still had.

Ser Jander Wyland entered the hall, hair wet and rubbing his hands vigorously together. "I do not recommend going for a swim," he said loudly with a grin, causing everyone to turn and stare at him. "That frigid black water does look inviting, I will concede, but I urge you to reconsider. If you value your chance of having children, stay clear!"

Several people chuckled. Jekil lifted a mug. "Some hot tea, ser?"

Jander strode over and clasped Jekil by the shoulder as he lifted the mug and drained it in one long pull. "Ah. Better than the finest Segian wine, if my Lady will pardon my saying so. Another cup, good Jekil! Our fortune rides on your tea-making services."

Jekil grinned widely and refilled the mug. Jander took it and stepped over to where Iskra was standing. "I'd ask how you slept, my Lady, but I fear I know the answer."

Iskra smiled. "How do you keep your spirits so high, Jander? Yours is the only smile I've seen since I awoke."

"How?" He turned to consider their small camp, mug held to his lips, his other hand on his hip. He stood straight and unbowed, smelling of lake water and looking rested and well. "This is life, my Lady. The wheel of fortune lifts us up and brings us down. You must free your happiness from its vagaries. Expect nothing, and everything is a gift." He hesitated, shrugged, them looked sidelong at her with amusement in his eyes. "Or something like that. Perhaps I'm just an irrepressible optimist. Or exhilarated by near-death experiences in freezing lakes. It's hard to tell."

Iskra's smile turned into a soft laugh and she sipped her tea. It was bitter and strong, exactly what she needed. "Well, I thank the Ascendant that you're with us."

Jander studied her and then spoke softly. "My Lady, I know the situation is dire. Your sense of responsibility for us must be crushing. Don't let that weight paralyze you. Everyone here looks to you for strength and leadership, not only as their lady but as a Sigean, whose soul has ascended the highest of us all. You must lead. You did well last night, giving orders, setting people in motion. You must continue that today. Keep them busy. Nothing creates tension and fear like idleness."

She stared down into her tea as if its dark depths might provide her with answers. Two weeks—they had two weeks before Mertyn sent a force to destroy them. Out of the corner of her eye she saw people watching her. What could they accomplish in two weeks? Should they flee into the mountains and evade destruction? Live in the wilds like animals?

Iskra took a deep breath and nodded. "You're right. We need action. Purpose. Direction. I must admit to being overwhelmed, but there is no room for that."

Where to begin? She fought the impulse to ask Jander to lead. He'd been in dozens of battles, had led men to war. Already the people here looked up to him. It would be easy to hand over the reins of power. Would he take them? If she wished it, she knew he would. And he would do well.

"Constable." She pitched her voice to carry. Brocuff looked up from where he was sitting by the fire, sharpening a knife. "Summon all your guards. Every one. I would speak with them."

Brocuff nodded and rose, sliding his knife into his hip sheath. "As you will, my Lady."

"Magister Audsley." She looked to where the plump Noussian was sitting almost hidden in the center of a massive knot of blankets and cloaks. "Bring me your map of the area." Audsley blinked and nodded, then turned to dig into his satchel.

"Ser Wyland. Find me Kethe, Ser Tiron, and Ser Asho. Bring them here."

Jander nodded smartly and strode away, handing his tea back to

Jekil as he passed the undercook.

Iskra looked at the remaining dozen men and women who were watching her from their places near the twin fires, faces open, expectant and hesitant both. "Where is Elon?"

One of the grooms raised his hand. "He's up on the wall, my Lady. Examining that ballista."

She nodded. "Good. Fetch him."

The groom nodded and almost ran from the room. Iskra cast about the room and saw one of the ancient Kyferin keep wheelbarrows close by. It would do.

After five minutes, everyone was assembled. Kethe's appearance tore at her heart—her daughter looked riven with grief, her face blotched and eyes crimson from weeping. Yet she stood resolutely at the back of the crowd, her face expressionless, staring coldly forward and ignoring everyone else. Ser Tiron in turn stood with his arms crossed, staring at the ground, clenching his jaw rhythmically and glowering. Something had happened. She'd find out what soon enough.

Stepping up onto the barrow, she gazed down at their faces. She saw fear. Doubt. Exhaustion. Numbness and apathy. "We have two weeks before Lord Laur comes knocking at our front door. Two weeks in which to prepare ourselves, in which to prepare a reception that will send him and his men running back to the Talon. I will not lie to you; our situation is dire, but not impossibly so. There is room here for tough, determined men and women to shift the odds in our favor. You have committed yourselves to my cause, and I will now drive you hard. I will not give up on any of you, nor will I let you think our situation lost."

Ser Tiron looked up, face dark with scorn. "If you think we can fight off his knights, you're lying to us and yourself both."

People stirred, looking back at him, then up to her for a rebuttal. "Agreed. Not in our present condition. But we will have accomplished much by the time they make their appearance. Magister Audsley."

Audsley came to attention.

"What is the closest town to our location?"

The Noussian raised his map and squinted at it. "That would be Hrething, my Lady. A good day's walk down the Erenthil River from where we are."

"Hrething." She nodded. "Therein lies our chance at salvation. They don't know it yet, but the good men and women of that town are going to help us fight off this invading force."

"Why would they do that?" Ser Tiron's face was as flat and hard as an anvil.

"Because I'm going to persuade them," said Iskra, voice cold.

"I'm going to send a group down today to begin negotiations. We shall ask for food, supplies, and labor to shore up our defenses. But more importantly, we will convince them to fight for us. I have brought enough gold with me to make each of them wealthy. They *will* aid us. Ser Wyland, I want you, Ser Asho, and Lady Kethe to lead four guards down to Hrething today. I will expect you to report back by tomorrow night."

Jander nodded, and she saw approval in his face. It warmed her, but she did not let that show.

"Master smith. What is your assessment of the ballista?"

Elon rubbed at his jaw line with his thumb. "It's in rough shape, obviously. The rope's useless, and it's hard to evaluate how much tension the bow arms will take. But if I work on it, I think I can get it to work once more."

"Good. Make that your sole focus. I want Lord Laur's men to be greeted by six feet worth of ballista bolts when they arrive. Constable, today I want one man to watch the causeway and a second to walk the castle walls. You are to lead the other four in cleaning out this hall and sealing the gaps in the walls. Everyone is to assist you in this. Then you are to begin investigating how we may block the gatehouse entrance. If necessary, we will send work crews to the mainland to cut trees with which to build a gate. Is that clear?"

Brocuff gave her a sharp nod and then turned to the crowd. "You heard Lady Kyferin! Ord, Janderke, Hannus, Haug, you're with Ser Wyland. Matzke, you're on watch up top. Ottel, walk perimeter. The rest of you, with me. Quickly, now!"

Jander stepped up to help her down from the barrow. "That was nicely done."

She inclined her head. "You're in charge of the expedition. I brought with me a small coffer of gold coins that you can use in your attempts at persuasion. Otherwise I will trust in your wisdom while dealing with these Hrethings."

"Of course. Don't worry. If there's any honorable way to convince them to help, I'll find it."

Iskra looked at where Ser Tiron had lowered himself to stare into the fire. "If not, I'll ask Ser Tiron to lead the second expedition."

"Hmm," said Jander, following her gaze. "He's not in a good place. Then again, how could he be?"

"Do you trust him?"

"He's an Ennoian. I trusted the man he used to be with my life. Now? I'm wagering there's some element of that man still left at his core."

Iskra inhaled and nodded. "Me too."

Jander turned to her. "Expectations will often help shape a man. I've seen green recruits fight fiercely beside veterans because their captain believed in them, and in so doing convinced them to believe in themselves as well."

"I don't know if I believe in him." Her voice was little more than a whisper. "I want to. But I don't know."

"Don't let him know that, then." Jander turned away just as Ser Tiron looked up. He smiled. "Lead. Set the tone. The rest will follow."

"Good luck, Ser Wyland." She smiled up at him. "I hope to see you back soon."

"You will." He stepped back and bowed, then turned and strode away. "Ser Asho! Lady Kethe! Come! Let us prepare for our outing."

Iskra watched the three of them gather with Brocuff's guards in the corner. Kethe avoided eye contact with her. Her daughter was holding herself stiffly, and looked as fragile as glass. Iskra felt a knot rise in her throat. Should she go to her? Press her to talk? No. The realization saddened her. Kethe needed to find her own path now, her own strength and self-respect. She was no longer just Iskra's daughter; now she was striving to be a warrior, a knight. Iskra had to give her the room to do so.

She took a deep breath and turned away. Ser Tiron was watching her, but he glanced away as if he'd been stung. Sensing the opportunity, she stepped up to him.

"Ser Tiron."

He rose stiffly and bowed. Was there a touch of mockery to his movement? "My Lady. You didn't give me a duty. I assume you either don't trust me or think I merit a day sitting by the fire."

She smiled scornfully. "You should be so lucky, ser knight. No, you have an active duty that will fill the entirety of your day."

"Oh?" He raised a dark brow.

"You are to be my personal guard."

He frowned, clearly taken aback. "Your what?"

"My personal guard." The idea had come suddenly to her, a wild idea, perilous, and shaped by Ser Wyland's words. "This is a dangerous land. Magister Audsley has spoken of these naugrim, and who knows what else may lurk in the shadows? Something has cleared the Hold of all life numerous times in the past. I would have your blade by my side should danger still stalk these old halls."

He stared at her in bewilderment. "I don't understand." Clearly, anger lurked just below the surface, ready to rear its head. "You're joking."

"I most certainly am not," she said coldly. "I am Lady Kyferin. It is fitting—no, necessary that I have a guard, whether I wish to have one or not. The success or failure of this endeavor rests on my shoulders."

Ser Tiron nodded dubiously. "Why not Ser Wyland? I could lead that expedition for you."

"You are not fit to enter into negotiations with strangers," she said. "Don't mistake me. I know full well how much pain and grief and anger you still carry within you. I see it, but I also see the man who labors beneath those burdens. That man once impressed me more than you can know. It is that man whom I am asking to stand by my side. Now, will you accept this duty?"

Ser Tiron stared at her with flat, dark eyes. "I told you: that man is dead."

Iskra met his gaze full-on. "I think you are wrong."

"Are you willing to wager your life on it?"

She raised her chin. There was no warmth in his eyes. It was like staring into the face of a sculpture. If only she were certain, if only she knew without a doubt that he could be trusted—but she didn't. Was this a terrible mistake?

Heart thudding, she fought to keep her expression severe. "Yes, I believe your sword will keep me safe."

Ser Tiron smiled, a feral expression that didn't touch his eyes. "Then I am your knight, my Lady Kyferin. Where you go, I shall follow, any my sword will always be at your back."

She nodded tightly. His words did not reassure her, but the die had been cast. "Come then. I would inspect the ballista."

She turned swiftly and strode out of the hall. She heard his heavy tread behind her, and fought the urge to run.

CHAPTER TWENTY-FOUR

Asho

The village of Hrething was bleak. Topping the final rise, Asho gazed down upon the ragged buildings that were clustered below. The glittering waters of the Erenthil plunged in a series of precipitous drops to join with another stream and disappear amongst the slate tile roofs. A water wheel was turning slowly on the far side of town, and a watch tower rose to a precarious height, three massive trunks bound together near the apex so that their final spars spread out and supported a mean platform. A watch fire was burning brightly up there, its flames streaming fitfully as the evening wind gusted down the pass.

"It's not quite the village of Emmonds, is it?" Kethe stepped up next to him, her hauberk glittering like fish scales beneath a heavy, black-furred cloak. With her auburn hair braided and coiled into a utilitarian bun and her sword at her hip, she barely looked like the young lady he'd known before.

"Not quite," he replied. She'd returned to being cold and distant throughout the day's march, keeping to herself and refusing to be drawn into conversation even by Ser Wyland. Old instincts bade him to walk on and not invite abuse. He chose to ignore them. "The odds of their having honeyed clover buns aren't favorable, I fear."

She smiled thinly and placed one foot on a sharp-edged rock, leaning forward, forearms on her knee. "Humor. I didn't think you had it in you, Ser Asho."

Asho turned and looked up the escarpment to where Ser Wyland and the guards were still making their way down. Even with his injured arm, he had proven more nimble then they. "You're being generous. That was a pretty poor joke."

"Still, not bad for a beginner. You've not had much cause for jests, have you?"

It wasn't a question. She was gazing at him solemnly, and he had the surreal sensation that she was truly seeing him for the first time.

"No. Not really."

He felt awkward. Ser Wyland would play the moment off with his habitual charisma, knowing exactly what to say to set Kethe at ease. He knew he should say something, anything, but all he could do was cross his arms and stare down at Hrething. He felt Kethe's gaze linger on him, and her scrutiny made him even more uncomfortable.

"Do you hate me, Ser Asho?"

He glanced over at her in surprise. Her color had risen, but she stood firm. "Hate you?" He stopped to consider the question. "No."

"You don't?" She seemed surprised. "Why not?"

"Why should I?"

Kethe swallowed and checked Ser Wyland's descent. "Because I've been cruel to you all these years. Because I'm Lord Kyferin's daughter. Because I've seen you as nothing more than an upstart Bythian slave since you first sat at our dining table."

Asho's head rocked back; he felt as if he'd taken a blow. "Do you still think that?"

"No." She looked away quickly. "Not any more."

His heart was beating quickly. It was rare for somebody to so openly discuss their disdain for him. "Why not?"

"Why not?" She spoke softly, staring down the scree to Hrething. "A lot has changed since my father died."

That was true, but it wasn't a complete answer. Her eyes narrowed, then relaxed. Her lips pursed, then parted as if she intended to speak only to close again. It was like watching the surface of a stream, flowing and fluid, mercurial and wild. He saw her then, the same slender girl he'd grown up with, if from a distance, for all her armor and coiled bun; saw the raw emotion she'd been concealing all day as adroitly as he had his whole life. She was barely holding herself together.

"I'm sorry," he said. "I never had the chance to tell you in person. But I'm sorry for your loss."

"You are?" She laughed bitterly. "You must be the only one. Everyone else is falling over themselves to tell me what a monster my father was."

Asho hesitated. Good manners would have him hold his tongue. A keening wind whipped down the escarpment, bringing with it faint curses from the guards and the sound of rattling stones. "I'm sorry for your loss. For the pain you feel. Not for Lord Kyferin's death."

Kethe nodded woodenly. "There you go. Very well. I suppose this is where you tell me all your personal grievances against my father."

He checked his sudden anger. Was that how he looked to Ser Wyland, so caught up in his own grief and sense of victimhood? He felt a cruel desire to hurt her, to force her to acknowledge anyone else's pain but her own, but he bit it down. "No. I won't waste your time."

"No? A miracle. Praise the Ascendant." She hugged herself tight. "I can only imagine the stories you could tell. Let me guess—you blame him for Shaya's abandoning you?"

There was just enough scorn in her voice to make him furious and enough raw pain to keep him silent. Was she truly so ignorant? He took a shuddering breath, held it for a moment, then released it.

"Thank you for reminding me who you truly are." He fought to keep his voice level. "For a moment there I had almost begun to forget."

Just then Ser Wyland came skidding down the last of the slope with a yell and staggered as he caught his balance. Asho stepped over the ridge and began to stride down alongside the whispering Erenthil.

"Asho," he heard Kethe call. He ignored her and fixed his gaze on the watch fire.

The watchman had sharp eyes. He spotted them while they were still a good distance away, and they heard the thin clamor of his bell as they reached the Erenthil's confluence with the other stream. Ser Wyland raised a hand and they stopped. A scant minute later a dozen men stepped forth from a narrow street. In the dark of deep dusk they were barely silhouettes, though it was clear they were large men. Standing beside Ser Wyland, Asho fought the urge to shiver.

Ser Wyland walked forward slowly, hands raised in a gesture of peace, and stopped a dozen yards from the silent men. "Good evening," he called, his voice amiable and deep. "We've come from Mythgræfen Hold by way of the Raven's Gate. Not a popular point of origin, I've been led to understand, but we're honorable folk and we've no wish to cause trouble."

"Mythgræfen Hold?" A tall man stepped forward, heavily bearded and clad in furs. He was holding a large ax in one hand. "That's an ill omen and a strike against you. What brings you to Hrething?"

Ser Wyland kept his voice friendly. "We're in need of food and supplies, and are ready to pay for them. I'd like to meet with your leader, seeing as we're to be neighbors for a spell to come. Are you him?"

"Me? No." The man laughed. "I'm not the headman. The Raven's Gate, you say? You come by way of Kyferin Castle, then?"

"Aye," said Ser Wyland. "Lady Kyferin herself is at the Hold."

At this the men turned to whisper amongst themselves, then the tall man turned back. "Lady Kyferin? Is she a Kyferin by blood?"

Ser Wyland frowned. "No. She married into the family. Why?"

"No matter." There was a thoughtful pause, then the man slung his ax back over his shoulder. "That's probably for the best. I'm Kolgrímr, son of Gunnvaldr. Come. We'll escort you to my father's house."

Ser Wyland led them forward, and up close Asho could see that the men were rawboned and lean like wolves, faces chapped by the cold winds, features heavy, with braided hair and thick beards. They were wearing thick furs and were armed with short, broad blades with no hilts and hand axes. Asho thought they had a durable look to them, hardy and resolute and dour. Ser Wyland introduced them all, but chose not to mention Kethe's ancestry, and Asho was unsurprised when she didn't complain. Kolgrímr nodded to each of them but didn't offer his hand. Then he turned and led them into Hrething, the other men following at his heels.

There was no talk. The street was little more than an alley, the houses leaning in close together as if for warmth and solace. The windows were all tightly shuttered. Occasionally Asho caught sight of the watch fire burning high above. There was no telling one house from the other; to his eye, there were no shops or government buildings, just uniform, hunched buildings with peaked slate roofs and raised doors as if the streets were prone to flooding.

Their group wound through the town and eventually fetched up before a house like all the others. Kolgrímr pounded on the door with his swollen knuckles, and it cracked open soon after to show an old woman's suspicious face. Warm red light and the scent of rich food wafted out into the chill air. Asho swallowed as his mouth filled with saliva.

"People down from Mythgræfen," said Kolgrímr. "They want to see Father."

"I can't fit all of you in here," she said. "You should know better."

Kolgrímr turned to Ser Wyland. "How about it? I'll go in with three of you. The rest are welcome to stand out here or wait in another home close by."

Ser Wyland nodded. "They'd be glad for the hospitality. Thank you."

The old lady cracked the door open wider and Kolgrímr entered, followed by Ser Wyland, Kethe, and Asho. Asho kicked the toes of his boots against the doorstep like Kolgrímr had done, causing caked mud and ice to drop to the street, then ducked under the low lintel to enter a baking warmth. The woman closed the door and Asho immediately felt the urge to shrug off his cloak.

The house looked to be one large room, low-ceilinged, with a ladder leading through an open square to the loft. The air was smoky from the two large fires crackling in opposite fireplaces, and the low beams were hung with dry vegetables and desiccated meat. One side was a clean kitchen, and a bench ran around the other walls, with two leather chairs set before one of the fires. The floor was covered with the pelt of a massive bear. Asho hesitated, trying to imagine how large it must have been while it was alive. Bigger than a horse, he decided. No, larger even than that.

"That bear turned man-eater before you were born," came a gruff voice from one of the leather chairs. Asho looked up, startled, and saw that an old man was staring at him with his one good eye, the other covered with a leather strap that cut across his face obliquely. "Would have been forty-three years ago now. No reason for it. Plenty of game and food for it up on the slopes. But it came down and started carrying away our goats, then after a while, even that didn't seem to satisfy it."

Asho slowly shrugged off his cloak and hung it on one of the well-worn pegs by the door. Ser Wyland and Kethe did the same, then they moved, stepping gingerly on the bear fur, to lower themselves onto one of the benches.

"It was when it took Torfa that we decided to hunt it down. We never found anything but her arm. We put together a war party and tracked it. Wasn't hard to do. It wanted to be found. It was waiting for us, knew we were coming. It was smarter than any bear had a right to be—doubled back on its own trail so that we passed right beneath where it was waiting on a ridge. Next thing we knew, an avalanche of fur and talons and teeth had fallen on us and everything was blood."

Asho blinked and looked down at the skin again. He could see numerous places where the pelt had been cut and then sewn closed.

"It killed three of us. Broke Ingvarr's leg. Dagr took off and ran. I understood, but I never forgave him. The beast backed me up against a wall. All snarling and bleeding, it was, but I knew it wanted me. Not to eat. Just to kill."

The old man's voice was mesmerizing. There remained in his gaunt features and his sunken eye a power that caused his voice to resonate. "I took up Ingvarr's longspear. Didn't have time to think. I set the butt against a rock and closed my eyes when the bear fell on me. It impaled itself. Didn't die, though. It kept roaring and slavering. Thank the Ascendant Ingvarr's spear was made of iron ash. Bent every which way, and still the bear came at me, pushing the spear through its own body. Then the spear did snap, and it fell on me and everything went dark. My last thought was a prayer for Ascension."

He shifted in his seat. Kolgrímr was in the kitchen, snooping under one of the pots. The old lady slapped at his fingers and the iron lid fell back down with a rattle. Gunnvaldr shot an angry look at his son, who ducked his head in apology.

"Anyway, I didn't die. Obviously. The bear's corpse kept me warm through the night. When Dagr came back with the others, they pulled it off me and there I was, hale and well. But the bear had rotted. Somehow it had putrefied in that freezing cold. Meat don't do that. We skinned it right there and discarded the flesh." He paused and narrowed his remaining eye. "Now, why do you think I told you that tale?"

Ser Wyland leaned forward. "All heroic deeds are worth sharing."

The old man sneered. "No. That would make me little more than a braggart. Young woman, take a guess."

Kethe was staring down at the fur. She looked up slowly. "Because you think only evil comes down from the slopes?"

"Aye, that's the right of it." Gunnvaldr leaned forward, and Asho half-expected his joints to pop and his sinews to creak. "I heard Kolgrímr say you've come down from the Hold. That's a bad place. It don't make you bad people, necessarily, but nothing good comes from those who stay up there."

Ser Wyland rubbed his chin and nodded as if these words were both wise and incontestable. "Unfortunately, we didn't have much choice in the matter. Lord Kyferin's dead, killed in battle, and his brother exiled my Lady to Mythgræfen against her will. We find it no more cheering than you do, and perhaps less so for having to actually stay there. So, if you're expecting us to defend the damned place, you're going to be disappointed. We'll leave as soon as we can."

Gunnvaldr was listening with sharp focus. "And when might that be?"

Ser Wyland shrugged. "The Ascendant knows. Lord Laur's strong and we're weak. So we've come to ask for food and supplies. We expect no favors. We'll pay for anything you've got to spare."

The old lady turned from her cutting board. "Are there children up at the Hold?"

"No," said Ser Wyland. "No children. Only adults loyal to Lady Kyferin."

"She must be quite the Lady to command such mad loyalty," said Gunnvaldr. "But we'll help you as best we can. We've not much to spare. Hrething is a small town, though there are many more farms scattered here and there about the land. Folk come here to trade and grind what crops they can grow at the mill. I'll have Kolgrímr put out the word that you're looking to buy. We'll see who comes forward tomorrow morning."

"Master Gunnvaldr," said Asho, leaning forward. "You've been here your whole life. You must know something about Mythgræfen Hold. Can you tell us something about it? Anything? We've forgotten almost everything about it."

Gunnvaldr stared hard at Asho. "You're a Bythian. One of them slaves from the underground city. What are you doing dressed in armor and sitting amongst these folk?"

Asho blinked. There was no animosity or rancor in the old man's voice, just plain, honest curiosity. "Lord Kyferin raised me from Bythos and made me his squire. I've since been knighted."

Gunnvaldr grunted. "Wonders never cease." He leaned back in his chair and took up a long-stemmed pipe from where he'd laid it down on the floor. He tapped the ashes out over the fireplace's grate, then unrolled a leather bundle and pulled out a pinch of herbs. "Listen, then, and listen well. Mythgræfen is a cursed place. We don't go up there. We don't talk about it. We don't even think about it. Death walks those walls. It's known nothing but blood since it was built. Pray you're quit of it soon. Nobody lives there long."

"Please," said Asho. "We're trapped there for the foreseeable future. What is this danger? What is going to attack us?"

"Hmmph," said Gunnvaldr. He tamped the herbs in, then reached forward again to take up a burning twig. He held the flame down into the pipe's bowl and inhaled sharply once, twice, and then puffed out sweet-smelling smoke. "It's been a long time since folk were foolish enough to muck around up there. We've little left but warnings and legends. Nobody knows what comes for those who man the Hold's walls during the Black Shriving, because none survive it. So, no, I can't give you details, because I don't have any."

Ser Wyland stirred. "Black Shriving?"

Gunnvaldr scowled, as if he'd been caught admitting something he'd intended to deny. "Nothing you have to worry about. Not yet, at any rate."

"Still." Ser Wyland spread his hands. "You can't blame me for being curious. Does it have anything to do with the Winter Shriving?"

Kolgrímr stepped forward and leaned one shoulder against a post. "Winter Shriving?"

"Yes. A holiday we'll be observing in two months' time." Ser Wyland hesitated. Asho saw no recognition on Kolgrímr's face. "It's an annual celebration of the process of Ascension. Our sins are cleansed throughout the night so that we may greet the dawn in a state of purity and spend the day rejoicing. You've not heard of it?"

Kolgrímr shook his head. "The Black Shriving falls two months from now. That's no celebration."

"Wait," said Kethe. "You've truly not heard of the Winter Shriving? Which is your city? Ennoia?"

Gunnvaldr shook his head. "We're Hrethings."

Kethe sat forward. "But then how do you know your current cycle of Ascension?"

Gunnvaldr and Kolgrímr shared a look. "We're Hrethings," said the son. "We pray for Ascension and to pass through the White Gate. That is all."

Kethe went to object, but Ser Wyland raised his hand and nodded. "That's fine. We're not here to discuss theology. So our Winter Shriving is your Black Shriving. What can you tell us of it?"

"It's a bad night," said Kolgrímr. "Legend has it that whoever's at the Hold disappears by dawn. Evil roams the land. Down here we lock our doors and pray to the Ascendant and hold a vigil till dawn."

Silence fell across the room, except for the crackling of the fires. Gunnvaldr puffed at his pipe, and his son turned back to the kitchen, where his mother was ladling soup into bowls. These were handed out, along with hanks of hard black bread that softened wonderfully when dipped.

"There's something else you ought to know," said Ser Wyland.

"There always is," said Gunnvaldr, staring into the flames.

"The man who banished us isn't content with letting us rot in the Hold. He's sending an armed force to finish the job through the Talon two weeks from now."

Gunnvaldr hissed smoke out through clenched teeth. "They'll have to pass through Hrething in order to reach the Hold."

Ser Wyland "That's why we're also interested in hiring whatever help's willing to come up to the Hold to shore up the walls."

Kolgrímr laughed warmly. "Hire Hrethings to come up to the Hold? Not likely."

"I thought as much," said Ser Wyland. He spooned some soup into his mouth. "Ah, that's good."

"You should quit the Hold," said Gunnvaldr. "You'll die there if you stay, whether at the blade of these enemies of yours or otherwise. We've no room for you here in Hrething, but if you move down into the lowlands you might find room in Dagrún. They might accommodate you."

Asho resisted the urge to set down his soup. "And save you the trouble of having warriors come through while we're at it."

"Aye," said Gunnvaldr calmly. "That's a welcome benefit right there. Do you blame me, lad?"

Asho looked down. "No, I guess not."

Kethe spoke, her voice quiet. "What is it you fear up in those mountains? Not just twisted bears. What else is up there?"

Silence fell. Gunnvaldr exchanged a glance with his son, but neither spoke.

"The portcullis of the Hold was torn down as if it were made of soft butter," said Ser Wyland. "What could do such a thing?"

"Nothing that will ever pass through the White Gate," said Gunnvaldr. "We don't speak of it. I'll ask you kindly to leave it at that, or leave my house."

Ser Wyland nodded and they subsided into silence once more, slurping their soup and enjoying the warmth of the fire. Asho mopped up the last drops in his bowl, and still he heard his stomach growl. Would it be rude to ask for another four bowls? He looked over and saw that Kethe had polished off her bowl as well. She caught his eye and made a face. Clearly she was still hungry too.

The silence was rent by a sudden pounding. Kolgrímr strode over to the door and pulled it open. One of the men who had welcomed them to town was there, a burning torch held aloft. "There's trouble. Einarr's found spoor along the west wood, moving in the direction of the Önundr farm."

Kolgrímr nodded and looked to his father. "I'm going after it."

"You are not." Gunnvaldr rose to his feet. He had clearly once been a powerful man, but his frame was now lean and bowed.

"I am. Of course I am." Kolgrímr smiled, but it was more grimace than smile. "How am I to earn my own floor rug and tale if I stay cowering at home?"

"This is no bear, Kolgrímr, and you know that." Gunnvaldr was shaking. "You will lock that door and stay here till dawn. The Önundrs will have to fare as best they can."

"No, Father." Kolgrímr moved over to where he'd propped up his ax. He took it up. "I won't leave the Önundrs to their fate. You know I won't."

Everyone stood. Asho took a step forward. "What's going on?"

"None of your damn business," snapped Gunnvaldr.

"We're handy with these blades," said Ser Wyland. "Perhaps we can help."

Kolgrímr hesitated at the door. "You don't know this land. What are the Önundrs to you?"

Asho felt a jolt of excitement run through him. He fought to sound calm. "Nothing, yet."

Kolgrímr stared at him, eyes hard. "All right. We're going to be moving fast."

Kethe rose to her feet, hand on her sword's scabbard just below the hilt. "Fetch our men."

Kolgrímr nodded and turned to the man who was waiting

anxiously outside. "Bring their friends. I'll be waiting for you at the edge of town. Hurry."

"Kolgrímr," said Gunnvaldr, and there was a tone of pleading in his voice. "This is no bear."

"I know, Father." Kolgrímr stepped forward, placed his hands on Gunnvaldr's shoulders, and kissed his brow. "I'll be back." He then kissed his mother's cheek, and stepped to the door. "Ready?"

Asho pulled his cloak on and tied it tight. Ser Wyland and Kethe did the same. They then plunged back out into the night, whose cold was almost shocking after the close and smoky heat of Gunnvaldr's home. Kolgrímr rushed down the narrow street and Asho hurried after, almost breaking into a run. A left, down a block, and then they entered the town square, which was dominated by the watch tower's massive legs. Back into another narrow alley, past a dozen houses, and then Kolgrímr stopped as the town came to an abrupt end and the night and the mountains loomed large before them.

"What are we hunting?" Ser Wyland's voice had changed. Gone was the amiable tone. Now he was all business, a seasoned knight, and Kolgrímr responded immediately.

"A creature of darkness. We won't know what it looks like till we see it, but it leaves large prints. Bare feet about this long." Kolgrímr held his hands almost three feet apart.

"A giant?" Asho couldn't deny the thrill that ran through him. Being a knight had always symbolized defeating Lord Kyferin. Suddenly it held a new potential, a chance to fight evil like in the tales of old.

"Like I said, we won't know till we see it."

Kethe stepped in closer. "How long has it been stalking your farms?" She was almost breathless, and Asho realized she was as excited and scared as he was.

Kolgrímr's response was somber. "Three weeks. Two farms have been destroyed."

Ser Wyland said sharply, "No survivors?"

"None," said Kolgrímr.

A band of men came jogging up, their torches startlingly bright. The four guards were with them, faces both alarmed and suspicious. The sight of Ser Wyland calmed them quickly. All told, they formed a band eighteen strong.

"Listen up," said Kolgrímr, taking a torch from one of the men and holding it aloft. "The beast's heading toward the Önundrs, but it's moving through the woods. We'll run along the forest's edge and cut to the farm at the Neck. With luck we'll get the Önundrs away and be ready for it when it appears. We move fast. Now."

Kolgrímr turned and jogged into the darkness. Ser Wyland nodded to the guards, assuring them that they were not being coerced, and together they set out, a ragged band of huffing men, three torches held up to light their way. The flames hissed and streamed in the wind, casting a fitful light across the rocky ground. Overhead, the moon shone brightly, one night past full, and Asho wished they could quench the torches and run by its silver light. If only the others could see as well as he in the dark. He ran, one hand on his sword hilt, eyes on the ground immediately before him. Soon his breath was coming in pants, his spit thick in the back of his mouth. It was hard work to run uphill in a full hauberk with a heavy shield on his back. To their right Asho could see the forest's edge, a black belt of evergreen firs. As they ran, the forest drew ever closer, until Asho saw the break in its line where they would plunge through to a higher meadow.

"Here," said Kolgrímr, breathing heavily. "Through the Neck and we're but ten minutes away."

He'd slowed to a fast walk. Asho drank down deep gulps of cold air. Sweat was running down his back beneath the padded coat he was wearing under his chainmail. This was dangerous, he knew; should that sweat cool, he'd grow dangerously chilled.

Moving forward, the group approached the wood. Rime-covered puddles crunched underfoot. Everything was still but for the hiss of their torches and their ragged breathing.

"Catch your breath," said Kolgrímr. "Steady. We've a steep climb before us, and then a hard fight."

They reached the edge of the forest. Asho couldn't see into it at all; the pines presented a solid wall of dark needles. It was sheer luck that he was staring at the right spot and thus saw it emerge from the woods. Like a nightmare unfolding into the heart of a dream, it was suddenly there, vast, silent, and impossibly hideous.

CHAPTER TWENTY-FIVE

kethe

Kethe's exhilaration was almost feverish. They'd accepted her amongst their number without comment, warriors all, men who knew no pity or remorse when it came to battle. This was no game, no rarefied outing. This was a hunt, a mission to save innocents, and the danger was all too real. There was no room here for her doubts and pain, her qualms and insecurities. All around her ran armed men with violence on their minds. The cold was shocking, but she barely felt it; she felt like she could run forever, so fleet of foot that she could leap up the cliff faces with a single bound. She was one with them. Grim determination steeled her exultation. She would not show weakness. She would not show fear. When the moment of truth came, she would be at the fore and would prove that she deserved the right to be counted amongst their number.

Asho ran by her side, breathing in harsh, controlled pants. His hauberk was a ponderous, unwieldy thing, easily twice the weight of her own. She felt lithe and agile in her armor, the leather supple, the chain so cunningly linked it felt like a second skin. The moon shone full and pregnant in the sky, and the land was silver and obsidian, ethereal and rife with the promise of danger and wonder both.

They veered to cut right by the edge of the forest. Kolgrímr spoke, gave his orders, and the band slowed. Kethe fought the urge to keep running, to take the lead and show them all how fearless she was. Instead, she cut her pace and inhaled deeply. The ground underfoot was uneven and hard, the dirt having frozen into iron ridges, and the puddles were slick and treacherous with ice. The moss and dry grass crunched with each step.

The forest drew close, a deeper dark against the night. Slowing down had been wise; she hadn't realized how hard she'd been pushing herself. She turned to smile at Asho and saw him go rigid with shock. Kethe started to turn to follow his stare, but then it was amongst them.

Yells and screams shattered the night. She heard the sound of tearing flesh. Hot liquid spattered across her face. She drew her blade, but then someone slammed against her and they both went down. The man stank of sweat and old fur and thrashed as he fought to stand, only to disappear as if something had simply yanked him up and away. Kethe battled the terror that was rising up within her, that wanted to clench her limbs and lock down on her mind, cause her to freeze and go still. She'd still not even *seen* the damn thing. Instead, she rose to a crouch, looked up, and saw it.

It was huge. Easily three times the height of a man, it towered over them, its skin black and satiny in the moonlight. Massive horns like those of some monstrous ox swept back from its head, then down and around, each longer than her arm and as thick as her thigh. But its face... Its face was utterly smooth, without features, a hard slope of bone with no eyes or nostrils. A jagged maw opened from horn to horn, filled with rows of fangs bigger than her thumb. Men were reeling all around it, trying to gather their wits, fighting to gain their feet and yelling hoarsely. It reached out with a muscled arm and snatched up one of Kolgrímr's men, raised him into the night sky and bit off his head. Kethe flinched as the sound of crunching bone hit her like a blow.

Stand! she heard her father bellow at her. *Stand and fight!*

She had no time to unsling her shield. Gripping her sword with both hands, she rose. Her guts were ice. She was going to die.

It spread both of its arms wide, bowed down and let out a hideous, soul-wrenching scream. The volume was overwhelming, the sound unnatural, like metal tearing. Men staggered back and a couple dropped their weapons and ran. Asho was one of the few men who were standing firm. She saw him unsling his shield, eyes wide with fear, but he refused to run. Kethe took a step back to steady herself and felt her heart seize in her chest. This wasn't possible. This wasn't real. She should run. What was she doing here?

Denial and fury arose within her chest. She could sense it now on some primal level, feel the wrongness of it burning off its skin like heat from a fire. Her mouth felt coated with rancid oil and her eyes were watering. She felt her father beside her, heard his roar echo within her skull, but when she opened her mouth it was her own scream of defiance that tore free.

The demon turned to stare at her. She raised her sword high with both hands and charged it.

A taloned hand swept down to tear off her head. She threw herself into a forward roll, came up right beside it and used her momentum to bury her sword into its side. Her sword slid in and stuck as if deeply wedged between rocks. For a brief moment it flared as if white fire had run down its length, but before she could look down at her blade, she heard the creature bellow and then it backhanded her.

The world spun. A white light eclipsed everything. She crashed down and tumbled, rolled, and fetched up against something hard. A tree? She blinked, tears filling her vision. She could hear dim screams amidst the ringing in her head, Ser Wyland bellowing orders, the thudding crash of feet coming her away. Wiping away the tears, ignoring the pain, she looked up and saw the monstrosity coming after her, her sword still sticking from its side.

She saw Asho hesitate—saw him glance at her, clearly wondering if he should come to her aid—then his expression darkened and he instead charged the demon, sword held high. He swung, but his blade bounced off its hide as if he had struck stone.

Undeterred, the demon came right at her. Instinct kicked in, and she scrambled to all fours and ducked around the tree just before the demon's claws slammed into the trunk. The pine shivered, and a rain of needles fell down upon her. She fell back on her ass and skittered away as the monster came after her, one hand closing completely around the trunk, its head coming round the other side, reaching for her with its free arm.

Talons sank into the dirt an inch from her foot, nails screeching on the rock beneath the topsoil. Kethe gasped, turned over once more and pushed herself up to her feet. She had to run, had to lose this abomination.

She could barely make out the trees in the dim light that filtered down from the moon. The ground was mercifully bare, completely without undergrowth and matted in a thick carpet of pine needles. She ran, dodging and racing around countless trees. It came behind her, faster than she would have thought possible. It roared as it slammed a shoulder into a tree, cracking the trunk, then another, then a third. Kethe's breath was scalding her throat, but terror gave her wings. She put on a burst of speed and ran as fleet as a deer. Branches sliced at her arms as she defended her face. It was easier to follow the slope downhill, and she leaped over a log, found a dry gulley and slid down to its bottom. It was an open road beneath the moon. Not daring to hesitate, she took off along it. The rocks that lined the gulley bed were smooth and firm beneath her feet. The sky was open overhead, and she could make out the obstacles as they came. Large rocks. Branches. She vaulted over them, nearly tripped, found her balance and ran on.

Yet still it came after her. She cast a desperate look over her shoulder and saw it charging along the bank of the dry stream bed. Kethe heard the sound of rushing water, and suddenly, her dry steam bed converged with a rapidly flowing river. Crying out, she scrambled up onto the bank and ran alongside the new river as it threshed its way between smooth boulders, gleaming like steel under the moonlight.

The demon was gaining on her, but she didn't dare cast a second glance behind her. One trip and she was dead. The river was four, maybe five yards across, fast-flowing, frothing and raging as it poured on. Ahead she heard a strange sound, a crashing roar. She leaped over a boulder, landed awkwardly and nearly fell. Pain lanced through her ankle as a rock exploded just to her left. The demon was hurling boulders at her. Moaning in terror, her lungs on fire, her head still ringing, she fought on, knowing she couldn't go much farther.

The river terminated suddenly in a sunken pool. Kethe caught herself at the bank's rim, arms windmilling. The roar was coming from the pool's center. It was pouring into a cavern underground.

She looked behind her. The nightmare was almost upon her. It palmed a rock larger than her head and raised it high. Kethe didn't think; she screamed and leaped forward, falling feet-first into the center of the pool.

The cold was stunning. The currents whipped her into a tight circle, battered her brutally against a rock and then sucked her down.

Her screams echoed as she plunged free-falling into a black and freezing void. She inhaled a mouthful of liquid ice, thrashed, was spun about and pulled underwater. Unable to see, she slid along the bottom, pulled over undulating swells of smooth rock. There was nothing to grasp, no ridges, no crevices. Her hands found only slick surface. Then she was sucked back up and her head broke the surface. She cried out, spat up water, choked. It was pitch dark. She was so cold she could barely feel her limbs. Shuddering, she fetched up against some rocks. She struggled out of the water, leather and chain pulling her down, and crawled over muddy ground to collapse onto her side.

The roar of the water was perpetual. She lay there shivering, teeth chattering, hair plastered over her face. She had to move. She'd die if she just lay here, but it was so hard to summon the will to stir. Her limbs wouldn't respond. Every reflex wanted her to curl ever tighter into a ball.

Slowly, painfully, she put a palm on the wet rock and pushed herself upright. Blinking, her entire body trembling, she looked up and saw a faint source of light: a waterfall cascading perhaps a dozen yards from the ceiling, where moonlight glowed softly, caught in the froth. Was that a frustrated bellow of rage? It was impossible to tell for sure over the crash of falling water. The echoes were confusing, but she felt space around her, a small cavern.

She couldn't go back up there. She couldn't sit here. She had to keep moving.

"Get up," she gasped to herself. But still, she couldn't move. "Get up," she said again, and thought once more of her father. How he would refuse to lie down, would refuse to give up. Summoning his strength, she forced herself up to her feet, reaching out blindly into the darkness as she did so.

The ground was treacherous. She shuffled forward, wanting to cry from the scrapes and bruises and the cold that was freezing her marrow. Her hands touched a wall, found it slick and wet. There was no indication as to where she should go.

Despair battered at her mind. What hope was there? She was lost. Nobody knew where she was. Alone in the dark, soaking wet and freezing to death. No sword, no food, her cloak torn from her neck. Should she strip off her soaked leather and chain? No; her woolens were soaked too. She needed a fire. She had flint and steel in her pouch, but that only made her want to laugh. What would she set on fire? Herself?

She stumbled alongside the wall, fingers too numb to feel the surface, only the resistance telling her the wall was there. Finally, the roar began to recede. She thought of her feeling of euphoria only minutes ago. She wanted to laugh at herself for feeling so tough, so ready to prove herself. She walked on, one arm pressed to her chest, the other outstretched. The wall guided her back to the river's edge, and she nearly fell back in.

She stood still, shaking, unable to think. The ledge had ended. The water was flowing furiously past her feet. She could turn around and go back, try to circumvent the waterfall, maybe climb back up and hope the monster was gone. In her heart, though, she knew she couldn't. A dozen yards of slick boulders in her condition? Impossible.

Minutes passed. She clutched at herself, wishing for heat. Once more she thought of her father, the most dangerous and powerful knight she had ever known, a monster like the one that had just tried to kill her. What would he have done if he'd stood here in her stead, soaked and alone and weaponless in the dark?

She heard his scornful laugh echo over the roar and saw him leap out to fall into the center of the river and ride its current down into the darkness, wherever it might take him. She hesitated. The river had to go somewhere. Come out somewhere.

Kethe closed her eyes, took a shuddering breath, and fell forward, back into the water.

It snatched her up greedily and bore her away. She flipped and tumbled, and then her head broke the surface and she gasped for air.

The sounds had changed. The cavern was gone. She was being pulled along in pitch darkness with a ceiling of rock barely a foot above her face. Her cries and gasps were loud in her ears. Then the ceiling smacked her scalp and she was shoved under. Tumbling, she flowed on. There was no air; she didn't know which way was up. Down and on she went, banging and bouncing against the rocks. She closed her eyes tightly. Her lungs ached; her head was pounding, her ears ringing.

Then, suddenly, the flow slowed and her head broke the surface again, and once more she gasped, spluttering and hacking for breath.

Her feet trailed over the riverbed. The river seemed to have broadened and grown slower. She fought for footing, lost it, fought again—then the water washed her up onto a shore. She collapsed onto her side on a bed of pea-sized rocks that crunched beneath her.

The echoes were liquid and confusing all around her. She lay still, heaving for breath. It would be so easy to just go to sleep. The water had become, if not warm, at least strangely soothing. The ground felt soft. She could relax. Let go.

A small kernel of light blossomed within her. She could visualize it perfectly: a tiny bud, beautifully formed, its petals wrapped tight. It hung in a void. Slowly the petals opened and a white luminescence spilled into her soul, filling her with true warmth. She heard a soft ringing sound like a bell being gently tapped, and the numbness began to recede.

Kethe's eyes fluttered. The inner light did not flood her with strength, but it felt as if she had gained a second wind. With a raw gasp she pushed herself up, sat, and then raked her hair from her face. Was that an opening up ahead? She could barely make out shapes and silhouettes in the darkness, the roundness of more boulders, gradations to the darkness. Crying out in pain, she stood, wavered, and then began to stagger forward. She kept her attention focused on the small flower of light that hung suspended within her soul. She stumbled and tripped but kept going until the ceiling pulled away and she felt fresh air on her face.

She stepped outside, and the river glittered anew beneath the light of the moon.

Knowing only that she couldn't stop, Kethe staggered on, following the water's course down and along the bank until it curled away to the left as the stream entered a narrow lake hidden in a cleft of rock.

A light was bobbing along the shoreline just ahead, pale blue and hovering over its own reflection in the water. Kethe swayed and sat. She could go no further.

The light came closer, and she saw that it was a lantern being held aloft by a young woman. There was no surprise on the woman's face. She stepped up and spoke, but Kethe couldn't make out her words. The blue light was emanating from a handful of insects that circled endlessly within the lantern, their abdomens glowing brightly. Kethe blinked. It was beautiful. Slowly, with a sigh, she toppled forward, and everything went dark.

Warmth seeped into her, brought her back to life. Kethe stirred and stretched. She felt soft furs beneath her, a heavy blanket above. A fire was crackling close by. She raised her hand to her temple and fluttered open her eyes. The slope of a roof was but a few feet above her, the beams carved with strange runes that beguiled the eyes.

Turning, she rose on one elbow and saw that she was inside a small cottage. A tidy fire was burning brightly in a stone fireplace, casting dancing light about the room. A brindled firecat lay before the fire asleep. The young woman was seated at a trestle table wrapping red twine around bundles of herbs. She was young but self-possessed, with a calm certainty to her movements and a maturity to her expression that made her seem as old as Kethe's mother. Her black hair was pulled back into a thick braid, and her high cheekbones and dark liquid eyes made her beautiful. Asho, thought Kethe, would be tongue-tied around her.

"You're awake," said the woman, not hurrying as she finished bundling a final sheaf. Her fingers were long and clever, her voice a sensuous, shadowy purr. "I was sure you would sleep through the night. It's not often I'm wrong."

"Who are you?" Kethe went to sit up and realized that she was naked beneath the blanket. She clasped it to her neck hurriedly as she rose. "Where am I?"

"Such gratitude. It never fails to warm my heart." The woman set the herbs down and leaned back. "I am your host. You are in my home."

Kethe bit her lower lip and looked around the cottage. It was filled with all kinds of intriguing objects and was deliciously inviting, from the crimson and burgundy wall hanging with golden glyphs painted down its length to the thick furs that covered the cottage floor. A pot of something savory was bubbling over the flames, and endless jars and vials glimmered on shelves in the firelight, holding everything from live frogs to small bones to herbs and inks and more.

"Your home." Kethe gathered herself. What had happened? She recalled a dancing blue light. Black rushing waters. A bellow chasing her through the night. She clutched tightly at her blanket. "We're not safe. Out there. In the night. A demon. We have to run."

"Yes, I know of what you speak." Perversely, the woman smiled. "You need not worry about that while you are with me."

"I don't?" Kethe blinked. "Who are you?"

"Questions, questions, questions. But I suppose it's natural. You may call me Mæva. But that's not what you're really asking, is it?"

Mæva rose gracefully to her feet. She was wearing a black leather skirt that that hid her feet, intricate patterns sewn along its hem with copper thread. A shawl of black and violet was wrapped around her waist, with a belt of worked bronze slung about her hips with numerous pouches hanging from it. Her midriff and shoulders were bare, for she wore only a wrap of similar black leather around her chest. Numerous bands and metal rings decorated her arms, and tattoos of swirling design adorned her shoulders. A leather choker was pulled tight about her neck, and the whole ensemble made her seem eldritch and fey, striking and wild.

Mæva stepped around her table to Kethe's bed and sat on its edge. Her irises were almost completely black, inquisitive and amused and piercing. She smelled of the forest, of bark and herbs, of soil and sunlight on leaves. She smiled, but the expression seemed only to make her all the more predatory. "You wish to know not *who* I am, but what. Am I right?"

Kethe swallowed and fought the urge to shrink back. "You live alone. Monsters stalk the woods. You don't seem afraid. Or mad. So, yes: what are you?"

Mæva's smile deepened. "I am one who has grown wise to the ways of the woods. Fortunately for you, or you might be face-down in the dirt right now, staring into the mulch, your last breath dissipating in the uncaring night air." Mæva reached out and traced the line of Kethe's jaw, and at this Kethe did flinch. Mæva laughed coldly and walked to the pot that was bubbling on the fire. Her firecat woke and shook out its wings before turning to study Kethe. Its eyes were a disturbing, curdled yellow, without pupils or sclera. "What were you doing, incidentally? Surely not hunting that beast alone?"

"No, not alone." Kethe tore her gaze away from the firecat, which was watching her with eerie self-possession, and looked around for her clothing and armor. She couldn't spot them. "My friends and I are trying to help a farm. That—that monster—was going to attack it. It attacked us, though. Took us by surprise. In a part of the woods called the Neck?"

"Hmm," said Mæva, nodding as she lifted the lid and stirred the food. Kethe's mouth flooded with saliva. "Yes. A thick stand of black balsams. I know of where you speak. Which means you must have entered the river through the Gouged Eye." She glanced over her tattooed shoulder at Kethe. "The sinkhole?"

Kethe nodded. "I jumped in. It was chasing me."

Mæva nodded and hefted the pot off its stand, then moved it to her table, where she set it down on a square of plaited rushes. "It's almost a mile from the Eye to where I found you." She pulled out two wooden bowls. "I'm impressed. Before tonight I would have doubted anybody could survive what you did."

"Yes, well." Kethe shifted uncomfortably. "I almost didn't. Um… where are my clothes?"

"Drying. Here." She brought over a bowl and spoon and handed them to Kethe. The bowl was filled with vegetable soup, which smelled exquisite. "Eat."

"Thank you." Kethe finally felt herself again. "And thank you. For everything. For bringing me here, for… saving my life."

Mæva sat and filled her own bowl. "How civilized. Gratitude after all. You're welcome. Though, to be honest, I was expecting you. I'm not in the habit of saving every drowned rat I come across."

"You were expecting me?" Kethe paused, spoon halfway to her mouth.

Mæva nodded. "Who are you, my little drowned rat? Why are you important?"

"Important? I'm not important. Not in any real way." Kethe wanted to shovel a hot spoonful of soup into her mouth, but Mæva's dark eyes held her trapped. "I'm Kethe Kyferin, daughter of the former Lord Kyferin, of Kyferin Castle and Mythgræfen Hold."

For the first time Mæva looked surprised and unsure of herself. "Are you now? A Kyferin? Of direct descent?"

"Direct…? Yes. Of course." Kethe finally ate some of the soup. It was delicious. Lumps of soft roots were mixed in with herbs and crushed nuts. Creamy and rich, it warmed her all the way down to the core and banished the last of her chill.

"Kethe Kyferin. You must have come through the Raven's Gate two nights ago, during the full moon. And already you're hunting demons in the Lower Wood with Hrethings. Why would a young lady of your rank do such a thing?" Mæva rested her chin on the base of her palm, eyes gleaming. "To help them, perhaps, from the goodness of your soul. Or perhaps you are short on knights who might do this hunting for you. And such a rapid descent from the Hold to Hrething speaks of need. Did you come ill-supplied from Kyferin Castle? If so, why? A hurried escape? Was the castle besieged?"

Kethe was shaken by Mæva's astute line of reasoning. *Demon?* "I applaud your wit, my Lady."

Mæva snorted. "I'm no lady. Mæva will suffice."

"All right. But yes. We're in dire straits up at the Hold. My father was killed in battle." It was the first time she'd managed to say that out loud in one go. "My mother and I were banished by my uncle, who took custody of my younger brother. We were forced through the Raven's Gate against our will." Why was she telling this strange woman all this? Mæva's dark gaze seemed to compel her. "My uncle is going to send an armed force against us through the Talon in two weeks' time, to make sure we never return. We need all the help the Hrethings can spare."

"And the Black Shriving only two months hence. I wonder if your uncle knows what wheels he's set in motion, sending a full-blooded Kyferin to the Hold." Mæva smiled cruelly. "Somehow, I doubt it. Men rarely think through to the true consequences of their actions."

"All right, enough." Kethe reluctantly set aside her soup. "What's going on here? Demons? Black Shriving? This all has to do with Mythgræfen Hold, doesn't it? And my family line?"

"Oh, yes, indeed." Mæva's amusement was evident. "Yes, child. Demons and more. Much, much worse than what you have seen. You've come to a dangerous and forgotten land. Some might say inimical to people like you."

"But not yourself?" Kethe fought her frustration.

The firecat rose and leaped into Mæva's lap, and Mæva began to stroke its neck. "Ashurina and I survive." The firecat—Ashurina?—was staring at her with its unnatural yellow eyes. The arrogant curl of Mæva's lips indicated she enjoyed the understatement. "But you won't last long if you set out hunting demons at night. I'd advise you to stop with such foolishness."

"That thing needs to be destroyed," said Kethe, trying not to sound sullen. "Now more than ever." She paused, and realized that she'd yet to receive a straight answer from Mæva on any of her questions. "I thank you, as I've said, for your help. You are clearly..." She hesitated, waving a hand as she sought the right adjective. Mæva raised an eyebrow as she waited. "Clearly a very competent lady. Would you please help me rejoin my companions?"

Mæva shook her head. "Not tonight. You wouldn't survive the trip. You need to rest. Perhaps in the morning."

Kethe curled her hand into a fist. "They'll be worried about me."

"As well they should be. But, no, I will not lead you outside, only to drag you back here again when you collapse. You were near death when I found you, girl. Only my skill as a healer has you talking and feeling remotely close to normal."

Kethe sighed. She sensed the truth in Mæva's words in the depths of her exhaustion—and the numerous aches and bruises and scrapes that seemed to cover her everywhere. "Fine."

"How gracious of you, allowing me to look out for your health and wellbeing." Mæva smiled mockingly down at Ashurina, which raised its chin to be tickled.

"Why do you exert yourself?" asked Kethe.

"Why? As I said, you drew me, as you no doubt drew the demon. I can feel it even now. You are to this world what the Gouged Eye is to the river. Which makes sense, now that I know you have Kyferin blood in your veins. I will see you home. Never you fear."

"What do you mean, I drew the demon?" Alarm flared through her.

"Hush. I told you that you're safe while you're with me. Enough for now. We can talk about this in the morning." Mæva's voice was firm. Ashurina leaped off her lap to lie down close to the fire and close its yellow eyes. "Finish your soup and sleep. Heal. You have the rest of your life to wrestle with your true nature."

Kethe tried to process that, and wanted to protest, but her exhaustion was making it too hard to think. She finished her soup, trying not to gulp it down. Had she thought herself ready to venture back outside? She yawned and set the bowl down on the floor. Doing so made it terribly easy to just lie down, so she sank into the furs. Mæva was watching her, but Kethe's eyes strayed to the flames. Their light grew diffuse and vague, and as the warmth seeped into her bones anew she sank back into a deep sleep.

CHAPTER TWENTY-SIX

tharok

Tharok awoke by slow degrees, emerging from a deep and soundless sleep into the dawn sounds of the mountain pass. He opened his eyes and gazed up at the bound branches that formed the apex of the hut, at the thick tan canvas stretched over them and over which in turn the goat furs were layered. The hut smelled of Wrok, of his hide, his sweat, and Tharok wrinkled his nose in distaste. Wrok's spirit lingered. With his body burned, he would never ascend to the Valley of the Dead, but would walk the world in misery, or rise at most to the slopes of the Dragon's Breath.

With a growl the kragh arose, realizing as he did that he was still clutching World Breaker. He would need a scabbard, he thought as he strode out of the tent, brushing aside the hanging fur to emerge into the pale mountain sunshine.

Golden light spilled down from the far eastern peaks. The sun had just crested and was casting great rays of diluted gold into the thin wisps of cloud that streaked across the heavens in furrows. A chill was in the air and a playful wind gusted, tugging at the furs that lay over Wrok's hut and the spirit banners that snapped from the apex of each other hut nearby. Wrok's hut was placed on the highest ground, and from where Tharok stood he gazed out at the two dozen other large clan huts and gauged how many had left during the night. Perhaps two or three, which meant some thirty kragh or so. They would be the core that had supported Wrok, his extended family members and closest allies. No matter. The heart of the tribe was his.

Tharok lowered his body into a crouch and wrapped his broad arms around his shins, gazing meditatively down as the camp came to life. A change of leadership might be afoot, but life proceeded anon. Life in the mountains was harsh, and there could be no respite from the duties of the tribe. The night would have been spent in festivity and finding mates. The darkest and largest kragh males would have fought and found willing females, then rutted for hours. Now, with the new warlord in place and the festival over, the males would spend the day recovering, eating the remains of the feast, enjoying the affection of the females while it lasted. Tomorrow they would form into their clans again and depart, to spend another three months ranging around the settlement before returning for the next mating feast.

High overhead he saw a small hawk hovering, stationary in the great sky, a speck of darkness against the unfathomable blue. He watched it until it folded its wings and plummeted down from the sky to disappear from view into a higher valley, focused on its prey. Musing, he scratched at his jaw. Normally a chieftain surrounded himself with brothers, uncles, grandsons, his clan serving as his enforcers and eyes and ears in the tribe. But he was alone, unprecedented for a chieftain, and would be without the traditional core unit with which he could administer his orders. He would need to recruit others to positions of trust quickly before he became too isolated and his position was thus endangered through lack of close support.

Rocking back onto his heels, enjoying the sensation of the sun on his still-bare skin, Tharok half-closed his eyes so that prisms of multicolored light played across his eyelashed view. His lies about Ogri's prophecies had struck a chord within his chest. For too long the highland kragh had been fragmented, fractious, at each other's throats and at the beck and call of the more numerous and wealthy lowland tribes. For too long they had served as the shock troops of the Tragon and Orlokor, taking herd animals and metal weapons in exchange for their blood and loyalty. The age of preying on and raiding each other had to end, along with the traditions of slavery and stealing wives, and the endless internecine fighting. Only then would the kragh as a whole rise to greatness once more.

He already had control of the Red River Tribe, a confederacy of some twelve clans that would follow him as long as his rule was of benefit to their fortunes. Twelve clans, perhaps fifty warriors in all. Not enough to do more than raid the other tribes, to engage in skirmishes and midnight thefts. He would need to swell their numbers before he could think of forcing the other chieftains to follow him, to fall in line. The traditional roles would have to be shattered, the expected way of life changed.

A figure was trudging up the slight slope toward him, hunched and twisted. Tharok watched him come, and did not move or stand but rather stayed silent with his eyes half-lidded as Toad presented himself, breathing hard.

"Tharok-krya, you have awakened." When Tharok refused to comment on that obvious remark, Toad continued, "I served Wrok well and faithfully for many years, and would serve you just the same. I hope I don't need to remind you that it was my storytelling that gave you the opportunity to rise to your current rank." Tharok turned slowly to fix Toad with one eye, and the small kragh stumbled back. "I mean, I'm sure you would have risen to this position by yourself. I am proud of the help I gave, is all, and would give more if you would have it."

"Food," grunted Tharok. "Clothing. And send kragh to open this hut and let the wind blow Wrok's spirit away."

"Yes, straight away," said Toad, grinning and moving back quickly, bobbing his head. "As you command!"

He turned and rushed down the shallow slope, then moved into one of the large tents. Good. For now, Toad would serve.

Over the next hour Wrok's hut was taken apart, the furs pulled free and the tarp removed from the branches so that only the framework stood, open to the sun and the air, allowing the wind to usher Wrok free of his belongings and to dance perhaps around the Dragon's Tear. Toad brought Tharok rough mountain clothing, new boots, and a heavy coat to guard against the cold, all of it of fine quality, donated by the Illkor clan, who were clearly currying favor.

Dressed, he descended to the great fire, where he dined on cold lamb and small, withered apples, eating heartily for the first time in days. It was important to eat meat. Too much time spent eating vegetables or fasting would lighten his skin. Other kragh gave him wide berth, watching him surreptitiously as they went about their business, and for now he was content to allow the distance. He was closely connected to none of them, and the distance and silence would serve to build his reputation more than chattering in a familiar manner ever could.

Tharok looked up as a figure approached, moving with confidence and lethal fluidity, the sleeve of his coat tied off just below the shoulder. The weapons master lowered himself onto a log across from Tharok. His sharp, black eyes studied the new chieftain, his harsh, drawn face revealing nothing of his thoughts. Tharok studied him in turn, chewing slowly on the last of the lamb, and then threw the great bare bone into the cinders of the fire and wiped his hand on his thigh.

"You could have volunteered to fight me last night," said Tharok. "You could have taken vengeance for your arm. Made me pay for the injury my father dealt you."

"As far as I can tell, you are not your father," Barok said.

"But his blood flows in my veins. You could have pressed to fight me, and old Wrok would have gladly let you. Why did you hold back?"

Barok pursed his lips, narrowed his eyes, and then finally shrugged one shoulder. "You are not your father, but, more importantly and in different ways, neither was Wrok. With your father and the Gray Smoke gone, Wrok would have led us to ruin, his choices dictated by other masters."

Tharok nodded. "Good. You saw which way the wind was blowing."

"I did, eventually. Maur and the women's circle understood the events before they played out, not just during the fact like myself."

"So, you do not wish to fight for the Tragon."

Barok was watching him with great intensity now, as if he were a hawk himself, hovering in the air. "Fighting for the Tragon would mean allying against the Orlokor."

"There could be profit in that," said Tharok, leaning back and opening his hands. "After all, the Orlokor are now the largest tribe, the most powerful. They control all of the slopes to the south, the whole arc above the human city. They have goats, sheep and horses by the thousands, and wealth from controlling the mountain passes, and they trade directly with the humans themselves. Many riches to be had for a bold tribe. Much shaman stone."

"I was one of the kragh who helped your father negotiate the Gray Smoke and Red River alliance with the Orlokor. I was there when your father became blood brother with Porloc, when your father swore to follow his lead. I'd honor that bond, even though it wasn't my blood."

Tharok nodded. "Good. That was the answer I wanted. Once you were trusted by my father, and you worked closely with him, making his goals your own. That you fell out and lost your arm lies between you and him, but I would have you work by my side and help me with your wisdom, your skill. I want you to remain the weapons master, but more importantly, I want to be able to count on you as I would a member of my own clan."

He stared Barok in the eye, chin lifted, waiting. The weapons master returned his gaze, taking his measure, and then, slowly, nodded. They reached out and clasped each other's forearms, squeezing as hard as they could, and then released.

"Good," said Tharok. "My first request is that you oversee those six kragh I delegated last night, and make sure they bring me Krol. I'm going to speak to the women's circle now, and if they agree, we march tonight for the lands of the Orlokor."

Barok raised an eyebrow. "The whole tribe?"

Tharok grinned. "The Little Sister Moon waits for no kragh, Barok. I will not let our clans disperse. We move fast because there is much to be done."

The weapons master nodded and rose to his feet. "I'll bring you Krol. Good luck."

Tharok watched him leave, chewing absently on the remaining sliver of lamb flesh that he had tucked away in the lining of his cheek.

Time was passing, so he rose, feeling pain in his side, his arm still weak, and took a deep breath, trying not to show any of it to curious eyes. He reached down to where World Breaker was slung by his side and briefly grasped the hilt. Warmth and power flowed into him, and he stood for a while, marveling at the blade. For the first time he wondered where it had come from, who had crafted it. Ogri had clearly benefited from its use, but there was no mention of how he had found it, or who had made it. Ogri the Uniter had simply appeared one day, as the tales told it, blade in hand, and had begun the unstoppable juggernaut that had been the united kragh tribes.

He heard footsteps, and he turned to regard the women's circle as they followed Maur into the clearing, moving to stand before him in a semicircle, Maur in the center. She wasn't the eldest, the largest, or even the meanest; that title belonged to old Ikrolla, who was given wide berth whenever possible, her tongue sharper than even the weapons master's blade. Still, Maur had been chosen to join the women's circle at the incredibly early age of nine, barely out of her childhood, and now at fifteen she was a woman in full, with an authority that had reined in Wrok and defied his father on numerous occasions when their tribes had met. Tharok had watched his father go toe-to-toe with Maur once, bellowing his commands and orders only to have them smash upon her implacable will as an avalanche would explode when it collided with a mighty boulder. He'd admired her then, one of the few to dare his father's wrath, and now here she stood, gazing at him in exactly the same manner.

"Maur-krya," he said, spreading open his hands and then looking to the six other females. Krilla loomed tall over the rest, and old Ikrolla stood hunched nearly in half, bent low over her iron walking stick, staring at him suspiciously with her knife-sharp eyes. He nodded to each, and then returned his attention to Maur. "It is good that we meet. There is much to discuss."

"Indeed," said Maur, her voice hard. "Such as your numerous lies, and how you, Tharok, who but yesterday was as brutish and forward as any kragh, are now standing before us wearing the title of warlord when we were sure that you were doomed to a life spent in slavery."

Tharok smiled and spread his hands again. "I have charm. What can I say? Charm and luck beyond my fair share." He sat, confident in having riled her further, and one by one the women found seats, whether it was on the log before him or on separate rocks. Only Krilla stayed standing, prodigious arms crossed over her prodigious bosom.

"Enough with the games. We only backed you last night because Wrok unfettered was an even worse option. Now you have to prove to us that we were right in our judgment, or you'll find your tenure as warlord a lot shorter than you think."

Tharok nodded, quickly adjusting his approach. Maur and the women's circle could prove his greatest ally, or his undoing if he stepped wrong. Maur was too sharp for bluster or misdirection. He'd have to move carefully. "I understand, and as warlord submit to the council's questioning."

"Yesterday, when we spoke, you said that your father had been summoned by the Tragon to go on a raid. You said that you went with him, that you were all ambushed, and you escaped with your life to flee into the mountains."

Tharok attempted to remain calm, collected. His words from before he had donned the circlet.

"Then Toad spins a tale in which Garok voluntarily searched out the Tragon, inspired by Ogri himself, and that you were sent to find the Blade in his stead. Perhaps you notice the discrepancies."

Maur jutted out her chin and waited. The other women stirred, and all eyes were on him. Tharok returned Maur's stare, his mind moving and spinning as quickly as it could, and then he made his call. There were no other kragh close by to overhear; none would dare intrude.

"The Tragon under the Throkkar brothers are moving to war. With the Hrakar smashed to the east, they are now the second largest tribe. Even so, they don't stand a chance against the Orlokor, who probably, what, double their number, if not triple it? But if they were to gather the highland tribes to them, tribes such as the Red River under Wrok, and the remains of the Hrakar under whoever leads them now, well, then they would form a coalition that could challenge even Porloc in his valleys and foothills."

The women had stilled. This, they had not expected.

Tharok pressed on, "Yet I ask myself, why now? Why do the Throkkar brothers move now against the Orlokor, who lie south of the Sky Mountains, a world away from their northern plains? What moves them to now gather the Hrakar to their side, to unite the highland tribes as the Orlokor once did when they moved against the Hrakar?"

Tharok stood now, energy seizing him. So much had become clear when he had donned the circlet, patterns emerging that he had never considered. It was a pleasure to finally speak them aloud. "It puts me in mind of the rise of the Orlokor. That was, what, ten years ago? My father was young, my age perhaps, when Porloc summoned him and Barok to his side, along with the Jurched, the Kilokar, the mighty Achorhai and all the other highland tribes. Did not the Tragon unite with the Orlokor against the mighty Hrakar, and together didn't they all move to smash the Hrakar grip of the Dead Sky Pass?"

He stopped pacing and stared at Maur, who watched him with an inscrutable expression. "The Hrakar were mighty, and now they are fallen. The Orlokor are now mighty, but should the Tragon unite with the Hrakar and the highland tribes, there is little doubt that they too will fall, in time, with much loss of kragh lives. I imagine, were one to go back in time, to ask the humans who keep records of such things, that before the Hrakar rose in power, no doubt another tribe was mighty, and they fell to the Hrakar. Which sets me to thinking."

He reached down and took hold of the hilt of World Breaker, drawing strength from the contact. "Our lives as kragh are one of cyclical war amongst each other. We are always taking down the strongest tribe. We are always reducing our own number. So, who benefits, in the long run? The answer becomes clear when you ask who now has access to the Dead Sky Pass? The humans out of their city of Abythos. Who trades with the Orlokor? The humans, bringing their Gate Stone and other goods through their magic portal. Who might be resenting how powerful the Orlokor have grown, and their control of the other two great passes through the mountains? The humans. And who might be now encouraging the Tragon to unite with the others and start the wars anew? The humans, safe and hidden away in their distant Ascendant Empire."

Tharok leaned forward and bared his teeth. "I, for one, refuse to be manipulated into killing my brothers. I, for one, refuse to kill the Orlokor so as to ease the minds of the humans. The cycle has to be broken. We have to stop killing each other. And the only way to do this is to unite the tribes as Ogri once did."

His piece now spoken, Tharok narrowed his eyes and gauged each female in turn. Silence hung among them as his words were absorbed, mulled over, digested. Maur turned to look at her sisters. Krilla stood with both brows raised, impressed. Old Ikrolla spat on the floor and looked away in apparent disgust, which meant, Tharok knew, that she too was impressed. Each female in her own way registered approval, and finally Maur returned her gaze to Tharok.

"Never would I have guessed that I would live to see a male string so many thoughts together. Wrok was a fool, and a puppet besides. Your father was powerful, but not given to depth of thought. Even Golden Crow has trouble going beyond the immediate. You, however, have in one small speech spoken the thoughts and guesses that have taken numerous women's councils years to put together. But yesterday, when I spoke to you, you gave no evidence of these thoughts. In fact, none of us here can remember any hint of your being so bright in all the years we have known you. Powerful, yes. Quieter than your brothers, true. But so deep, so wise? No."

Tharok leaned forward, cutting her off before she could continue. "I lied about Ogri coming to my father. He went down into the north valleys to meet with the Tragon as I told you, and he died there because of simple treachery on Wrok's part. I was with him, and I fled for my life. I fled from the Tragon kragh, and went up the Dragon's Breath to lose them, to die in the Valley of Death. That much I did lie about. However, I told the truth when I said that Ogri's blood runs in my veins, and that his spirit came to me and gave me World Breaker and gave me a vision of the world that has burned my mind and revealed much to me."

Tharok stood and took a slow, menacing pace forward. The women did not shrink back, but they lifted their chins in response. "Do not doubt me. The sword and my new vision are proof of Ogri's blessing. Do not doubt the spirits. I will unite the tribes. I was once slow, given to battle and little else, true. But now I am more. You can sense this. You hear it in my voice. I will break the pattern. I will break the traditions that defeat us. I will lead us to a new age of ascendancy. All I need is for you to not stand in my way, but rather to help me. What say you?"

Maur stood, and for the first time Tharok had the pleasure of seeking her discomfitted, unsure of herself. A thought struck him out of the sky: had she mated the night before?

She sniffed loudly and turned to the others. They were rising as well. Maur nodded to them and turned back to Tharok. "We'll speak of this amongst ourselves. There is much for us to discuss. For now, though—for now you have our support. See to it that you do not lose it."

"Fair enough," said Tharok. "I am at your service until then."

The women nodded, Old Ikrolla spat on the floor again, and then they moved away, talking quietly amongst themselves. Tharok waited as long as he could and then grinned widely, immensely pleased with himself. His father had never stumped Maur in such a manner. To see her hesitate mid-speech like that was a first. She would probably make him regret it later.

He took a deep breath, then turned his mind to more serious matters. He had to put the word out that the tribe was to move before the clans dispersed. They would head south come first light. They would avoid their normal hidden trails and travel openly down the Chasm Walk, giving time for rumor of their coming to precede them. That should give Porloc advance notice of their approach and allow the lowland warlord to form an opinion before Tharok could present his case. It would allow word of World Breaker's coming to agitate the Orlokor, to strike fear into their hearts, and force them to rise in response so as to crush the Red River tribe completely.

Tharok smiled. *Perfect.*

CHAPTER TWENTY-SEVEN

audsley

Audsley sighed. It was the second bitterly cold and bleak morning since Ser Wyland had left, and Mythgræfen Hold was beginning to weigh on his spirits. The island was tiny, barely large enough to contain the Hold and its ruined bailey. At first it had been entertaining to walk amongst the fallen masonry and gaze at the improbable trees that grew here and there, to watch Aedelbert stalk amongst the ruins and listen to the melancholy cry of the ravens. To dream of what the Hold must have been like a century or so ago. Now, however, he longed for a bath, a hot meal of grilled rosemary pork with jellied currants, and his favorite armchair back in the Ferret Tower in which to snuggle down under three or four blankets with a good treatise or history book.

No such luck. He pulled his blankets tighter around his shoulders and shifted his posterior where it had grown numb with cold on the block of stone on which he sat. The dry cold made him wish he'd brought his tub of ingka nut butter he used to have imported from Zoe. His poor skin. He felt like he was flaking all over. That and Aedelbert was refusing to come out from under their heaviest blanket.

Brocuff was working on the wall with two of his soldiers, seemingly impervious to the atmosphere, his laughter raucous and as lively the flames. Lady Kyferin was, as always, up somewhere on the walls, shadowed by Ser Tiron as she waited and watched for the return of her daughter. Elon was tinkering with the ballista, which left Audsley alone and without much of a purpose.

Glum, Audsley stared into the fire and thought of his home city of Nous. Had it really been over a decade since he'd left it to enter Lord Kyferin's service in Ennoia? No, more than that: twelve years. He rested his chin on his palm. How he missed the Emerald City, with its great towers rising directly out of the ocean waves to challenge the peerless blue skies. To think he might never again row out at dusk to turn and watch sun the set with all its refulgent glory behind the copper domes, that he might not walk down the thousand winding stairs carved into the sides of the towers to the great balconies on which the markets were held. The smell of salt, the tang of fish, the cry of men singing at dawn to bring the women home safely in their cockleboats.

He wondered where she was now. The young women with gems

in her hair, the mysterious lady who had smiled at him so sadly from her solitary window. Each morning he'd passed across from her as he climbed toward his studies, and each morning his heart would race as he wondered if she would be there, alone and gazing out over the forlorn sea. Usually her window was empty, which filled him with a longing sense of loss, yet when she was there he was filled with terror, and would hurry by, turning his face away with mock disdain even as he tried to catch glimpses of her beauty.

Audsley smiled, feeling a tender sadness for his youthful folly. How hard would it have been to stop and say hello? The one time he'd dared slow his pace she had smiled at him, that one precious smile, and he'd panicked and run on. Ah! The folly of youth. He should have invited her down to the spice markets, have been bold and dared ask her to dive off the Fisherman's Ledge with him into the azure waters. Read her poetry, done something - anything.

Instead, he'd been timid. And when his commission to serve at Castle Kyferin was served, he'd passed one last time by that window, but it was shuttered and when he'd asked at the door the servant had told him the lady had left to travel the empire. Alone.

Feeling the faintest echo of that shame all over again, Audsley reached into his pack and drew forth his Nousian disc. It was a squat glass cylinder that held within its center a reservoir of Nousian water. Like all the others given to every journeyman Magister when they left Nous for a post in one of the other cities, it had a silver triangle embossed on its surface and was meant to remind each Nousian of their true home and ultimate loyalty. Instead, it reminded him of the vow he had ever since sought to observe: *be bold*.

Reaching into his pack, he drew forth a candle and lit it at the edge of the fire, then placed the flame beneath the glass disc. The light caused the ripples in the water to glow, and by squinting so that his vision blurred, he could almost see the watery glow of refracted light dancing across the ceilings of the flooded rooms at the bottom of Nous. The corridors and hallways and ballrooms and lecture halls, filled with the cold water of the rising sea.

Sighing, he blew out the candle and stored it and his disc back in his pack. "Come on, Aedelbert. We can't sulk all morning."

Aedelbert chirped and snuggled down deeper beneath the blanket.

"Fine, you're not sulking, but all the same. Don't force me to play the role of cruel taskmaster. Come along."

He pulled the blanket off his firecat and scooped him up. Aedelbert glared up at him and snorted out a small tongue of flame in annoyance.

"None of that. Here. Have a little breakfast." He squatted before the fire and scooped up a coal with one of Elon's misappropriated tongs. He held the glowing rose stone before Aedelbert's nose; the firecat sniffed it and then set to licking it cold. When he was done, Audsley dropped the ashen coal back in the fire and set Aedelbert on his shoulders. He gathered his cloak about his frame and drifted out of the great hall.

Audsley walked around the ash saplings, stepping absentmindedly over rusted weapons and armor as he went. What use was a learned man during a time of action? This was a time for swords and derring-do, not perusing ancient scrolls. Audsley fought back a sigh. Everybody had been given a task, save him. He was superfluous, really.

Audsley froze. What was that? He'd just walked past the entrance to a small room they were using to store their food supplies. He'd seen something. Movement. He stood still and listened. Aedelbert had tensed as well. Was that a subtle scuff on the ground? He gulped. One step was all it would take for him to return to the archway and peer inside.

Audsley hesitated. Naugrim? The sensible thing to do would be to call for others to join him. Some of Brocuff's men. Audsley frowned. Surely a quick peek couldn't hurt. He turned and peered into the room. Aedelbert peered around him in turn.

There, in the back, by the barrel of apples. Audsley pushed his spectacles up and peered intently into the gloom. A creature was barely visible behind the sacks of turnips. Too robust for a Bythian, but its pale skin and white hair gave it away. Naugrim. Audsley felt his heart pounding in his chest like a hammer. This was it. His first encounter with the supernatural. There, right before him, was a creature from myth and legend.

He couldn't let it get away. "Excuse me? Hello?"

The naugrim froze, then whipped a glance over its shoulder, lank white hair flaring around a hideous face. *Bad idea*, thought Audsley, eyes going wide. The anger in its eyes was shocking. *Bad idea!* He saw a massive nose, tiny gold eyes, and a slit of a mouth filled with sharp teeth and chunks of apple. Its frame was not just robust, but muscled, and its eyes were lit with a malevolent cunning. Before Audsley could react, it grabbed another apple and ran through the wall.

Aedelbert hissed and flew into the room to land on a tall stack of crates, fur puffed out, wings slowly beating. Audsley reached out to steady himself against the archway and turned his head from one side to the other in a vain attempt to catch sight of the—the thing. It was gone.

Audsley gulped and took a step into the storeroom. Never had a collection of bags and barrels looked so ominous. The room was damp, its ceiling low and made of rotten beams of wood. He took another tiny step. Silence surrounded him. He rounded the turnips and stared at where the creature had stood. He *had* seen it. He knew he had. Right there, eating an apple. He waited a full minute, listening and watching, and finally walked up to the barrel and examined the wall. Plain stone, like the rest of the Hold. He ran his fingers over the blocks. Not even a rat could get through. And yet the creature had done exactly that. Crouching, he picked up a chewed-up chunk of apple and felt a wave of pride wash through him. Evidence!

He reached into his pouch, drew forth his nub of candle and held it out to Aedelbert, who lit it with a fiery breath. "Thank you," he murmured, and scrutinized the dirt floor, where he found bare footprints, long-toed, with little dimples at the end to indicate claw tips. Audsley quickly sketched the sign of the Ascendant and tried to track the prints. They led right to the wall. Holding his candle aloft, he couldn't help but smile. So it was true: they really could pass through stone.

Then he stopped. Was that a vertical seam? He traced it with his fingertips. It was so subtle he wouldn't have spotted it without being this close. "How strange," he said to Aedelbert, who leaped onto his shoulder. "A hidden door?" He tapped his chin. A small wedge of stone was inserted between two larger blocks as if to fill a gap at about the height of a door handle. Audsley pressed it. The stone sank inward, he heard a muted click, and a section of the wall swung inward, revealing a dark space beyond.

"Oh, my," said Audsley. He stood, hand outstretched, straining to hear or detect anything, but heard only silence. Had the naugrim run through the closed door and into the passage beyond?

Before he could change his mind, he gave the door a firm push, and it swung in all the way, the light of his candle revealing a small landing at the top of a flight of stone steps. Moving forward, he peered into the darkness below. Exhilarated, curious, and trying not to think about how afraid he was, he stepped through the narrow portal onto the landing. The door was actually made of wood, he saw, with a facade of stone stuck to the front to cunningly emulate the wall. The little stone triggered a simple bolt; pushing it in caused the bolt to recede. "Very nice," said Audsley, working the bolt two or three times. There was no actual lock; from within, he saw, one simply moved the bolt back manually and the door would open.

"All right, now's the time to go tell the others. Enough of this foolishness, Aedelbert! We are not cut from the same cloth as heroes.

We're common men, you and I." He looked down the steps. The darkness into which they descended was terrifyingly inky and absolute. It reminded him of the sunken stairwells in Nous that led to the flooded levels below. Audsley shivered, goose bumps breaking out across his skin. "Yes, indeed. Time to go tell Lady Kyferin. And Brocuff. Right now. We've done our part. This is an amazing discovery, but we'll let someone with a sword finish the exploring."

Aedelbert rubbed his head against Audsley's cheek and purred.

"What? Go down there? You and I? You can't be serious." He stared down into the darkness, mesmerized. His candle flame stood tall and still. No draft. It was probably a contained chamber down there, then. "Hello?" His voice echoed faintly, but no response came. "Hello? We might very possibly be coming down."

He hesitated. What would he do if they saw that pale little monster again? Well, it *had* run from him. He swallowed again and looked back out into the storeroom. *Fetch someone else*, he thought. *Don't be a silly fool.* Let someone else have this adventure. Let someone else play the hero, while genial and boring Magister Audsley and his firecat stood at the back, anxiously watching over someone else's shoulder.

Audsley tugged his vest down and smoothed its front. "Feel free to convince me to do otherwise at any moment," he whispered to Aedelbert—then he began to descend the steps.

"Hello?" His voice was muted, as if absorbed by the darkness. "We really shouldn't be doing this, you know. Coming down here. Just give the word if you don't want us to come down, and we'll happily run back upstairs, screaming the whole way."

His mouth was dry. His little candle wavered as he took step after step. A complete rotation, and then another. Aedelbert perched tensely on his shoulder, claws digging through the fabric of his cloak. He imagined returning upstairs after making some fabulous discovery, finding Lady Kyferin and Ser Tiron together, and recounting his adventures coolly and carelessly. Lady Kyferin would gaze at him admiringly, and Ser Tiron's surprise would turn into grudging admiration. *I didn't think you had it in you, Magister, but by the Ascendant, I see now that I was wrong!*

The stairs turned once more and then opened up into a small chamber. A single Gate stood in the room's center, a desiccated corpse lying stretched out on the floor before it. Audsley covered his mouth with his hand. Half a corpse. Whoever had passed through the Gate had been killed when it had closed, cutting them neatly in half. The floor around the body was still dark with the ancient shadow of dried blood.

The Gate was clearly closed now, for he could see right through it.

"Oh, my," whispered Audsley. "Aedelbert, perhaps you shouldn't be seeing this."

There were three further rooms off this central chamber, which seemed to act as a central hub. Audsley craned and tried to peer into each room, but his candle's faint radiance failed to penetrate their gloom.

How long had the body lain there? It had been a warrior of some kind, he saw; it was wearing dusty black plate armor. A vicious-looking sword lay beside it, the lower half of one side serrated, the upper half curved into a wicked point. The corpse was holding a scabbard in the other hand.

The silence served only to heighten the pounding beat of Audsley's heart. He took a final step down into the chamber proper and looked at his candle flame. It burned steadily. There was still no draft.

"Hello? Ser naugrim? Are you down here?" There was no response. Audsley bit his lower lip. "What do you think, Aedelbert? Should we press on in pursuit of further glory, or allow discretion to bludgeon valor into submission?" Aedelbert leaped from his shoulder and glided down to land beside the body, where the firecat lowered its head to sniff at the dried blood. "Ah. Very well."

Audsley approached the Gate. It was beautifully carved from freestanding obsidian, its surface catching the candlelight in a thousand small planes and sharp edges. Where did it go? What had this stranger fled in such haste that he had risked leaping through just as the Gate closed?

Audsley squatted beside the body. The face was little more than mummified skin stretched taut over the skull. He reached out to touch the sword and snatched his hand back as Aedelbert suddenly hissed loudly at him.

"No? Don't touch it? All right." He rubbed his hand as if he'd been burned and rose to inspect the Gate more closely. The Gate glass contained enough sand for a one-minute opening. A great distance, then. There'd been no mention of this Gate in *Alastair's Lunar Almanac*. He felt a frisson of excitement. A new discovery! Wait till his old masters in Nous heard of this!

Aedelbert suddenly wheeled and hissed. Audsley spun and nearly jumped as a pale form darted back into one of the rooms, disappearing from sight. He stood frozen, staring, waiting for it to emerge. A minute passed in silence, and finally he exhaled. "Perhaps we should explore a different room first. Stay in that one, ser naugrim, if you will!"

He approached the first archway and peered into the room

beyond. He stopped, eyes wide, breath caught in his chest, and felt a giddy sense of excitement rush through him. The walls of the small chamber within were covered with shelves groaning with a huge collection of books. A desk was placed front and center, with a number of candlestick holders lining its edge. Audsley didn't know where to begin, what to look at first. There was no sign of the pale little monster, but even if he'd seen it lurking in the corner he wouldn't have paid it much attention. Hesitantly, not quite daring to believe what he was seeing, he stepped up to the desk and peered down at a large map that was pinned to its surface by several books. He'd never seen its like. It depicted no Ascendant city, or any of the lands he'd seen before. Audsley lit several of the candles set about the table, and as their pale golden light bloomed he blew out his own and shoved it into his pocket. Aedelbert hopped up onto the table just as Audsley walked around it so as to study the map properly.

"No title or key. Shoddy work, that. But here we have a scale. All right, so a relatively small area. Mountains. A lot of them. Nice sense of elevation, nice ink work. Not complete, I see. And—ah. Oh, my." His finger hovered just above a diamond-shaped lake, in whose center a small island was drawn, the words *Mythgræfen Hold* elegantly lettered beside it.

"Extraordinary," he whispered.

He traced the course of the Erenthil down to where the name *Hrething* was marked beside a small 'X'. Excited, he lowered his gaze to the bottom of the map, cast around, and then sighed contentedly. A small town was marked with a fortress beside it. *The Talon*. Checking the scale, he tried to estimate the distance. Forty miles? There was a faint dotted line rising from the Talon to Hrething. A path?

Suddenly lightheaded, he straightened and combed his hair away from his face. This was amazing, far more detailed and accurate than his own shoddy little map. He wanted to do a little dance, to imitate that Aletheian waltz once more. But he was too anxious to see more. What else was there? A few villages were marked higher in the mountains. *Ostwald. Thestin*. Former mining towns? Would they be ruins today?

The land around the Hold was terrible. The elevations were incredibly steep and composed of an endless series of tiny valleys, waterfalls, blinds, ridges, escarpments and cliffs. It must have taken years to explore and map. Marveling, Audsley let his eye wander over the spines of the books being used as paperweights. A slender black volume was entitled *The Chaos Years*. A fat little red leather book chased in gold was entitled *Agathanasius, the First of His Name: A Biography*. A large brown tome that was falling apart bore the faint title of *The Age of Wonders*. The fourth corner was held down by an elegant green book, its wooden covers wrapped with muslin. *The Cleansing and the Shaping: A Primer*.

"Oh, my," whispered Audsley. He'd never even heard of these books, yet he had thought himself erudite. Blinking rapidly, he walked over to a shelf. One wonder after another greeted his eyes. *A Bestiary of Zoe. The Song of Alstarus. The Battle of the Souls. The Sealing of the Black Gate. The Diseases of Will Workers. The Letters of Abelard and Heloise.*

Audsley stopped and closed his eyes and stood perfectly still. If this banishment to Mythgræfen Hold were to last ten lifetimes, it would still end too soon. He counted ten beats of his heart and opened his eyes once more. Works of history. Biographies. Philosophical texts. Travelogues. Spiritual tracts. Allegories. Fables. Poetry collections. He felt dizzy. He recognized one name in ten. He had thought the Great Library at Nous to be complete, but it lacked most of these volumes. Where had these books come from? Were they forbidden texts? Might he find copies of them in the Black Vaults in Bythos?

Audsley laughed weakly. Had he thought himself learned? Had he? He didn't know where to begin.

He drew down a slender black book, *The Path of Flames*. He opened it at random and held the book up so that he could make out the text by candlelight. The script was strange, curiously elongated, and barely legible. "For wisdom, both absolutely and in relation to what is known, lies in seeking the greatest good at the cost of the least corruption. Thus one who walks the Path of Flames, while dealing with great forces, must learn to pay attention to the subtlest of signs, so as to avert the encroachment of darkness. As corruption gains a foothold, so does our ability to discern the truth become warped, resulting in an inability to diagnose the very malady against which we must guard—"

Audsley dropped the book as if it had turned into a snake and stepped back, wiping his hands on his tunic. Aedelbert leaped up in surprise and flew to the top of a bookcase. *Sin Casting.* A primer? What had gone on here in the Hold so many centuries ago? Had it been a hotbed of sin? Audsley took a breath and restrained the urge to simply flee upstairs. No, there were answers to be had here. Answers to the many questions that had been bubbling through his mind ever since he'd passed through the Raven's Gate. Everybody upstairs had their duties: shoring up walls, watching the causeway, cooking the meals. Well, this room was his own personal battlefield, a realm of hidden knowledge across which he would lead his armies of enlightenment!

Audsley smoothed down his tunic. He would not turn tail and

flee like an ignorant Zoeian. He was a magister, trained in the finest of arts in the city of Nous itself, and by the Ascendant, he would wrest the secrets from this mysterious Hold with zeal and determination!

He bent down, picked up the book, and quickly replaced it on the shelf. "Now, we need a plan, don't we, Aedelbert? An orderly series of objectives that I must seek to accomplish, a road to guide my feet."

He tapped his lips and walked back to the map. The Hold was clearly marked. If his earlier speculations were correct, then the Hold predated Kyferin Castle, which meant it had been built here ages ago for a singular purpose. What purpose was that? The Talon's location was suggestive. A supporting role? It had remained, after all, within the Kyferin family.

Audsley leaned down and studied the steep valley in which the Hold was situated. Why here? Why on this tiny island? A protective feature, to be sure, but terribly awkward and isolated. He studied the contours and high passes, the peaks and ravines. The Hold was situated, so it seemed, almost equidistantly from each of the high mountain villages or mining towns. Just as the Talon supported the Hold, did Mythgræfen support those towns? Was it a center of operations? No, its presence was clearly military in function. Was it the highest location at which a castle of this size could be built?

Audsley straightened and rubbed his head, then took up the candle and stepped back outside to the mysterious Gate. A score of naugrim fled into the walls, gone so quickly Audsley nearly screamed. There had been, what, five of them? Seven? He stood shaking, candle flame wavering. How many were there here in the bowels of the Hold?

He took a deep breath. They still seemed more afraid of him than anything else, and his curiosity was too strong. He'd take a quick look at the other rooms, then report upstairs immediately.

He moved to the next archway and peered inside. Aedelbert moved ahead of him into the smaller chamber, similar to the first in that it contained a desk and shelving on which numerous old scrolls were laid. Had they run out of space in the first room?

Audsley stepped inside and moved up to the desk to find no map, but rather a heavy ledger. He blew off the thick coating of dust, set down his candle with care, and after wiggling his fingers to make them limber turned the heavy wooden cover.

The words were terribly faded and written in an elegant hand. Leaning down, he read the cover text slowly.

Financial Ledger
3210 YG

Kept by Joenius Kyferin

"Hmm! Of passing interest, I suppose." He turned a massive page using both hands, and then again. Columns, figures, and entries ran down the left-hand side. Double bookkeeping, he saw. Quite sophisticated. But what was being tracked?

He studied a dozen pages carefully, taking his time, and finally pulled out a chair and sat. The entries seemed to concern mining extracts. What set his heart to racing was the name of what was being dug: *Gate Stone*. He'd never heard the like. Was that what was used to build the Gate frames? Most suggestive! If so, then this was a find indeed—the source of the Gates! Audsley leaped to his feet and struck a daring pose.

"Mysteries, I assault you! Enigmas, be gone!" He relaxed and tapped his chin. Why were the mines abandoned if their ore was so precious? And 3210 YG... That was no calendar year he knew of. It was currently 317 FOE—Founding of Empire. What could YG mean? The previous calendar, of course. But how to convert it to FOE? More mysteries.

Turning back to the ledger, he flipped to the very end. The final third was blank, and the final entries did not indicate a dwindling in supply. If anything, the extraction of Gate Stone was remarkably constant. So, why cease with the operations?

Audsley closed the ledger and idly read through some scrolls that were lying on the table. He winced each time they cracked beneath his fingers. A truly respectful magister would leave everything alone and send word to Nous for a proper team of investigative scholars, but the situation being what it was...

Half an hour passed as he read on, jumping ever quicker from scroll to scroll. Fascinating! While the dates were set in that confounded YG, the events related within were clearly set during the Unification Years, approximately 0 FOE. Most of the scrolls were addressed to this Joenius Kyferin, who had no doubt been the Lord or Lady of the Hold at that time. The tone was urgent. Finally, Audsley found the last scroll and sat to read it in full.

Dear Joenius,

I write to you with grave news. Aletheia has fallen to Agathanius, the first of his Name and promulgator of Ascension. The high halls of that floating city are drenched in blood, and word has reached me that the fanatics have transported Lord Pallindar to Bythos, where he has been cast through the Black Gate. That makes him the last of the Great Lords to fall. Every city is now under Ascendant control. The age of knowledge is drawing to a close. Bonfires fill the halls of Aletheia with choking smoke. They are destroying countless texts and volumes, Joenius, anything that does not agree with their philosophy.

I'm not surprised that your Will Workers have departed. They have all retreated to Xatos, choosing isolation over combat. I fear this a poor decision. I cannot help but believe that Agathanius will soon turn his attention upon them. For now, however, he is content to punish the Agerastians, branding them heretics and lashing them with his wrath.

I've left the worst for last. The Ascendants have declared the mining of Gate Stone to be anathema. All who engage in this practice are ordered to cease and destroy their operations or be subjected to punishment. You should know by now what that would entail. Already I have received several blunt questions from self-righteous officials demanding to know the status of our operations. I have tried to explain the dual nature of our work, that we both extract and defend, but they do not care for nuance or subtleties. I fear our tenure at Mythgræfen must end, and the Gate Stone and minor Black Gate be damned. We must call back our men and return to Kyferin Castle, lest the Ascendants come visiting with their fire and kragh.

Yours as always,
Alyssa

Audsley set down the scroll and leaned back in his chair. He was trembling. His firecat leaped into his lap and looked up at him with concern. Carefully, he took off his spectacles and cleaned them on his tunic. "Oh, my," he whispered. "A minor Black Gate? Oh, my, Aedelbert. Oh, my."

CHAPTER TWENTY-EIGHT

ISKRA

My life, thought Iskra, *has been spent waiting for the return of those dear to me.* She stood in a corner of the battlements, almost out of the cruel wind that swept in off the lake, her thick cloak pulled tightly around her. It was bitterly cold, but she paid that no mind. The brutality of the landscape appealed to her: the slate-colored waters, the ragged, terrible mountains that clawed at the sky all around her, their peaks clad in glittering ice and snow. Ravens croaked and shook out their feathers, watching her with cold and calculating eyes. Even the ruin of the Hold felt fitting; it perfectly reflected her fall from grace, the collapse of her dreams, her inability to offer protection to those who served her.

Burying her chin deeper into the folds of her cloak, she slitted her eyes and focused on the far point of the lake, where it birthed the Erenthil. It was from there that Ser Wyland would return, bringing with him uncertain news and her daughter. Her fear that he might fail in this task served only to fuel her determination to be present when he appeared; she would see her daughter's red hair as they walked along the edge of the lake toward the causeway, or hold him to account.

Her emotions flickered through her like dancing flames. Fierce resolution gave way to hesitancy and doubt, only to fold into mourning and anger as she thought of her son, and then return to determination to rescue him and safeguard those she loved. How was she supposed to wrest an advantage from her situation? What could wit or wisdom make of such a poor position? A handful of guards, two knights, a daughter who thought herself—and might actually be—a warrior, a ruined castle, and an army on the march to destroy them within two weeks.

It was enough to make her want to laugh, to cry, to hide away in some dark corner and declare herself done. And yet there was Roddick. He was a hook in her soul, a chain that held her at her post. There had to be a way to free him. Ser Wyland would see it done. He would return with good news—locals willing to help, something, anything for her to capitalize on, so she could wrest an edge over Lord Laur.

Iskra blinked and leaned forward, resting a hand on the frigid crenellation. Something was approaching from the lake's edge. Not a boat. Was it a trick of her eyes? It looked like two people were walking toward the Hold, right over the water's surface. Goose bumps ran down her arms, and her stomach clenched. Impossible. Perhaps there was a causeway beneath the water for those who knew where to tread?

"Ser Tiron," she said. "Come. What do you see there?"

Ser Tiron clanked over from where he'd been lounging a dozen paces away and leaned forward. His grim features knitted as he squinted, and then he scowled. "That can't be."

Iskra turned back to the lake, resting her hands on the lichen-stained stone. The two figures were striding ever closer. One of them looked familiar, even at this distance. Iskra raised her hand to her mouth. Auburn hair, a familiar frame. Her daughter was returning home to her.

"Kethe," she whispered, then turned and hurried down the steps. Her heart was thumping. Was that her daughter's ghost, come to bid her goodbye before passing through to the next life? Where were the others? Who was she walking with?

She descended the steps as quickly as she could, Ser Tiron right behind her, and rushed along the interior wall of the bailey to the front gate, out past the twisted oak, through the knee-high stalks of dried grass and brittle goldenrod, onto the gravely spit of sand that served as a beach.

Ser Tiron came after her, hauberk clinking, and hopped down off the grass onto the beach with a heavy thud. He strode up to her and followed her gaze out over the water. "I never thought my madness was contagious. You see what I'm seeing?"

"My daughter," said Iskra, her voice faint. "Walking on water."

Ser Tiron scowled. "There must be a second causeway hidden beneath the surface."

Iskra was glad for his presence, his solidity by her side. Whatever was walking toward them, Ser Tiron would meet it with unflinching defiance.

"Perhaps. But the water would flow differently over it." She took a deep breath and tried to force her stomach to settle. "And I don't see that sign."

"Well, they can't literally be walking on water." Ser Tiron's voice was flat. "Can they?"

"Regardless, they are approaching. We'll have our answers soon."

She could see them both clearly now. The stranger was a woman; she could tell by the sway of the stranger's hips, the narrowness of her shoulders. A firecat was draped over her shoulders. Who was she? She was wearing a dark cloak, possibly green, with a hood thrown over her head; while Kethe's hair smoldered in the morning light, Iskra could make nothing out of her companion.

"My Lady," called out a voice from behind her, and, turning, she saw Brocuff had emerged from the gate with three guards. Two more appeared at the walls above, bows in hand. "Your orders?"

"Stay where you are. Wait for my signal before approaching."

Brocuff nodded. Iskra heard the guards up top mutter oaths of incredulity, but she ignored them and turned back to wait.

"Look around their feet," said Ser Tiron, his tone turning harsh. Iskra stared and saw silvery shapes bobbing up alongside the two women. Fish, each about the length of her forearm. Clearly dead, they rose and floated belly-side-up, leaving a trail of bodies in the women's wake. Ser Tiron straightened, and she sensed tension coil within him. "That can't bode well. Must be Sin Casting of some kind."

She could make out Kethe's face now, and to her immense relief her daughter gave a wave, said something to her companion, and then broke into a jog. Each footstep sent out concentric ripples and summoned more dead fish from below. Ravens exploded out of the oak, crying raucously and beating their wings as they wheeled and flew away, swooping around the Hold and out of sight.

"Mother!" Kethe's voice was faint, but it carried over the water. "Hello!"

"She doesn't seem... cursed," said Ser Tiron.

"No."

Iskra took a step forward, right to the lake's edge. Kethe ran up, only to hesitate where the last wavelets washed up onto the beach. For a second Iskra thought, *She can't step on land. She drowned, and her uneasy spirit is doomed to walk this lake*—and then Kethe hopped off the water to crunch onto the gravel and right into Iskra's arms. Iskra hugged her tightly, closing her eyes as she squeezed hard.

"You're back," she said. "You're back."

"Yes," said Kethe, pulling away. "Of course." She smiled, new complexities in her expression, and turned to look at where her companion had stopped and now was standing a dozen yards away. "In large part due to Mæva's help. You won't believe what happened, Mother. A demon! We joined the Hrething men in hunting it, and I got separated from the group, and it chased me and I fell into an underground river, and then—"

Ser Tiron's growl was harsh. "How by the Black Gate are you two walking on water?"

"Oh," said Kethe. "Right. Of course. Mæva is... I guess the word would be a wise woman? A witch? She saved my life, healed me, and then escorted me home. I don't know where Ser Wyland and the others are, but she said she'd see me back safe, and she did."

"A witch," said Iskra softly, turning again to study the stranger who was standing perfectly still, watching her in turn from the dark recesses of her hood. Her firecat was watching the dead fish bob around them in the water.

"Well, I know exactly what to do with witches," said Ser Tiron. "Invite her in close, and then I'll chop her head off and we can burn her to ashes."

"No!" Kethe turned to her mother. "I know it looks frightening, but she saved my life. I gave my word that she would be safe."

"Peace," said Iskra, not looking away from the figure. "She saved your life. I'll not have anybody killed in payment for such service. Bid her approach."

"Look at those dead fish, Iskra," said Ser Tiron. "You can't think she means us any good. Send her away if you won't let me kill her, but don't let her step onto this island."

"Please, Mother." Kethe touched Iskra's arm. "I swear to you, I'm not under any spell, and she saved my life. She might be able to help us! At least talk to her. Get a sense of her yourself. The Hrethings won't do more then sell us food. We can't turn Mæva away."

Iskra nodded and gestured that Mæva approach. Ser Tiron stiffened as the woman did so, but didn't draw his sword. Step by step, the witch approached, and when she was a few yards away she stopped again and drew back her hood. Her firecat leaped up into the air briefly, wings flaring, only to land once more. Iskra gazed at her. She looked to be in her twenties, but her eyes were those of an older woman. There was an intelligence, a cunning, a depth of experience and wisdom in them that Iskra would have sworn had come at a terrible price.

"You saved Kethe's life," Iskra said, speaking as if they were in the Lord's Hall back at her castle. "You have my deepest gratitude."

Mæva inclined her head. "Hers is a life worth saving."

"I would agree," said Iskra. "But, then, I am her mother. What is her value to you?"

"Her value? Why, she's a charming conversationalist, and her earnestness is so endearing." Mæva paused and smiled. "Is that not enough?"

"No," said Ser Tiron, shifting his weight subtly on the sand as if anticipating an attack.

"Your daughter has a powerful wyrd," said Mæva. "You won't understand or appreciate what that means, but for one like myself who can sense some of the invisible forces at work in the world, that makes her important. That she's a Kyferin and stands in Mythgræfen Hold makes her all the more notable." She paused, examining Iskra carefully.

"And makes the boon owed to me for saving her life all the more valuable as well."

So we come to it, thought Iskra. "And what boon would you ask of me?"

"Nothing as of yet. Let us say that I shall claim it in the future. For now, I am pleased to have returned her to you, and ask for nothing more."

Ser Tiron went to respond, but Iskra raised her hand. "Why did you cross the lake on foot rather than circle to the causeway?"

Mæva gave a sinuous one-shouldered shrug. "I've walked enough for one day. That, and I knew a demonstration of my power would be requested once we got to talking. Two birds, one stone."

Iskra nodded. "I welcome you to the Hold, Mæva. I offer you guest rights and give you my word that you'll be safe here as long as you give me no cause for grief." She turned to stare at Ser Tiron, who scowled at her and nodded, then back to Brocuff, who was watching wide-eyed. "Constable, see to it that your men understand what I've said." She turned back to Mæva. "Now, I see there is much for us to discuss."

"My Lady!" Audsley came running out of the front gate, puffing for breath, his firecat flying overhead. "Dire news! We have to talk at once—I—ah —" He stumbled to a stop at the sight of Mæva standing calmly on the lake's surface. "Oh."

Mæva simply smiled at him and stepped forth onto the beach.

Audsley's firecat hissed and beat its wings furiously at the sight of the witch, then rose up quickly to disappear into the branches of the twisted oak.

"Enough." Iskra's voice was firm. "Follow me into the Hold. We'll have this discussion in private." She stepped back up onto the turf and strode back into the Hold, then turned off into one of the small, ruined guard rooms. Ser Tiron positioned himself just before her and to the side while Audsley shrank back against one wall. Kethe stood next to him, and Mæva stood at ease, arms crossed, firecat dropping to the ground to sit beside her, wings folded back across its brindled coat. Its eyes, Iskra saw, were a hideous yellow, like a rancid egg yolk. She'd never seen their like.

"Magister," said Iskra. "You're agitated. Do you want to go first?"

"Oh," said Audsley, eyes still wide as he stared at Mæva. "No. I mean, it is urgent. But she, er, I mean… Ahem. She can go first."

"Very well." Iskra turned back to the witch, who met her gaze with amusement. "Then let us begin with you, Mæva. You claim my daughter has a powerful wyrd. Do you care to explain further?"

"First, let it be noted that Kethe is a fine, strong young woman," said Mæva. "I'd like to think I'd have saved her regardless of these other factors."

"You'd like to think?" asked Ser Tiron.

Mæva smiled. "My actions aren't entirely predictable, noble knight, even to myself." She hesitated. "How to explain? You are all dumb to the world. I do not mean that in an entirely insulting way, though it is hard not to feel superior. You are insensate like most people, and notice only the crudest and most obvious parts of this world. You feel the wind on your skin, enjoy sunlight on your face, can feel rough stone or piercing cold. Sometimes I am sure you feel quite intensely alive, but believe me, you are apprehending only the very surface of reality."

Iskra found the witch's arrogance equal parts amusing and grating. "Poor us. I assume it is otherwise for you?"

"Oh, yes." Mæva lowered her chin, and her eyes gleamed with a dangerous light. "Very much so. There are energies that flow through this world that are undetectable only to a unique few—that eddy and ebb, that surge and pool. When I walk past your Raven's Gate, I feel a roar akin to a waterfall. This entire Hold—" She extended her arm and turned, looking around the room. "It throbs and vibrates with this power. But it's fractured. The energies mimic the form, though that's not always the case." She narrowed her eyes as she concentrated. "I can feel a vortex out there in the courtyard. A sinking sensation, as if the energies were being pulled down."

Audsley started. "Down?"

"Hmm. Yes." Mæva cocked her head and looked to her firecat as if for confirmation. "Is there something below?"

"I... ah. Um." Audsley stepped back. "In a moment. Please continue."

Mæva shrugged. "In short, I can feel the play of these energies, and in some manner manipulate them, coax them into doing what I wish. It is a perilous thing to do, and it would surely kill me if I did not deflect the worst of this energy into other living creatures."

Iskra narrowed her eyes. "The fish."

"Indeed." Mæva's smile disappeared. "They paid the price of my casting."

"Sin Casting," said Ser Tiron.

"Names." Mæva shrugged impatiently. "Suffice to say there's a reason I live alone. But my point is, just as I can sense the weft and weave of these energies, I can also sense how they flow into Kethe. Pour into her and disappear."

Kethe blinked. "Disappear?"

"As I told you, my dear, you seem to be a sinkhole for this power. Conflate that with your being a Kyferin, and you become a very important individual indeed."

Iskra stepped forward. "What does it mean, for her to act as a sinkhole?"

Mæva gave her one-shouldered shrug again. "I don't know. I've lived most of my life in solitude with Ashurina, mastering my own control of magic so as not to die. I've never met anybody like her. But I know it holds great import. Especially in light of her being a Kyferin."

Iskra fought to keep her expression calm. Inside, however, her thoughts were roiling. "And why is that?"

To her surprise, it was Audsley who spoke, his voice wooden. "The Kyferins used to defend this land centuries ago from the dangers of the Black Gate."

Everyone turned to stare at him. Ser Tiron shifted uncomfortably. "The Black Gate is sealed."

"The one in Bythos is," said Audsley. He smiled tremulously, but failed to hide the terror in his eyes. "But not the one high up in the mountains here."

Iskra felt the shock like a slap. "What are you talking about?"

"Downstairs. I, ah, might have followed a naugrim into a set of hidden rooms—in which I found a lost Lunar Gate and a study and office. Scrolls. Books. Far too many for me to read in one sitting, unfortunately, but I—how shall I say—perused a number of the last message scrolls left on a desk, and learned much." Two spots of color had appeared on Audsley's smooth cheeks. "There is and might always have been a smaller Black Gate up in the mountains. The Hold was built by your ancestors to protect the land from it, as well as mine something called 'Gate Stone' from the ground. I still have much to learn, but I believe your ancestors were guardians against the evils that came through it, as well as benefiting later from mining this ore, which might quite possibly have been used to build the Lunar and Solar Gates, amongst other things."

Nobody spoke. Audsley smiled apologetically. "So, um, yes. Which might explain why the Hold has been wiped out again and again since it was originally abandoned. Without a continuous presence here, the forces from the Black Gate would mount and prove impossible to resist when they attacked."

Kethe passed a hand over her brow. "The demon that nearly killed me. It came through this Black Gate?"

Audsley nodded. "Yes, I'd imagine so."

"Why was such a vital defense abandoned?" demanded Iskra.

"Well…" Audsley hesitated again. "It seems that the first Ascendant—praised be his name—was against the mining of Gate Stone. When he founded the Ascendant Empire, he ordered that all such mining operations cease."

Kethe pressed her fingertips to her temples. "But why?"

Audsley shrugged. "I don't know. He thought it violated the tenets of Ascension. The why of it has been lost, though the answer may lie below."

Ser Tiron's eyes were darting from side to side as he tried to piece this together. "But why did the Ascendant abandon this smaller Black Gate?"

Audsley shrugged helplessly again. "I need more time with the scrolls. But from their tone, I think—and this is very awkward—I think its presence was overlooked or ignored. Perhaps it was inconvenient? There is talk of the early Ascendants violently enforcing their beliefs, even at the expense of knowledge and nuance. But I really don't know."

Kethe looked to her mother. "While we were in Hrething, they revealed that they don't celebrate the Winter Shriving. They call it the Black Shriving instead. They said that's when the forces of evil sweep across the land, and when those in the Hold disappear." She suddenly flushed in remembered outrage. "And they don't even believe in the cycles of Ascension – they said they simply hope to lead good lives and go straight through the White Gate when they die!"

Audsley blinked rapidly. "Is that so? Fascinating. That creed was espoused by an Ascension cult over a century ago called the Jogomils, name for Jogomillin, a heretical Noussian who disappeared when his movement was, ah, suppressed by the kragh. No-one knows to where he went, but now I'm sure we can make an educated guess…"

Iskra closed her eyes and fought for calm, for control. All her life she had relied on her Sigean education and upbringing to guide her during times of peril. The world operated according to logical and ineffable laws set down by the first Ascendant, laws which set each and every living being in their place and gave them a simple and elegant system to follow in order to Ascend. There had been no mention of this chaos, this bloodshed, or of Black Gates overlooked during Ascendancy's rise.

The situation was slipping through her fingers. There were too many questions, too much uncertainty. "This changes nothing." She opened her eyes and gazed from one person to the next. "Lord Laur is still marching on us in twelve days. The Winter Shriving is almost two months away. We must survive his assault before we can concern ourselves with these older matters."

Audsley spluttered, "But Lord Laur pales in significance beside these revelations—"

"Lord Laur," said Iskra, "wants us dead. All the knowledge in the world won't save us from his knights. Unless you have discovered a means to defeat them below?"

Audsley stepped back almost sulkily against the wall. "Well, there was a sword."

Ser Tiron perked up. "A sword?"

Audsley nodded. "Nasty-looking thing. Somebody got cut in half by the Gate down there. Dropped their sword as they died."

Iskra raised her hand. "Excuse me. A Gate?"

"Yes." Audsley blushed. "I was going to mention it. A Lunar Gate, of course. I don't know where it goes or to which phase of the moon it's attuned, however."

"A new Gate. In the bowels of the Hold." She paused to process this information. "Incredible. Audsley, see to it that someone watches this Gate whenever the moon is in the sky."

"Yes, my Lady," said Audsley, bowing low.

"And I'll come take a look at this sword," said Ser Tiron.

"Mæva." Iskra turned to the witch. "You know our situation. Will you help us against Lord Laur?"

Mæva had been watching and listening with a neutral expression. She drew herself up as if considering the question, then nodded. "Of course. Though I will not engage them in direct combat, and with the understanding that down the road your family will extend me the same amount of aid that I do you."

Iskra nodded. "We shall provide you with commensurate aid if it is within our power to do so and does not sully our honor. Now. How can you help us?"

Mæva's lip curled into a defiant smile as she held Ser Tiron's gaze. "What are you seeking to accomplish first?"

"Secure the help of the Hrethings," said Iskra.

"Then, yes. Perhaps I can help. The demon they hunt is impervious to normal weapons—"

"No," cut in Kethe. "It isn't. I wounded it."

Mæva stopped, her annoyance at being interrupted changing into curiosity. "Did you, now?"

Kethe nodded. "Nothing mortal. But I left my sword buried in its side."

Mæva tapped her lips. "Yes. I can see how you might have been able to. But not the others. No one else will be able to harm it. I could perhaps lead a small group to the demon and enchant their weapons so that they could wound it." She hesitated, glanced at Ashurina, then gave a firm nod. "Yes. That I could do."

Ser Tiron smiled. "Now we're talking. How many weapons could you curse?"

"Curse?"

"Sin Casting is evil," said Ser Tiron sweetly. "What else would you call it?"

Mæva smiled sweetly back. "Oh, I can see you *are* going to be fun. Fine. I could perhaps 'curse' two blades. Maybe three."

Ser Tiron grimaced. "Only two or three?"

Her gaze hardened in irritation, but before she could respond, Iskra stepped in. "Very well. We descend to Hrething immediately. I will speak with their headman myself and strike this bargain. The demon's head in exchange for their support."

Audsley blanched. "Me too?"

"No. I want you to stay here and continue your research. Ser Tiron, Kethe, prepare your packs. We leave immediately."

Kethe groaned even as Audsley beamed. Mæva gave a mocking curtsey. "I am pleased that you have chosen to accept my help."

"Yes, well..." Iskra regarded her coldly. "I have sworn to use every tool at my disposal. Don't think I've forgotten the nature of your magic, Mæva. Everything I have learned since I was a child tells me that accepting your help damns my soul."

"Then why accept it?"

Iskra couldn't help but glance at her daughter before answering. "It's a price I'm willing to pay. Now come. There is a demon in need of slaying."

CHAPTER TWENTY-NINE

TIRON

Ser Tiron walked at the back of the group, his boots crunching on fallen twigs and dead leaves, his face and beard damp with the fog that wreathed itself through the bare trees and swallowed those in the distance whole. They were high up above Hrething, though it was impossible to tell; the few craggy bluffs they'd reached that might have offered views of the land below instead gazed out into nebulous gray nothingness. The smell of black earth and rotting wood filled the air, and sounds were muffled and indistinct. He couldn't stop glancing over his shoulder, not sure what he half-expected to be creeping up on them, but unable to control the suspicion that something would the moment he let down his guard.

The group moved in silence, following the witch as she picked a path ever higher into the mountains, a small goat walking behind her on a tight leash. Jander walked a few paces behind her, hand on the hilt of his sword, with Asho and Kethe in the center of the group. They'd been climbing for hours. No one spoke. Clearly, all of them felt the ambient menace that suffused the forest. Even Jander seemed on edge. The fact that there was an actual demon up here with them only made their fears all the more cloying.

"This will do," said Mæva, coming to a stop.

Ser Tiron looked about. A small group of shattered rocks lay to one side, their rough sides smothered in rust-colored lichen. Pale golden leaves lay strewn everywhere over the dark dirt, barely hiding the knobby roots and elbows of rock that made footing treacherous. Skeletal trees rose up the slope before them, their naked branches blending into the fog. Distant trunks were reduced to shadows, then vague intimations of columns, then nothing at all. For the life of him Tiron couldn't guess why she'd chosen this Ascendant-forsaken spot.

"I can sense the demon not far from here." Mæva pushed back her hood. Gone was the persistent mockery, the aloof amusement. "It rests during the day, and won't stir for at least another six hours."

"Good," said Jander. He removed his helm and raked his fingers through his hair. "That gives us time to prepare. What can you tell us of this area? Are there any geographic features that we can use to our advantage?"

Mæva nodded. "We're not far from a cliff face that drops over a thousand feet to the forest below. Mountain goats can be found grazing across its ledges, and there's a hunter's trail that hugs the cliff tightly and makes its way across to the far side. It's treacherous, but passable."

Asho had fallen into an easy crouch, his white hair lank over his shoulders. "Not to the demon, though."

"No," said Mæva. "It's too large to follow you onto the trail."

Jander looked over at Tiron. "What do you think?"

They all turned to him, and Tiron fought the urge to scowl. What did he know of battling demons? "That trail could serve as our means of retreat. Could we draw the demon to the cliff?"

Mæva gave her one-shouldered shrug. Her goat tested the leash, then resumed nosing at the leaf litter. Tiron saw a glimpse of bare skin beneath her cloak. Did she not feel the cold? "The demon moves quickly, despite its size. But yes, there is a clearing by the cliff's edge."

Kethe placed one hand inside the other and pushed her palms toward the foggy sky, stretching out her back and then twisting once to each side. Her movements were sinuous and controlled. "What would happen to the demon if we managed to push it over the cliff? Would that be enough to kill it?"

Mæva shrugged again. "Perhaps. Hurt it, definitely. Kill it? I don't know."

Asho looked around the sparse forest. "If we could draw it to this clearing, we could attack it from all sides. We just need a way to slow it down to ensure it doesn't catch whoever we send as bait."

"I'll go," said Kethe immediately. "It already knows me. It chased me once before. I'm sure it would do so again, and I'm the fastest of all of you."

Asho looked at her sidelong. "Are you sure?"

She glared at him. "You're short. My legs are longer. So, yes."

Tiron snorted. "So eager to throw away your life, are you? Well, then, let's come up with a means to slow it. Trip rope?"

Kethe shook her head. "It smashed its way through trees the last time it chased me."

Jander moved off to where a tall sapling stood. He gripped it with both hands and hauled back on the slender trunk. It bent, surprisingly supple. He hauled it nearly parallel with the ground and then let go. With a *whish* it snapped back upright. Jander looked over at them. "What do you think?"

Kethe opened her mouth, confused, then shut it again.

Tiron rubbed at his jaw. "A large enough tree, perhaps. Tie it to a rock. Whoever's running cuts at the rope as they go by. We'd have to weaken the cord till it could be severed easily with one strike."

Asho moved over to the tree and pushed on it. The bare branches swayed over his head. "Kethe. Would something like this stop it?"

"Stop it?" She hesitated. "No. Slow it down for a moment? Maybe."

Jander shrugged. "We'll see what we find along the route to the cliff. It's a possibility. What else?"

Mæva circled around Jander, trailing a finger along his shoulders. "If you don't find it overly cowardly, I could disguise the presence of those waiting in the clearing. Allow you to surprise the demon when it blunders forth."

Jander stepped away from the witch, brow lowered. "Why would I find that cowardly?"

She shrugged and smiled. "You knights have bizarre understandings of honor. I don't claim to understand it, but I know you will often refuse to do the most expedient thing, like killing an enemy when he is unarmed."

Jander's frown deepened. "You're right. That would be dishonorable. But this creature is no enemy knight. I'm willing to take any advantage we can get."

Mæva nodded. "Then I shall see it done. Come. I shall show you the cliff and the path to where the demon slumbers. Then I shall need some time to prepare."

"Prepare for what?" asked Asho.

"Prepare to curse your blades." Mæva glanced over at Tiron, her gaze inscrutable. "So that you may destroy it."

Four hours later Tiron let out a shuddering breath and sat on a damp rock. His arms and back ached from their labor, and sweat was already cooling on his brow.

The clearing was about the size of the Hold's courtyard, barely large enough for them to dance with this demon. Its far side ended in sharp rocks—and then nothing. He'd stood at the very edge and gazed out and down, and though the clouds had hidden the depths which yawned before him, some primal sense of intuition had caused his balls to tighten and his throat to close. He'd backed away carefully.

Now they were ready, or as ready as they could get before nightfall drew any closer. Jander was standing in the center of the clearing drinking from his flask. Kethe was kneeling to one side, eyes closed as she prayed to the Ascendant. Her blade wouldn't need Mæva's attention. Asho and Jander had both reported that hers was the only wound that had been dealt to the demon before it had turned to chase after her.

The witch was sitting cross-legged by the cliff's edge. She had discarded her cloak altogether, and seemed completely at ease in her thick leather skirt and minimalist top. She wasn't faking it, either, he knew; the few times he'd walked by her, he'd not seen her shiver or any sign of goose bumps. The cold and damp didn't bother her at all.

As he watched Mæva, her eyes opened and she focused on him. "Come," she said, and his balls tightened all over again. "It's time to prepare your blades. Place them before me."

Jander and Asho exchanged a look, and Tiron knew that neither of them was comfortable with this Sin Casting, but Iskra had made it clear that they were to accept Mæva's help, and all of them knew that without it they were doomed. So they stepped up to where she was sitting, and one by one set their blades before her.

"Where did you get that blade, Tiron?" Wyland's voice was almost sharp. And no wonder; he'd retrieved the blade Audsley had found below the Hold. Its surface was black and gleamed as if oiled, and its serrated lower edge and wickedly curved tip made him uneasy just to hold it, as if it might animate at any moment and lash out at him.

"I brought this for our newest knight," he said, turning to Asho. "It was below, in the rooms the Magister found," he said. "Asho asked me about glorious swords of old. Well. This ugly blade should suit him just fine."

"Why?" Asho stepped forward, his face a cold mask. "Is this meant to be a clever jest as to my soul's proximity to the Black Gate?"

"No, fool." Tiron stared down at the wicked sword. "It's a comment on knighthood. Though it's clearly going over your head. Catch." And so saying, he tossed the sword through the air.

Asho caught the blade adroitly, and as soon closed his fingers around the hilt the air around the blade began to shimmer like that around Elon's forge. Runes began to glow where before there had only been matte-black metal, intricate and fiery, as if they were windows onto a bed of superheated coals. Mæva let out a gasp, leaped to her feet, and almost stumbled clear off the edge of the cliff.

Asho was staring wide-eyed at the sword. His pale hair was stirring as if moved by a breeze, and his silver-green eyes reflected the burning glow of the runes.

Jander's face betrayed his shock. "By the Ascendant, Asho. What did you do?"

"I—nothing!" Asho dropped the sword and leaped back. Immediately it returned to its matte-black self. He stared at it, eyes wide. "What was that?"

Mæva stood in a half-crouch, looking for all the world as if she were ready to spin and race away. Slowly she straightened. "Who are you, Bythian?"

"Me?" Asho blinked. "I'm—I'm Asho. What do you mean, who am I?"

Kethe had risen and moved over to stand with them. "What was that? I felt something. Like... a surge of heat."

Mæva studied her. "Pick up the sword, Kethe."

"What?" Jander stepped forward. "No! Why?"

Mæva regarded him without concern. "We don't know what she is, but she has power. I'm sure the sword cannot hurt her." She turned to Kethe. "Pick it up."

"Don't," said Jander, but then he clamped his mouth shut as Kethe crouched and picked up the blade.

She rose slowly, sword extended, brow furrowed. "It feels... strange. I feel strange. Feverish." She was breathing deeply. No runes appeared on the sword's surface; instead, it began to turn a dull iron gray from the central fuller out.

"Drop it," said Mæva sharply. "Quickly!"

Kethe's eyelids lowered slightly. She took a heavy step backward, and the sword began to waver. "Strange," she said. "I feel...strange."

Tiron took a step forward and slapped hard at her wrist. Her arm jerked down and the sword fell to the ground. Kethe gasped sharply, and her eyes snapped open. She blinked, put her hand to the side of her head, and then sank down into a crouch.

"Kethe?" Asho was immediately by her side. "Are you all right?"

"Yes," she said. "Yes. I'm feeling better." She inhaled deeply through her nose. "It felt like a wave of nausea. It's passing now."

Jander turned angrily on Mæva. "You said it wouldn't harm her."

"Well, I guess I was wrong." The witch stepped up to the blade and stared down at it. The matte-black color was returning slowly. "The demon actually stirred when she held it. Fascinating."

Tiron felt irritation and fear stir his soul. "You have no idea what that sword does, do you?"

Mæva looked up. "An idea, perhaps. Kethe drains magic from the world. In Asho's hand the blade lit up. In hers it turned gray. It is clearly a weapon of power. Beyond that? Idle speculation. The kind I know you love so."

Her smile was beyond irritating. He turned back to Asho, who helped Kethe stand and then moved over to where the blade was lying. His pale face looked gaunt. "Why do you think it did that when I held it?"

"She's already said she doesn't know," said Tiron. "It was a mistake for me to bring it. Come, I'll toss it over the cliff's edge and we'll use our normal blades."

"No," said Asho, his voice quiet but firm. "It felt right for me to hold it. Like I was opening my eyes for the first time." Before anybody could protest, he scooped the blade back up. Again the air began to shimmer along its length, and the red runes blazed into existence. Without a word, he walked to the edge of the clearing. Nobody followed him. He stopped before a sapling, bit his lower lip, then swung the blade with both hands.

The sapling fell, its four-inch-thick trunk neatly severed in twain.

"Well," said Jander after a pause, "looks like Ser Asho has found a new blade." Tiron saw deep concern in his eyes. "It surely falls under our Lady's order to use whatever tools we have at our disposal. I just hope it doesn't damn his soul."

Kethe stepped closer to Jander. Asho was still studying the sword at the clearing's edge. "He's a Bythian. He's got nowhere left to descend to but through the Black Gate."

Jander grimaced. "I know."

"We're running out of time." Mæva stepped forward again and sat. "Bring me the goat and let's be done."

Kethe walked over to where the goat was tethered and brought it over. Nobody wanted to look at it. The creature sensed some impending danger and began to bleat. Jander's sword and Tiron's family blade lay before the witch, who closed her eyes and placed her hand over them in the air.

"Sin Casting," said Tiron with disgust. "As if we couldn't fall any further."

Mæva opened one eye and glared at him. "Shut up."

Tiron turned away. She'd better not ruin his sword. Well, it wasn't like he was bound to be reborn in Nous, at any rate. Not after the life he'd led. With a little luck he'd just be reborn one step down in Zoe. Or maybe Agerastos. Who knew? Who cared.

He turned at the edge of the clearing, Jander by his side, and together they watched the witch. She sat in silence, brow furrowed, her whole body taut. She had a good body, he had to admit: lean, muscled arms, full breasts under that leather wrap, a slim torso. He shook his head in annoyance. What was wrong with him? He scowled and crossed his arms, then the goose bumps raced down his back and the hairs on the back of his neck stood up.

Green light wove its way down from her palm in undulating waves to sink into the blades. The goat's bleat took on a plangent tone and it began to tug fiercely at its leash. Kethe grimaced and held on with both hands. The light continued to fall lazily from Mæva's palm, and Tiron saw thick beads of sweat form on her face. Her entire arm was shaking. He realized he was forming the triangle with his fingers, and saw that so was Jander.

The goat let out an agonized bleat that tore halfway through into a wet gurgle. It collapsed suddenly onto its side and lay heaving for breath. Tiron grimaced in disgust as it flopped its head about and then lay still. Its ribs ceased rising and falling. Even in this thin mountain air Tiron could make out the stench of spoiled meat.

Mæva let out a cry and fell back. Kethe dropped the leash and crouched by her side. The blades now oozed a faint green necrotic light.

Tiron's heart was pounding like a battering ram at a castle gate. He took a step forward, then another. "Is it done?"

"By the Ascendant, it had better be," rasped Jander.

They approached cautiously. The surfaces of their blades roiled and bubbled as if a cauldron of green muck were boiling just under their metallic skins.

The witch pushed herself upright and stared down at the swords with an expression halfway between a snarl and a frown. "Toss the goat over the cliff." Her voice was husky. She was still breathing hard, Tiron realized, her chest rising and falling rapidly. "Your swords are safe to pick up as long as you don't touch the blades." She stared at him and Jander as if they were to blame for some personal affront. "Don't stand there gaping like village idiots. Pick them up. The magic will only last half an hour. You'd all best hurry."

Kethe's face paled. "All right. So—now?"

Mæva nodded. "Follow the path I showed you. Keep your mind open. You should sense it when it senses you."

Asho had rejoined them. "And if she doesn't? She didn't last time."

Mæva reached out and curled a strand of Kethe's auburn hair behind her ear in a surprising display of affection. "Oh, she will. This time she's alert; she's looking for it. And I get the feeling she's coming into this power of hers quite rapidly."

Tiron scowled. "The same feeling you had over her holding the blade?"

"Enough," said Kethe. "I'm going. I'll be back in ten minutes. The demon will be right on my heels, so you'd all better be ready." She hesitated, bit her lower lip, then turned to go.

"Kethe," said Asho, reaching out to touch her arm but then drawing back his hand at the last moment.

She turned to look back at him. "What?"

Asho hesitated. "Nothing. Just be careful. And good luck."

Kethe stared at him suspiciously, and then nodded. "You too." Then she turned and jogged away from the clearing.

Tiron watched Asho. "Be careful? And good luck? She's way above your station, boy."

Asho blushed and turned away, moving quickly toward his designated hiding spot.

Tiron grinned, amused, then saw Jander's hard look. "What?"

"Nothing. Get in position."

Tiron wanted to spit. Now even the emotions of the Bythians were sacrosanct? He stomped over to the outcropping of rock he was to hide behind and crossed his arms once he was behind it. Sin Casting. Flaming swords. Tender Bythians. The whole damn world was going to hell.

The next ten minutes took an age to pass. Tiron resisted the urge to peer out from behind his rocks. He'd been in too many campaigns to make such a greenhorn mistake. Instead, he settled in as comfortably as he could, relaxed, and listened carefully.

His mind wandered. What was he doing? Why? He thought of Iskra, her back to him as she gazed out over the lake all yesterday morning. Then he thought of Kethe, running bravely to face a demon out of legend. These Kyferin women were worth a hundred Erlands. Were they worth more than his Sarah and son?

He pressed his forehead against the damp, rough rock. He was avoiding the decision he had to make, busying himself with this suicidal hunt so as to not think of his oaths and obligations. And if they killed this demon, what then? Would he continue to help Iskra on her impossible quest?

Tiron gritted his teeth. He'd grown weak in that cell. He'd lost his resolve, his courage to do what was right. No, to *know* what was right. Down in that cell, he'd been clear on his loyalties and loves. Up here in the waking world? He pressed his brow harder against the rock till it hurt. He didn't know. Sarah. Iskra. His son. Kethe. What should he do?

Fight. That, he understood. That was simple. Battle. Killing. No room for thoughts, doubts, stupid quandaries. If he should die here, now, fighting this demon? A noble death! He'd take that. He'd let that answer his questions.

Tiron's heart stilled as the thought hit home and resonated powerfully. Death would solve his problems, and solve them honorably.

He straightened and stared at his glowing blade. This was a way out, the only way to end his torment without betraying someone important to him. He grasped his cursed blade with both hands and felt a powerful surge of certainty and calm.

This demon was his answer. This demon was his escape.

CHAPTER THIRTY

kethe

Kethe walked slowly through the trees as if wandering through a dream. The fog wreathed the trees and hid the canopy, muffled the few sounds that filtered through the trunks and filled her nose with the rich scent of loam and rot. She held her blade out before her with both hands, taking scant solace from its clean, sharp length. Now that she was alone, their plan seemed ludicrous. How was she to find this demon? Was the Ascendant to guide her to its lair? Would she truly be able to sense it before it attacked her?

There was the faintest hint of a path beneath her feet. Raw rock rose almost vertically to her left, damp and dark and scrawled with pale green lichen. Knobby branches reached down to pluck at her cloak and catch at her armor. To her right the ground fell away sharply, dropping down ten yards to a rough slope covered in rocks and evergreen shrubs.

Her heart was beating with slow, powerful thuds. Her breath came in light gasps. It was too easy to recall her headlong flight from the demon last time. How it had bowled over trees in its determination to kill her. Now she was walking toward it.

Madness.

And yet, there was nowhere else she'd rather be. This was her chance. On some level she didn't quite understand, she knew that this one deed could somehow redeem her father. She thought of him as she stole forward: massive, booming, strong beyond all measure and afraid of nothing. She knew now that there had been sides to him that she had never guessed at, aspects of his character that were beyond abhorrent. And yet on some base level, the man he had been revealed to be was not the father she had loved. If she could only succeed at this mission, if she could only master her fear long enough to defeat this demon, then her valor would reflect glory back onto her father, and in so doing vindicate his approach to life.

He had stood alone, strong and brave, needing nobody and fearing nothing. He was her exemplar, and this was her last opportunity to finally stand beside him and not find herself wanting.

The trail bent around to the left, curving around the rock face, and then climbed a steep rise to a shallower slope. Kethe swallowed. The fog was so dense that the demon could be standing twenty yards away and she'd not see him. Instead, she was surrounded by looming and threatening shapes. To her left a massive shadow resolved itself into a tumbled boulder. Up ahead, a vague silhouette laden with menace became a simple blasted oak. Kethe wiped her brow and quickly gripped her sword again. The demon was somewhere out here. Somewhere ahead.

Then she felt it: a vague prickling on the borders of her mind. An itch. She stopped and stood still. Was it her imagination?

The feeling faded, and there was silence. The fog drifted past her slowly, reminding her that it was in truth a cloud that was dragging itself across the mountain's rough face.

She took a few more steps forward and felt it again—there.

Her mouth was dry. The pit of her stomach was as taut as a drum. The urge to turn and flee caught her by the throat and she took a step back. Her sword shook. This was no game. That demon had stood over fifteen feet tall. Had it sensed her? Was it raising its head even now, turning its great horns from side to side as it tried to fix her location?

She would not run. *She would not run.* This was her last chance. She had fled the tournament field, and she had fled the demon during its first attack, but she would not flee now. Not until she had secured its attention for sure.

Kethe forced herself to take a step forward. Then a second.

The itch remained. Upslope a bit, to her left, not too far. She bit her lower lip and approached, moving slowly, trying to avoid stepping on dry branches or rustling the dead leaves. She reached out and grasped the trunks of slender saplings to help her climb. She could barely breathe from the fear.

The ground rose and then peaked. A ridge? The itch was growing stronger. It wasn't moving. Had it sensed her yet?

She gained the top and fought the urge to drop to her stomach and crawl forward. Moving slowly, wishing she were a ghost, she stepped forward and then stopped. The ground dropped away suddenly into a deep hollow at whose end a cave was carved into the mountain in the form of a deep, diagonal slash. The darkness under the beetling brow of stone was absolute.

The demon was inside. She knew it like she knew her own name. It was resting away from the light of day. It hadn't felt her yet, hadn't moved. She stood swaying, knees weak, holding on to a branch to steady herself. What should she do? Call out? Throw something? She saw a large branch not far from her feet, but she couldn't move toward it.

What would her father have done?

Slowly, she released the tree, took her sword with both hands, and raised it high overhead. Her father had been fearless and strong. *He'd been a rapist and a murderer*. No, she told herself firmly. He'd been a *warrior*. Shaking, she took a deep breath, held it, and yelled, "Demon! Come out and die!"

Her voice rang off the stone flanks of the hollow. The itch in her mind grew stronger. Her eyes were locked on the cavern entrance. It had heard her; she knew it had. Should she run now?

The darkness swirled. Something was emerging. A black, clawed hand reached out of its depths to clasp an outcropping of stone, and then she saw a hint of horns, the wide gash of its mouth, the massive shoulders and narrow waist.

It stepped out into the weak daylight. Even below her in the hollow as it was, it seemed impossibly huge, a creature alien to this world. Its blank face was all the more terrible for lacking eyes, something she could fix on. It raised that smooth surface of bone up to her and its lips peeled back from its razor-sharp teeth.

Kethe felt her heart seize within her chest. Had she dared summon this monster from its slumber? Had she threatened it? She had to run, now, but she couldn't look away. As long as it simply stood there, gazing back up at her, she felt mesmerized, paralyzed by her terror.

It stepped clear of the last rock and rose to its full height, extended its muscled arm and pointed a taloned finger at her. Claiming her. Marking her as damned. Kethe took a step back, and it crouched, preparing to spring up at her, each movement slow and graceful, laden with power and lethal intent.

"Run," Kethe whispered to herself, her voice a horrified whisper. "Run, Kethe. Run!"

The demon roared and leaped. Kethe lunged back, tripped, and fell. She rolled down the steep slope, careening off rocks, battering against trees, and by fortune or instinct managed to come to her feet, blade still in hand, and half-fell half-sprinted down the rest of the slope. The demon crashed into the trees amongst which she had stood but seconds ago, and then she heard it roar and leap again.

Gasping, praying she wouldn't trip, she reached the narrow trail and tore to her right, following the path back along the small cliff face as fast as she could go. The demon landed behind her once more and came right after. She could hear its passage. There was nothing subtle about its pursuit. The narrow trail she was racing along, however, was too narrow for it; she sensed it move above and behind her, charging along the cliff top.

Kethe's fear turned into a mad exhilaration. Arms pumping, she opened up her stride. Her whole body was tingling. She was fast, but she had never run like this. She vaulted over rocks, her footing sure, sprinting around the curvature of the path. The demon came after her, bursting through all obstructions. Come, then! Did it think her easy prey?

She broke free of the narrow trail and hit the slope that led to the clearing where her companions were waiting, a final mad dash. There was silence behind her, and then the canopy overhead exploded into a roar of breaking branches as the demon's leap brought it crashing to the ground like some fell meteor bursting down from the heavens. She felt the very ground shiver as it landed. She glanced back. It was ten yards behind. By the White Gate, only ten yards!

Her confidence left her, and she lowered her chin and ran for all she was worth. Her breaths were the rasp of Elon's bellows. There: the first of the sapling traps. She angled toward it, raised her blade, and swiped down with all her strength as she sprinted past.

The rope severed. The ten-foot-tall sapling sprang up and smashed into the demon just as it was about to fall upon her. It roared, stumbled, fell behind her once more.

There were two more such traps. She ran on. The fog smothered her, made her feel as if she were running within an illusory world with no end. Her thighs burned. The demon came at her from the side, not close enough for the second trap. She immediately discarded the decision to slow down so as to be able to spring it and ran on to the final tree. The largest of the three, it had taken all of them to bend it down while Wyland secured it.

She heard a hiss of air, and instinct caused her to throw herself into a forward dive. She hit the ground hard, rolled tightly and threw herself forward again as she gained her feet, slashing desperately to the side as she passed the rope.

She landed outstretched on the ground, the impact driving the breath from her. The tree remained bent down. She hadn't cut through the rope.

The demon reared above her, arm raised high to pound her skull into the ground. Kethe screamed, a primal sound of denial, and lunged to one side to slice at the rope. It gave, and with a *whoosh* the tree sprang up like a catapult right into the demon. It staggered back, shrieking its fury. Kethe didn't hesitate. She popped back up onto her feet and raced toward the clearing.

The fog thinned, and the trees pulled away. Dead leaves and dirt gave way to bare rock. "It's coming!" Her scream was ragged, barely intelligible. "Now! Now!"

CHAPTER THIRTY-ONE

Asho

The sword called to Asho. Like the moon to the tides, it pulled on him, made him want to place his hand on its hilt and feel that surging connection once more. It was unlike anything he had ever felt. That rush that had washed over him when he'd stepped out onto Mythgræfen Hold that first time was nothing compared to this. It was almost overwhelming, transfixing him with a sense of potential and possibility. When he held the blade, he felt as if he could hew the world itself in half. He felt inebriated, as if he'd drunk a large cup of firewine on an empty stomach.

His hand kept straying toward the hilt. It was this very awareness of his lack of control that made him fight back, keep his hand clenched in a fist and refuse to succumb.

The ten minutes it took Kethe to draw the demon lasted an eternity. He felt completely alone, so high above the forests below. The wind howled as it rushed down the peak above them and threw itself heedlessly over the cliff's edge, carving whirls in the fog and filling the air with its lonesome cry. Everything was damp and cold.

He focused on his breathing. That demon was coming their way. It was hard not to remember his terror when he'd faced it last, surprised and panicked in the dark. He could remember with chilling clarity that moment in which he'd had to choose between moving to help Kethe or attacking it directly, risking her life in hope of glory. His blade had bounced from its black hide as if it had struck rock. He'd fallen back, shocked, and had stared in horror as it had chased Kethe into the woods.

Had it been just for glory that he'd risked her life? Alone, wrapped in the fog, Asho stared grimly at the rock behind which he hid and pushed himself to honesty. No, in that moment his pride had held him back. His whole life, she'd mocked and disdained him. That moment had been a test, and he'd allowed his anger to guide his blade, to keep him from moving to protect her. As a result, he'd not only failed utterly to hurt the demon, but he'd spent two days consumed by guilt thinking that she had died.

What manner of man was he? What manner of knight? What had he really accomplished in Lady Kyferin's service?

Asho clenched his jaw and looked down at the black sword. It was his means to kill the demon. He knew it would pierce its hide. This was his chance to finally prove himself. He would strike the killing blow.

There—a crash. Was that...?—no.

A moment passed and he stiffened, tension coiling within him like an iron snake. That was a roar. Undoubtedly the demon. It was coming. Their plan suddenly seemed like madness. He wiped sweat from his brow, then heard another crash, the sound of an entire tree being riven apart. Was that footfalls?

Kethe suddenly burst into view, running full out, her sword cutting the air with each swing of her arm, blood running down her brow.

"Now!" she screamed. "Now!"

And the demon came after.

Asho rose as it passed him. Even in this dim light, it was terrifying. It was vast, fifteen feet tall and built like a mountain, its flesh not black but leaden gray in the thin daylight, gleaming wetly and stretched taut over its vast musculature. There wasn't an ounce of fat on the thing, each muscle picked out as if it had been flayed and its meat turned gray over time. Massively horned, its maw slavering, it ran into the center of the clearing only to stop as Ser Tiron burst out from his hiding place, fouled sword held aloft, and roared, "For the Black Wolves!"

Asho drew his blade. Power ran down its length from hilt to point, lighting the runes the color of Hell. It felt like an extension of his arm, and the world seemed to grow a fraction more vivid. Terrified, exhilarated, Asho raised it over his head and screamed, "For the Black Wolves!"

He ran forward. Ser Wyland was a large shadow that ran in from the far side. Kethe had turned and backed away, sword held low and at the ready. The demon lowered itself into a crouch, swinging its head from side to side, arms out wide, claws splayed.

They converged on it at the same time, and Asho lost sight of his friends. Holding his blade with both hands, knowing that a shield was beyond useless, he sprinted up to the demon's flank and swung with all his strength.

His sword's wicked edge split open its flesh into a black smile. The demon screeched, beset on all sides, and sprang straight up. Asho staggered back, following the arc of its leap as it sailed up thirty feet and latched onto the cliff face above them. Its claws dug into the rocks and sent a spray of them falling and bouncing to the clearing below. Three great wounds had been opened on its thighs and back. It released its grip with one hand and swung out to stare down at them with its sightless, bony facade of a face. Its mouth opened wide, revealing its fearsome fangs, and it roared its fury.

The others fell in line with Asho, gazing up, completely taken aback.

"Fuck me," said Ser Tiron. "What the Hell do we do now?"

Nobody had time to answer, because the demon let go and fell upon them. They scattered, throwing themselves aside so as to not be crushed, and the ground shook when it hit. Asho threw himself into a roll, came up into a crouch and turned. The demon was impossibly fast. Nothing that large should be able to move so. It swept its fist through the air into Ser Wyland's large shield. It crumpled and he went down, bowled over like a child. Ser Tiron roared again and ran forward, ducking under a second fist, and dragged his sword across the demon's stomach, opening up a seeping black wound.

Asho grunted, rose, and ran forward. His sword singed the air as he swung it, but the demon sensed him coming. It stepped out of his reach and then lunged forward to bite his head off. Asho yelled and dropped desperately to his knees, leaning back and barely avoiding its snapping jaws.

Kethe screamed and brought her sword two-handed through the flesh of its upper arm. Where she cut, a flash of white light bled out into the air. The demon recoiled, but Tiron was racing up on its other side. He had his sword reversed in his grip, holding it point down. Making no attempt to protect himself, he leaped up, back arched, and buried his cursed green blade to the hilt between the demon's ribs.

It reared to its full height and threw its head back to roar its pain, pulling Tiron's sword out of his grip as it did so. Despite the numerous wounds that had been opened up across its body, it didn't actually seem to be hurt. Asho fought to his feet just as it snatched Tiron off the ground, both clawed hands wrapping around his chest. Asho took a deep breath and ran in under its arms and sliced at its knee; his sword cut deep, and the monster dropped Tiron, who fell heavily to the ground in a crash of plate.

"Get up!" yelled Asho, grabbing Tiron by the arm.

"Let go of me!" Tiron shook his arm loose. His eyes widened, and he scooped Asho's heel out from under him, causing Asho to crash to his back just as claws swooped through the air where his head had been. "Idiot!"

Asho rolled to his side as claws dug deep into the rock where he'd been lying, got on all fours and scrambled out of range. Ser Wyland wasn't moving. Where was Kethe?

The demon took up Tiron again and raised him high. The older man laughed savagely even as his chest plate buckled under the demon's strength, then screamed in pain.

Asho's eyes flared wide as time seemed to slow. He sensed a new presence above him on the cliff face. Like a candle glow seen in the night, he felt the rushing pull of a presence call to him. Kethe. She was climbing to a ledge above the demon. Burning like a white bonfire in the darkness of his mind, he felt her pride and fear, her vulnerability and guilt, her determination and pain. *Kethe.* And he knew that she sensed him too.

Every instinct bade him reach out to her, to forge a connection with her fierce vitality. *No. I stand alone.*

Her burning light dimmed and then disappeared.

"Tiron! Catch!" Even as Tiron looked over at him, Asho lobbed his sword up into the air, a move born of desperation. There was no chance. There was no—but Tiron caught it, fingers wrapping around the naked edges of the sword. Blood immediately splattered into the air, but he brought the sword around and took it by the hilt with his free hand.

"You want me?" He sounded almost joyous. "I'm yours!" He drew Asho's sword back and thrust it right into the demon's head just before it could bite him.

The demon shrieked again. Its hands flew open, and Tiron fell ten feet onto the naked rock, where he rolled over and lay still. The demon whipped its head from side to side, the sword's pommel jutting out from the smooth carapace of its face.

Asho heard a scream and saw Kethe leap out from the ledge to which she'd climbed. Fifteen feet up, she soared through the air, lithe and agile as a cat, to land on the demon's back, her own sword raised high. Asho cursed and frantically looked around for a weapon. There— Ser Wyland's blade. He raced over to it and picked it up, turning just in time to see Kethe bury her sword to the hilt in the back of the demon's neck. White fire erupted from the wound and the demon screamed, a sound so shrill Asho could barely hear it, then reached up and seized Kethe by the back of her armor. It tore her free and threw her violently to the ground.

Asho cried out in alarm. Nobody could survive being thrown onto rocks like that, but even as he prepared to run to her, he saw Kethe push herself up, arms shaking, face bloodied, and her expression was grim. Relief surged through him. How had she survived?

The demon fell to its knees. His blade was still buried in its head, Kethe's embedded in its back.

They both rose and staggered toward it. The demon seemed blinded, turning back and forth as it clawed at the air. Guided by instinct, Asho darted in and seized the sword's hilt with both hands. It flamed to life, embedded even as it was within the demon's head. It shrilled in agony. The single rune that was visible just above the point where the blade disappeared into its head burned so brightly that it seared Asho's eyes. The demon's head was glowing from within, light spilling out its open maw.

Kethe stepped in behind it and grabbed hold of her own sword. White fire burst forth again. Asho closed his eyes and strained to keep his grip on the sword's hilt. He sensed a terrible energy flowing between the two swords, building and building as the demon screamed ever louder, until with a cacophonous explosion the demon's head simply burst.

Asho cried out and let go of the sword. The demon's corpse thudded over onto the ground, and Asho gazed, wide-eyed, at Kethe. For a moment she held his gaze, and he saw in her eyes an awareness of what had happened, of how they had connected. Then she turned away.

Ser Wyland rose stiffly and staggered over to where Ser Tiron lay on his back, his helm crumpled around his head, dark blood seeping from the rim and pooling over an eye.

Asho wanted nothing more than to lie down, but he forced himself to walk over. "Is he alive?"

Ser Wyland crouched by Tiron's side and frowned. "Looks like his armor has been crushed. Bones are likely broken. I don't see how we can move him down to Hrething without killing him."

Stones skittered down the slope, and Mæva slid down and fell beside them in a graceful crouch. Her eyes were locked on Ser Tiron, and she moved to his side without hesitation. Asho felt a stirring of hope. He stepped back, watching her face, seeking some comforting sign of confidence.

"Not good," she said. She pressed her fingers to his neck, then ghosted her hand down his chest to where one of his legs was bent the wrong way. Asho shuddered at the sight of it. That injury alone guaranteed an end to Ser Tiron's career as a fighting man.

"Can you help him?" Kethe's voice was flat. Asho couldn't tell if she was disappointed or hopeful.

Mæva shook her head. "I could, but at too much expense to myself. I've no animal to cast the taint into. It would warp me beyond anything I'm willing to suffer."

"Your power is selfish beyond measure," said Ser Wyland.

"If survival is selfish, then, yes, by all means." She looked up at him, her face pale. "Are you any different?"

Ser Wyland gave her a mocking smile. "I'd like to think so. I'd sacrifice myself for Ser Tiron or any of my companions willingly."

Mæva returned his smile coldly. "All right. Then I'll cast the taint into you and heal him."

Ser Wyland paled, but nodded. "Do it."

"Wait," said Asho. "There has to be another way."

Mæva rose to her feet and stood in front of Ser Wyland. She reached out and cupped his cheek, then ran her hand down his breastplate. "It will warp you, my heroic knight—your body and mind. You'll be become a sniveling, whining, broken creature. Your bones will twist and your mind will break. Everything good about you will turn to ash. Are you so sure you're willing to take this on?"

He caught her wrist and stared down at her. "Are you taking pleasure in this?"

Asho wanted to intervene, but he didn't know what to say.

"No," said Mæva. "But your self-righteousness sickens me."

Ser Wyland smiled. "Well, you won't have to stand it for much longer. Hurry."

Mæva crouched beside Ser Tiron again and placed a hand over his chest. She calmed her breathing and closed her eyes. "Goodbye, Ser Wyland."

Asho felt panic rise up within him. Was this right? He looked up to protest, but Ser Wyland's expression stilled his tongue. The man was iron and flint.

"Stop," said Kethe. Her voice was cold with command. "Cast it into me."

"No!" Ser Wyland wheeled on her, brow lowering. "I won't—"

"Now," said Kethe. She looked impossibly slender and battered in her leather and chain, but her eyes matched Ser Wyland's in determination. "I can take it. Go!"

Mæva stared at Kethe with flat, hooded eyes, then nodded. "There are no assurances here."

"I know," said Kethe hurriedly. "Just do it. Quickly."

The witch nodded and cast a sidelong glance at Ser Wyland. "Looks like I won't be rid of you yet."

"Lady Kethe, you can't—" Ser Wyland cut off what he was about to say as Mæva crouched beside the fallen knight and placed her hand above his body, closing her eyes and muttering to herself. Kethe widened her stance as if expecting a blow, her face pale, staring at the witch with fierce focus.

"Kethe," said Asho, but she ignored him.

Ser Tiron gave a wheezing gasp and his back suddenly arched. Mæva leaned forward as if against a great wind, forcing her hand down against an invisible resistance. Crimson and sickly green energy erupted from Ser Tiron's chest like a wildfire and rose up to stream toward Kethe, who lowered her chin, closed her eyes, and took the taint full in the chest.

Asho and Ser Wyland stared helplessly as she staggered back. A faint green glow enveloped her, and she writhed in agony. The weight was too much; she fell to her knees, one hand planted in the dirt. Shaking and shivering, she dropped her head so that her hair fell over her face, and Asho cursed and took a step forward. But what could he do?

Then, with a soft cry, Kethe rose to her knees. Her eyes were locked shut, her face contorted with effort. She raised both hands, and the green glow seemed to concentrate itself between her palms. She closed them together, and the glow grew all the brighter, right up until she smothered it. With a gasp she dropped her hands and fell over onto her side, just as Mæva grabbed Asho's arm.

"Hurry! Remove his helm!"

Kneeling again, he and Ser Wyland pulled Ser Tiron's armor off. The man was breathing deeply, and Asho saw that his wounds were healed. It was impossible but true. Blood was smeared over his face and matted in his hair, but there were no cuts. His leg had straightened out. He was breathing smoothly, and his color was good. Asho shook his head and looked up at Mæva, who was staring in disbelief at Kethe.

"That's not possible," said the witch. "Even for one such as her."

Ser Wyland rolled Kethe onto her back and checked her pulse. "It seems our Lady is full of surprises. She destroyed the taint of your magic. There's only one kind of person I've ever heard about who can do that."

"A Virtue," said Asho. He stared down at Kethe in wonder. He thought of the Virtues he had seen at the Battle of Black Hill, clad in resplendent armor, glowing with might, figures out of legend and surpassingly wondrous. "But…" He couldn't string his thoughts together. "But that means she has to go to Aletheia."

"Or die," agreed Ser Wyland, voice heavy. He wiped at his face, his expression weary.

"A Virtue," said Mæva, her voice soft with respect. Or fear. "Is that what Ashurina sensed? No wonder she told me of your coming."

"It won't make much of a difference if we don't stop Laur's army." Ser Wyland rubbed at his face. "They won't care what she is. They'll only want her dead."

Asho rubbed his hand over his head. Too many complexities were manifesting themselves too quickly for him to understand. They had an inkling as to Kethe's potential nature, but what of his own? Had the sword spoken to him? What had he sensed within himself? What had he turned away from? Doing so had almost cost Kethe her life…again. He rubbed his face and turned to the demon. "Let's focus on the next step for now. Maybe we can grab one of its horns as proof of what we've done."

Ser Wyland stood, looking twice his age. "Indeed. We'll work on removing one while the others recover."

Asho nodded with gratitude, raised his blade high overhead, and brought it down with all his strength at the great, winding horn's base. The shock of the blow shook him right up to the shoulders.

CHAPTER THIRTY-TWO

tharok

Chasm Walk was a vast and perilous gorge that had carved a route through the mountains, making it one of the primary passes through which one could traverse from the rich pastures to the south to the wild and desolate plains to the north. It opened deep in the heart of the territory of the Orlokor, who exacted high tolls on the human and kragh merchants who were loath to travel the four hundred miles to the east to the Dead Sky Pass. Orlokor greed, however, resulted in exorbitant tolls; as such, the gorge was perhaps less frequently traveled than its easy gradient would lead one to assume, its vertiginous walls rarely echoing with the passage of mules and wagons.

The Red River Tribe moved as one, the twelve clans strung out behind Tharok, who was riding at the front astride a great mountain goat, one of the many tamed bucks whose great spiraling horns could skewer a bear from belly to spine. The rest were, for the most part, on foot; large bundles of furs were strapped to the backs of donkeys while heavier loads were carried on supple slings hitched between other mountain goats. They moved at a good pace, striding with the mile-eating steps of kragh given to lengthy periods of travel, and the crushed rock that filled the savage depths of the gorge and formed a rough and ready road proved easy ground for them to cover with their roughly made boots.

On the third day they reached the first Orlokor outpost, a crudely amplified series of caves set into the base of the chasm wall from which some thirty lowland kragh had spilled, hastily pulling on their human-crafted chainmail and readying their spears and swords. Not an axe amongst them, Tharok had noticed as he pulled the goat to a halt. He watched as the Orlokor fell into a rough, humanlike formation and approached.

"Who goes there?" roared their leader, a broad and stocky kragh whose forehead would have reached no higher than Tharok's sternum.

"The Red River tribe," he called back in return, not deigning to dismount.

The leader surveyed the few hundred kragh massed behind Tharok, eyes running over the goods, the children and women, and then settled once more on Tharok. "The Red River are led by Wrok, or if he's dead, by his brother Krol. You are neither."

"No, I am not." Tharok resisted the urge to scowl at Krol's name. The large kragh had never returned, tipped off no doubt by the clans that had left during the night. "I am Grakor's son, Tharok, wielder of World Breaker and warlord of the Red River. Wrok is dead and Krol has fled. We go to the Orlokor warlord."

The leader absorbed this as the lowland kragh muttered to themselves. "World Breaker? You can't be—"

Tharok drew his great black scimitar and pointed it at the lowland kragh. "You call me a liar, Orlokor?"

The leader stepped back, eyes opening wide in fear and amazement. "No! Is that—is that really—? I—good fortune to you, then, Tharok, son of Grakor. Mighty Porloc will be happy to receive your tribute."

"Your expectations mean nothing to me." Tharok sheathed World Breaker. The gesture hadn't been subtle, but it would get the rumors moving. "Now move aside."

And without waiting for the stocky lowland kragh to respond, Tharok urged the mountain goat forward. Its neat hooves clipped along the crushed rock road, and the Orlokor leader growled, baring his diminutive tusks, but at the last moment stepped aside. Tharok didn't even glance down at him, but looked serenely over the heads of the other lowland kragh as their group of thirty parted. He rode through them and his tribe followed, forcing the Orlokor to stand along the cliff walls and watch as they passed, until the last of the highland kragh were through and they regathered to mutter angrily amongst themselves.

Tharok set an easy pace. He wanted Porloc to have plenty of time to react. Five days and three checkpoints later, the Chasm Walk began to level out, the peaks around them subsiding into mere mountains, their tops no longer encased in snow and ice. The trees began to show greater variety, fir and pine giving way to oak and aspen, and the air grew warmer by slow degrees.

Each night they made camp off the Walk, striking out for an hour to find hidden, higher ground, and mounting a perimeter set by Barok and enforced by numerous kragh who patrolled throughout the night. Each night Tharok had Wrok's hut assembled and he sat brooding in the gloom, the darkness dispelled by a solitary lamp as he turned the circlet around in his hands, examining the plain iron surface, wondering at its nature, its history, its origin. He found that the more he wore the circlet, the harder it became to take it off, and he had grown to relish its clarity of thought, the breadth of the knowledge it gave him. Yet in the depths of the night, doubts assailed him. Which of them was truly making the decisions? Was he, when he wore it, or somebody—or something else?

It was almost two weeks after setting out that they reached the mouth of the Chasm Walk, the snowy peaks but a memory behind and above them. They stopped at the sight of a new construction. A massive wall extended from side to side, blocking the last of the gorge as it flattened out into a wider valley. Two great guard towers had been built along the wall, their skilled construction unlike anything kragh could erect, human-carved blocks of stone cemented tight and built to last. Orlokor kragh were striding along its top and manning the towers, and the few hundred Red River kragh stopped and marveled at its presence. To have had humans build this wall must have cost a fortune in coin, and hinted at Porloc's concern for who might come over down the pass toward his lands.

Tharok spurred the mountain goat forward and rode the last few hundred yards up to the wall. A great gate of ironwood was set in the center, its surface banded by steel and sporting great pointed rivets, a fearsome entrance that would take much effort to force. Sitting astride his goat, Tharok glanced up at the light green faces that peered down at him from between the crenulations and waited.

Finally a kragh of some import appeared, dressed in the black uniform of Porloc's personal clan. The kragh was slender, slight, no bigger than an eight-year-old highland kragh, but normal perhaps for the lowlanders. "Who are you, and what do you want?" he called down, his voice harsh and rough.

"I'm Tharok, warlord of the Red River clan. You know who I am. Word has preceded me. Open the gates and let me pay my respects to Porloc."

"We know who you are, son of Grakor," called the kragh. "Porloc demands to know: do you come in peace like your father, or is this a time for blood?"

"Time for blood?" Tharok laughed. "I have with me only two hundred kragh, many of them women and children. Do you so fear the highlanders that you think even our old women could break down this wall?"

The kragh stiffened. "You claim to carry World Breaker, Ogri's blade. Word has reached us that you claim that Ogri's blood runs through your body. What are your intentions?"

"Nothing but respect," said Tharok, spreading his arms. "By Ogri, I swear that I have come to pay my respects to Porloc and nothing more."

The kragh thought this over and then disappeared from view.

Several hundred lowland kragh had gathered along the top of the wall, and they now were gazing down with bows and arrows held ready. Tharok could practically taste their fear.

The front gate opened, and a delegation moved out to greet them. Some sixty kragh mounted on horses emerged, the human-provided steeds speaking of wealth and power. At their center rode Porloc, his great fat body mounted on a large draft horse clad in black silks.

Tharok turned to look at the Red River kragh behind him. He found Barok amongst their number and nodded at him, and the weapons master marched forward, joining Tharok out before the Tribe. Moments later Maur detached herself from the tribe as well, so that the three of them stood ready and waiting as the Orlokor reached them.

The sixty warriors halted their horses in a gradual curve before them, and from their center Porloc and six guards continued forward, stopping only ten yards from where Tharok was waiting. Porloc was dark for a lowland kragh, and even had a hint of tusks emerging from his broad mouth. He was fat and soft, clad in green finery and uncomfortable with the blade slung over his back. He fixed Tharok with a beady glare.

The sun beat down on the kragh, both lowland and high, and everything was still except for a cool breeze from the higher slopes that blew down the Chasm Walk at their backs. Porloc raised himself to his full if still insignificant height, and Tharok nudged his mountain goat forward, indicating by his willingness to approach Porloc that the other was of higher station. This seemed to reassure the great warlord to some degree, but his eyes were filled with wariness.

"Greetings, Porloc of the Orlokor, greatest warlord of all the kragh tribes," said Tharok. "I've come with the Red River tribe to speak with you, to introduce myself to you, and renew old bonds."

"You are well received," said Porloc, smoothing the silk over his belly. "Welcome to our lands. You look familiar. What is your name?"

"Tharok, son of Grakor, who has been killed by Tragon treachery."

Porloc spat. "The damned Tragon. Grakor was a great kragh, tough and smart. I counted on him, depended on him. His loss is bad."

"But you have gained me," said Tharok. "A new warlord of the Red River tribe."

"Grakor was of the Grey Smoke," said Porloc. "Why is it that you lead the Red River?"

"Because Wrok of the Grey Smoke is no more," said Tharok loudly. "For his treachery I burned his body and was chosen to lead his tribe."

Mutters swelled along the wall.

"I see," said Porloc, eyeing Tharok with veiled eyes. "Is it true, then, that you carry Ogri's sword?"

In response Tharok reached down and drew it forth in one smooth sweep so that he could hold World Breaker high and allow the sun to gleam from its ebon blade. It seemed to hold the moment, the attention of hundreds focused on its length, as if it were more real than anything around it, making the whole world seem insubstantial by comparison.

"World Breaker," said Porloc, his voice quiet. "It is true, then. You have it—the Uniter's sword. I've heard whispers that you wish to unite the tribes, Tharok. That you are Ogri come again. That you even want to rule the Orlokor in my place. What do you say to that?"

Tharok held the blade high for a moment longer, allowing the tension to mount, and then he lowered it so that its point was directed at Porloc's chest. The fat-bellied warlord drew his mouth into a silent snarl, and his six guards bristled. Tharok ignored them. He swung the blade so that its point swept the battlements of the wall, and then finally lowered it.

"World Breaker was given to me by Ogri," he said, calling out so that his voice rang across the chasm. "Ogri told me that whoever wielded it would unite the tribes, and that they would usher in a new era of glory for the kragh."

Tharok fell still. Barok stirred by his side, shifting his weight to his back foot, turning subtly so that his profile was presented to the six kragh. Maur was glaring at him, her eyes livid.

"I've come from the highlands with Ogri's blade because I believed him," called out Tharok. "The kragh must unite under one ruler, under a kragh who has proven himself worthy of the blade. A true leader, one who will make history. That's why I've come to present it to you, Porloc of the Orlokor. I've come to give you World Breaker."

The stunned silence was filled by a roar of delight from the kragh along the wall, who banged their weapons against the battlements and stomped their feet on the rock. Porloc blinked, and then a wide smile split his circular face, his eyes gleaming with pleasure and delight. Tharok slipped from the canted saddle and dropped to the ground, and there he reversed his grip on World Breaker so that he was holding it hilt out, then walked toward the Orlokor warlord.

"I've come to renew our vows of alliance," he said in his avalanche voice, so that even those cheering on the wall could hear. "I've come to follow you when the war against the Tragon breaks out." He stopped just short of the chieftain, who shifted his weight in barely hidden desire to grip World Breaker. "My father had the honor of being your blood brother," he said. "He fought by your side and helped you carve your empire from these lands. As such, I bring you World Breaker not just as the warlord of the Red River, but as your blood son."

Everybody stilled. Maur hissed under her breath, and Porloc froze. Tharok went down on one knee and raised World Breaker for the chieftain to take it. From the crowd spread a ripple of hushed voices as kragh whispered to kragh what had been said. Nobody moved, until finally Porloc reached out and closed his small fingers around World Breaker's hilt. He let out a sigh of pleasure as its strength flooded him, and lifted the sword from Tharok's grip, raising it to the sky before lowering it and gazing full upon its blade. He turned it around, marveled at how it caught the light, and then laughed, a sound that was young and filled with delight and heady pride.

"Your gift is well received, Tharok, son of Grakor, who was my blood brother. You give me a gift straight from Ogri himself. You give me the means to win the war against the Tragon, for war is coming, and with this sword I'll not just win the war, I'll unite the tribes under the Orlokor banner! I renew our alliance to the Red River, I recognize you as warlord of your Tribe, and more—I recognize you as if you were my own son, blood of the kragh with whom I shared blood so many years ago. Come!"

Tharok rose to his feet and stood by the horse so that Porloc could grab him in a bear hug, squeezing him with surprising strength before clapping him hard on the back and laughing once more, holding up World Breaker for all to see. The Orlokor kragh exploded into bellows and roars of approval, pounding on the battlements, and Porloc turned his mount in a slow circle.

Which was why only Tharok, who alone did not cheer, heard Maur as she whispered, "You fool—what have you done?"

Porloc had ridden north from his great tent city specifically to meet Tharok as he emerged from the mountains. Word had traveled quickly of World Breaker's appearance, and rumor had swelled until it was said that the Red River tribe moved at the head of thousands of highland kragh, come down from the mountain to sweep the Orlokor into their grip and then to smash their way south into the human city of Abythos. Porloc had gathered as many warriors as he could and ridden hard for the north, to guard the wall at the mouth of Chasm Walk and await the worst.

His relief, therefore, was immense. He insisted on having Tharok ride by his side as he returned to the south, a ride of some five hours down from the high valley into the broader and gentler slopes below, the low mountains giving way to foothills and long ridges that eventually sank deeper into the ground before becoming the plains upon which he and the Orlokor lived. Gold, his great tent city, sat in the heart of the largest valley, a great conglomeration of huts and tanned hide tents, the permanent home of almost a thousand kragh who formed the heart of the Orlokor tribe.

A part of Tharok wondered at this, at males who lived settled and still like female kragh, not roaming and roving with other males of their clan as they hunted and fought and protected their territory. Always remaining stationary, the world about them never changing, always seeing the exact same sight from the entrances of their tents.

As they descended the last slopes toward the tents and the few stone houses, Tharok discovered another reason why the sedentary life would never appeal to him: the place reeked of waste and filth. Clearly they had not figured out how to deal with the accumulation of trash and sewage caused by staying in one place indefinitely. Numerous solutions presented themselves to Tharok as he gazed upon the refuse. He chose to voice none of them.

"Gaze upon Gold, young Tharok, and marvel. Here stands my court, the center of our tribe, the center of the world. Around this valley the stars swing, and I sit in my hall and allow the humans to send their ambassadors to me. Food there is in plenty, and wealth pours in from all the lands we now hold. Ten years ago we conquered this land from various loose tribes and clans that held it, your father and I, and then we went on to smash the Hrakar themselves! Now? Never has a tribe grown so strong, so numerous, so powerful!"

Tharok nodded, turning to study the high ridges of the valley and note the guard outposts and the flocks of sheep that grazed on the lush grass that seemed to billow from the ground like smoke from the peaks of volcanoes. Everywhere he looked, there were lowland kragh, hundreds to be seen at any time, herding, going to and fro on unknown business, driving carts down into Gold or leaving on horseback on urgent missions.

"There are indeed many of you, Porloc-krya," he said.

"Yes, and by the Sky Mother, our numbers grow every day, every year. I myself now have more children and grandchildren than I can remember, and trust me, that is saying a lot." He paused. "I can see it in your face, Tharok—I can sense your disgust. You are highland kragh. You don't understand why we sit still, why we Orlokor don't roam as your clans do. I saw the same expression on your father's face when I told him of my plans to build a city. He thought I wanted to copy the humans, but no. There is an advantage to it."

"I see the advantage," said Tharok. "That much is clear. You establish yourself in a central location, and that allows you to begin to organize your power and lands. You begin to create a system to control your tribe as it grows. You gather wealth, you gather your males, and there is safety in numbers with the Tragon and Hrakar and others watching you for signs of weakness."

Porloc glanced at Tharok out of the corner of his eye, his face neutral. Finally, he nodded. "Yes, indeed. The humans have much to teach us, I've always said. Look at the marvels they build, how they work with rock and stone. True, they have much longer lives in which to master such things. They write their strange language down on paper and preserve knowledge that way. They are able to do things that I don't even understand, but that doesn't mean we can't learn, can't grow."

Porloc warmed to his topic. They were getting closer to Gold now, a mere ten minutes from passing between the first tents. "Look at our greatest source of income. Tolls! Who would have thought, ten years ago when your father and I took this land by sword, that I would hold it with such a strange practice. If somebody wants to cross the mountains, humans looking to trade with the Tragon, say, we demand coin or shaman stone. They pay; we let them pass. So simple! It is like shaking wealth from the trees. We don't even need to fight any more – especially not after that disaster in the human land of Ennoia."

"Disaster?" Tharok roused himself, suddenly interested.

"It is not worth speaking of," said Porloc, waving a hand as if warding away a bad smell. "The human empire came as they do from Abythos and paid good shaman stone for the help of our clans in one of their conflicts. Yet they lied to us. They did not tell us we would be fighting against human shamans. They rained down spirit wrath upon our kragh, who naturally fled and were destroyed. Shameful. Even now their warlords and high priests are begging for us to return and fight for them. But we need not fight their shamans! We don't need to work! Why die for humans in a far away land we shall never walk to, never conquer ourselves? All we need do is put some sixty kragh at the mouth of the pass and demand payment. And the wealth comes in. The humans grumble, but what can they do? They promised us riches if we destroyed the Hrakar, and did we not? Who today fears the grubby Hrakar? Not I. Not I and my great tribe in our city of Gold!"

The path leveled out, and together they rode into the city. The first few tents were mean raw hide assemblies that Tharok would have refused to house a goat in, but soon they were riding past greater huts, huts of such size that it would have taken bending fully grown trees down to create such space and architecture. Kragh by the dozens and then hundreds lined the path, pushing their heads out of hut entrances or simply filling in the spaces between houses or lining the path proper, staring at Tharok and then pointing at the blade at Porloc's side. Kragh began to call out their warlord's name, and Porloc raised his fist in a signal of victory. The warlord had returned.

Behind them the kragh horde fragmented, the hundreds of warriors that Porloc had gathered splintering and moving into Gold to find their families or to spend coin on food and drink. The Red River tribe were to camp just outside Gold and await Tharok there, though Maur and Golden Crow and a few select others were to come later that night to join the celebration at Porloc's compound. Tharok sat tall, with his chin raised as they moved forward, followed only by Porloc's own honor guard, some fifteen lowland kragh in metal armor that clinked and clanked as they walked.

Porloc chattered on, but Tharok barely heard him. Thoughts assailed him as he saw more of the city, strategies on how to take it if ever he should attack Gold, the benefits of siege, of fire, of using pestilence as a weapon. Conversely, he saw dozens of ways to improve the city, ranging from the benefits of paving the roads to establishing regular patrols by trusted clans to ensure peace and order. He wondered at the lowland mating rituals, at the authority of their women; for the first time he questioned why lowland kragh didn't grow tusks or swell in size with stature, why their skin didn't darken when they ate flesh. Theories presented themselves, and he tried to piece together a history from the fragmented tales he had heard as a child. How many centuries ago had the lowland kragh descended from the mountains and begun to change?

The thoughts came faster and faster, stimulated by all he saw. Tharok felt almost nauseated. It didn't help that Gold stank. Offal and refuse filled the streets, and children ran and played without regard for the filth underfoot. They passed a large market in which vendors hawked and sold their wares, where the sizzle of meat on a spit competed with the stench of feces, and there Tharok saw his first humans manning a stall, their tall, skinny bodies seeming to be without muscle or mass, their delicate skin the color of pale wood. Three of them were selling weapons, metal swords and axes that gleamed as if newly polished in the sun, and a deep crowd was formed before them, kragh reaching out to try to grip the wares only to be admonished by the humans in crude kragh. One of the human men turned to watch them pass, his face bearded like a mountain goat's, almost as tall as a highland kragh and dressed in rich robes of brown and umber. Tharok held his gaze, studying the man, and then they were past.

There was a slave gallery to their right, where a number of lowland kragh were being sold alongside three bedraggled humans. One of the humans was female, standing naked in the thin afternoon sun, and Tharok stared hard as they passed, marveling at how slender her legs were, how thin her forearms, how slight her body. She looked like a bird, so frail that were he to roll over her in the middle of the night he was sure he would snap every bone in her body beneath his weight. That was no woman; Maur was a woman. That human wouldn't even be able to lift a pack, much less carry it all day through the mountains. Still, there was something to that smooth, sunburned skin, to the mass of white hair that looked like moonlight caught in a web.

Out of the corner of his eye he saw a towering figure in irons. It was a highland kragh, chained up behind the humans, his skin impressively black, his physique powerful and ponderous. Tharok drew his mountain goat to a halt. Porloc stopped his own steed a few paces on, looking back at Tharok with impatience and surprise. This wasn't the time to make inquiries about a slave. This wasn't the time to show Porloc anything but decisiveness and solidarity. He couldn't start questioning Gold's practices within moments of arriving.

And yet, a deeper part of Tharok wanted to know that highland kragh's tale, and flet disgusted at seeing him chained up like a common lowland kragh. So what if it was a poor decision to walk over there and demand answers? To free him, perhaps?

No, one single highland kragh was not important in the grand scheme of things. There were hundreds like him being sold and used across the land. Tharok's true goals would lead to a revolution in this system of slavery. He couldn't risk his current standing with Porloc by acting belligerent and demanding here in the square. He should put this highland kragh out of mind and move on.

"Is there a problem, Tharok?"

Porloc's honor guard were milling around, uneasy and watching Tharok with suspicious gazes.

Tharok forced himself to shake his head. "No problem, my warlord. I was just admiring the size of this square. Very impressive."

Porloc nodded and turned his horse to continue riding. A second later Tharok urged his mountain goat on as well. He wanted to glance back at the slave. He forced himself not to, but felt a rising sense of frustration within him that he couldn't explain to himself.

Another market, more huts, and then finally they came to Porloc's own hut, built of thick stone and painted black, two levels high and with a huge wall around it enclosing a compound. It was practically a fortress. Tharok stopped his mountain goat and stared, giving his mind a moment to adjust to the sight. It was all hard angles and rough stone, tanned hides falling to obscure the windows, guards standing at attention at the open gate.

"Welcome, Tharok of the Red River, to the Heart of Gold, my home." Porloc studied him to gauge how impressed he was. "You will stay here as my guest. Tonight we feast, but for now I'll give you time to yourself. I must meet with my clan and prepare for the next few weeks. Rest now. We will speak again soon."

Porloc dismounted, allowed his horse to be taken away, and then headed off even as several other lowland kragh moved forward to talk to him.

Tharok sat on his mountain goat and considered the compound, the rough rock from which it was built, the various lowland kragh guarding it. It felt alien. Too human. He studied Porloc's fat figure as he walked away, World Breaker strapped to his back, and plans revolved in his mind. He closed his eyes and allowed his thoughts to expand and contract, interweaving in a manner he could barely comprehend even as they evolved. Everything was going according to plan, he thought.

But whose plan is it? Is this the circlet thinking, or is it me?

Tharok growled, reached up, and tore the circlet from his brow.

CHAPTER THIRTY-THREE

Asho

Dusk was falling when they stumbled into Hrething, Ser Wyland and a completely recovered Ser Tiron hauling the horn along the ground behind them with two thick ropes. The demon had rotted away before their eyes, shrinking and diminishing until only a putrid mountain goat's skeleton was left.

Kethe hadn't spoken a word since awakening, and Asho couldn't help but cast worried looks her way every few moments, although he received no acknowledgment in return. It was as if she were walking in a dream, her brow furrowed in thought, her eyes never lifting from the forest floor.

Mæva had excused herself, explaining that she wasn't interested in being pilloried by the Hrethings. Despite Ser Wyland's protestations of protection, she laughed, blew him a kiss, then disappeared back into the forest. Ser Wyland had blushed and muttered something ungracious beneath his breath.

Shadows were lengthening and the high peaks were catching the last of the setting sun's rays, causing the ice that clung to the cliff faces to glimmer and glint with a crimson light. Down in the valley the wind had taken on a cruel chill, such that when they finally sighted the hunched and cluttered roofs of Hrething they all breathed a sigh of relief.

Two guards were posted on watch at the edge of town, and at the sight of their small band one raised a cry and ran back into the street, while the second jogged up the gradual slope to join them, slowing to a walk when he was ten paces away. It was Janderke, Asho saw, and his eyes were wide with wonder at the sight of their battered armor and the huge horn they were dragging behind them.

"Ser knights—" He stopped, unsure how to continue.

"We're well," said Ser Wyland with a weary smile. "And the demon is slain." He stopped and straightened with a sigh. "Dead and rotting. How goes it below?"

"Well enough," said Janderke, eyes locked on the horn. "Lady Kyferin is waiting in Gunnvaldr's house, and everybody is tense. I think wagers were being made as to whether you'd return."

Asho stepped forward. "And what did you bet, Janderke?"

"That you'd be returning victorious, of course!" He grinned.

296

"You've made me a handful of copper. My thanks!"

"Well, earn it by putting your shoulder to this rope," growled Ser Tiron. He'd been subdued since awakening, though he'd confirmed that he'd healed completely. "You're half my age. You should do twice the work. Get over here."

Together they finished the last descent. A crowd emerged from the streets to flood out onto the hillside. Hrethings and folk from Castle Kyferin all stood intermingled, and at the sight of them Ser Wyland stepped back, slid his hands under the twisted horn, and with a grunt hefted it high into the air. The evening light caught the wicked striations along its sinuous length and everybody let out a ragged cheer. Ser Tiron stepped up, Asho behind him, and, forming a line, they lowered the horn onto their shoulders. It was long enough to span the three of them. As one they marched down, Janderke and Kethe trailing them, and into the crowd. Men and women were grinning, bowing and cheering, and then the crowd opened and revealed Lady Kyferin, composed yet unable to hide and her pride and relief, hands laced together before her and her chin held high.

They dumped the horn down onto the rocky dirt, and Ser Wyland stepped forward and knelt. "We've slain the demon, my Lady. Its body has rotted away, leaving nothing but the bleached bones of a mountain goat."

Again the crowd let out a cheer and Asho stepped forward to kneel. He felt hollow. How he'd dreamed of a moment like this, where he might be celebrated alongside other knights for performing a heroic deed. Yet now that it was happening, he felt like an imposter. It had been Kethe who had killed the demon. Kethe who had drawn it to the clearing. All he'd done was throw his blade to Tiron.

"I wish that I could say I never doubted your success," said Lady Kyferin, her voice carrying, and the crowd felt silent. "But I feared for your lives. I worried that even the greatest four knights in the land might perish before such a terrible foe. I see now that I was foolish to do so." She smiled, and Asho looked down. "Heroes of the land," she called, her voice bright in the evening air. "You honor us with your valor! You bring safety to the land! Never were there truer knights!"

Again the crowd broke out into cheers, bold and celebratory. Asho looked back to where Kethe was kneeling. This moment was hers, but she was distant, gazing at her mother but seeming to look through her.

"Headman Gunnvaldr," said Lady Kyferin, catching the crowd just as the cheers began to die down. "We have killed the demon that plagued your people and your land. Will you now help us as we have helped you?"

The old man stood straight, and for a moment Asho had a glimpse of the warrior he must have been in decades past. His son, Kolgrímr, was standing by his side, and both looked grave, proud, and fierce.

"It's been years since something like this has prowled our woods," said Gunnvaldr, his voice quiet. People grew silent and strained to hear. "We'd have lost many innocents and good men before we were able to bring it to ground. You have our thanks, the four of you. We'll be singing songs of your deeds for years to come."

Asho could almost hear Lady Kyferin's thoughts: *It's not your song we want.*

"But we made an agreement, and you've upheld your part in it, so the Hrethings will come to your aid. The Hold might be cursed and the high lands steeped in evil, but it's clear that we're no safer for being down here. We'll do what we can to help you against those who are coming for your heads, and I'll put the word out amongst the far farms so that good fighting men will gather to help in this struggle." He looked up at his son, then back to Lady Kyferin. "Give us three days, and we'll have a force assembled that should give any invading army pause."

Lady Kyferin nodded, her expression grave. "You have my thanks, headman."

"Now," said Gunnvaldr, raising his voice at last. "It's time we mark this moment with a feast! Kolgrímr, butcher one of the cows. Afildr, Leifi, broach two of the mead flasks from under my house. Rauðr, get the fire pit going in the square. Everyone! Tonight we gather to celebrate these men and women who have fought for us. Let's show them our gratitude, and celebrate!"

Asho climbed to his feet. The crowd swirled past him, some even clapping him on the shoulder as they went. He saw Lady Kyferin step forward to speak with Kethe and then quickly draw her aside, her brow contracting in alarm.

Ser Wyland stepped up beside him, watching the two women. "Her powers are a death sentence unless she can get help."

Asho felt his insides knot up. Should he mention what he had felt? The voice that had spoken to him? His failure to seize the moment? "All the more reason to defeat Laur's men."

Ser Wyland rubbed at his jaw. "Even if we defeat this invading force, we still won't be in the clear. Laur holds Kyferin Castle, and he won't leave the Raven's Gate unguarded. The other Lunar Gate is in the Talon, and they won't open their gates to us just because we've killed their knights."

Asho nodded. "I guess not. Though there's that Gate Audsley found beneath the Hold."

"True. But only the Ascendant knows where that leads."

Asho nodded soberly. "How long do you think she has?"

"That's a question better put to the Magister. He might know. But not too long, I fear."

Asho watched as Lady Kyferin shepherded her daughter away. Kethe looked lost, her eyes still blank with shock. Anger rose within him. "There must be something we can do."

Ser Wyland arched an eyebrow in surprise. "I hadn't realized you cared so much about her wellbeing."

Asho started. "I—what? I don't, I mean—of course I want the best for her."

Ser Wyland stroked his mustache. "Mm-hmm. I must have misread the coldness between you two."

Asho felt his face burn. "She's a great knight. She's proven herself again and again in battle."

"She has, indeed."

"Right. So. Now that we've got the support of the Hrethings, we can work on defeating the invading force."

"Laur's not going to take this attack lightly. He'll send in an overwhelming force to make sure the deed is done quickly and thoroughly. Even if we get a hundred locals with bows and axes, I don't think it will be enough."

Asho watched the men and women as they hurried back into the town, laughing and with a spring in their step. "But it vastly increases our strength."

"True. But think: How would you deploy those men? What would you have them do?"

Asho frowned. Lining them up into a regiment and having them face the invading knights in pitched battle would lead to their slaughter. "Their strength lies in their knowledge of the land," he said. "They could shadow the invading force, attack them from a distance, and then fade away when the knights gave chase. Pick off stragglers." Ser Wyland's face remained impassive. "But... then the knights would fire Hrething when they passed through it and massacre the women and children—unless we had them sent up to the higher farms. But they still wouldn't have anything to come home to."

"Right." Ser Wyland looked at the last of the villagers as they disappeared into Hrething. Ser Tiron had stepped away without a word. Only the two of them were now left standing outside the town. "That's why Gunnvaldr was so reluctant to help us. He knows that his people can't afford to pay the price of fighting Laur's men. The fact that they're willing to do so speaks to their honor."

Asho felt anger flare within him. "So, what are you saying? That we shouldn't use the Hrethings?"

"Not at all." Ser Wyland smiled tiredly. "Who knows where they rank on the cycle of Ascension? I would wager as low as a Zoeian, perhaps even an Agerastian given their heresy. They would benefit in dying for our cause. It's simply that we're going to need to have an excellent plan if we're to use them effectively. Fortunately for Lady Kyferin, she is served by some of the bravest knights I have ever had the privilege to fight alongside."

Asho looked away.

"What is it?"

Asho felt helplessness rise up within him. "Nothing." He hesitated. "I just feel the fool."

"The fool? What are you talking about?"

Asho turned away. "I thought myself strong. That I could become Lady Kyferin's most valuable knight." He snorted. "Instead, I've fumbled every opportunity, and worse yet, risked the lives of my friends through my actions."

The silence drew out between them. Asho could feel the weight of Wyland's gaze. He fought the urge to kick at a stone. It had been a mistake to open up.

"You've fought bravely." Wyland's voice was stern. "Why are you denigrating your accomplishments?"

A great wound tore open in Asho's soul, and his bitterness came flooding forth. "Bravely? I was beaten soundly at the tournament. I failed to help Kethe when the demon attacked. Then, all I did in today's fight was throw Tiron my sword so he could stab the demon. Every time I'm faced with a chance to act nobly, I throw the chance to the winds. I don't trust my instincts. I don't know what to do." He wanted to laugh. "And I thought I'd become Lady Kyferin's greatest knight. How pathetic."

Wyland didn't answer right away. Asho fought the urge to glance at him. Finally he spoke. "I cannot help you."

Asho started. He'd expected to hear something about 'true knights' or the like. "What?" Pain cut into his chest. "So, you agree. I'm beyond hope."

"No, I don't agree." Wyland sat with a sigh on a rock. "Quite the opposite. But I can't help you until you're willing to listen."

"But I am listening. Right now. Go ahead. Try me."

"No," said Wyland, pulling off a boot. He shook it, and a pebble fell out. "You're not listening. There's no room in your head for my advice."

Asho bit back on his frustration and crouched in front of the older knight. "There is. I swear there is."

Wyland pulled off his other boot and laid his foot over his knee. There was a hole in his sock. He began to massage his foot. "Your head is so filled with bitterness and anger that you won't listen. Do you remember when we first spoke? You told me that all you needed was your sword. I tried to caution you, but you couldn't listen."

Asho opened his mouth to retort, but he had nothing to say. He closed it. Was Wyland right? He hung his head. "Maybe I can't be a true knight, then. Maybe my background prevents me from being one."

"All evil and lazy men have excuses for their actions, and many claim hard circumstances. The mark of a real knight is his disdain for excuses. He takes full responsibility for his actions. He knows that the only thing he can control is himself, so he does exactly that."

Asho wanted to protest. It was too much to ask. Throughout his whole life, his outrage and fury had given him strength, fueled his determination. Was he supposed to simply forget it all? Put Shaya behind him?

The wind tugged at Ser Wyland's cloak. The knight pulled on a boot, then the other. "You've had a hard life, Asho. I don't deny it. Harder than most. But don't let that pain drag you down. Embrace it. Be grateful for it."

"Grateful?" Asho couldn't believe it. "For a lifetime of pain and loss and abuse?"

"Yes. Tell me: why do we Ennoians fight when violence is forbidden by the Ascendant?"

"Each cycle has its role." Asho fought down his irritation. "Ennoians are warriors."

"Yes, but it is clearly stated that violence is forbidden. Hence the use of the kragh. But still, how do we Ennoians hope to Ascend to Nous when we flout so grave a law?"

Asho scowled. "It's sanctioned. It's your role."

"Not quite." Ser Wyland smiled grimly. "Our dedication to war is justified by the suffering it brings us. That suffering cleanses us of the sin of murder. The more we suffer, the greater our sacrifice. Hard campaigns. Painful wounds. Violent death. We honor the Ascendant through might in arms, defeating his opponents, and by suffering for him before we die. The more we suffer, the greater our reward."

Asho nodded reluctantly. "All right. So?"

"You, Bythian, are blessed. As unnatural as it is, your ascension to knighthood affords you the greatest chance to suffer." Ser Wyland grinned and placed both hands on his knees. "Your suffering elevates you. If you are to serve Lady Kyferin truly, you will disdain excuses. You will ignore insults. You will let nobody drag you down. You will fight with all your heart, and when your death comes, as it surely will, you will die at peace with your life and your deeds, knowing that you have brought more light into the world than dark, that your suffering had purpose, and that you have served the Ascendant with all your soul."

Asho's heart was racing. Ser Wyland's words resonated with power. He wanted to deny them, decry them as unfair. To scream his resentment and pain. But the words would not pass his lips.

Ser Wyland smiled and stood. "Don't forget your sister. Honor her. Don't forget the insults; rise above them. Don't turn away from your companions; embrace them. Don't hate Lord Kyferin. Prove him wrong."

Asho couldn't breathe. His every instinct fought Wyland's words. But, whose fault had his failures been?

He saw Shaya turn and ride away into the night. He saw Kyferin's broad face with its mocking, hooded eyes. Heard the thousand insults. Felt the blows. Remembered the endless nights he had spent staring up at the moon and vowing futilely to never cry again, to never ask why the world was unfair--instead, to get revenge, to hurt everyone as much as they had hurt him. He felt that pain, sharp and vital and burning within his core, that anguish and anger that had fueled him through so many challenges, lifted him when he wanted to give up, given him strength when he wanted to die.

It was him. He was that rage.

He reached for it. He sought that anger, but Wyland's gaze was inscrutable, and the older knight's words stood between him and that bitter strength. He couldn't embrace it. Couldn't hide in it. Couldn't lose himself in its all-consuming self-righteousness.

Again, Asho saw Shaya's face. Her silver-green eyes. Her heartbreaking love for him. The sorrow he'd seen in their depths for abandoning him. His whole body shook as he was suffused with his overwhelming love for his sister, his soul mate. That final look—it had been the last time anybody had looked at him with love.

Who had she seen? What was it in him that she had loved?

Asho gave a terrible cry and covered his face with his hands. *Shaya*. At his most basic level, he still wanted to merit that love. He didn't want to be alone.

He dropped his hands to see that the larger knight was watching him carefully. The wind gusted past them, and finally Wyland nodded.

"I see you, and mark you as my brother. I shall help you stand if ever you should fall. My shield shall always be at your back and my sword at your side. We are Black Wolves. We live and die for the Kyferins."

A shiver ran through Asho, but he straightened. "I see you, and mark you as my brother." His voice shook with emotion. "I shall be here to help you stand if ever you should fall. My shield shall always be at your back and my sword at your side." His voice grew strong and sure, and a thrill ran through him. "We are Black Wolves. We live and die for the Kyferins."

Wyland grinned and clasped Asho's forearm in the warrior's grip. "Brother."

A happiness Asho had never dared dream might be his own flooded through him. He grinned foolishly and laughed. "Brother."

Wyland grinned and crouched down by the horn. "Now, there's much to do. Let's not leave this out here to foul up the field. Help me get it to the town square. It'll serve as an ongoing reminder as to the course the locals have chosen."

Asho grabbed one end, glad for his leather gloves, and hefted it with a grunt. Following Ser Wyland, he felt light and clear and focused like never before. In some ways nothing had changed, but in others he felt like he'd been given a chance at a new beginning. It didn't matter that they were opposed by seemingly insurmountable forces. Together, he knew that they could somehow defeat all of it—and would.

CHAPTER THIRTY-FOUR

ISKRA

Iskra pulled Kethe behind her, fear driving her through the crowd without regard for her station. She fairly ran through the streets of Hrething, but in her mind's eye she seemed to be racing down the streets of her peak city in Sige once more, diving through the solemn crowd in the desperate hope of catching a glimpse of her brother Bron as he was led away to be consecrated.

She turned into Gunnvaldr's doorway without bothering to knock, simply stepping up and through and then turned to pull Kethe in behind her and slam the door shut. The house was empty, the fireplace filled only with ashes and coals, and in the sudden stillness she examined her daughter and wondered how she hadn't seen the signs. Kethe trembled, her eyes moving from side to side in minute movements that betrayed the panic just beneath the surface. Reaching up, Iskra touched the smoothness that had appeared around her eyes, noting for the first time how the skin there had lost its texture. Just like Bron.

"Oh, my dearest love," she breathed, and then pulled Kethe into a tight hug. She didn't care about the chain and leather, the sword at her hip. This was her daughter, her precious child. Too many memories and images cascaded through her mind, a life spent loving someone, caring for them, feeling pride and hope and a terrible tenderness in light of the cruelties of the world. She held Kethe tight, breathed her in, and wished there was something she could do, anything at all that lay within her power to spare her daughter from her coming trials.

"Mother," said Kethe at last, pulling away. "What's happening to me?"

Iskra pulled her down to sit beside her on one of the wall benches and held her hand tightly. "You're manifesting an affinity for the White Gate, my love." It was so hard to say those words, but she managed, speaking smoothly and calmly, to her own surprise. "My brother suffered the same fate. When I was just fifteen, he started to show the signs. Since we were both in Sige, those signs were quickly recognized, and he was taken."

"Your brother?" Kethe frowned. "I have an uncle?"

"Had, my love." Iskra brushed her cheek. "He was taken from us before I met your father. When we realized what was happening, it was too late. Not that we could have done anything. It's meant to be a source of pride, to have a member of your family taken and consecrated and raised to Aletheia. My father acted proud, but I know he was crushed, as were we all. I always meant to tell you about him. Bron." How many years had it been since she'd said his name out loud? "But there never seemed to be a good time." She looked down at her hands. "Perhaps on some level I hoped that I could protect you and Roddick from his fate if I simply pretended he'd never existed."

Kethe was sitting very straight. "He became a Virtue."

"No." Iskra sighed. "He didn't survive the consecration. We never saw him again."

She felt the old shock and horror rise within her again from when word had finally reached her family, the blank nullity of knowing that smiling Bron was gone, dead, and that she would never, ever, no matter how long she lived, hear his voice or see his face again.

Kethe rocked back as if weathering a blow. "I thought…" She paused, swallowed, and tried again. "I thought that manifesting this power meant you were destined to become a Virtue."

"No, my love. It only means that you are destined to be put through the consecration. Nobody outside of Aletheia knows what that involves, but very few survive the process. They say that it is a mercy, that if the candidate is not worthy of becoming a Virtue, that it's better they pass away quickly so as to earn the glory of direct Ascension with all honors, regardless of their current cycle." Her voice shook. Never had the rites and dogma of Ascension struck her as more foul than when she'd heard the smug Aletheian deliver those words to her family.

"So, I have to go to Aletheia?" Kethe tried to steel her voice, but Iskra knew her too well. Far too well. She knew how close the tears were, could feel them.

"Yes. As soon as we can get you there. They say the sooner you are consecrated, the higher your chances of survival. But I don't know how we're going to get you to Aletheia." Iskra felt her heart cramp. "I will go through the Raven's Gate when it next opens to explain the situation to Laur. He won't kill me in plain view above the keep. He'll understand that this transcends our struggles. He'll give you safe passage to Ennoia."

"No!" Kethe pulled her hands away. "I won't abandon you. Not now, not with everything that's going on."

"You must." Iskra tried to smile. "Don't you see? It would kill me more surely than anything Laur could throw at us to see you suffer. And, my love, this is something you cannot fight. The White Gate will claim you, slowly but surely. You have to go to Aletheia. You have to be consecrated as soon as possible."

Kethe stood and backed away. "You don't know me if you think I'll leave."

"You will leave." Iskra fought to keep her voice soft. "You have no choice in the matter."

"I do have a choice!" Kethe clenched her hands into fists. "Everything I've fought for these past few years, everything I've done, was to assure me that I'd always have a choice! That nobody would ever be able to force me against my will again, that nobody would ever make me feel helpless or weak! If I have one thing, one single thing under my control, it's my own life! And nobody, not even you, can tell me what to do with it!"

"Oh, my love." Iskra stood, and would have taken her hands if she could. "Your choice was taken from you the moment you started to manifest your powers. You've been chosen by the White Gate. Like my brother, like your father's ancestors. If you don't go, you will die. You will age faster and faster as the life is sucked out of you, until you are a withered husk. You'll burn brighter than any flame, but your fall will be terrible. You must do this. Ascension requires that you accept your destiny."

Kethe opened her mouth to retort, and then looked down and away. Iskra strove to find something with which to comfort her. "Think of it this way: if you become a Virtue, then you'll be able to end this war between Laur and me. You will discover abilities beyond that of any normal warrior - you will become a force for good to which all must bend knee. This could be our best way to find peace."

Kethe snorted bitterly. "I'm not a child, Mother. I know it takes time to become a Virtue. Time we don't have."

"Time *you* don't have." Iskra placed her hands on Kethe's shoulders and forced Kethe to meet her eyes. "What's happening to you is more important than any of this. You have to understand that. You have to see that you've been chosen to perform mighty deeds. This is a terrible honor, and you can't damn your soul by turning away from it. You must accept your fate. You must get to Aletheia. You have to survive, you have to live, and you have to respect the force that singled you out from amongst the millions alive today."

A flood of emotions washed across Kethe's face; Iskra saw panic, fear, fury, denial, and helplessness. Iskra pulled her into a hug again and held her tight. "We'll survive Laur's attack, then I'll go through the Raven's Gate when next it opens. There's no choice. I swear, if there was any other way, I would take it in a heartbeat. But there isn't. Promise me you'll go. Please, Kethe. Promise me."

Kethe stood stiff and awkward, but finally nodded. "All right." Her voice was soft, and Iskra felt something break deep inside her.

"Good." Iskra pulled back and smiled. "Now, go help the others with the feast. We have to make the most of the time we have left. I won't have you hiding in here. I'll be out in a moment, and then we'll celebrate your victory. I want you to tell me all about it."

Kethe nodded, but she didn't really seem to hear. She walked to the front door, hesitated, then pulled it open and stepped out into the dusk.

As soon as she was gone, Iskra's knees gave away and she nearly collapsed to the floor. She managed to pull herself to Gunnvaldr's armchair and sank into it, misery rising up to clutch at her throat. First Roddick, now Kethe. How could she keep fighting when the most precious things in her life were being torn away from her? She wanted to bury her face and weep, wanted to crawl into a small, dark place and curl into a ball. What sort of world was this that wed you to a beast and then tore your children away one by one?

Iskra closed her eyes tightly and focused on her breathing. There was no time for weakness, no room for breaking down. Survival depended on her being strong. Her men and women looked to her for leadership, to justify the faith they had placed in her and see them through this challenge. The Hrethings needed her strong so they could justify the sacrifice they were about to make. Everything would collapse in a second if they thought her broken and weak.

The door opened. She stood, wiping away the few stray tears that had slipped down her cheek, ready to greet Gunnvaldr or whoever had entered with a cheerful tone—and stopped. It was Ser Tiron. He was standing in the doorway, his expression haggard, his shoulders hunched, eyes sunken and staring at her.

"Ser Tiron?" Her voice faltered. "What's wrong?"

"Iskra," he said, his voice a pained rasp. She saw him look to the door as if he wished to escape, but then he shoved it closed and stepped deeper into the room.

"What is it?" She moved closer, alarmed. He had the look of a man who had received a mortal wound. His hard face was ashen and his hands were trembling.

"Iskra." He took another step forward, and fell. She almost cried for help, fully expecting to see a dagger protruding from his back, but then saw that he'd fallen to his knees. He hung his head. "I'm a foul man. I've come to apologize, to confess. And then I'll take my leave. I'll go and I'll never return." He stared fixedly at the floor.

"Ser Tiron, what's happened?" Had he betrayed them somehow?

He'd just finished slaying a demon, for Ascension's sake. "What's going on?"

"I swore." He spoke in belabored gasps, as if each word was being dredged up from the dark depths of his soul. "In that hole your husband put me in, I swore to kill you and your daughter and son." His words were bloody and raw, and the intensity of them made her flinch. "I swore by the love of my dead wife that I would kill you all to avenge her, no matter what happened. I swore an oath. A sacred oath to her memory." His face worked as misery flowed through it. "And then you freed me. By the Black Gate, I hated you for that mercy, though it was only to help yourself. That made it easier to keep on hating you."

Iskra took a step back. She was unarmed. His sword was buckled at his side. "Yet Kethe and I still live. You haven't moved against us."

"No." He looked up at her then, and his smile betrayed such depths of self-loathing that Iskra stopped cold. "And I found that I could hate something more than your husband—myself. When Kitan told me to kill you and yours, I told him to go to Hell." He laughed. "But his words echoed my own resolution. A resolution I've failed, that I've been too weak to uphold. Ever since then, I've cursed myself for being an oath-breaker. A coward. A traitor to her memory."

Iskra didn't know what to say. She stood still, eyes wide, watching. Listening.

Tiron lowered his gaze to the ground once more.

"It grew unbearable. I couldn't kill you. I couldn't even kill your daughter when she attacked me. The Ascendant knows I wanted to fulfill my oath, but—I just couldn't. So, today, I decided to find release. I'd die killing this demon. I'd die, and then I'd be free of my oath." He smiled, and it was an awful grin, mocking and derisive. "And I failed to even do that. Here I am—and what's worse, when I thought I would die, when I was sure it had me, when the damned thing lifted me up to bite off my head, I thought of you. Of you!" He looked up suddenly and glared at her. "What kind of man am I, to think of you when I should have only thoughts for my Sarah?" He rose to his feet. "I'm scum. Oath-breaking, faithless, wretched filth." His words brimmed over with hatred. "I can't even kill myself," he said, and laughed weakly again before covering his face with his hands, shoulders heaving. "I can't even die."

"Ser Tiron," whispered Iskra. She didn't know what to do, whether to run away or move to him. Whether to stay silent or speak— but what words?

"No." His voice was raw, his fury simmering beneath the surface. "Don't say a damned word. I don't want your pity or your scorn. I don't even know why I came here, not any more. Maybe it was a need, a need to finally tell the truth." His eyes searched the walls as if for an answer. "It grew inside of me till I couldn't bear it any longer. But now it's done. You know my shame. I'll go."

"Wait!' She almost reached for him, but he whirled at the last, eyes blazing dangerously. "Wait." Her mind raced. She was losing him. She had to speak. "You may have betrayed me in thought, but never in deed. You've served me well."

He shook his head with disdain and turned again to go.

"But not well enough!" Her voice snapped like a whip crack, and he froze. "You came here to confess. Now I demand that you perform your absolution." She felt a power rising within her, felt her shoulders push back and her chin rise. "If you think you can slink out of here like a worthless dog, then you are wrong. You are my knight. Mine! And I demand you serve me with the honor I deserve. Once you are done, then I will discharge you if you still wish to run, but not yet. You are not released, ser knight!"

Ser Tiron hesitated by the door, clearly aching to throw it open and depart, but finally looked over his shoulder. "You are mad if you think to use me further."

"Perhaps, but I'll do just that if it means saving my people." She took a deep breath. "You said Kitan came to you. That he asked you to kill me."

Ser Tiron nodded reluctantly.

"We can use that." Iskra felt excitement quicken her pulse. "He'll be leading Laur's force." She looked down, staring through the floor, sensing her opportunity. "You will meet him halfway. Claim that you were en route to the Talon."

"I will?" Ser Tiron sneered. "To what end? Challenging him in combat?"

"No. He asked you to kill me. You will tell him that you have done so."

Ser Tiron narrowed his eyes. "He'll demand proof."

"And you will give it." She paused. "I will cut off my hair. You will take it to him, soaked in blood. And Ser Wyland's family blade as well. You will convince him that you slew me, slew Ser Wyland, and then fled."

He turned at last to fully face her. "But why? What will that gain you? He'll still come to make sure."

Iskra smiled. "But his guard will be down. He'll believe you. He'll enter Mythgræfen unaware of the trap we'll be laying for him."

"What trap?"

"Go fetch Ser Wyland, Ser Asho, and Kethe. We need to discuss this, now."

He stiffened.

"I won't tell them what you told me." She held his gaze. "I'll simply tell them that you came to me immediately after Kitan approached you. I've kept this knowledge quiet to safeguard your honor. But now that I have a plan, it is time to speak openly of this matter." Ser Tiron hesitated, and Iskra took a step forward. "Go. Now."

Ser Tiron clenched his jaw, looked down, and then nodded once. He turned and shoved open the door. It was dark outside, and he disappeared into the street.

Iskra hugged herself tightly, trying to keep her jangled nerves and fear and hope contained within her frame. She moved to the window and stared outside into the narrow street. It was a slight chance, a narrow opening, but it was all that they had, and she and her war council would need all their cunning to craft a doom from it for Ser Kitan Laur and his men.

CHAPTER THRITY-FIVE

τϽΑROK

Tharok gasped. The world contracted to a point, and suddenly there was nothing more than this dirty compound, the filthy lowland kragh, the Sky Mother above, and his mount between his legs. He felt hunger, anger, and an ornery stubbornness. The clamor in his mind had ceased. The thoughts of campaigns across the mountains into Tragon lands were gone. He had known why he had given the World Breaker to Porloc, but no longer. It had been something about setting him up. But why? How could giving Porloc the greatest weapon ever wielded by kragh be a way to set him up?

Tharok turned the circlet around in his hands. The answers lay within it. All he had to do was slip it on and it would all come roaring back. Why he had led the Red River tribe down the Chasm Walk instead of through the wilderness so as to surprise the Orlokor? Why he had pressed to be recognized as Porloc's blood son? All of it lay within the dull metal, the answers to every riddle. He thought of the highland kragh in the slave market, and stowed the circlet in his pack.

Tharok then swung one thigh over the saddle and slid to the ground. He landed heavily on purpose so as to feel the shock of impact through his bones and enjoy the thud. A lowland kragh approached, dressed in metal armor, and bobbed his head. The thing was half Tharok's size, his skin as green as grass. No tusks. No dignity. No strength or presence. An Orlokor kragh.

"Tharok-krya," said the guard, "I'm to show you to your quarters."

"And if I don't want to go?"

The kragh stopped and blinked. "What?"

"What if I don't want to go to my quarters?" asked Tharok. "Are you going to force me?"

The kragh blinked again, and began to back up. "No, of course not."

"Are you sure?" Tharok took a step forward. "No? Then get out of my way." He almost wished the lowland kragh had pressed him, shown some backbone, but of course he hadn't. Tharok reached behind his saddle and drew his great half-moon axe and slipped it over his shoulder. "I'm going to look around. If Porloc wants me, tell him I'm in town." He walked right at the guard, who quickly scrambled aside.

Tharok strode out through the main gate and into the city of Gold. What a name. It said everything one needed to know about its warlord. He stared around with fresh eyes, bereft of all the information that had flooded through him before. A myriad of scents, a constant hum of noise punctuated by the occasional distant roar or clangor of metal, tents and huts on every side blocking his line of sight. Faded crimson, mud-splattered yellow, bright green skin, rutted streets, the haze of countless campfires filling the air. This was strange, this was novel, and the equanimity with which he had viewed it before while under the spell of the circlet was gone. Nothing here was natural; all of it had been made by hand. Great paths led between the buildings and huts, and everywhere was the stink and clamor of kragh filth. Standing in the entrance to the compound, Tharok rolled his head around his neck, causing the great vertebrae to snap and pop, and then set off.

First he went to a tavern. The highland kragh were given to drinking fermented goat's milk during certain key revels, but he had heard from the older kragh that the lowlanders made liquids with more fire. He took a coin from his pouch and set it on the warped wooden bar that was set before the hut's entrance.

"What will it be?" The kragh behind the bar was small, bald, and suddenly very nervous.

"Give me whiskey," said Tharok, leaning forward. "And no small cup like you lowland filth drink from. Give me a cup fit for a highland kragh."

The bartender paused. There were other Orlokor drinking at the bar. They all turned to stare at him. Tharok turned to stare them each in the eye. "Anybody have a problem with my words? Speak up, now. Don't be scared."

The kragh looked at each other and then away, shaking their heads.

The tender came back with a wooden mug filled with clear liquid in his hand. "Here you go. Whiskey fit for a highlander."

Tharok took up the mug and wrinkled his flat nose. It stank so bad that it made his eyes water. Then, without further thought, he tossed the whole mug back, pouring rank tar fire into his gullet, searing the flesh, sending a shuddering, coughing roar through his whole body. He couldn't breathe, and with a gasp threw the mug to the ground.

The bartender began to laugh. Tharok grabbed him by the throat, smashed his head down onto the bar and held it there. He leaned down and stared the kragh in the eye.

"What," he growled out, voice like soft rolling thunder, "is so funny?"

"Nothing," gasped the bartender. "Nothing."

"Were you laughing at me?"

"No, no, I wasn't."

"Oh. Good."

The fire was spreading through his belly like dragon's fire. He released the tender, who immediately began to stand back up. As soon as he was standing straight, Tharok cupped the back of his head and smashed him down so hard, he drove the kragh's head right through the wood, splintering the bar in half so that both sections of wood collapsed to the ground, sending cups and bottles crashing to the dirt.

Tharok stepped back. The bartender lay still in the ruins of his bar. "Good," he said again. "Because I'm not laughing." Then he gave lie to his words by throwing back his head and letting a belly laugh ring out. Turning, he saw that kragh had stopped and were staring. There were no highlanders amongst them, so he shrugged and began to walk down the street, leaving them behind.

The street led him down past endless houses and huts until it opened out into a marketplace. There was the human weapons vendor. Tharok approached by shoving smaller kragh aside; they quickly realized what was happening and stepped out of the way. Tharok moved right up to the front and stared the human in the face.

The male was slender like a sapling tree, his hair fine like flax, his features delicate like melting ice that would crunch easily under the heel of his boot. Pale skin, eyes blue like the Sky Mother herself. There was no strength in him, and he looked old and wrinkled. These were humans? thought Tharok. These were the leaders of the plains, the makers of empires and wonders?

"How can I help you, mighty warlord?" The human spoke passable kragh, though his throat had difficulty with the harsher sounds.

Tharok lifted his gaze and stared past him at the weapons on display. There were fine metal blades as long as his arm. Axes, daggers, spears, all gleaming like weapons from a dream, like fish caught from the freshest stream.

"What's to stop me from taking what I want?" Tharok placed both hands on the board and leaned forward, putting his weight on the wood so that it creaked.

The human stepped back and lifted an eyebrow. "Other than the laws of the marketplace?"

"I don't know of any laws."

"They're simple. Porloc has given us right of trade. You break them, you offend Porloc."

"Porloc isn't here."

"No, but Grax is."

"Grax. Who's that? A highland kragh?"

The human took a whistle from around his neck and gave it a sharp blow. Tharok could barely hear the sound, but that was of no matter. From around the back of the hut emerged a hulking figure who would have been easily twice Tharok's height if it had been standing straight. Even hunched over as it was, it loomed massively. It was no highland kragh. It was wearing a carapace of blue stone embedded into the flesh all along the back of its arms, shoulder and back. Its skin was a pale blue, and its face was a nightmare. A massive nose nearly hung over its lips, its tiny eyes were piss yellow, and its bat ears stuck out nearly a foot on each side of its great head. It was dragging a hammer behind it so large that Tharok doubted he could lift it.

"This is Grax," said the human with a quiet smile. "He helps keep things in line."

"By the Sky Mother," breathed Tharok. "That's a stone troll."

"Indeed," said the human. "*My* stone troll. Now, are you going to give me trouble? If not, buy something or get lost."

Tharok eyed Grax. It stared back at him without animosity or much interest. It was surreal to see it here, amongst these tents in a marketplace. Stone trolls were beyond rare, almost legendary, and terrifyingly dangerous. Even up on the peaks where he lived he'd not heard of anybody seeing one in decades. Some whispered that the stone trolls were gone altogether, faded into the dark like other monsters of yore. Stories spoke of their delight in shaman stone, but how they hungered even more powerfully for flesh and would waylay travelers by throwing great boulders at them as they tried to make their way over narrow passes.

Tharok almost decided to loosen his axe, almost decided to test how fast this Grax could move, the fire in his belly urging him on. But he held back. "No," he said, and backed away slowly. Grax's eyes followed him, and it pulled the hammer off the ground and hefted it with both long, ropey arms. Tharok nodded, once, twice, and then moved away altogether.

By the peaks, a stone troll. Under the control of a human. A marvel.

Tharok wandered, looking for the other market, unsure how to get there and not wanting to ask. For an hour he simply moved from stall to stall, pausing to marvel at a deep well, to consider fighting a handful of belligerent lowlander kragh, until he finally fetched up before the slave gallery.

Ah, yes, this was what he had been looking for. The hour was growing late, and the number of slaves on display was greatly diminished. There were three Tragon kragh, their foreheads branded, their faces broken and bruised. Who knew where they would end up. The human female was also there, swaying where she stood, so weak she could barely keep her chin up. At the back, a silent shadow, stood the highland kragh. Nobody had bought him. He was of prodigious size, larger even than Tharok, and his skin was nearly coal black. His heavy shoulders and deep barrel chest hinted at his strength, but he stared fixedly at the ground and made no move to assert himself.

Tharok raised his hand and beckoned the slave owner over. The Orlokor kragh came rushing over, eager to please.

"Why is this highland kragh enslaved?"

"I don't know why. He was delivered to me a week ago by his tribe. He was of the Urlor, and as you can see, is in great health. He could do the work of five Orlokor."

"Don't tell me things I already know. Why has he not been purchased?"

"He's not... he's been problematic. A couple of offers were made, but he gave them trouble, so they were withdrawn. I'm going to sell him for a pittance to the humans if nobody else makes an offer."

"How much." Tharok phrased it not as a question but a flat statement.

"Him?" The slaver's eyes gleamed. "For you? A bargain. No more than two gold."

Tharok didn't question or haggle. Instead, he took his pouch and simply handed it to the Orlokor. "Here. Put the balance toward freeing any other highland kragh that come through your hands. Now release him."

The Orlokor stammered, opened the pouch, and quickly nodded. "Yes, yes, but I can't just release him. He'd run away. Here, I'll give you the key—"

Tharok grabbed the slaver by the throat and lifted him from the ground. "I said, release him."

The smaller kragh gurgled in Tharok's grip and waved frantically at his assistants, who rushed forward to remove the shackles from the great kragh, who had watched all this with a neutral gaze. The metal shackles fell heavily to the dirt and the kragh stepped forward, rubbing his wrists.

Tharok released the slaver and then, on a whim, pointed at the human woman. "Her as well. She comes with me."

The human was so weak she could barely understand what was

happening to her. "Am I to go free?" she asked as she was unbound, trying to focus on the kragh. "Xavier? Has he come for me?"

The highland slave sniffed deeply and stepped up to Tharok. "You bought me."

"No," said Tharok. He wasn't used to having to look up at anybody. "I freed you. Your fate is your own now. Go your own way."

The highland kragh frowned. "Your name, your tribe?" His voice was so deep it was akin to boulders shifting deep within the earth.

"Tharok, warlord of the Red River tribe. You?"

"My name and tribe are behind me now."

"Then give yourself a new name and find yourself a new tribe. And don't shame yourself by being enslaved again." Tharok turned to consider the human woman. She was looking around in confusion, clearly overwhelmed and gripped by terror. Tharok grunted, reached out, and took her by the arm. "Come," he said. He was already regretting his decision.

A sudden blow crashed into the back of his head with such power that it pitched him forward. The human woman screamed as his world exploded into bright white light and he crashed to the ground, face digging deep into the dirt.

A deep growl rumbled in his chest. He slowly pushed himself up to his knees, then his feet, and only then turned to stare at his assailant. The highlander slave was rubbing his knuckles pensively, watching him with hooded eyes. Tharok's growl deepened, and he drew his axe. "It is time for blood."

The highlander slave shrugged, his massive shoulders rolling. "You weren't watching your back."

"So? Is that an insult to your honor?"

"No. But it was easy to take you down. Where is your clan? You walk alone, making it easy for me, and so easy for anyone else too."

Tharok paused, the dull beat of his bloodlust demanding that he move, that he attack. He forced himself to hold back. Perhaps the circlet really was rubbing off on him. "Come to your point."

"I've nowhere to go. No name. No clan. No tribe. No honor." The massive kragh eyed him carefully. "I think you have no clan. Like me. So I'll watch your back."

Tharok continued to growl just beneath his breath, but the other kragh's words resonated. It was true; no highland kragh would walk such a place without his clan around him to watch his back. Despite his resolutions a week ago, he'd not built a clan of his own. There was Toad, there was Barok, but for the most part he'd stayed aloof, caught up in his thoughts. The urge to bury his axe deep in the other kragh's chest dissipated, and he shook his head to clear the last of his rage and lowered his weapon.

"Come up with a name, then." The sheer size and darkness of this kragh spoke of his having been a warlord in his own time, but he showed no desire to challenge Tharok. In time his skin would lighten and his mass would shrink, bringing him in line with his new station. Tharok would watch him carefully until that happened, however.

"Why did you buy the human?" The freed kragh stared at the gold-haired woman, who was hugging herself and staring at them both with fear.

"I don't know." He examined her. She was emaciated, small, weak, and fragile. It was a miracle that humans managed to live for so long. A mixture of curiosity, pity, and disdain tugged at him. "Perhaps I want to learn more about humans from one of them instead of from the tales kragh tell each other. Bring her and follow me."

Still blinking away tears from the blow, his head still ringing, he turned and slipped the axe over his shoulder. It was time to get back to Porloc's.

CHAPTER THIRTY-SIX

ᴛıʀᴏɴ

Ser Tiron guided his pony using his knees, letting it amble forward at its own pace. The animal had been loaned to him by Gunnvaldr's son, who'd told him it was called Biter. A good name. It spoke of spirit. It had yet to have a go at him, however; perhaps some dull instinct told the pony that biting this particular knight would prove a dangerous move. The beast was a far cry from his old destrier, Night Fall, but still Tiron found himself growing fond of it. There was something about its implacable manner, the way it seemed to have no difficulty making out the trail despite the thick and tangled mane that fell across its eyes. Rugged—that was the word. Biter, Tiron had decided, was the kind of pony that would lower its head and march all the way to the Black Gate if it had to.

Luckily, that wasn't in the cards. The road from Hrething down to the lower plain where the Talon beetled out over Lake Crescent was little more than a cart trail, two ruts carved deep into the rock with a hummock of long grass between them. The slope had at first been precipitous, and Tiron had leaned as far back as he'd been able, grasping the cantle with both hands behind his back to stop from sliding right over the pommel, but finally he'd given up and just walked alongside Biter. He could have sworn he'd seen a victorious gleam in its eye somewhere beneath its mane. Still, a few miles down, the path had begun to level out, the mountain slopes pulling back and turning into merely steep, verdant hills. Easier riding, and they'd made better time.

Not that Tiron was in a rush. There was something about this preceding time before his encounter with Kitan and his men that appealed to him. There was nobody to speak to but Biter, nobody to judge his thoughts and doubts. Since his confession to Iskra he'd felt all hollowed out, like the rind of a fruit from which all the flesh has been scraped. He'd spoken barely a dozen words this past week, and instead focused on his swordplay, training each morning for several hours and then spending the afternoons and sometimes the evenings hiking around the shores of Lake Mythgræfen, working up a sweat, pushing himself till his thighs and calves and lungs all burned.

In Kyferin's dungeon, the isolation had been a way to cultivate his hatred; his solitude had been active, made bearable by hopes of revenge. Now he saw how true solitude could be its own goal. If he spent enough time away from people, he could stop thinking so many thoughts. The busyness in his head would subside. He'd felt it during his long hikes, long stretches of time when he stopped reflecting or remembering, and instead was simply aware of the trail, of the obstacles before his feet. Given enough time, he supposed, maybe his very sense of self could merge with the wilderness, till he was little more than another dangerous predator, living from sunrise to sunset, resting, eating, and spending hours gazing up at the sky or following the passage of the wind across the forest canopy on the lower slopes.

Biter stopped walking. Tiron blinked and looked down at him. "Move." He got no response. He flicked the reins, then dug his heels into Biter's incredibly rotund sides. The animal was wider than a feasting hall ale barrel. Still, the beast failed to respond. "Hey. Get a move on."

Then he heard it: the subtle clink and tramp of soldiers on the move. Coldness crept through him like mist over a dawn lake. He slid a leg over Biter's saddle and slid to the ground. He was wearing his hauberk over leather armor, but had left his plate behind. It fit his story better. He drew his sword and stepped out before the pony.

"If this gets ugly," he said over his shoulder, "run. Don't wait for me. Save yourself."

Biter shook his head from side to side, causing his mane to flop around, then lowered his muzzle to crop the grass.

The sound grew louder. Ser Wyland had been right: Kitan was coming up straight and center, making no attempt to hide his approach. Of course, he thought his attack a surprise; why would he waste his time skulking through the woods this far out from the Hold?

The first men came around the curve of the path and halted at the sight of him. They were on foot and clad in hauberks similar to his own, their gleam bright in the morning sun. Mail coifs covered their heads, and each was wearing a tabard bearing his own heraldic emblems. Knights, then, not common militia. They were marching four abreast. As one, the lead men drew their blades and unslung their shields. Tiron saw the Golden Vipers standing at the front, twin faces mirroring their hope for violence.

Voices called up from behind, and one of the lead knights raised his hand without turning, demanding silence. They took their time examining the woods to both sides, which was wise; a common ploy would be to hide archers in the shadows and stop the column with a lone man up front, turning them into vulnerable prey.

"Good morning," called the lead knight as he stepped forward and broke rank. He was tall, broad-shouldered, and looked to be in his mid-thirties, which meant he had enough experience to avoid rash or novice mistakes. His face was broad and marked by a pale vertical scar that twisted one eye almost closed and his mouth into a permanent sneer. Still, Tiron liked the look of the man. He had the air of a competent professional.

"Decent enough," Tiron called back. "You lot marching from the Talon?"

"We are. I am Ser Dirske, of Laurel Mount. And you, ser knight?"

"Tell Ser Laur that Ser Tiron would like a word. Tell him I bring good, if bloody, news."

Ser Dirske raised the tip of his blade. "How did you know Ser Laur marches with us?"

"An educated guess. Don't make me spell it out and finish making you look like a fool. Now tell him."

Ser Dirske stood still, lips pursed, studying him. Clearly, he was not a man used to being insulted. Too bad; insults came too easily to Tiron's lips. To cement his confidence, Tiron slid his blade back into its scabbard.

Ser Dirske spoke over his shoulder to one of the men, and Tiron saw the message being passed back. A sizeable force, then. Ser Wyland had guessed thirty knights with perhaps twice that number in men-at-arms. Ser Tiron had thought it the opposite: twice the knights and half the soldiers. No matter. He'd find out soon enough.

Five minutes passed, and then a familiar figure pressed his way forward. Ser Laur had chosen to march in his plate armor, it seemed; the man was either preternaturally resilient or a complete fool—or both. His enameled blue plate gleamed like the ocean beyond Zoe's harbor, and the other knights opened a path for him with respect. His sumptuous blue cloak nearly brushed the dirt, and his hand was resting on the pommel of his sword.

"Ser Tiron!" His voice was cheerful and pitched to carry. "It's a pleasure to see you. And all alone? Don't tell me you were en route to the Talon?"

Tiron took hold of Biter's bridle and began walking forward. "Meet me halfway, Kitan. I've words for you alone."

Kitan turned to his men and spoke a command; Tiron saw protest form on Dirske's lips, but then the man bit them back. Reaching up, Kitan removed his helm, then tucked it under his arm and marched up to meet Tiron perhaps two dozen yards ahead of his men.

"Nice pony," said Kitan. "How good is he at a charge?"

"Biter?" Tiron turned to consider him. "Vicious. Once I can

convince him to get moving. Now—" He turned, opened a saddlebag, and pulled free a bloodstained roll of blue cloth. "A gift for your father."

Kitan narrowed his eyes as he took the cloth. "A gift, you say? He does so like gifts." He carefully unrolled it, and stopped at the sight of the auburn braid. It was as thick as a man's wrist and coiled like a snake, easily two feet in length. One end had been rudely hacked, and most of it was dark and crusted with blood. Kitan took it up in one hand, then brought it to his nose and inhaled. His eyes remained locked on Tiron. "Ah. I recognize that scent." He pressed the braid to his lips, then dropped it back onto the cloth. "Now, this will merit a true reward. But why only hair? Where is the pretty head that goes with it?"

"Crushed and lying in Mythgræfen Hold." Tiron felt something coalesce within him, a dangerous and cold certainty that he would see this man dead. "I'm not in the habit of carrying body parts with me."

"A pity. Did you ruin the face?"

Birds called overhead and flitted through the branches of a mountain ash, causing their shadows to dart across the trail. The light was syrupy gold, the colors of the forest around them rich and vibrant or drowned in shadow. Surreal, to be surrounded by such natural beauty while faced with such a man. Tiron shook his head slowly. "No. I struck her from behind while she was praying. Why?"

"While she was praying? Oh, that's rich." Something entered Kitan's eyes then. "And good. I'd like to see her face, cold and still. Eyes wide with that final flash of pain and shock. And Father demanded I bring back her head. Nothing less, not even this golden braid, will suffice." Carefully he wrapped the hair in the blue cloth once more, but made no sign of giving it back. He glanced down at it, then back up at Tiron with a smile. "A keepsake. Now, what of the others? I'm sure they objected to your revenge."

"They did. Or would have, if I'd let them." Turning again, Tiron reached for the hilt of a blade that was strapped alongside the saddle, and drew it forth with a rapid flourish. Kitan immediately stepped back and drew a foot of his sword before stopping. Tiron smiled. "What's wrong, Kitan? Afraid of me?"

Kitan bared his teeth in what might have passed for a smile. "No, just amused at your sense of humor." He straightened and took the sword. "I know this crest. It's Ser Wyland's." He paused, eyebrows raised. "Well, then. You are a most thorough man. Ser Wyland is dead?"

Tiron nodded. His disgust made it easy to look hard and cruel. "He is. I left thereafter."

Kitan sighed. "A pity, really. Ser Wyland might have offered me some amusement. I'd hoped for a good fight to justify all this effort. Still, you've done well. What of the others? The squire? Kethe?"

"They live. I didn't set out to massacre the whole group. They must still be back at the Hold with the remaining three guards and Brocuff."

"Only three? I thought ten guards went through."

"They did. Seven of them had a change of heart upon seeing their new home. They disappeared two days in."

Kitan nodded. "Pathetic. And you? You were marching to the Talon?"

Tiron's smile was wry. "You promised me a reward and a pardon. I was coming to collect."

"Let's delay that reward a few days more. Lead us to Mythgræfen. We need to kill the survivors and collect some heads. Then I'll send you back with a token force to feast and celebrate to your heart's content. Agreed?"

Tiron frowned. "A token force? You're not returning to the Talon?"

"No, unfortunately." Kitan sighed dramatically. "My father must be most displeased with me. He's tasked me with rebuilding the Hold and garrisoning it properly as once our family used to do. Foolish of him. He's spending a small fortune on gathering supplies and hiring craftsmen to send through the Raven's Gate two weeks hence. It seems he takes our old family legends quite seriously."

Tiron laughed harshly. "He clearly doesn't take the legends seriously enough. Hasn't he heard how every force that's tried the same has disappeared?"

"Oh, yes." Kitan's eyes were cold. "But he's no fool. He's petitioned his Grace for assistance. With the kragh refusing to take the field, the Grace is only too thankful for the several hundred men-at-arms we've sent to help with the Agerastian siege, along with the knights we've promised once this expedition has been seen to. In exchange, he's lent us one of his Virtues."

Tiron's mocking grin froze on his face. "His what?"

Kitan shrugged, as if it were of no matter. "Makaria, the Virtue of Happiness. He rides with us. You'll meet him soon enough." He paused. "What's the matter, Ser Tiron? You look almost ill."

"Nothing." Tiron forced himself to relax, though his mind was racing. A Virtue? Riding with Kitan? "It seems a waste, though, sending a Virtue here when the Agerastians are at our throats."

Again, Kitan shrugged. "My father has promised his Grace access to something high up in these mountains that has secured his unwavering support. Regardless, it is done. Now, shall we proceed? The quicker we reach our destination, the sooner you can return to civilization."

Tiron nodded. By the Black Gate, he thought. A Virtue.

They marched all day back up the trail and camped in the lee of a granite ridge. Tiron marched at the front of the column, leading Biter by hand, and didn't catch a glimpse of the Virtue until dusk had fallen. He kept to himself and was ignored by the others, which suited him fine.

It felt strange to be on the march again in the company of knights—the comments, the conversation around the campfires, the jokes and abuse, the rasp of whetstones on blades and the hurrying of squires as they cleaned and cooked and served. If he closed his eyes, he could almost imagine he was amongst the Black Wolves once more, marching toward some distant encounter. But these men were not striding into battle; rather, they were headed toward a slaughter. Which made the familiarity strangely nauseating; it was hard to hate these men when they made the same kinds of jokes or offered familiar complaints.

Tiron lay on his bedroll, far from the fire and crowd, and watched Makaria. The Virtue sat apart from the knights, his back to a knotted iron ash, wearing pure white and slowly plucking chords on a lute that fit into the palm of his hand. He wasn't playing a song, but seemed rather to play notes almost at random as they suited him. He exuded a serenity that fascinated Tiron; the dark-skinned man seemed his perfect opposite, at peace with the night and the world and himself.

Tiron thought of rising and approaching him, engaging him in conversation. The Virtues were the ultimate warriors; every knight on some level wished to emulate their prowess in combat. They were the stuff of legend, the military chosen of the Ascendant, and their roles in history and the founding of Ascension were the stuff of children's tales and myth. And yet, the one time Makaria had gazed upon Tiron it had been with disgust, and no wonder, if Kitan had told him that Tiron had murdered Iskra while she was in prayer.

No, it was best not to tempt fate. Instead, Tiron turned and gazed up at the stars. They were brilliant, this high up in the mountains. The sound of the knights' laughter washed over him. Had he been like these men? They followed Kitan without question, just as he had followed Lord Kyferin right up until he'd killed Sarah.

Tiron scowled and rolled onto his side, staring into the black vastness of the woods beyond the ridge. Had he ever felt qualms about razing another lord's lands as part of a campaign to defeat him? No. He'd burned farms, had cut down farmers who had run suicidally at him with rusted blades or thin spears. He'd never raped, never tortured, but there had been those amongst their company who had. Tiron had simply turned away from that, telling himself that such atrocities were the reality of war. Those men would be punished when they died, being reborn in Zoe or farther down the chain. Agerastos. Bythos, even, for the worst.

Tiron closed his eyes, but still his memories plagued him. Old screams, torn from throats over a decade ago, the deaths forgotten by the world now except for him. He'd been following orders. That was what a knight did. Your lord said march, and by the Black Gate, you marched. You lord said charge, and you slew. Burn, and you burned. These knights had been ordered to massacre, and they were cheerfully marching to do just that.

Would he have done any different if Lord Kyferin had given him this order four years ago?

In his heart, he knew he'd be sitting amongst these men, complaining about rust and the quality of the food, laughing at the tales of brothels and swapped sisters. The familiarity and faint nostalgia suddenly sickened him. He thought of Iskra, alone and defiant in the Hold, beautiful and calm and disdainful. He was too steeped in blood and ruin to ever be worth such as her. And to think she had belonged to Enderl Kyferin, all these years. The Ascendant's ways were beyond cruel.

Closing his eyes, he tried to sleep, but even after the other knights had settled down in their tents and the fires had been quenched, sleep was a long time coming.

CHAPTER THIRTY-SEVEN

TIRON

They passed Hrething just before noon. The trail peaked over a small rise and afforded them a view of the huddled houses. Smoke was trailing from numerous chimneys, though Tiron knew those homes to be empty. Most of Hrething had been moved to the high farms, leaving behind only a skeleton force to tend the fires and give the impression of a populated town.

Gunnvaldr was sitting on a tree stump at the edge of town, smoking his pipe, and rose to his feet at the sight of the first knights appearing over the rise. He shook his fist at the sight of Tiron. "Murderer! You'll be rewarded for what you did when you're thrown head-first though the Black Gate!"

The knights slowed, amused smiles on their faces, and many turned to watch Tiron's reaction. He gave none. Shaking his head, he looked to where the trail continued up along the Erenthil. Kitan, however, stepped out of the column to confront Gunnvaldr. *Damn fool,* thought Tiron. *The plan was for him to retreat after calling out his insults.*

"Ho, there, old father. Why do you accuse the good and honorable Ser Tiron of such a foul deed?"

Gunnvaldr drew himself up, quivering with outrage. It was a good performance. "Why? You should string him up from the closest tree. Traitor! Oath breaker! He slew Lady Kyferin, turned on her, and then killed all the other knights in her guard!"

Kitan turned to regard Tiron with false amazement. "All that? Well, I suppose we'll have to give him his just rewards. But regardless of what he did, he *is* a knight. It's a punishable offense for a commoner such as yourself to speak to him so. Ser Cunot, Ser Cunad, string this old man up by his neck. Let him serve as a warning to all who would impugn Ser Tiron's honor."

Tiron tightened his grip on his reins. To object would seem bizarre.

Gunnvaldr had taken a step back, eyes wide as he realized his sudden peril. The Golden Vipers stepped away from the column and began to march in his direction.

"Wait!" Tiron's voice was harsh and cruel. Everyone turned to stare at him.

"Surely you don't object, good Ser Tiron?" Kitan's voice was dangerously light.

"Not at all. But it was my honor who insulted. I should be the one to avenge it."

Kitan pursed his lips, then nodded. Cunot and Cunad stopped, and Tiron patted Biter's neck and drew his blade. "Come here, old man. I'll show you what happens to peasants with loose tongues."

Gunnvaldr stared at him, fear riveting him in place. Tiron tried to walk as slowly as he could without drawing notice. Nobody could see his face now but Gunnvaldr. *Run!* he mouthed. *Go!* Gunnvaldr blinked rapidly and backed away a step, then a second, but he'd lost his chance. There was no way he could outdistance Tiron now. He was going to have to slay the old fool. He thought of the knights' laughter around the fires the night before, and realized he couldn't. He'd have to let Gunnvaldr go, and face the consequences.

Forgive me, Iskra.

"Enough." The voice was rich and redolent with power. Tiron froze, then looked over his shoulder to see the white-armored Virtue stepping forward.

"Is there a problem, Ser Makaria?" Kitan's voice barely hid his annoyance.

"There is. This man will not be hanged for speaking the truth." Ser Makaria raised his visor and gazed coldly upon Tiron. "This knight did murder Lady Iskra and Ser Wyland both. If he cannot live with that, he should not have done the deeds."

Ser Tiron gulped. Makaria's gaze was as pitiless as the glare of a hawk. Even though he hadn't committed those crimes, he still felt himself judged and found terribly wanting. Still, relief flooded through him. He sheathed his blade and nodded. "Fine. I've no problem with what I've done. After all, we both serve the same master now: Lord Laur and his goals."

"No," said Makaria, voice inflexible. He fairly radiated power. "I serve the Ascendant and his Grace. Our interests align with Lord Laur's, but he is not my master."

Tiron glanced over at Kitan, whose smile had grown sickly. "As you say, Ser Virtue." He moved back to where Biter was standing, indifferently chewing on the grass.

"Very well," said Kitan. "We've greater tasks to attend to. Let's be on our way. March!"

He rejoined the line, and Tiron began to stride forward once more, but even as he walked he could feel Makaria's harsh gaze upon his back.

He felt a grim sense of satisfaction. Let the Virtue judge him when Iskra and Jander stepped into sight, hale and ready for battle.

The climb up alongside the Erenthil took up the remainder of the day, so it was nearing dusk when they finally reached the banks of Lake Mythgræfen. The Hold looked spectral and ghostly on its remote central island, steeped in shadows and with a ring of ravens circling about its keep. A cold wind was scything off the waters, and more than one knight shuddered and pulled his cloak closer around his frame.

Kitan stepped up alongside Tiron and frowned, jutting out his lower jaw. "What a miserable place. Seems a complete waste of stone and lives."

"That it is," said Tiron. "It's claimed more Kyferin blood than any other enemy can boast. A curse, I'd call it. A curse nobody understands."

"Madness," said Kitan. "I'd pull every stone into the lake and shatter the Raven's Gate so as to remove all temptation for future folly." He hawked and spat. "Let's get this over with. Quick march!"

They hurried around the lake, boots crunching on wet sand and gravel. The sun sank at last behind the far western peaks, and the colors grew subdued and sullen, the world bathed in slate blues, velvety grays, dark forest greens and black, inky shadows. Tiron's gut began to tighten as they rounded the final curve to the causeway. The white stones seemed almost luminous in the falling dusk, the water lapping about the lower rocks. All was silent. No lights were burning in the distant Hold. No sounds filtered across the waters.

"Abandoned," said Ser Dirske. "Nobody there but corpses, I reckon. You think the survivors took to the hills?"

"If they did, they were fools," said Tiron. "Not one of them knows how to survive a night in this wilderness. No, I'll wager they're hunkered down like mice, terrified and taking scant comfort from a small fire in the main hall. Grief and fear will have undone them."

Dirske nodded and smoothed down his mustache in an attempt to hide his own fear.

Kitan leaped up onto a small boulder by the lake's edge. "All right, this is how the next ten minutes is going to proceed. We're going to cross that causeway at a run. No war cries. Not a sound. When we reach the island, fifteen men will slide to the left, fifteen to the right. Thirty will proceed through the main gate into the courtyard. The remaining twenty will stay on the causeway itself to prevent any escapes. Kill all that you find, except for Kethe Kyferin. You'll recognize her by her red hair and her mulish eyes. You can rough her up, but bring her to me alive. Beware: she's handier with a blade than you'd think. Once we secure the island, we'll grab our keepsakes and turn right back round. We'll camp a half mile back down the trail. That should be far enough from this cursed place for it to not disturb our sleep." He paused. "This isn't a battle. This is mere housecleaning. Dirty, fast work that will see you well rewarded. Those who show the proper enthusiasm will be noted. Are we ready?"

Makaria was staring at the Hold, and for the first time Tiron saw him frown. "There is power in that castle. I can feel the world pouring into it. Even if we only face a dozen people, be careful. All is not as it seems here." He looked up at Kitan. "Follow your plan. I'm not here to kill scullions and girls. If there is any cause for me to intervene, I'll do so, but do not count on my help in accomplishing your task."

The knights had been about to chorus their agreement, but now they looked uncertainly to the castle, then back to Kitan, who was fighting to control his annoyance. "As you wish, Ser Virtue. Just remember that you were sent with us to help claim the Hold for Lord Laur and the Ascendant."

"I've not forgotten," said Makaria coldly.

"Well, then," said Kitan, raising his voice again. "Who's ready for a quick fight, then riches and a hot bed? Let's get this done, men. Let's get this done."

The men nodded, and a forest of blades was drawn, shields unslung, and helms pulled down onto mail coifs. Packs were dropped, squires busied themselves tightening straps and adjusting armor, and then Kitan stepped forward. His blue cloak billowed out around him, his azure armor gleaming softly in the dusk. He looked like the consummate knight, thought Tiron. The thought made him want to spit.

Kitan raised his sword high. Everyone held their breath. Then, turning, he dropped it so as to point it at the Hold, and broke into a run. Tiron felt the need to yell swelling amongst the ranks, the need to give voice to their anger and fear and hunger. But they bit it down and instead ran forward in silence, the rocks and gravel of the causeway crunching beneath their heavy steps. Tiron ran at the front, Kitan by his side. It was a good distance, but they covered it in what seemed to be the blink of an eye. Breath rasping in his throat, Tiron led the knights onto the island. As they had been commanded, men split left and right to surround the walls, disappearing into the undergrowth. Tiron ran past the twisted oak tree and into the courtyard.

It was empty but for the ethereal ash trees. Moving slowly, allowing Kitan's men to bunch up around him, he pointed to the storeroom entrance with his blade, beside which a single lantern was burning. Kitan nodded and allowed him to lead the way.

Tiron moved to the door and lifted the lantern from its hook. Fear arose in his chest. The darkness of the doorway seemed as forbidding and dangerous as the Black Gate itself. He knew he couldn't hesitate, couldn't give Kitan reason to doubt, to question. Taking a deep breath, he strode through the doorway and lifted the lantern high.

A massive pile of apples gleamed wetly in the center of the room. There had to be hundreds of them, the few remaining crimson fruit that Lady Kyferin had brought and the twisted little crabapples from the Hrethings' store. The whole lot of them glistened with honey. Two dozen small figures had been feasting on them, but they had frozen and were staring at Tiron, eyes narrowed against the light. Pale, albino little monsters, with hunched shoulders like miniature blacksmiths, lank white hair like that of drowned folk, noses protuberant like potatoes and mouths little more than gashes filled with sharp teeth. Their golden eyes glittered as if filled with their own inner flame.

"The Ascendant protect us!" Kitan had stepped up next to him, others crowding in behind. Tiron drew his arm back and hurled the lantern into the far corner, where it smashed and fell into a barrel filled with oil.

The barrel exploded. The darkness was hungrily consumed by a billowing ball of fire that roared out with enough force to send the naugrim rolling. The wave of heat baked the sweat on Tiron's face and drove him back and down onto one knee, an arm raised to protect his face.

Yells and roars surrounded him. Gathering his wits, Tiron rose to his feet and plowed forward through the madness of chittering, furious naugrim. He nearly rolled his ankle as he stepped onto an apple, regaining his balance just as a naugrim suddenly blinked into existence in midair before him and crashed into his chest. Tiron crashed onto his back, the small demon tearing at his chain with hooked claws that cut through the metal as if it were packed dirt. Tiron roared and slammed his elbow into the creature's head, sat up and lifted it bodily off him and tossed it away. It blinked out of existence before hitting the ground, but he saw another half-dozen converging on him. The others were throwing themselves at Kitan and his knights. Rising, Tiron ran to the secret door, tore it open and stepped through. When he turned to pull it shut, he saw Kitan and his men yelling and flailing as ever more naugrim swarmed out onto them.

Grinning despite himself, he hurried down the spiral stairs and out into the Gate chamber where Iskra, Asho, Brocuff and the eight remaining Kyferin guards were waiting. Audsley was watching from a far chamber, looking terrified.

"Success?" Asho stepped forward, hand on the hilt of his new sword.

Tiron was glaring at Iskra. "What the Hell are you doing here?"

She raised her chin haughtily. It was still shocking to see her with a shorn head. If anything, it made her all the more striking. "You expected me to hide?"

Tiron tore off his helm. "There are men upstairs with swords looking to cut off your head!"

She took a sharp step forward. "My husband would not have hidden. Neither shall I."

"You are *not* Enderl bloody Kyferin."

"Enough!" Iskra's eyes blazed in her pale face. "These are my people! They fight for me!" She took a shuddering breath. "I will not hide. Perhaps I cannot wield a sword, but I will *not* hide. Now. The naugrim. Did our plan work?"

"Aye," said Tiron sourly. "Too well, perhaps. They've gone mad."

"Good," said Asho, face grim. "Five more minutes and we'll head up. With a little luck, we'll be the hammer to Ser Wyland's anvil."

"Yeah, sure." Tiron turned back to Iskra. "But we've got a problem."

Brocuff stepped up. He was wearing a heavy chain over a suit of leather so thick that Tiron doubted a battle ax would be able to cut through it. "What? More men than anticipated?"

Tiron nodded. "Yes, there's that. But Kitan's brought a Virtue with him."

Asho's naturally pallid face somehow paled even further. "A Virtue? Which one?"

"Does it matter?" Tiron wanted to laugh. All this work for naught. "Makaria."

Brocuff went to make the symbol of the Ascendant's triangle, then stopped. "Does that mean the Ascendant is against us?"

"No," said Iskra. Her voice sounded hollow. Tiron knew she was quick; she'd have already worked out what this meant. "Merely the Ascendant's Grace. But this cannot be. He knows our cause is just. That we are the wronged party." She shook her head. "I will speak with him. This Virtue. I will reason with him, and he shall see the justice of our cause." She began to push through the men. "Let me pass-"

"No, Iskra." Tiron set himself before her. "You are mad if you think there is still time for words."

She stopped before him, trembling, chin raised. "Let me pass, Ser Tiron."

A deep sadness swept through him. A sense that she was still lost in the rationale of a world that no longer made sense. "No, my lady."

"I am of Sigean birth! By right I should rule from Kyferin Castle, by right the Ascendant's Grace should send his Virtues to my aid!" Tears filled her eyes, and she dashed them away. "I will reason with him!"

"He has come, if not to kill you himself, then to take the Hold and support Lord Laur's claim." Tiron felt a terrible tenderness welling up within him. "I'm sorry, Iskra."

The room was hushed. Iskra held his gaze, eyes wide, and then turned away abruptly. "The chaos has infected us all," she whispered. "Madness stalks the empire. I do not understand it any more."

Tiron wanted to take her in his arms, to hold her close, and an outpouring of words rose to his lips, a desire to tell her how the empire had never made sense, how this madness had always lurked beneath the surface. But movement caught his eye, and he looked to the Bythian.

Asho had drawn his blade. The runes caught fire, and waves of impossible heat radiated from the sword. His hair began to shift and interweave as if he were underwater. "Makaria may be a Virtue, but he is also mortal." He climbed two more steps and then turned to address the small group. Tiron could sense how much his news had shaken the guards. Even the stalwart Brocuff looked uneasy. Asho stared at them, face grave, his pale silver-green eyes flat and determined. "You all know I was fighting beside Lord Enderl when he died, that the Grace himself knighted me for my valor. But what you don't know is that the Grace was mortally wounded that day. I saw him fall with my own eyes. He should have died. Instead, he took a black potion from an Aletheian advisor. He magically healed and rose to flee the battlefield."

"What?" Brocuff's face darkened with anger. "You're lying."

"No!" Asho pointed at the constable with his blade, the black, cruel length of it glimmering with hellish intensity. "I swear it by my hope for Ascension. I don't know what's going on in the halls of Aletheia, but I know this: the Grace is but a man, and he is weak. He turned away from his destiny and betrayed our deepest beliefs. Now he sends a Virtue to do Lord Laur's dirty work. Maybe once the Virtues and the Grace were holy men, but now they've become pawns in mortal politics. That man upstairs may be worth ten knights, but he's just a man. Noble as he may seem, he's become the enemy. Our enemy. He's come here to kill Lady Kyferin, and I for one don't intend to let him succeed. Do you?"

There was a minute of silence, and then the guards drew their swords, first one, then two more, then all at once. Brocuff growled beneath his breath and drew his wide, chopping blade.

Tiron watched Asho grudgingly, with newfound respect. The Bythian bore no resemblance to the sullen squire he'd once been. He was no war leader like Enderl or Jander, but here and now, in this cramped, dark room with his fiery blade and demons above and a Virtue opposing them, he managed to stir even Tiron's heart.

Tiron grinned nastily and turned to the others. "Come on. Let's go show them what happens when they arouse the ire of the Black Wolves."

The guards turned to him, wide-eyed. "Ser, we're not—"

"Tonight, you are!" Iskra's voice rang in the small room. "Each and every one of you! Tonight you are Black Wolves, the Black Wolves of Lady Kyferin! Tonight you hunt, tonight you kill, and tonight we all will show Lord Laur what happens when he places his hand in the wolf's maw!"

The guards growled their assent. Before Tiron's eyes they seemed to swell, growing in confidence and lowering their heads as they broadened their shoulders.

Asho reached his hand into a worn pouch by his belt and pulled free a folded crimson cloth. He let it unfurl, and Tiron felt a sudden pounding in his chest.

"The Everflame," he whispered.

Asho bared his teeth in a feral smile. "Come, then. Honor to Lady Kyferin! Honor to the Ascendant, to his truth, and death to those false ones who oppose us! Let us hunt! Follow the Everflame to war!"

He turned and ran up the stairs, and with a roar the others followed right behind him.

CHAPTER THIRTY-EIGHT

kethe

Kethe felt herself a fell queen of war as she watched Kitan's men march to their doom. Their armored shapes looked small on the causeway below, which pointed accusingly at the Hold like a dwindling finger. Standing high up the slope on the mainland behind them and surrounded by the Hrethings, she knew deep down in her bones that not one of those knights would return from that causeway alive.

This had been the most dangerous part of their plan; had a single knight noticed Kethe's force high up on the mountain slope, then battle would have been joined immediately and without the choke point that was so necessary to their victory. But they hadn't. Tiron's tale had lulled their senses, and they'd been taken by the mystery and horror of the Hold.

Perfect.

Turning, she nodded to Elon, who grunted and began to haul the branches off his pride and joy. All week he had labored at his forge, directing others as they worked against the clock to repair and strengthen and improve upon the ancient ballista. Now it was crouched on the mountain slope like a massive predatory bird, its arms thick and broad like the wings of an eagle, its hammered black iron body riveted and exuding a lethal power.

With the last of the branches tossed aside, Elon took up a rope as thick as his wrist as seven other men moved into place to do the same. This procedure had been rehearsed time and time again. Each wrapped the rope around his forearm and then looped it around his waist. They were the strongest men of their group, each built like a bull, broad-backed and barrel-chested. Even amongst such company, Elon stood out like a giant. Once they were all ready, he nodded to two other men who were waiting with mallets. They raised them high, then swung and knocked the wooden wedges out from the ballista's two great wheels.

The massive construct lurched forward and stopped as the eight men leaned back against the pull. Sinews corded and muscles rippled as they arrested the massive machine's descent down the slope. They'd spent several mornings clearing and beating down the earth, laying down flat rocks and building as smooth a ramp as they could to the platform below. Now they fought to lower the ballista slowly, foot by foot, the wood creaking as it descended ten feet, then twenty, then came to a stop on the cunningly disguised earthen platform that stood just fifteen feet above the causeway itself.

Kethe watched the distant Hold. A group of some twenty or thirty knights had remained to plug the entrance to the Hold, while others had swept out and around on both sides. A central force had plunged into the Hold proper, and any moment now they should hear the explosion.

Everyone held their breaths and leaned forward, waiting, watching. Staring into the gathering dusk as if they could pierce the stone walls of the Hold into the storage room itself.

But nothing happened. Had Tiron been caught? Had the barrel failed to ignite?

Sweat prickled Kethe's brow, and then, suddenly, they all heard it. The explosion was muffled, a flattened *crumph* that sent ravens cawing into the air, but still Kethe felt a thrilling surge of excitement. It had worked!

She raised her hand and pointed down the slope. Seventy Hrething bowmen rose from where they had hidden behind rocks or lain in depressions to descend to a point ten feet above the ballista. They each stabbed five arrows into the dirt and then knelt so that they would be right at hand.

Kethe heard the first cries and roars. The madness had to be total. She was the sole remaining fighter left this high up on the slope, but she was loath to abandon her vantage point. She stared into the night, where the high peaks were now deep purple and glittering ice. Night had nearly fallen. Voices were echoing across the waters in their panic and fury. She saw movement at the Hold's gate and heard an indistinct command being yelled in anger. The knights on the causeway hesitated, then turned to race back to the shoreline.

Below, she saw Elon and the second strongest man slide their oak staves into the hubs of the ballista and crank them down. Even in the dusk she could see the effort it took both men to draw the thick rope back along the main groove. The huge arms bent back, an inch at a time, and still Elon drew back the cord. It had taken Elon and his team a full day to disassemble the ballista and carry its parts out of the Hold and up to this height, another day to assemble it and run tests. Now she shuddered to think what that massive spear would do to the knights racing obliviously toward their deaths.

There was a final, straining crank, and then Elon released his oaken spar with a gasp. A massive spear was dropped into the groove. It was three yards long and two inches thick, with a leaf-bladed head six inches long. Elon sighted down the groove, watching, waiting, hand on the catch that would release the cord.

The knights were pounding toward them, forty, fifty of them. Kethe felt like crying out with impatience, but she bit down on her tongue. On came the men who had sworn to murder her and her mother and their followers. They were killers all, cold-blooded monsters. They deserved no mercy. Still, Kethe dreaded what was about to happen to them.

"Fire," whispered Elon, and pulled the catch.

The ballista convulsed, jumping in place with the violence of its release. The spear simply vanished. There was a high, keening sound, and then the knights in the front simply lifted off their feet and flew backward with a scream. Six of them fell to the ground, with many more tripping over their bodies.

Elon wasted no time. He was at the cranks, working his stave in and out as he drew the cord back. Another spear was dropped in.

The knights at the fore had frozen in shock in the middle of the causeway. Shouts came from the back of the group as more of them fled the Hold. Those in the front were at a complete loss as to what had happened. They knelt by the fallen men, then leaped to their feet in alarm.

Wait, Kethe urged them. *Waste more time. Just stand right there.*

Sweat gleamed on Elon's bare arms. He grunted and locked the ballista in place and checked the sighting. The knights were running around their fallen companions now, swords catching the moon's first light in quick flashes like a fish spied briefly in the depths of a pond. They ran on, yelling their war cries at an invisible foe, and again Elon whispered to himself.

The ballista launched its second spear.

Another half-dozen men were abruptly knocked back, but this time Elon's aim had been a little high. He caught the front three in the head, bursting helms and shattering skulls before the spear punched into the men behind them. Down they went, like puppets whose strings had been cut. More men tripped over them, but this time nobody stopped to ponder their sudden deaths. On they came.

Elon and his men got to work, cranking back the ballista. They'd have time for one more shot, thought Kethe, just as the lead knight passed an innocuous marker that stood erect beside the causeway.

"Draw," called out Kolgrímr. The seventy Hrethings drew their arrows back, the air growing taut with tension. On charged the knights, and then Kolgrímr cried out, "Fire!" and as one the archers released. A dark cloud sprang forth into the night sky, darker even than the purples and slate blues overhead, and fell amongst the knights.

Kethe had examined one of the Hrething arrows before. As thick as a finger and fletched with goose feathers, they were used to hunt the large cliff goats or turned toward grimmer purposes when monstrosities descended from the slopes. They hit with terrible force, and the leading knights crumpled under their onslaught. Kethe tried to guess the number of dead. Thirty or forty knights lay still on the bloodied causeway. Another twenty or thirty were still pounding forward, shields raised now to ward off any more arrows.

Something caught her eye. A single man was walking down the length of the causeway, his white armor glowing like the moon. He exuded a sense of purpose and calm that chilled Kethe even at this distance.

She slid down quickly to where Elon was working. "Your next bolt. Take out that man at the back."

"Just the one?" Elon hesitated, but nodded. He cranked the hub one last time and then jumped back to align the ballista. The spear was dropped into the groove.

They had precious seconds left. She had to run down and lead the attack, but she waited, frozen.

Elon angled the ballista with great care as the man in the white armor continued to walk unhurriedly toward them. Elon hesitated, exhaled, then released the catch. The ballista leaped again with a crack. Kethe's stomach clenched as that high, keening sound filled the air. The bolt sailed over the knights, almost too quick to follow, a fleeting shadow.

The knight in white armor strode forward, seemingly oblivious. Then, impossibly, alerted by some sixth sense, he brought up his shield with inhuman speed and twisted his body. The great spear smashed into his shield and shattered, fragments spinning away into the night.

Kethe gaped. Her tension curdled into disbelief and then fear. The white knight looked up at where the ballista was placed and she felt his gaze fall upon her. Her fear turned to terror, which finally sparked her fury.

Kethe drew her sword. "For Lady Kyferin!" she yelled. "For the White Gate!"

She ran nimbly down the slope and threaded a path through the archers and the band of men who stood awaiting her with Ser Wyland. She sprinted past them, sure-footed, down the last slope and across the beach to smash into the knights just as they were about to step off the causeway.

The bottleneck was key. The first four enemy knights charged off the causeway and into a wall of waiting swords. They screamed their defiance and swung their blades, but were parried even as others stabbed past their shields. The knights screamed. Two fell, one pressed forward his attack, while the fourth tried to retreat.

Ser Wyland wielded his blade with both hands, eschewing his shield, and he roared as he swung, hammering his opponents as Kethe darted forward behind the guard of one knight and slid her blade into his armpit as he raised his blow to parry Ser Wyland. The man grunted and died and another stepped into his place.

The ground around the choke point became slick with blood. A number of the enemy knights abandoned the causeway to wade knee-deep through the shallows and gain the land. The Hrethings fired a hail of arrows down upon them, and while some cried out and fell back into the water with a splash, many more reached the shore.

"We're being flanked!" Ser Wyland cast wild looks in both directions.

The sheer number of the enemies had become apparent. A score remained on the causeway, stepping over the bodies of their fallen to clash with the defenders, but the enemy knights were now moving in to envelop them on both sides. Ser Wyland grabbed the ram's horn that hung around his neck and put the tip to his lips. A moment later the dusk was rent by the clear call of the horn, and was answered on the slopes above by a ragged cry from the archers.

"Charge!" Kolgrímr's voice was faint, but the sound of seventy men racing down the slope, hatchets and stabbing blades in hand, filled the air like a small avalanche.

The pressure that Kethe's group was feeling from the sides and even behind suddenly lessened as Kitan's knights turned to face the new onslaught, and Kethe laughed and plunged forward, feinting high and then bringing her blade in a sweeping cut across her enemy's thighs. She didn't stop. She was the flickerflash of lightning in the belly of a storm cloud, light and free to dance and whirl amongst these tottering and stumbling men. Each was ponderous and slow in his armor, their swords coming at her as if they were moving through water.

Something was burning within her, a white and banishing flame that fed on her soul even as it gave her wings. She felt alive, truly alive, as the darkness seemed to lighten around her and details became almost painfully salient. Wide eyes within polished steel helms. The cold, mineral tang of the lake water mixed now with the coppery taste of blood in the air and the churned-up silt. The raw, ragged sound of men killing each other all around her. The sharp, harsh clang of blade on blade, the wet, sucking sound of flesh being opened. Screams. Curses. Pleas for mercy. The mix of sand and gravel beneath her boots. The burn in her arms, in her throat, in her lungs. Her blade was a serpent's tongue, darting here, stabbing there. Not for her the fixed combat, going toe-to-toe with a foe till one of them died; she dealt blows and moved on, slipping and leaping and ducking and spinning. Brocuff would have groaned at the number of times she showed her back, but nobody was fast enough to deal her a blow.

Kethe pressed deeper into the ranks of the enemy, leaving Ser Wyland and their guards behind. They constrained her. Here, with knights on all sides, she could truly relax and flow. The last of her fear receded, and she found herself relaxing, sensing her enemies as they moved around her. She didn't fight to keep them all in sight; instead, she simply kept moving, stepping and twisting, never remaining in one spot for long. Men turned away from the fight in a vain attempt to follow her, to strike back at her lithe form, and in doing so blunted their own charge off the causeway.

Suddenly she was through, out the rear of their pack, with the Hold rising before her in the gloom of dusk, its upper towers illuminated by the soft light of the waning moon.

The white knight was striding down the causeway toward her. His plate armor was beautiful. It seemed to glow with a soft, silver light all of its own, and his blade was a shard of starlight. His shield was shaped like a kite, its tapering point nearly reaching his shin, and on its front was emblazoned the ancient rune for Happiness.

Kethe stood still, chest rising and falling as she regained her breath. Behind her the melee continued, a sinkhole of violence and blood. The causeway, however, gleamed like a road of bone, strangely pure and simple. It was here that she would fight this Virtue. It was here that he would kill her.

Makaria lifted his visor. He was a handsome man, dark skinned, with a manner both solemn and grave. "A clever plan." His voice carried almost eerily over the sound of battle. "Was it Ser Wyland's?"

"No," said Kethe. "My mother's and Asho's."

"So, she still lives. Your Ser Tiron is a most convincing liar." He smiled sorrowfully. "Good. I grieved when I heard she had been slain in prayer."

Kethe fought to regain her breath. "What are you doing here? *Why?*"

Makaria's sorrow seemed to deepen. "We must secure the Hold. There is a danger in these mountains that we must counter, and the Grace has accepted Lord Laur as the rightful lord of Kyferin Castle. I wish that it were otherwise." So saying, he raised his blade, presented himself at a three-quarter angle and began to approach her, sliding his feet forward.

He was as relaxed as she had been but a moment ago, but now Kethe found that her fear and bewilderment were making it impossible to grasp that joy. This was a *Virtue*. How was she supposed to fight him?

Kethe raised her blade and clasped it with both hands. Makaria continued to approach, his visor still up, face stern.

"Forgive me, Lady Kethe."

In that moment, he attacked. Kethe felt a pang of horror and fell back in disarray, fending off his strokes with desperate parries. His strength was terrible, and each blow sent a shock up her arms. He cleaved down from the diagonals with such speed that she couldn't regain her balance; she fought to simply parry left and then right and then left again, never able to raise her sword completely. Her heels caught at the rocks and she nearly fell. She had never fought anybody this powerful and fast. A great overhead blow knocked her sword aside and he rammed his shield forward, smashed it into her chest and knocked her sprawling onto her back.

Just like that. It had taken him less than five seconds to drop her. Kethe fought back a groan and thanked the Ascendant she'd managed to hold on to her blade. Makaria stepped back, giving her room to rise. She tasted blood and rose to a crouch.

Makaria wasn't even breathing hard. He watched her carefully, sword held at the ready.

How is he so calm? Brocuff's words came back to her: *I've seen some real killers in my time. Men to whom fighting was as natural as breathing. You can mark 'em out in a battle when you know what to look for. When everybody is gasping like fish out of water, leaping around and waving their swords like fools, these men are as calm as you please. They're in control of themselves. And as a result, they're aware. They're masters of the battle*

Kethe felt herself defeated before even swinging her blade. He was dominating her with just his presence. Furious, she let out a cry and lunged forward, spearing her sword straight at his face.

Makaria's sword flicked across in a neat parry and he stepped back, but Kethe kept after him. A slash at his neck, three quick chops at his side, a stab at his thigh and then a reverse slice at his face. He blocked most of them with his shield and parried the others with his blade, but still he stepped back, giving ground before her onslaught.

Her fear fed into her anger and became a white bonfire in her soul. She thrilled to feel her confidence return. She pushed herself, swinging harder and faster. Over and over she slashed and cut, and Makaria continued to retreat, blocking with his shield and now actually forced to duck and dodge.

She was a conduit. He might be an accomplished Virtue, but she could touch that selfsame fire. She let it burn her, consume her, exulted in her strength, embraced the battle fury that was her curse and her blessing. With a scream she smashed his shield aside. Makaria's eyes widened in shock, and Kethe whipped her sword up high and clutched it with both hands, ready to bring it down with all her strength and smash his helm in twain.

Somehow, impossibly, Makaria recovered his balance and planted his boot straight into her chest, putting the strength of his hips behind the blow.

Her breath exploded from her lungs, and she flew back to crash onto her shoulders a good five yards away. She rolled, a rag doll, and came to a stop face-down, a searing cut opened on her cheek. Her head rang, and she couldn't inhale. Her gut was an aching void, her lungs frozen in a permanent spasm. She tried to crawl to her knees, but it was hard to move, hard to do anything but fight back the panic.

Makaria stepped up and gently rolled her onto her back with his boot.

Her sword was gone. She lay on the rocks heaving and retching. The white fire in her soul had disappeared. The stars overhead grew vague and diffuse as tears flooded her eyes.

Makaria appeared over her, the moon behind his head, his face dark. "This is... unexpected. I can sense the white fire burning in your soul. And with such strength." He hesitated. "Perhaps this is why the Ascendant guided me here. Perhaps finding you was the true reason behind the Grace's command. If I spare you, will you swear to put aside your blade and come with me to Aletheia?"

Kethe blinked away the tears. Her lungs finally unlocked and she inhaled furiously, a desperate wheeze that brought life back into her body.

Makaria waited, poised, sword held at the ready. Could she lie to a Virtue?

"No," she whispered. "Never."

Makaria pursed his lips in disappointment and nodded. "Very well. I pray we meet in our next lives." So saying, he swept his blade high and then brought it scything down to take off her head.

CHAPTER THIRTY-NINE

AUDSLEY

The screams of men dying had grown muted and then stopped altogether. Audsley sat hunched before the map of Mythgræfen Hold and its local environs, Aedelbert clasped tightly in his lap, staring into the middle distance in shock. He could hear a lone man begging weakly from above. It was driving him mad.

"Mother? Mother, please." The man's voice was barely audible, but despite himself Audsley strained to hear his every word. "It hurts. Ah, it hurts so bad. Someone, please. Please!" The man's voice rose to a shrill scream of anger and terror and then dwindled away into a sob. "Mother," he began again. "Mother?"

Audsley bolted to his feet and strode out into the central chamber where Iskra was standing, hands clasped together, staring up at the dark stairwell. Aedelbert flitted up to land at the top of the dead gate. "This is intolerable, my Lady." Audsley's voice shook. "That man…"

"I know," said Iskra softly, not looking at him.

"Hello?" The man's voice was devoid of hope, but still he called out. "Hello? Someone? Water. Please. Don't leave me here. Hello? I don't want to die." Again his voice was drowned in sobs. "I don't want to die," he said, and repeated it again and again.

Audsley paced back and forth, running his hands through his thin hair. He felt furious. Couldn't the man die in dignity and silence? Did he have to torment them down here with his pleadings?

"Calm yourself, Magister," said Iskra.

"Calm myself? My apologies, dear Lady, but I find this situation intolerable. Not only must we wait blindly here in the depths to learn the outcome of this battle, but we're to be subjected to this aural torture?"

Iskra looked over at him at last, pity on her beautiful face. "Have you forgotten your training, Magister? School yourself."

"Yes, yes." He sighed and straightened his back. Then he closed his eyes and pressed his fingers into the form of a triangle. He was being irrational. It wasn't the man's fault that he was approaching Ascendancy with trepidation. That was normal human weakness. Audsley thought of the glimmering, limpid waters of Nous, how they reflected wavering light across the ceilings of the drowning rooms. *Ascension is mine own responsibility; though the Ascendant loves me, it is by my own word and deed that I rise and fall through the cycles of immortality...*

"Mother!"

"Oh, by the bleeding Black Gate!" Audsley tore off his spectacles and set to cleaning them furiously on the edge of his tunic. Aedelbert chirped, but Audsley refused to be soothed. He rammed his spectacles back on. "I'm sorry, but—"

"Mother!"

"Enough! I'm going to go reason with him."

"Reason with him?" Iskra stared at him as if he'd gone mad.

"Yes, well, if not reason, then at least give him some water." Audsley turned to the stairwell. "If he's one of ours, I shall bring him down to tend to his wounds. A most charitable deed, yes? If he's not, then—then I'll—" He mimed thrusting a knife, then dropped his hands in despair. "I'll drag him a little farther away so we can't hear him."

"Audsley." Iskra stepped up to him, her face grave. "You'll risk revealing our location if you go upstairs."

"Oh, kill me now, it hurts, it hurts!"

Audsley drew himself up as tall as he could. "My Lady, I cannot sit down here and listen to that man die. It is driving me insane. I shall employ the utmost discretion, I promise you. And think—we've not heard fighting for minutes now. The action has most surely moved out into the courtyard, if not the causeway, as planned."

Iskra frowned and then nodded. "All right. But be careful."

Audsley felt a pang of fear quiver through him. Was he really going to go up? He'd sworn to hide behind the table throughout the duration of the fight. Now he was going out into the open?

He steeled himself, gave a nod, and turned to the steps.

Combat was ghastly. He'd always known it had to be a sordid affair, what with men opening each other up with their weapons—and the Ascendant knew that had to hurt—but to actually *hear* it? The screams? The clash and clangor of swords on shields? The yells, the curses, the weeping? *Ghastly* didn't do it justice. Bestial? No, beasts were above waging war. Though some were rumored to engage in organized violence, such as the infamous Zoeian crimson ant, which would apparently sweep out over the land like a crawling carpet, clashing with an opposing hive with both building up into a glistening wall of gnashing pincers...

Audsley blinked. He'd reached the landing at the very top of the secret steps. Aedelbert was at his heels. Frowning, he leaned forward and tried to spot the locking mechanism. He wrinkled his nose as he focused, brushing his hair back. *Where...?* Aedelbert chirped and blew out a tongue of flame. "Ah, there we go. Thank you. Now, go downstairs. It's dangerous up here."

Aedelbert stared up at him with obvious disdain.

"No, I'm serious. Go down, now. If I have to battle for my life, I can't be worrying about your safety. Down!"

Aedelbert gave a sulky chirp and then leaped from the top step, wings stretching out so he could glide back down into the darkness with a flick of his tail. Audsley sighed. It would take him at least a week to get back into Aedelbert's good graces. Ah, well.

Carefully he reached out and laid his fingers on the latch. The dying man had gone silent. Had he died? The darkness around him was jellied. He strained to listen. Was that a yell in the distance? How was the fight going? Even if the dying man were truly dead—the Ascendant guide his soul—shouldn't Audsley engage in a little sly reconnaissance? Get the lay of the land? He saw himself returning below, perhaps wounded lightly but dramatically on the upper arm, his clothing scuffed, to report back to Lady Kyferin in a bold and dashing manner.

He bit his lower lip. He'd take a peek to see what was going on. If he saw anything dangerous, he could slink back through the door and be back downstairs with Lady Kyferin in the blink of an eye.

Audsley inhaled and held his breath. He thought of his younger self performing that ridiculous waltz on Fisher's Landing back in Nous, too terrified to dive into the azure waters below. He could go back down now, return to the shadows as he'd always done. The man had gone silent after all. Nobody expected him to go out there. In fact, it was foolishness to risk discovery! What was he doing? He could go below and use this time productively. Read a scroll. Begin the long and laborious process of apologizing to Aedelbert…

Audsley pressed down on the latch and pulled the door open a crack. Heart hammering away, he peered out into the chaos of the storage room. Embers from the explosion glimmered here and there like swamp lights. Bodies lay strewn across the floor. Sticky apples were everywhere underfoot. Everything was still. He could hear now the distant cries and yells of the battle. It was still ongoing.

He gulped and opened the door wide. He'd peek out into the courtyard at the very least. Maybe climb up to the battlement to catch a bird's-eye view…

A shadow detached from the wall and stepped before him. Audsley saw dark plate armor, a torn cloak, a visored helm and a naked blade in hand. His throat clamped shut so that he could only squeak as he tried to slam the door closed. The knight punched the swinging door with such force that fragments of stone fell from the facade and the door smacked out of Audsley's hand to swing open again.

"There. Thank you, Magister." Audsley knew that voice. Terror was pulping his stomach, kneading it with such force he couldn't do more than gurgle. The knight stepped forward. "I knew Tiron had gone in through here somewhere. Cunning wretch. What's below?"

"Ser Laur?" Audsley backed away, unable to tear his eyes from the blade.

"At your service." The knight pushed up his visor and Audsley saw his cruel eyes. "Where's Iskra?"

"I won't—" Audsley let out a cry as Ser Laur suddenly smacked him across the face with the flat of his blade. He threw up his arms and staggered back. "Stop that! How dare you—"

Kitan stepped through the doorway and with a growl kicked Audsley in the gut. Audsley staggered back, tripped on the first step, and fell into the darkness. With a cry he tumbled down the steps, knocking his elbows and back and head on sharp edges, unable to stop himself, slipping and clattering down till the curvature of the wall finally stopped him.

Sobbing, he tried to rise, but Kitan was there. The knight placed a boot on his shoulder and shoved him again, and down Audsley went, wailing piteously till he spilled out into the central chamber, heaving for breath, dizzy and stunned. He crawled away from the descending knight. "Iskra!" he cried. "Hide!"

Iskra did no such thing. She was standing in front of the dead Gate, a slender blade in her hand. Where had that come from? She glared at Kitan as he stepped out into the torchlight.

"Ah," said Kitan, ignoring Audsley completely. "You don't know how delighted I am to find you at last, dear aunt. I was so sad when Tiron told me he'd killed you already."

"For some reason I find that hard to believe, Kitan." Audsley was impressed. Iskra's voice didn't even waver.

"Oh, believe me, I was distraught. You see, I'd wanted to kill you myself." He smiled. "A little morbid, I'll admit, but there you have it."

Iskra took her blade in both hands. "You always were a degenerate."

"Yes, it's true. By normal standards." Kitan began to advance, completely unconcerned with her blade. "But, come. I've been trained to kill since I was a boy. Is it so strange that I enjoy actually doing so?"

Audsley clambered painfully to his feet. "A true knight doesn't—"

"Shut up," said Kitan evenly, never taking his eyes from Iskra.

"A true knight," said Audsley, stepping quickly between Iskra and Kitan, "is noble and does not fear death, and—and—"

Kitan stopped, eyebrows raised. "What are you doing? Do you want me to kill you first?"

"Audsley," said Iskra. "Step aside."

"No my Lady. It is my honor to defend you." He couldn't believe he was doing this. He drew himself up. He didn't even have a knife. "You won't go one step farther, you Ennoian thug."

Kitan laughed. "What? Do you honestly expect me to respect your higher station? You fat, blubbering, effeminate idiot?" He smacked his blade across Audsley's shoulder, causing him to cry out. "Pathetic. Look at you." He smacked Audsley again, and then stabbed the tip of his sword into Audsley's thigh. "Let's hear you bawl, Magister. Let's hear you beg."

The pain was shocking. It was really, incredibly, intensely overwhelming. *So this is agony.* Audsley let out a strangled scream and stumbled to one side as his leg went weak.

A terrifying yowl filled the chamber, raucous and feral, and a streak of winged flame descended upon Kitan from on high. Kitan yelled in surprise and backed away, slamming down his visor as Aedelbert swooped past him, lashing him with a whip of crimson fire.

"What the Hell—"

Iskra didn't wait. She lunged forward, left foot gliding over the smooth stone floor, and stabbed her slender blade at Kitan's neck. While she was no warrior, she had grown up amongst knights, and surprise was on her side. Her form was smooth, her control admirable, her aim true.

Kitan parried her strike with such force that her sword leaped from her hand to skitter across the floor and fetch up against the wall. "Enough of this," he growled, and backhanded her.

Iskra didn't make a sound. She stumbled back and fell to the ground, the skin of her left cheek split open.

Audsley felt fury, genuine, palpitating fury, blossom in his chest. He screamed incoherently and ran forward to bull-rush Kitan against the wall. The knight glanced at him with disdain and swung his blade at Audsley's head. Instinct made Audsley throw himself to the ground, but he still felt the side of his scalp erupt in wet, fierce pain. The room spun, and he hit the ground. Was he dead? No. Dying? He didn't know. His head... He reached up to touch the wound. It was wet and messy. He could barely think. Was he dying?

He heard Iskra cry out, partly in anger, partly in pain. Audsley blinked away his tears. Where were his spectacles? He levered himself up onto one arm. Aedelbert landed beside him and hissed in terror. He wanted more than anything in the world to comfort him, but there was no time. He could just make out Kitan. He was a blurring mass. The knight was wrestling with Iskra, pinning her by the throat to the ground.

"I wish we had an entire evening to enjoy this," he gasped. "But I'll wrest what pleasure I can from—ow! How dare—"

Audsley heard the sound of Iskra being struck again. Trembling, he moved forward, forcing himself to do so silently. He blinked furiously, but couldn't make out details. Where had Kitan's sword gone? He was holding a dagger. For what? Detail work? Anger and icy disgust curdled within Audsley, and he decided there and then to die before letting this beast go any further.

A gray shape darted past him, as silent as a ghost. Aedelbert. His firecat stopped alongside a long shadow and exhaled a sliver of fire so as to draw his eye. Kitan's sword! Audsley crept up another step and scooped it up with both hands.

Kitan must have heard him. The knight turned to look up, his face a pale smear. "You've got to be kidding me."

Audsley didn't waste any time. He brought the sword down with all his might and heard the crash of it smacking Kitan's armor. It was like striking a wall. The sword bounced aside and Audsley nearly fell.

Kitan lurched to his feet. "All right. Now I kill you. Come here, fat man."

Audsley backed away, swinging furiously in great empty sweeps. This was it. He was going to die. *Please, let it be quick.* "Run, Iskra! Run!"

"Here you are." A new voice, coming from the stairwell. Audsley stopped. He could only make out shadows. Ser Tiron and a few others? Audsley felt a wave of relief pass through him that was so strong he almost whimpered. "We've been looking for you, boy."

Kitan turned toward the stairwell. "Tiron. Well, well. It seems I must take all my pleasures at once." His voice was tight with displeasure. "You find me at a disadvantage. Magister, give me my blade."

Audsley backed up against the wall, holding the sword tightly. "No."

Kitan sighed with impatience. "Now, Magister. This is a fight I've been relishing."

"No sword, Kitan?" Tiron sounded darkly amused. Audsley could barely make him out as an approaching shadow. "What a pity." He spoke to his companions over his shoulder. "This is between him and me."

"A moment, Tiron, and we'll see which of us is truly the best. *Now*, Magister!" Kitan stepped forward, and Audsley swung. His sword clanged against Kitan's armored arm, knocking it away, but was followed by a blow that smashed across his face. Audsley cried out and crumpled, but did not let go of the sword.

Then Kitan let out a cry of pain and shock and whirled away. "How dare you?"

Tiron laughed. It was a dark and frightening sound. "Come on, Kitan. Time to see what the Ascendant's got in store for you."

"I don't have my sword!" Kitan sounded outraged. "This is—" He cut off and stumbled back, swiping his dagger in front of him as Tiron lunged at him.

Aedelbert scooted up along the edge of the wall to where Audsley was lying. He pressed up against Audsley's cheek, and Audsley felt something cold and smooth in his firecat's mouth. "Oh, bless you!"

He took his spectacles with trembling fingers and fumbled them on. The world leaped into focus. Kitan was dancing back, face livid, while Tiron stalked after him, blade slick with other men's blood. Three of their guards were standing at the stairwell, their faces hard, watching the fight. Audsley took the sword with both hands. The pain in his head was nauseating him, yet it strangely felt very far away. Kitan kept backing away, long dagger held before him. Tiron was wounded, Audsley saw; his armor was dented and spattered with blood, his cloak torn, and he was hunched over as if his side pained him. But his expression was clear, his eyes bright and focused on Kitan.

"You coward," said Kitan. "Give me a blade. Fight me with honor!"

"I don't want to fight you with honor," said Tiron, voice calm. "I just want to kill you. See the difference?"

"I hope Enderl killed your wife slowly," spat Kitan. "And you know, I bet she enjoyed it, getting it hard by a real man—"

Tiron let out a roar and charged awkwardly forward, his wound hampering him. Kitan spun, his dagger flashing, and somehow Tiron was staggering past him, his blow evaded. Kitan raised his dagger to strike down at Tiron's back.

Audsley closed his eyes, stepped forward and swung his blade. It connected with another clang across Kitan's back and knocked him into a stumble.

Catching himself, Audsley gasped and backed away in time to see Tiron recover and slam his blade deep into Kitan's side. He stepped in close and shoved the sword in another six inches.

Kitan gasped and rose to his tiptoes, dagger falling from his hand. "Almost had you, Tiron." He somehow managed to smile. "Even with just a knife."

"True." Tiron didn't seem concerned. "But you're the one who's dying, aren't you?"

"Taken down by a fat magister." Kitan grimaced. "Pathetic." He winced and rose higher on his tiptoes as Tiron twisted the blade. Blood ran out of the corner of his mouth. "Promise me, as one knight to another. Promise you'll have my body sent to my father."

"No," said Tiron, his face made brutal by his disgust and hatred. "I'm going to dump your body in the woods for the animals."

"Please," whispered Kitan. His hands were clasped around the blade. "Mourning. My father."

"You don't deserve it."

Tiron placed his foot on Kitan's stomach and shoved. His blade tore free and the other knight collapsed loudly to the ground. His blood spilled out over the older stain. Kitan gasped, his breath bubbling wetly, and then lay still.

"Iskra?" Tiron dropped his sword and staggered to where she was rising to her feet, her sword held before her. She was staring at the fallen knight, eyes wide, jaw clenched. "Iskra, it's over. It's done."

She shook her head. "Never. I swore nobody would ever touch me like that again." Tears filled her eyes and spilled down her cheeks.

"He's dead. It's all right. He's dead." Audsley had never heard Tiron sound so tender. He took the blade from Iskra's hands and pulled her into an awkward embrace. "It's over."

Iskra shuddered, but couldn't take her eyes away from the fallen Kitan. The side of her face was swelling horribly. She rested her hands on Tiron's breastplate, but seemed unable to relax.

Audsley suddenly dropped his sword. It bounced loudly on the rock. Tiron glared at him sharply over Iskra's shoulder, but Audsley ignored him. "The Gate," he said. "The Gate."

The empty arch had flooded with black, undulating ink. Its surface was choppy, as if gusts of wind were blowing sharply across its surface. How long had it been open? Moments, Audsley thought. Ten seconds, perhaps. Fifteen?

Iskra pulled away from Tiron. "A Half-Moon Gate. How long do we have?"

"Forty seconds," whispered Audsley, stepping up to it. "Maybe less."

His pain was a distant throb. He felt nothing but unmitigated wonder. His first true mystery gate—it could lead them anywhere in existence. Any city. Any ruin. He'd spent his whole life reading about mysteries, lost stoneclouds, hidden Lunar Gates, the myths and legends that might or might not have had a grain of truth to them. And now here he was, face to face with magic and wonder. He could barely breathe.

He turned to Iskra. "I'm going through."

"Absolutely not," she said. "You're wounded. We don't know what's on the other side. You can't just—"

"I'm going through." He felt absolutely certainty wash over him. "Even if we defeat Laur's men tonight, you know we can't go back. Not with a Virtue and the Grace on Laur's side. We need help. Something. Anything. I'm going to get it."

Iskra opened her mouth to deny him, to argue, but there was nothing for her to say.

"Fifteen seconds," said Audsley. "Look for me a month from now. I will return, my fairest Lady!" He felt giddy with excitement—and, possibly, blood loss. "I, Magister Audsley, do hereby swear it!"

"Then we're going too," said Tiron. "You're not going alone."

Audsley blinked. For a moment he thought Tiron meant Iskra, and then he realized that Tiron was talking about the three guards, who had all gone pale. "You are? I mean, are you sure? Because—"

"Ten seconds," growled Tiron. "Go!"

Aedelbert flew up onto his shoulders and dug in his talons as Audsley turned toward the Gate. He took a deep breath as he heard the other four men step into place behind him. "Our souls to the White Gate," he whispered, and then, with awe and terror rising to a crescendo in his soul, he stepped into the rippling surface of the Lunar Gate.

CHAPTER FORTY

Asho

Asho ran. The causeway stretched interminably before him, a hundred miles long and Kethe at the far end of it. He'd never reach her in time. The rocks crunched under the balls of his feet, his armor felt weightless, and the Everflame trailed behind him like the tail of a comet. They had cleared out the Hold, had fought brilliantly, bravely, madly against the remaining knights and against all odds destroyed them all—but he'd spotted Kethe falling on the causeway far too late. The Virtue stood over her, sword raised, his intent clear. A hundred miles had contracted to fifty yards, but he was still too far away. She was going to die, and there was nothing he could do to save her.

The Virtue's sword began its downward swing, and the world seemed to slow. A rushing roar filled his head as he saw Kethe raise her arm in a futile attempt to block the blow. Everything sprang into terrible, lucid detail: The swirling melee beyond them where the causeway reached the mainland. The Virtue's dark features, grim and remorseless. Kethe's own terror and desperation, her eyes wide, her mouth pulled into a feline snarl of defiance.

Asho could *sense* them both. Twin suns burning brightly in a jet-black sky, each called to him in the same way that heights made him want to jump. He felt a heady, feverish desire to bleed his very essence into their souls. The Virtue was the roar of a tremendous waterfall, drowning out the world, obliterating his ability to think—and yet, beside Makaria's annihilating force, he could still sense Kethe, smaller, fiercer, and familiar.

The Virtue's sword continued its inexorable descent, but Kethe sensed him. She tore her eyes from her imminent death to look at where Asho was approaching. Their eyes met, and he felt a shiver pass through him as if his whole being were a bell that had just been struck. Her eyes widened. The Virtue's blade was but ten inches from her neck. There was no time, left, no time at all.

Asho held Kethe's gaze and reached out to her. Through the cacophony and madness of the invisible forces at play, he struggled to connect, to latch on to her brightness—and he felt her reach right back. Their souls locked tight and mingled, and in that instant he felt a terrible power surge up within him which he channeled through his sword.

The causeway erupted.

Rocks flew up into the night sky in a straight line from him to the Virtue. The roar was shattering. The force of Makaria's blow was lost as he reacted with impossible speed, spinning and crossing his arms over his chest, forming an 'X' behind which he steeled himself just as the line of power smashed into him.

Asho felt the Virtue absorb his force, drink it deep, and destroy it. Asho screamed and staggered to a stop. The rocks and boulders that had been thrown high into the sky, some the size of Asho's fist, others as large as the ballista, came crashing back down. They plummeted down from the sky, sending up white gouts of water which flowed into the jagged scar he'd carved through the causeway.

Asho slowly straightened. Water surged around his feet. Kethe scrambled up and away from Makaria, who was staring at Asho with a mixture of shock and disbelief.

The waves surged and slowly settled. Thirty yards of cratered water lay between them, broken by the occasional rough ridge or outcropping of stone. Makaria straightened from his crouch and lowered his arms. Asho heaved for breath. Kethe backed away, sword in hand once more, eyes wide.

"You." Makaria pointed with his sword. "I know you." He paused. "Ser Kyferin's squire. The Bythian."

Asho took a deep breath and stepped up to the water's edge. "I'm Ser Asho. Lady Kyferin's knight." His voice sounded tremulous in the darkness, nowhere near as rich and confident as Makaria's.

"You're no knight," said the Virtue. "You're just a Sin Caster."

Asho clenched his jaw. He couldn't refute it. "And you're no Virtue. You're Lord Laur's dog."

"Brave words," Makaria said, and stepped back. "Say them to my face." Then he ran forward a half-dozen steps and *leaped*.

Asho raised his black blade as he stumbled back. The Virtue sailed through the night air, his white cloak snapping behind him, impossibly high, and landed on the ragged end of the causeway with a crunch. He fell into a crouch, one fist planted on the rock to catch himself, and then stood. This close, his power was oppressive, the sense of his inhaling the magic from the world a muted roar that sounded like a thousand tree trunks splintering.

Asho stepped back again, fear flickering within him. The runes of his blade were muted, a dull cherry red. He couldn't sense Kethe.

Makaria swung his blade in a tight circle by his side and advanced.

"Why are you doing this?" Asho gave way before him. He had

no hope of besting him in a fight.

Makaria came on, implacable. "How did you sin cast without suffering?"

Asho thought of the Agerastian Sin Casters, how they had grown sick and vomited blood by the end of the battle. He felt winded, raw, but nowhere near as devastated. *Kethe*, he thought. *She's draining the sin from… from my magic. Why can't I feel her now?*

"Work with us," he said. "Join with Lady Kyferin. Don't fight us."

Pity flickered across Makaria's face. "Work with a Sin Caster? No. This corner of the world needs cleansing and healing. I am glad now that the Grace saw fit to send me here. There is much work to be done. Starting with your death, Bythian, and the reclaiming of the Everflame."

Asho stopped backing away. There was no retreating from this fight. He took a deep breath and felt his anger churn within him. Makaria symbolized everything he'd always admired and resented about the world: the unfair system of Ascension, the pinnacle of knighthood, the perfection of an enlightened soul.

"I never wanted this," said Asho quietly. "I never asked for any of this."

"If you expect my pity—"

"But a true knight does not blame his circumstances." Asho could feel Shaya's presence close to him, all but speaking to him. "A true knight is always himself, regardless of what others may think. Regardless of what they call him."

His sense of self was deepening, widening, as if his mind were falling through a trapdoor from a cramped attic into the expansive vastness of a great hall. His thoughts seemed to echo. He wasn't alone; something else was deep within him, watching him, biding its time, waiting for the right moment. He dimly heard Makaria say something and lash out with an attack. He blocked it almost absent-mindedly, giving ground, focusing his energies on himself. On this presence within him.

Are you ready to listen?
Who are you?

Makaria pressed his attack. Asho was knocked out of his reverie as his sword nearly flew from his hands. Each blow he parried sent a shock through his arms all the way to his shoulders. The Virtue's face showed no signs of effort, yet his attacks came from all sides almost at once. Asho's heel caught on a stone and he nearly fell, stumbling instead back into a crouch and then leaping away as Makaria followed through flawlessly, lunging to impale him where he'd squatted.

"Enough of this," said the Virtue. He spun his sword as he rose, and white flame ran silently down its length. Asho gulped. "Your soul to the Black Gate, Sin Caster."

And then he leaped. Another of his huge, impossible leaps, raising him high in the sky to come crashing down upon Asho, leaving him no hope of evasion. Asho cried out and raised his black sword in desperation.

The clangor of their impact was tremendous, and white flame dripped down Makaria's blade even as Asho's sword flared into black fire. Where the two touched, they hissed and spat sparks. The Virtue's strength was punishing. Asho quickly fell to one knee, eyes slitted against the painful light, shoulders burning, arm shaking. The white sword descended toward his face. This was a Virtue, he thought—and he was almost holding his own against him.

There was the sound of footsteps, and then Kethe appeared, leaping high to fall like a vengeful spirit upon Makaria, who spun away and blocked her attack with a furious upward parry.

She landed lightly, spun away from Makaria, and came to a stop beside Asho. Together they faced the Virtue.

"A worthy fight," said Makaria. "I welcome it."

Kethe's eyes smoldered. "Then you're a fool."

Asho took a deep breath and again reached out to Kethe—and felt her quick and welcome response. At once white fire blossomed along the length of her blade, and he couldn't help but feel a thrill as he raised his own sword and black fire ran down its edges. Energy infused him. His bond with Kethe was a surging, tumultuous flow, raucous and wild and unstoppable. Asho had never felt so close to another being—not even his sister Shaya. He could sense Kethe without looking at her, read her intentions. When she threw herself forward to attack, he joined her seamlessly on the assault.

Their blades cleaved the night with white and burning ebon arcs. Makaria backed away, ducked and sprinted aside, spun and parried, pressed the attack and then retreated again. Asho and Kethe harried him on both sides, coordinating their attacks flawlessly, trying to get past his guard, stumbling back from his brutally strong ripostes, recovering and learning to work together. Asho found himself swinging high so Kethe could attack low, reaching out to parry an attack that would have opened her shoulder, swaying aside to allow her to swing through his space.

But it wasn't enough.

Within moments the Virtue's strength and training began to tell the tale. He was one of the Seven, and while Asho and Kethe had just discovered their power, he had been training and refining his own for years. Makaria forced Asho back with a wild swing, then turned with impossible speed to hammer his fist into Kethe's face. She was knocked back into the water. Asho yelled and gathered himself to attack, but Makaria wasn't done. He drew a dagger from his hip and threw it with unerring precision right at Asho's face. There was no time to block it. Asho's eyes widened as it flew toward him.

Power flooded into him from the blade, and Asho acted on instinct. He leaped up and soared fifteen feet into the night sky. As he hit the apex of his leap, he swung his sword down at Makaria and unleashed another surge of force that cracked the causeway, tore rocks back up into the sky and blasted open a channel under the Virtue's feet. Makaria flew back to crash into the shallows of the ruined causeway.

Asho hung suspended in the air. His cloak fluttered around him, and black flames swirled and surged off his glowing blade. He felt a terrible power growing within him and felt a moment of lucid fear over what was happening.

Kethe was rising out of the lake, climbing up the causeway's slope, still connected to him and drinking deep of his taint even as she stared up at him in shock.

Asho felt his fear spike into terror. Makaria was rising from the water, blade still aflame despite being soaked. Eyes wide, Asho stared at the sword's black surface and its fiery runes, feeling the power that radiated from its edges. Makaria crouched, eyes glittering, preparing to leap up at where Asho was hovering. Without knowing what he was doing, Asho pointed his blade at the Virtue.

Yes.

Makaria let out a cry of defiance and surged up, white blade cutting the night like a tongue of lightning. Power roared through Asho's body, a torrent of such magnitude that it caused Kethe to scream and topple senseless to the ground. Asho's connection to her was immediately severed, but a deluge of black flame shot through with the deepest crimson blasted from the point of his sword even as he started to fall. It scalded the air, filled the world with its deep, guttural roar, and enveloped Makaria completely.

They both fell.

The Virtue screamed. The force of the fire deflected his approach, knocking him back so that his enveloped frame crashed into the water.

Asho dropped like a stone, falling down to the causeway and landing with a crash on the rocks. He lay still, head ringing, mouth slicked with a patina of foul grease, stomach roiling. What had he done? The sword lay dead in his hand. He couldn't sense Kethe at all.

Groaning, head pounding, he rose to sitting and stared out at the water. Makaria lay still, just under the surface in the shallows, but he was still burning. Steam and bubbles swirled the water above him.

Disgust and horror rose in Asho's soul. He was shaking with terrible force. The battle at the causeway's head had ground to a standstill. Pale faces in the light of the moon were staring out at him.

A voice spoke quietly in the deepest recesses of his mind. **I am yours, and you are mine.** The words were shot through with gloating triumph. Denial arose within him, and with a cry he cast the sword from him and fell on his back, then lay gasping and staring up at the moon.

I'm damned, he thought, over and over again. *I'm damned.*

CHAPTER FORTY-ONE

Tharok

Tharok returned to the compound late that afternoon. He'd spent a few hours simply sitting and watching Gold revolve around him, trying to understand with his own intelligence what had seemed too obvious with the circlet on. Finally he'd given up and returned to Porloc's homTharok returned to the compound late that afternoon. He'd spent a few hours simply sitting and watching Gold revolve around him, trying to understand with his own intelligence what had seemed too obvious with the circlet on. Finally he'd given up and returned to Porloc's home. The festivities were beginning outside, but he had no heart for them. His thoughts were filled with memories of his departed family, his dead clan, his destroyed Tribe. He thought of the Tragon, freely wandering the northern steppes without fear of retribution. That thought filled him with a slow-moving anger that he could do nothing about. He didn't know how to injure the Tragon. The Red River tribe was but fifty fighting kragh. The answer, he knew, lay in the circlet—but he didn't wish to put it on.

He froze upon entering his room. The slave girl—he'd forgotten her. She was sitting in the corner, slender white arms wrapped around her shins, her forehead resting on her knees, shivering in a thin shift she'd found. Tharok stood looking at her for a moment, uncertain, and then moved to the bed, where he slowly removed his axe from his shoulder and set it against the wall, then took off his belt and laid it around the post. The girl seemed oblivious to him, so he stared at her, examining her fine, pale hair, the hollows between her shoulders and neck, the delicate, bird-like fragility of her bones.

"Human," he said. The slave started, raised her head, then scrabbled to her feet, almost climbing the wall. She stared around herself as if she was blind, and Tharok realized that she couldn't see in the dim light. "Girl," he said. "Calm down. I'm not going to hurt you."

She was breathing quickly now, small, shallow breaths through her mouth. Her palms were pressed against the wall, and she was staring in his direction. Suddenly impatient, Tharok moved to the door, opened it, and strode down the hall till he came to the closest lit candle. He took it, returned, and entered the room, casting everything in warm tones of umber and gold. The girl stared at him, put her hands to her mouth, then shook her head and sank back down into a crouch.

Tharok set the candle on the floor in the middle of the room and retreated to the far wall, where he too sat and crossed his legs. She was like a panicked young mountain goat, liable to leap off the edge of the cliff in its attempt to escape. He sat still, and saw that by slow degrees she calmed down, or at least returned from the edge of panic. Her skin was burned by the sun, deep red and blistered along her shoulders, cheek and nose. Her lips were flaking. She had stood for too long in the marketplace.

"Do you understand me?" he asked.

"Yes," she whispered, her voice strange, reedy and thin, her kragh crude but clear.

"You are mine now. I bought you." He tried to not make his voice cruel, to simply explain the situation, but tears brimmed from her eyes and overflowed down her cheeks. She bit her lower lip and lowered her head. For some reason her weakness made him angry.

"What do you want from me?"

"If I were to set you free, what would you do?"

"I would… I would head south, to Abythos."

"Do you have money?" he asked, and she shook her head. "A horse, then, to carry you?" Again, she shook her head. "You are so weak you can barely stand. How would you move so far south and not be caught again by Orlokor slavers?"

"I wasn't caught," she said, her chin rising and her tone growing defiant. So there *was* some strength to her. "I was given. And I would find a way." Tears glimmered in her eyes, but her mouth was set.

"You have nobody to speak for you. Porloc does not grant you safe passage."

"You could speak for me. Speak to him. Ask him to give me safe passage."

Tharok mulled that over. "No. He would think you important to me and keep you to use against me. It would go worse for you."

"Then what? I am to be your slave."

"Perhaps. Perhaps I will free you regardless. But you lack strength. Are all humans so weak?"

"No," said the human, and she looked away. "Some are strong. Or, at least, they appear to be so. Now I am no longer sure."

"You could stay with my tribe for now if you wish. It won't be easy, but you will be protected. You can tell me of humans, and in exchange we will feed you and help you regain your strength. Then, later, you can choose to leave when there is a better chance of your not being caught."

357

"Are you giving me a choice?"

Tharok yawned, and the girl flinched at the sight of his tusks. He stood up, his knees popping, and with a wince he reached up to unshoulder his heavy hide shirt. He would be wearing finery for tonight's feast. Finery by highland kragh standards, at any rate. "You can do what you like. Come with my tribe or try your own luck escaping Gold and making your way south alone. Highland kragh do not own slaves. That is a lowland kragh tradition." He reached down and dropped his pants, stepped out of them and kicked them to the side. She quickly averted her eyes, and Tharok looked down at himself, then at her. Was she in her mating season? Did humans have mating seasons? Was she a grown woman? He thought she was, but who knew with humans?

He shrugged and moved to the bed, picked up the heavy goat- and sheepskin cloak, the leather vest and pants. "I won't have time in the morning to deal with you. Leave or stay; it's all the same to me. But make your decision tonight. Come morning, if you are here, I will assume you intend to march with us. Understood?"

She stood up, uncertain, and wrapped her arms around herself again. "Yes. What—what is your name?"

"I am Tharok, son of Grakor, warlord of the Red River. My own clan was dispersed and killed." He watched her as, slowly, she allowed herself to slide back down the stone wall till once again she was seated. "What is your name?"

"Shaya," she said. A name from a different language.

"Shaya." He grunted and began to dress, then took hold of a large sheepskin and tossed it onto the ground in front of her. She startled, but then carefully reached out, took hold of the fur and pulled it around herself.

"Thank you," she whispered.

Tharok didn't respond. His mind had already turned to Porloc and the Tragon. There had been a plan, a means to his own advantage—but it was gone now. Irritated, he dressed quickly, picked up his axe, and left without giving her another glance.

The feast was magnificent. Ten pigs had been slaughtered and spitted through the mouth over open flames, turned by Tragon slaves who were bent to the task by whip-wielding chefs. A central bonfire was burning in the center of the Heart of Gold's great yard, and cushions were cast everywhere for the guests to sprawl on. Twelve musicians were playing on drums of varying sizes in the corner, from small pock drums to a single mighty peak drum that loomed over its player. Everywhere wine and whiskey was flowing, and the mightiest kragh of the Orlokor tribe were gathered, from Porloc's clanmates to distant and subordinate warlords. It was a war council, a celebration, and a coronation all at once, and at its center stood Porloc, raised high on a wooden dais and surrounded by his family. World Breaker was prominently displayed.

Tharok was sitting to one side, by the far wall, with Maur, Toad, Golden Crow and Barok sitting beside him. The freed slave had chosen the name Nok, after the dark son of Sister Death, and stood to one side, alert and brooding. They dined on steaming flesh and drank from copper cups until Maur could take it no longer and leaned over to Tharok.

"Great and mighty and oh-so-wise warlord of the Red River tribe." Her tone belied her words. "What by the Sky Mother are we doing here? What is your plan?"

Tharok bit down on a leg of lamb and crunched right through to the marrow. It was delicious. He slurped and then waved the leg in annoyance. "Why must everything be planned?"

Maur's brow lowered. Golden Crow shuffled back in alarm. "Then why, I ask you, are we here? Why did you put World Breaker in Porloc's hands? What benefit does this bring to the Red River Tribe?"

Tharok could only shrug and take another great bite from the leg he was holding, enjoying the juices as they ran over his jaw. The circlet remained off his head, in a pouch affixed to his belt. Much remained a mystery to him without it, but he enjoyed being simply himself, eating and eyeing the women without thoughts of politics and maneuvering distracting him all the time. He'd tried eyeing Maura when she'd first arrived, but had quickly thought twice about it.

Toad had carefully filled a bowl with garlic roasted goat tongue bits, and popped one into his mouth. "Tharok-krya's plan is obvious. Look at where we sit! We are honored and protected. We are now tied closely to the Orlokor tribe, and as they rise, so shall we. Very wise!"

Maura scowled and sat back, sipping from her cup of wine. "When Tharok spoke to the women's council up in the peaks, he told us of a different dream. He spoke of uniting the tribes and breaking traditions. Of turning against the humans." She glared at him over her cup. "What happened to those dreams, Tharok?"

Tharok shrugged and tossed the bone over his shoulder. He remembered that conversation, but now it seemed both ridiculous and like too much work, a dream built of smoke. What was real was this ribcage carved from one of the spitted pigs, how the fat bubbled and the hide gave off a pleasing aroma. What was real was the fire, the music, the way the drums caused his heart to beat faster. Was Toad right? Was this enough? Was this what he wanted?

Porloc rose, raised a hand, and the drums went silent. Kragh ceased dancing, so that only the great fire was moving and broke the silence.

"Tonight, we have much to celebrate! We are the greatest kragh tribe in existence. Our wealth overflows, our city of Gold is a wonder, and I have at my call thousands of dangerous kragh warriors. We are feared! We are mighty! And this is all just the beginning, for now we move to even bigger and better glories. I have been given a sign by the mighty Ogri himself that the Orlokors' fortunes are to rise to dizzying heights!"

The crowd roared and kragh pounded their fists against the floor. The sound echoed hollowly in Tharok's chest and he did not cheer.

"There are those amongst you who share my concerns over the Tragon," continued Porloc. "Those who think that the tides of fortune rise against us, but no longer! Fate has delivered into my hands this wondrous blade, this powerful weapon, this symbol of kragh unity. I show you World Breaker! This sword was wielded by Ogri himself! Think of that, my Orlokor. This is the sword that cut off the head of the great human shaman himself in their floating city of white stone. This is the edge that brought every kragh tribe to heel. This is the very blade that drank the blood of thousands, and now it is here, amongst us, in my hand. With it we shall conquer all, and become richer and more powerful than our dreams could ever have imagined!"

Again the crowd roared, working itself up into a frenzy. Kragh fell to all fours and pounded the floor, and some even rose to beat at their chests. Tharok resisted the urge to spit. The lowlanders looked idiotic acting this way.

Maur hissed and kicked Tharok. He frowned at her, jutting out his lower jaw so that his tusks emerged prominently, and then looked back to Porloc, who continued speaking.

"Word shall soon spread of World Breaker being in my hands, and the other kragh shall flock to us. Once our numbers are truly great, we shall sweep up all the tribes and clans to the west, and then I shall lead a strike against the human city of Abythos like Ogri himself one did, deep in our ancient past. We shall take what we will from their city, and give those riches to our followers. Even more kragh will follow us then, when they see our success. Gold, women, metal—wonders all will we bring home. This dawn marks the beginning of our new era, and we shall accomplish it beneath the Orlokor banner!"

Maur leaned in close, gripped him by the back of the neck with one iron hand, and hissed in his ear, "If you do not act now, I will do everything within my power to remove you as warlord and have you cast from the tribe, you miserable, drunken sack of piss!"

Tharok shook her free and glowered. Porloc would never have dared strike against the humans without World Breaker. Tharok had set these events in motion, but now he had lost control. He could only dimly recall his previous plans. His chance to act was slipping away, almost gone. His former plan was almost ruined.

Porloc stood with his arms raised as if he was already celebrating his victory over the humans. His round face gleamed with leftover fat. World Breaker was raised aloft in his fist. Glory to Porloc! But something told Tharok that this planned raid would end badly for the kragh. Still, what was that to him? He could face down Maur... probably, and take the Red River tribe back to the peaks. Let Porloc dash himself against the human walls, then find a chance over the next few years to get revenge on the Tragon for his father's death.

Barok was staring at him. Maur had looked away in disgust.

Tharok took out the circlet and turned it in his hands. Which future did he wish for? A glorious one, filled with revenge, unification, and conquest on a scale not seen since Ogri's Ascension? Or a natural one, quieter, humbler, filled with his own pride and strength? He glanced sidelong at Maur. She would see him cast down. A yearning to earn her approval filled him. More than that—to conquer her, to capture her desire, to make her his mate, to be the kragh who could stand by such a female as an equal, to be the kragh she had glimpsed these past few days.

Tharok took a deep breath. He'd already set events in motion. He would not back away now. He placed the circlet on his brow.

"For now, I invite you all to eat and drink, to rut and to break bones as you will," continued Porloc, and hundreds of brutish voices cheered and roared in approval. "For we—"

"Porloc!" roared Tharok, stepping forward from the ranks of the kragh into the firelight to stare up at the warlord. He used his avalanche voice, deep-throated and powered by lungs more powerful than Porloc's, drowning out all words so that silence fell over the crowd. Orlokor kragh turned to stare at him, brows lowering, hands going to their weapons. Porloc himself stood still, arms still raised, taken aback by the interruption.

"I would say a few words to honor your greatness before we fall into feasting proper and lose ourselves," said Tharok, turning to the encircling crowd with spread arms, grinning at them so that his tusks hung low. "After all, tonight is a night to be remembered, and in the days to come, let it not be said that the mighty Orlokor began their revolution alone. The highland kragh stand with you, or shall as soon as this is done, and I would have it noted, that I, Tharok of the Red River, who did have the honor and the glory of bringing World Breaker to you, was the first!"

His words hung in the air, and then several kragh cheered, the rest catching on as Porloc lowered his arms and nodded his head. "Yes, Tharok, this is true. We Orlokor are glad to have the Red River tribe by our side." He opened his mouth to continue, but Tharok interrupted once more.

"You honored me beyond all measure when you named me your blood son," he roared, turning so that all could hear him clearly. Porloc made a sour face. "And I would earn your approval right away. As you fix your keen eyes on the western tribes and Abythos in the south, I would fix mine on the north—where the Tragon still gather and cause trouble. They killed my father—your blood brother—and stand unpunished. I would see my father avenged! The Red River tribe will march to war, and if this cause meets with your approval, I would request that you send kragh with me to swell my numbers and see to it that the Tragon are made to pay for killing a member of Porloc's own family!"

Tharok, who had been turning in order to address the whole crowd, finished this last facing Porloc, lowering his arms in the sudden silence. Porloc stared down at him, his frown etched deep into his face, and then he laughed. "But of course. Your father's death has not been far from my mind. Tomorrow we will discuss how we can avenge him. Tonight, however—"

"Porloc-krya," said Tharok, drowning him out once more as he went down on one knee. "My thanks to you. You honor your bond to your blood brother. I would take the Crokuk clan with me, and bring you back Tragon heads. Does the honor of your own brother merit such an undertaking?"

Porloc's face darkened. "The Crokuk clan? That is a mighty clan, indeed." Porloc hesitated and allowed his eyes to drift over the crowd. Everyone was staring at him: Kragh leaders, lesser warlords, the great and small of the Orlokor tribe, watching to see how he would respond. Porloc laughed stiffly. "Of course, Tharok. I was about to suggest that myself. Tomorrow, the Crokuk will march against the Tragon with the Red River by their side, and they will teach the Tragon a lesson that they will never forget!" The warlord seemed to warm to this now that the decision was made. "For none can hurt the Orlokor without retribution! They will know pain for having dared go against us. We shall crush them and kill them all!"

Again the assembled crowd erupted into roars of approval. Tharok rose to his feet, smiled at Porloc, and bowed low once more. Porloc held his gaze for a moment, and then forced himself to smile, raising World Breaker into the air before turning to speak to one of his brothers by his side.

Tharok moved back to where his tribemates were standing. Without looking at any of them, he sat down, took hold of his copper cup and raised it to Maur. "Satisfied?"

Maur stared pensively at him, arms crossed over her chest. "The Crokuk clan."

"Indeed," said Tharok, grinning at her. "That's some five hundred warriors. We shall march tomorrow morning. I can't wait to leave this filthy town."

"So soon?" asked Golden Crow, taking up his slab of pork once more.

"Aye, shaman. We move tomorrow. There's no time to waste."

Maur's expression was complex, her eyes gleaming in the firelight. "Now I see. That's why we came down from the highlands—so that we could gain Orlokor swords with which to fight the Tragon?"

Tharok drank deeply of the wine, then set the cup aside. He had had enough alcohol for the night. Still, he couldn't resist goading her. "Obviously."

Her expression darkened, but Barok leaned forward. "And World Breaker? Why give it to Porloc? That I still don't understand."

Tharok gazed out over the crowd. The drums and alcohol and pride were causing more and more of the Orlokor to join the circle that was dancing around the fire. They leaped and fell to all fours, spun and threw their arms up high. In the light of the fire they were little more than silhouettes, shapes out of time, ancient and primal. He felt a shiver wash over him. For all that they were lowland and weak, they were kragh. Blood of his blood, if one went back far enough. And they would be his.

"We were not strong enough to hold World Breaker," said Tharok softly. "If not Porloc, then some other, larger tribe would have come for it. Then another, and another. We would have been destroyed within months."

The other Red River members thought this over. Finally Maur nodded. "Agreed. But by giving it to Porloc, you have set loose his ambitions. If he attacks the humans…"

"Trust me, Maur. Things will not proceed as you imagine. I have a plan."

Maur snorted and shook her head. For the first time, though, she didn't sound angry at him. "I can only hope."

Tharok leaned back against his cushion and turned his gaze to consider the kragh before him—perhaps a hundred of the leaders of the Orlokor, a hundred kragh who represented some ten thousand across the far sweep of the southern foothills, entrenched in deep valleys and hanging above the humans like a sword. Ten thousand Orlokor, of which he now had some five hundred.

As the drums beat and the dancing around the fire became faster and more fevered, as flesh was torn from the flanks of the roasting swine and sparks drifted through the air from the tongues of flame that spiraled into the night above the bonfire, Tharok stared at Porloc. The Orlokor warlord sensed the highland kragh's gaze upon him, and he turned and stared at Tharok over the crowd. Their eyes met, and for a long moment they simply held each other's gazes. Then Tharok raised his copper cup, and Porloc did the same.

CHAPTER FORTY-TWO

ISKRA

Iskra bade her men bring their dead and wounded into Mythgræfen's courtyard and assemble the captured enemy on the thin curvature of beach in front of the Hold. The dawn was cold and raw, the sun not yet having risen over the eastern peaks, and the colors of the land were muted and somber. Wrapped in her heavy white-furred cloak, she strode out through the ruined gatehouse, accompanied by Brocuff and Kolgrímr, and came to a stop on the bluff overlooking the sand on which the prisoners were kneeling.

There were seventeen of them. None were bound, for they had given their word as Ennoian knights to conduct themselves honorably after surrendering their swords. They were kneeling, backs straight, faces alternately arrogant or drawn with pain, nervous or carefully expressionless. She recognized the Golden Viper twins, Ser Cunot and Ser Cunad. A pity they had not died, she thought.

The wind whipped in off the scudding wavelets, and ravens croaked in the branches of the twisted oak.

"You came here under the command of your Lord to kill me and mine." Her words sounded thin in the morning chill. "Now the causeway and the lake shore are littered with your dead. Ser Kitan and the Virtue Makaria are no more. You have surrendered and acknowledged yourselves defeated."

She paused. She felt as hard and cold as the bare branches that the lake had washed up on the narrow crescent of a beach. None of the prisoners spoke; they were all waiting to hear her judgment. "It is customary for captured knights to be held for ransom. I shall not follow the custom, as I do not have the resources to house you or any interest in your gold."

The men stirred. None of them dared show fear, but she could read their doubts regardless. Only the promise of gold safeguarded a captured knight's safety. The beach was ringed with Hrethings and her remaining household guards. Ser Wyland was but one step to her side. All she had to do was give the word, and the sands of this pale beach would be drenched in blood.

"Instead, I shall release you and send you back to the Talon, where you may await the next opening of its Lunar Gate to return home.

I shall allow you to take your mounts and squires, though the carts and resources you brought with you so as to equip your stay here at the Hold will remain, as shall all weaponry but your daggers. Those too injured to make the journey may stay and be tended here at our infirmary. When next the Raven's Gate opens I shall allow them to pass through the Kyferin Castle."

Men from both sides stared at her in confusion and wonder. The captured knights on this beach were easily worth several years' income from all her former holdings, farms, and lands. To simply let them go? Unfathomable.

"Ser Wyland, have each man released and escorted across the causeway to their squires after they've give their solemn oath to cause no further mischief and make a direct return to the Talon."

Ser Wyland nodded wearily. His armor was battered, his shield missing, his face carved with deep lines of weariness and pain, but he stepped forward to execute her commands without complaint.

Iskra turned and walked back to the Hold. Bodies were being hauled out to be laid in rows in front of the Raven's Gate, where they would be stripped of their armor and weapons by dull-eyed Hrething warriors. They straightened and nodded respectfully to her, but she gazed past them. She didn't want to see any more blood or corpses. She'd seen enough to last her a lifetime.

With Brocuff following dutifully at her heels, she passed through the gate's short tunnel and out into the courtyard. As agreed, Mæva had come after the battle to ensure that she could heal the men, and had turned the open space into a field hospital. Over two dozen men lay wrapped in blankets and cloaks on the courtyard stones, cushioned only by the long grass and the numbness of sleep. Kethe was sitting against the base of the largest ash sapling, her head titled forward in a dead sleep.

Mæva rose at her approach. "I did what I could until Kethe could take no more. Most shall live, and will even wield a weapon again if they should so choose. I fear for the lives of only three."

"And Kethe?" Iskra couldn't keep the tremble from her voice. "Is she all right?"

Mæva turned to follow her gaze. "That I cannot answer. She allowed me to heal time and again, absorbing the darkness of my magic without complaint. These men owe their chance at health directly to her. I've never seen the like."

Iskra had to claw back the urge to rush to her daughter's side. "Will you stay and tend to them?"

Mæva nodded. "I shall." She hesitated, then said, "To be honest,

I didn't think we would survive the night. That we did speaks to me of miracles. I shall do what I can to aid you and yours."

Iskra knew she should respond with greater warmth, but all she could manage was a nod. "Thank you, Mæva. I will be calling a meeting later this afternoon to discuss our future. I hope that you can join us."

The witch smiled tiredly. "Here is where I should make a mocking comment about my surprise over having earned your confidence, but I am too tired. I will be there."

Iskra returned her tired smile and walked to her daughter. Kethe's face was drawn, the hollows under her eyes a dark purple, and her lips were bloodless. Her face was like a waxen death mask of its normal, vital self. Iskra's breath caught in her throat. "Brocuff," she said woodenly. "Please take my daughter to her bedroll."

"Yes, my Lady," said the constable gruffly. Had his voice caught in his throat? He picked up Kethe carefully, and then preceded Iskra into the great hall. She half expected to see Tiron standing to one side, glowering and alone, or Audsley hunched over the fire, spectacles reflecting the flames. Where were they? She felt a pang in her heart, loss and hope inextricably intertwined.

Brocuff laid her daughter down by the fire and pulled a blanket over her shoulders. "Will there be anything else, my Lady?"

Iskra forced a smile. "No, Constable. See to your duties, then rest. I will require your presence at this afternoon's meeting."

"Very well." He turned to go, hesitated, then turned back. "If it's not out of line for me to say—well done, my Lady. Well done. You saw us through the night."

Iskra sat down alongside Kethe and gazed at her wan features. "Thank you, Constable. I can't take too much credit, but I appreciate your words."

As Brocuff walked away, Iskra brushed a lock of hair from Kethe's face and felt a sob well up deep within her. She fought it down. What was happening to her darling girl? How much was she suffering? If she could take Kethe's pain and exhaustion into herself, she would in a moment, but there was nothing she could do. Too much had happened for her to understand all the implications, but one thing was clear: her daughter's trials were just beginning.

Iskra lay down beside her daughter and pulled her close. She smoothed down Kethe's hair over and over again while humming a song she used to sing to her when she was little and couldn't sleep.

She thought of Kitan looming over her, knife in hand, and Tiron as he had cut the knight down. How it had felt in that moment to step into his arms. She saw again the rippling black ink of the Gate fading away, claiming him and Audsley both for the next month, if not forever. Would she ever see them again?

Too many questions. She closed her eyes and let exhaustion steal her away.

CHAPTER FORTY-THREE

Asho

Asho pulled open the secret door and stepped into the narrow passage, where the smell of blood and death hung thickly in the air. He held aloft his candle, but in truth he barely needed its light to make out the steps as they descended down to Audsley's secret rooms. He walked slowly, one hand held out to trace the rough stone walls. He moved down and around, down and around, till he finally stepped out into the central chamber.

He stared down at Kitan's fallen body. The knight lay on his side, his azure armor gleaming in the candlelight like a treasure spied in the depths of a well. His blood had already turned black, a broad puddle that overlapped the centuries-older stain.

Asho looked past the dead man to the now-dead Gate. Where had Audsley and Tiron gone? Would they return? What mysteries were they encountering now? They could have stepped out anywhere in the known world or beyond. Asho prayed that the Ascendant would grant that they not only return in thirty days' time, but bring back a flicker of hope with them.

Had it only been a few hours ago that he'd stood here with Brocuff and the other guards, intent on defeating Kitan's forces, their breathing echoing off the vaulted ceiling, their torches casting dancing, menacing shadows across the walls? Waiting and not yet knowing that Makaria himself was stalking toward the Hold, bringing with him the key to unlocking Asho's own damnation?

Asho forced himself to swallow, and set the candle down on the floor. The sword was buckled at his hip. He hadn't drawn or even touched it since sheathing it last night. Its weight had pulled at him. He'd fought desperately to keep himself distracted ever since he'd pulled himself to his feet on the causeway and gone to help Kethe rise. She'd been insensate and, cradling her to his chest, he'd staggered back to the Hold. He hadn't dared to look closer at Makaria's remains—the remains which had burned beneath the water, consuming what was left of the Virtue's body with a terrible and dark hunger.

Exhaustion assailed him. He'd kept moving ever since. No matter that he was battered and wounded, no matter that his body craved oblivion. He hadn't dared sleep for fear of his dreams, hadn't dared stop for fear of his memories. But now, with the wounded seen to, the enemy knights released and the dead laid out and hauled onto the far shore, he could no longer avoid his fate.

Asho took a deep breath, closed his eyes and focused. Slowly the rushing roar of the world grew around him. It was as if he were standing in the center of a vortex, and all the magic in the world was gathering and draining down through the Hold. Whatever role this ancient castle had played in defying the Black Shriving, it was playing it still. Dimly, he could sense Kethe asleep above him in the great hall, a faint resonance that barely registered on the far edges of his mind. She was a flickering candle in the dark reaches of his mind. Could he reach out to her even while she slept? He didn't dare try.

Instead, he lowered his hand to the hilt of the sword. He hesitated, then clasped it firmly and pulled it free. Just as when he had first drawn it during his demon hunt, the runes smoldered to life and the air around the blade began to shimmer as if it were being superheated. Asho brought the blade up and studied it carefully. It was jet black, but by turning it from to side, he could make out ripples in the blade. The runes were in no language he had ever seen before.

Asho took a deep breath, held it, and pushed from deep within his soul, cracked open his soul and poured his essence into the blade. With a *whoomph* the length of the sword caught fire. Ebon tongues of flame poured up its length, shot through at their very core with the darkest veins of crimson.

It was the same fire he had seen the Agerastians wield on the battlefield. Hell fire. Flames from beyond the Black Gate. If ever there was a weapon of evil, if ever there was a tool of damnation, he was now holding it in his hand.

Asho's skin was crawling. Makaria had fallen to this fire. He had killed a Virtue with the fires of perdition. He wanted to laugh, but could feel hysteria lurking just beneath his panicked mirth. He extended his arm. The flames wavered and dripped from the blade, vanishing as they fell. Turning, he drew the sword's tip across the wall. Where the tip connected with the living rock, the metal whitened and he left a thin cut behind.

Heart pounding, he ceased feeding the flame with his will, and the flames flickered out of existence.

His exhaustion crashed down upon him, followed immediately by a crippling sense of nausea. Asho dropped the sword and fell to his knees, palms flat on the ground, to retch and gag as his stomach churned and rebelled. For long minutes he spat up nothing but bile, and finally fell over onto his side. He felt awful.

A memory came to him of the Agerastian Sin Casters keeling over, one by one, spitting up blood as their magic took its toll. Without Kethe, he realized, he would die. Without Kethe, his own magic would be as lethal to him as his enemies were.

He lay still and stared at the sword. Its blade was once again matte-black.

He recalled the fire pouring in a torrent from its blade to engulf Makaria mid-leap, a fire that had continued to burn even underwater. A fire that had destroyed the Virtue of Happiness.

Revulsion swarmed through him. He was a Sin Caster. He was damned to fall through the Black Gate upon his death. He was anathema to his own religious beliefs, and there was nothing he could do about it.

With a cry he sat up and seized the blade. His horror and fury welled into a crescendo, and the blade caught fire anew. Holding it reversed in both hands, Asho slammed it down into the stone floor. It sank down till only a hilt of flaming metal was left showing.

Gasping, he rose to his feet and snatched up the candle. A splitting headache assailed him. He had to get out.

He turned and staggered up the steps.

Behind him, the blade guttered and died. The chamber was plunged into darkness anew.

CHAPTER FORTY-FOUR

keтhe

Kethe awoke reluctantly. For a long while she simply lay still, eyes closed, allowing the murmur of conversation in the great hall and the crackle of flames to wash over her. In the near distance she could hear the soft moans of the injured as they tried to sleep, and beyond that the cruel caws of the ravens. They had survived the night, but to what end? An arm was draped over her shoulder; for a moment she thought it might be Asho's, and then she recognized her mother's breathing.

She carefully extricated herself, stifling a groan as the pains in her body flared back to life, and rose to her feet. Wan sunlight was filtering in through the high cracks in the wall and ceiling. Early afternoon, she guessed. Several guards turned to nod in her direction. Kethe didn't want company, needed to be alone. With a tight smile she picked up her cloak, swept it over her shoulders, and padded out of the room.

She climbed to the battlement and walked to the side opposite the lone guard. There she huddled down in the lee of the wall to sit with her knees beneath her chin, arms wrapped around her shins. She could see the massive mountain slopes that cupped the lake and the Hold just over the walls; their stark cliff faces and ice-bound peaks were walls that she could not escape. A sob formed deep in her chest and fought to escape her throat. Biting down, she lowered her face to her forearms and closed her eyes.

She was going to die. That thought beat at her like Elon's hammer at the anvil, over and over. She was going to die, and badly.

Last night she had helped kill a Virtue. Again she saw him go down, wreathed in impossible black flame, Asho suspended high over the causeway, hair flaring and eyes blazing. She'd been connected to him, had enabled his final attack. How was she now to present herself to Aletheia and ask to be consecrated? That road was forever closed to her. There was no escaping her fate. Her powers would continue to manifest until they burned her out and left her a guttered ruin.

Tears brimmed and then spilled down her cheeks. Her soul wanted to cry out at the unfairness of it all, but she bit down that cry, refused to let it sound. The world was anything but fair. She wouldn't shame herself further by mewling like a child.

Asho emerged from the far stairwell and turned to her, and she wiped the tears from her cheeks. Had she known he was coming? On some level she must have, just as he seemed to know where she was sitting. He approached slowly, trailing a hand over the battlements, his face guarded, his mouth a thin line. He looked battered and low.

She pushed herself to her feet. He was the last person she wanted to talk to, but she knew there was no denying the need for them to talk.

"Hello," he said, his voice little more than a rasp.

"Asho." She pushed her shoulders back. She was her mother's daughter, even now.

He moved up beside her and turned to gaze out over the lake, so she turned to stand shoulder to shoulder with him. She could barely make out the thin line of knights as they reached the faraway Erenthil, their squires and pack animals a ragged line behind them.

"We won," he said simply.

"Yes." Neither of them sounded overjoyed.

The wind whipped up and caused small waves to scud across the lake's surface toward them. Asho hunched his shoulders, but Kethe welcomed its cruel chill as they stood in silence watching the retreating knights. A raven circled the Hold and disappeared into the oak tree's canopy to roost.

"We need to talk about last night," he said at last.

She fought down the immediate rejection that arose within her and instead simply tightened her hands into fists. "What about it?"

"What about it?" He chuckled. "Well, you've got the powers of a Virtue. I'm a bloody Sin Caster." Kethe opened her mouth to interrupt, but he powered on. "You're the supposed pinnacle of goodness, while I'm damned and doomed for the Black Gate when I die." He stared down at his pale hands. "We're bound, despite all that. I can sense you. We can connect, somehow, and when I cast my magic, you drain away the sin."

Kethe looked away. "We killed him—the Virtue. You and me. We're both damned. I'm not the pinnacle of anything."

"Damned and stuck out here together," he said softly. "The only way I can make sense of what's happening is if we use our... powers... to help Lady Kyferin."

She felt her eyes burn and wiped at them angrily. "Obviously."

"We're going to need to work together," he said, his voice growing harsh. "I know you don't like that, but you're going to have to get over it. We're bound, you and I. By—"

"Shut up!" She rounded on him. "We killed a Virtue! I saw you burn the flesh right off his bones! He's still there! Nobody's dared touch his body. You and your black sword, throwing Hell fire, and me helping you!" She shook him. His face was closed off, his silver-green eyes flat. "Don't you understand? We're going to die, and we're going through the Black Gate. There's no Ascension for us, no eternal bliss. We're damned, and yet here you stand talking about—"

"You think I don't know that?" He stepped forward, and despite herself she gave ground. "My whole life, people have been falling over themselves to remind me how close I am to damnation. I'm a Bythian, one step away from Hell. And now I discover I'm a Sin Caster. You think the subtleties elude me? I've been one step from Hell my whole life, and now I know I'm going to be hurled into damnation the moment some Virtue manages to cut off my head." He was glaring at her, showing true anger for the first time. "And, you know what? Fine. I'm damned. These are the cards I've been dealt. But I'm done with apologizing for who I am. I'm done with accepting what others think of me. I'm going to do everything I can to help get us out of this situation. So, the question is, are you going to do the same? Or are you going to spend your time sulking and feeling sorry for yourself?"

"Sulking?" Her fury and pain was a storm that was buffeting her to pieces. "Feeling sorry for myself?" Her outrage knew no bounds.

"What else are you doing up here?"

Kethe let out a cry of pure fury and threw a punch toward his face as hard as she could. Asho caught her blow in the palm of his hand an inch from his face, stopping it cold—and in that moment their bond exploded to life, washing out from their hands to flare out into the world, a wave of blinding white that thrummed with power.

Kethe's eyes widened in shock. Their energy was endlessly circling through them. Her fist was burning with white fire, his with black, and the harder she strove to push through his palm to strike him, the brighter the flames grew.

Asho was forced into a fighting stance, legs bent, thighs flexing as he leaned into her punch, his face drawn with effort, his eyes narrowing. Black fire coruscated around his hand, and despite herself she could feel the taint of his strivings sinking into her, bleeding out of the world and saving him from the worst of the backlash.

She could sever that bond. She could kick him out into the cold to suffer the full effects of his sin casting. Punish him by turning away.

Slowly, she backed off, straightened and pulled her fist away. The flames remained around their hands, but they had diminished in size. Their bond remained, however, vital and true. She could feel him, sense him as if he were an extension of herself. It was as intimate a feeling as if their naked bodies had been pressed together, a union that verged on terrifying.

Asho lowered his hand. His face was grave. His silver-green eyes had turned flat white, burning with the same fire that wreathed her fist. His frame trembled as power flowed through him.

"I'm not asking you to like me," he said. "I don't need or want that. But work with me. Help me understand this thing we can do. Accept that we are bound to each other."

Kethe raised her hand and stared at the pale fire that flickered over her skin. Her weariness was washing away. The longer she stayed connected to him, the stronger she felt, and it felt good. It felt right. She stared at his somber face, at his burning, blank eyes, and reluctantly nodded. "All right. We're bound to each other. But if you dare accuse me of sulking, I'll pound your Bythian face in."

He grinned and ended their connection. The white fire flickered out of existence, leaving only his mocking silver-green eyes in its place. "Agreed."

Kethe sighed and turned back to the lake, gazing out at where the last of the knights were finally disappearing from view. "Be honest with me, Asho. Do you think we have a chance of surviving this situation?"

Asho stepped up next to her. "I don't know. But I intend to do my best."

As they watched, the last of the enemy knights turned to gaze back at them. The tiny figure stood still for a moment, then stepped down and disappeared from view.

CHAPTER FORTY-FIVE

ISKRA

Iskra had only just fallen asleep when someone shook her awake. Kethe was gone, and Iskra rose in confusion. Afternoon sunlight was pouring thinly through a high crack in the wall. Ser Wyland was crouched by her side, hauberk over his aketon but without his plate.

Moans of pain came from the courtyard. People were gathered around the two fires, holding plates that were being filled by Jekil.

"Food's being served, my Lady." Ser Wyland smiled apologetically. "I've come to learn that a full stomach does more good on the campaign than sleep. Can I fetch you a plate?"

Iskra rubbed at the corners of her eyes and rose. She felt like she'd been sleeping on a bed of rocks, which wasn't far from the truth. "Thank you, yes. Have you seen Kethe?"

"Yes. She's up top. Taking some time alone, I believe." He stepped away and cut to the front of the line, and returned with a bowl of stew. "Kitan's men weren't planning to rough it. No more black gruel for us, I'm happy to say. At least not for a few weeks."

Iskra took the bowl. The warmth leached into her fingers. "I wouldn't put it past them to poison their own stores as a last strike against us." He greeted that with a raised eyebrow, and she nodded. "I know, I know. Have you eaten?"

"I have."

"Good. Please summon Brocuff, Kethe, and Ser Asho. Ask them to join me in the guard room of the main gate. Mæva and Kolgrímr, too."

Ser Wyland bowed and stepped away.

Iskra ate as she walked. She stepped outside into the courtyard and stopped. Two dozen men turned to gaze at her from where they were lying. She recognized the first man: Ord, one of her own guards. Smiling sorrowfully, she stepped up beside him and cast around for something to sit on as he struggled to sit up. She managed to pre-empt him by sitting on a small chest, and spent the next few minutes asking him about how he felt. She then moved on to the other men, most of whom were Hrethings. She had precious little to say to them other than to offer her thanks, but they received her words with awkward smiles and bobs of their heads.

When she left the last man, she found the small guard room full.

Brocuff and Ser Wyland were standing to one side, while Asho and Kethe were standing awkwardly beside each other, as if they were unsure how to inhabit the same space. Mæva was leaning against the wall, her firecat twining itself between her ankles, while Kolgrímr stood by himself close to the door.

"Good afternoon, everyone."

Part of the ceiling was missing, and it was from there that the light and fresh air was flowing. She moved to stand in the sunlight, and for a moment simply stared at a burst of purple flowers growing from a crack in the wall. She turned at last and linked her hands behind her back.

"Thank you, all of you. Thank you for your role in last night's events. All of us have played a crucial part in our success. This victory is ours."

She looked from one face to the next. "I will come to the point. Ser Kitan came to destroy us with a far larger force than was necessary. He planned to remain and rebuild the Hold. It seems Lord Laur takes our family responsibilities more seriously than my late husband did. Worse, he came accompanied by a Virtue."

Iskra looked to Ser Asho and Kethe. Neither matched her gaze. "Makaria is dead, but what he symbolized cannot be ignored. Lord Laur has procured the complete support of his Grace."

Everyone stirred at this. Ser Wyland rubbed at his jaw. "Bad news indeed. It makes our return to Kyferin Castle all the more… difficult."

"Difficult?" Brocuff shook his head. "Impossible."

"Do we need to go back?" Kethe's voice was hesitant. "Perhaps we can make a life for ourselves here."

Iskra shook her head slowly. "His Grace won't leave us alone. He can't afford to. We've defeated one of his Virtues, and he can't afford to let that stand. Despite everything that's going on, he will have to make a lesson of us. The next army that comes through will be far too large for us to defeat alone."

Kolgrímr stepped forward. "You aren't alone. The men and women of Hrething stand with you."

Iskra smiled. "And I welcome that support. Without you and your men, noble Kolgrímr, we would not be here today. But Lord Laur will desire to avenge his son, and the Grace his fallen Virtue. We cannot stand against them."

"Then what do you suggest?" Asho's voice was almost a whisper. He was still wearing his battle armor, and if anything his face was more drawn than her daughter's. "Flee the Hold and live in the wild?"

Iskra shook her head. "I have been foolish. I realize now that I made two mistakes. The first was to rely on the Ascendant and his Grace. The second was in trying to emulate Enderl and defeat our foes through strength alone. But I'm not him, nor do I wish to be. We need allies with whom we can stand against the Grace. We cannot survive alone."

Brocuff shook his head. "That's a bad business, turning against the Grace. You might as well ask all of us to jump through the Black Gate now."

Kolgrímr raised an eyebrow. "As different as our interpretations of Ascendancy might be, you've got to admit that the Grace isn't acting as a spiritual leader. He holds no authority over us Hrethings; only the Ascendant himself can judge us. I don't think resisting him and striving for Ascendancy are at odds."

Mæva gave her one-shouldered shrug. "The Grace is just a man, and all men are fallible. The loss of his Virtue proves that."

Iskra turned to Asho. "You shared something in the rooms below before leading the charge against the enemy. Why don't you tell us again what you saw during your first battle?"

Asho frowned. "The Grace was mortally wounded. He drank a potion that healed his wounds and saved him from death."

Ser Wyland smiled tolerantly. "I find that hard to believe, Ser Asho."

"As hard to believe as his aligning with Lord Laur and sending a Virtue against us?"

"That - well. That is political manuevering. Every man, even his Grace, must make hard decisions on occasion." Ser Wyland's flace had grown flushed. "But cheating death? That I cannot believe."

Iskra slashed at the air with her hand. "Enough. I believe Asho's tale. I find the scales are dropping quickly from my eyes. If we are to survive the coming onslaught, there is only one group that is large and powerful enough to stand against the Ascendant: the Agerastians."

Even Ser Wyland looked taken aback. "The Heretics? The men who killed your husband and are besieging Ennoia?"

Iskra nodded. "Before he left, Audsley told me more about the Hold's final days during the rise of Ascendancy. Not enough for me to understand the particulars, but enough to realize that what we've been told about our past may not be completely accurate." She raised her hands to forestall argument. "I'm not questioning Ascendancy, but rather the details behind its rise. We've been told our whole lives that the Agerastians are called heretics for their role in fighting the first Ascendant's rise to power. For their wicked role in that war, they were banned from using their Solar Gate, prevented from ever leaving their city of Agerastos, and treated only one step above Bythians."

"Aye, and rightly so," said Brocuff. "They destroyed their Solar Gate, for crying out loud!"

"And in doing so freed themselves from oppression," muttered Asho.

Brocuff glared at him. "Their doing so has threatened Ascendancy itself – who knows what destroying the Gate has done to the souls that must rise from Bythos or fall from Zoe?"

Asho's face burned and he looked at the floor. Once he would never have responded. His days of silence were over, however. "We've spent centuries punishing them for the actions of their ancestors and branding them heretics. Why are we surprised when they fail to care about our religion?"

Brocuff threw up his hands in disgust and turned away.

Iskra stepped forward. "There is much for us to learn. They have used Sin Casters in battle, yet Asho has cast magic in our defense. Does that make him evil? If not, then why must we condemn them? I don't claim to have answers. I merely have questions and a complete lack of options. If we are to survive, we will need to learn more about the Agerastians - and perhaps side with them."

Kolgrímr shrugged. "I don't know much about this war that is happening in Ennoia, but I have no problem with allying with the enemy of my enemy."

Mæva scritched between her firecat's ears. "And they have Sin Casters of their own. Perhaps they can provide us with answers."

Asho opened his mouth to say something, then closed it and looked away. Iskra raised an eyebrow. "Asho?"

"I—something doesn't add up. I've only been able to sense— magic, I guess—since arriving here at the Hold. Yet the Agerastian Sin Casters were able to throw black fire on Ennoia." He rubbed at his jaw. "Doing so caused them to sicken near to the point of death."

Kethe glanced at him sidelong. "They didn't have a Virtue-in-training to drain the taint from their magic, obviously."

"Right," said Asho, blushing. "But there haven't been Sin Casters in nearly two hundred years. Not since the Black Gate was sealed. I can cast magic here because I'm close to this minor Black Gate. So how are the Agerastians suddenly casting magic now?"

Mæva pursed her lips. "Did they have any pets with them?"

"Pets?" Asho blinked. "On the battlefield? No. Though… they did eat some black rocks before casting. I'd almost forgotten."

"Black rocks?" Iskra felt something nearly connect in her mind.

If only Audsley were here.

"Right," said Asho. "They'd chew on some right before they threw black fire."

"Gate Stone," said Iskra. "That has to be it." Elements connected within her mind, points of information forming lines, diagrams, a perfect explanation. Excitement surged through her. "Which was why the Ascendant ordered our mines here to be shut down. Gate Stone is mined close to the Black Gate. Perhaps it absorbs the power that comes through, and stores it up. Eating the stone then releases it and powers their spells."

"If that's the case," said Ser Wyland, "then we're sitting on a huge reservoir of untapped magical might."

"If you can get to it," said Kolgrímr sourly. "Don't forget that the upper passes and mountain ranges are infested with demons."

"If we could close the Black Gate, or clear it somehow," said Asho, "if we could secure the old mines—we might have something that the Agerastians would be willing to fight alongside us for."

"*If* you can clear the Black Gate," said Kolgrímr. "That's a very big if."

"We can clear it," said Kethe. Her voice was cold and certain. "That's what Virtues can do. That's what I can do. Fight demons and destroy centers of magic."

"None of you has any idea what lies up in the Skarpheðinn range," said Mæva, voice cutting. "None of you."

Iskra raised her hands. "We have perhaps a couple of months' time before we can expect retaliation from Laur and the Grace. The Ascendant willing, we should hear back from Audsley and Tiron before then, and with a little luck they will bring us good tidings. In the meantime, we will do what we can to learn more about the upper passes, this Black Gate, and how best to acquire Gate Stone with which to bargain with the Agerastians." She lowered her hands. "Unless anybody else can suggest a better course of action?"

Kolgrímr scowled and shook his head. "I'm all for an alliance if it doesn't involve our cutting our own heads off first. You don't know what you speak of, Lady Kyferin. Mæva is right. You've yet to even live through one Black Shriving, much less attempt an assault on the high peaks."

Ser Wyland gave a rough smile. "I don't think anyone here truly thought it would be possible to survive last night, yet here we stand. So what if our next course of action seems equally if not more daunting? I say we attack this next impossibility with as much determination as we did the first."

Mæva's voice was cold. "I believe it folly to believe we can 'cleanse' the Skarpheðinn range… but I can help with learning more about them. I could lead a small group."

Asho rested his hand on the pommel of his castle-forged sword. "I will do this, if my Lady requests it of me."

Kethe glanced at him and nodded. "I will, too."

Iskra nodded decisively. "Very well. It's settled."

"Remember, my lady." Mæva's gazed at her with piercing intensity. "One day I shall come to collect. These favors do not come freely."

Iskra felt a shiver run through her, though she fought to show no sign of her unease. "Understood, Mæva. Thank you for your… honesty."

"And the Black Shriving?" asked Kolgrímr.

Iskra gazed around at her small band of followers and felt a surge of fierce determination. "We shall strive to defeat the forces arrayed against us, to break free of this impossible situation where all others foresee our death. The odds are against us, but we shall not be deterred. We shall fight with everything we have, and risk all in the pursuit of justice. You ask about the Black Shriving, Kolgrímr. I tell you this: come what may, we shall not run. Let the darkness boil down from the high peaks. Let the worst of the Black Gate attack our walls. Let demons howl, shadows crawl, and the Doom itself seek to sweep us away. For the first time in hundreds of years, that evil shall not find Mythgræfen Hold unprotected. Kyferins once more shall guard the walls—and I swear to you, we shall not fail."

19622880R00213

Printed in Great Britain
by Amazon